POP KULT
WARLORD

Other Books by Nick Cole

Soda Pop Soldier   *The End of the World*   *Fight the Rooster*
CTRL-ALT Revolt!   *As We Knew It*

The Wasteland Saga

The Old Man and the   *The Savage Boy*   *The Road is a River*
Wasteland

WYRD

The Red King   *The Dark*   *The Pawn in*   *The Lost Castle*
Knight   *the Portal*

Galaxy's Edge
by Jason Anspach and Nick Cole

Legionnaire   *Sword of the Legion*   *TIN MAN*
Galactic Outlaws   *Prisoners of Darkness*   *Imperator*
Kill Team   *Turning Point*   *Requiem for Medusa*
Attack of Shadows   *Message for the Dead*   *Chasing the Dragon*

POP KULT
WARLORD

NICK COLE

CASTALIA HOUSE

Pop Kult Warlord

Nick Cole

Published by Castalia House
Kouvola, Finland
www.castaliahouse.com

ISBN: 978-952-7065-79-2

Contents

Chapter One

A million-dollar jackpot is moments from going up in smoke in a firefight inside a make-believe simulation called *WarWorld*.

That's as real as real gets.

Digitally rendered bullets are chewing Hemingway's Bar and Steaks to shreds all around me, and the rest of Havana is burning to the ground, when they redirect me to take out a high-value target. I'm down to twenty heavily armed grunts and a couple of new pros who've just signed on with ColaCorp.

Game Over is looming and the winner is still undecided even in these last moments.

Ubermart is throwing everything they have at us, trying to push ColaCorp off the objective. It's the bottom of the ninth. The fourth quarter. Whatever works to paint the picture that the entire *WarWorld* season has led up to this frantic machine-gun free-for-all moment. We went for broke and punched through their defenses around a simulated Havana. Now all we have to do is hold the objective for twenty minutes, and we'll win the first ever *WarWorld* Super Bowl.

RangerSix comes over the gaming suite speakers. "Question, this is Six…"

On-screen, within my HUD, Ubermart Ubermarines are storming the front entrance of an in-game digital representation of an actual restaurant that exists in the real Havana. Supposedly, it's one of the fanciest dives in New Havana City. And right now, Super Bowl partiers sit in that very restaurant, watching via holographic projection as the battle between ColaCorp and Ubermart goes down live. Tens of thousands more partiers are packed in the streets all around, viewing the battle on the big-screen PrismBoard.

We're fighting in a digital facsimile of the same world they're drinking themselves blind in. It's like the sweatiest, most drunken hour of Mardi Gras in full riot, and I can hear the noise of it all even through the concrete-reinforced walls of my gaming suite beneath Conquistador Light Stadium. This was already the party to end all parties, and then suddenly a war broke out for everyone's amusement. Which is how pro gamers get paid. Fight to the digital death using state-of-the-art weaponry for corporate teams while half the world watches via gaming streams.

What can I say... it's a living.

Our heavily armed avatars—combat troops skinned in camo-tattoos and carrying high-tech automatic weaponry while fighting alongside bots, tanks, mechs, and close-air-support crafts—are being broadcast holographically throughout the world. But right now, right here, right above me, New Havana is this moment's capital of the world. Ground Zero. Party Central. Everyone at Conquistador Light Stadium cheers and roars and stamps their feet or waves their sonic bolo noisemakers as directors' cuts play on the ultrajumbotron and a rock band threatens to deafen half the island of Cuba. I think it's ACReduxC. Good stuff. Old-school war metal.

"Say again... Question, this is RangerSix, stand by for priority mission tasking." The cacophonic assault rifle chatter across the bar slash objective we're holding, in-game, is making the BattleChat cut in and out. Plus we're slowly getting slaughtered by wave after wave of Ubermart Ubermarines.

I'm down to eighteen grunts now. With fifteen very long minutes to go until Game Over. I see a Marine come through one of the bar windows and try to block out what that must be like for the spectators who paid big bucks to watch murderous holograms invade the bar in real time and blow each other to bits with lethal weaponry.

He's carrying a Mossberg Tactical with Dragon's Breath rounds. I know they're Dragon's Breath rounds because of the hot liquid napalm covering the machine gun team he just knocked out. The digital grunts, just bots really, die horribly for everyone's entertainment, on fire and screeching as they blink out on my roster list inside my HUD.

"Little busy right now, Six," I reply over BattleChat as I burn through half a can of ammo.

I don't even sight the Ubermarine as he weaves through the debris. Just drag the roaring M249's stabilized laser sights across the bar in front of me, rounds chewing up simulated teak and mahogany and shattering cut crystal glassware, until the three red targeting beams land on the muscle-swollen Ubermarine, Predator-style as we say. I think I hit him with about forty rounds all at once.

"Player kill!" shouts the bombastic in-game play-by-play announcer. CoCoBoom's dog tags suddenly appear in the bottom corner of my screen with a flourish of triumphal trumpets. Cash floods into my account, but there's no time to count it. Too many of his buddies are coming through the walls. They're rushing the objective.

I have fourteen grunts left.

The money I just earned for taking out another player doesn't really matter anyway. It's not much compared to the big prize we're all fighting over, and besides, I'm already loaded these days. Still, the old me never stops adding it all up, because I was so poor for so long.

The million-dollar bonus ColaCorp will pay for winning the end-of-the-season Super Bowl, on the other hand... that matters. That's a lot.

And then there are the endorsements.

"Barely holding on here, Six," I manage as I rake the far side of the bar with suppressive fire. "Support would be nice right about now."

"Yeah, about that, Question. Jolly and Kiwi are inbound with Wolverine armor to support your left flank. They'll take command of the action and draw fire from the Plaza Real. Highlighting on your

HUD... now. But son, we've had a major development. And holding that objective won't matter in about ten minutes."

"Why's that?"

I'm burning through the rest of my ammo as more and more Uber-marines rush the marbled steps that lead up from the Plaza Real into the famous nightclub that is Hemingway's. In real life as holographs; in-game as enemy players. One of my fellow ColaCorp players goes down when a grenade goes off inside the bar. Eleven grunts left. Three players.

More Marines coming through the doors.

The M249 goes dry and I discard it with a quick tap on my key-board. I pull my AMT .45 Longslide, a sponsor item from Vintage Weapon Systems, and engage as many as I can. This thing puts holes in the digital super-roided Ubermarines' chests like there's no tomorrow. Which is an appropriate turn of phrase. Because if we lose, a lot of people will think there *won't* be a tomorrow. People who've gambled quite a bit more than they can afford to lose.

Still more Marines are coming through. This is it. This is the big push to dislodge. It's about to turn into a real knife-and-gun show in just a few seconds.

We're being overrun.

RangerSix is talking but I'm not hearing anything because I'm dropping Marines as we fall back toward the kitchens. Everything is splintering teak, bullet-smashed metal, and smoke as tracers from both sides mix and form a crossfire hurricane.

A big Ubermart Marine, a player by the looks of his tats and camo customization, closes and pulls a knife, hoping for a glorious webwall kill he can be proud of. I've heard the networks are paying bounties to get kill cam footage of me in particular. So this guy's just greedy.

I ventilate him with a dozen rounds after pushing in a fresh mag and notice I have enough rounds for two more full mags. My grunts have fallen back to the secondary line of defense and are opening up from behind the kitchen.

We're killing three to one, so I can only imagine Ubermart is going for broke right here, right now. They have to. This is for all the marbles. The first ever *WarWorld* Super Bowl. There used to be another Super Bowl, someone told me, before the Meltdown. But it got all Social Justice and no one watched it anymore.

All the game-streaming networks and the directors are cutting in close, looking for that spectacular moment to capture the victory that's just minutes away. For either side.

"Enigmatrix is going for the old fort, Question. We believe Ubermart rolled the dice and got an orbital gun positioned above the battlefield. She puts eyes on the objective and we lose. That's it. She'll vaporize what's left of your combat team, never mind how many of her own troops she takes out in the process. Not to mention she can strike our assault carriers off shore, and just about everything else we've got on the board. Gotta stop her right now, Question. We're tasking you."

"Airstrike?"

I'm reloading. Waiting for the big push that'll throw us out of Hemingway's. Beyond the shattered windows of the opulent party palace, Ubermart tanks and mechs are shooting across the Plaza Real and into the defenses on this side of the square. Everyone on both sides is on full auto and crawling, dashing, surging forward to rip the enemy players' guts out live on TV, phones, SoftEyes, PrismBoards, and ultrajumbotrons.

Whatever happens in the next few minutes, the network will get their big finish. And the world will go nuts.

"Negative, Question," replies RangerSix. "Nothing mission-capable on station for an airstrike at the moment. Plus she's got anti-air on all the buildings."

Well what do you want me to do, I think as my fingers dance across the keyboard getting out commands to what assets I still control. I'm pinned down on the objective, pretty much out of ammo, and one physics-computed digital bullet away from being Game Over-ed and beyond the ability to make a difference in the match. That's what I'm thinking as I drop down to no players and nine grunts on the roster in my HUD.

"Well, son, it's your lucky day. We're airdropping a vehicle package just for you. I need you to make it out of the AOC and get to the coast road. You can intercept and stop her before she reaches the fort above the city. She needs a high vantage point to target for strike. Leave your team to guard the bar. Your ride is arriving now at the rear of your location."

Suddenly Kiwi is in my HUD. A small video chat window.

"Cheers, Question. We got this, mate. Now take her out and let's finish this thing." I can see he's leering intently at his screen. I can hear his fingers slamming at the keys like there's no tomorrow. Like he's composing a symphony of bullets and destruction one kill a second. And I know he's down here with me in another immersion suite. My best friend. Not half a world away in Australia like normal. They flew us all into Havana to do this in real time.

"Roger, Six. I'm on it." I roll my shoulders and head for the back door to the restaurant in-game. On screen, all hell—rendered in explosions and gunfire—breaks loose behind me.

Chapter Two

The dropship, a ColaCorp supply-variant Albatross, is just climbing off
into the firework display of artillery and rockets that is New Havana
City's skyline in the middle of our virtual online battle. Missiles streak
up from blocks away to knock it down, but the dropship lumbers on,
popping flares that rain like sparklers and reveal my ride by their color-
shifting lights.

My ride. It's not uncommon for corporate sponsors to lie in wait
for just such an in-game moment in which to promote their product.
In the executive "party suites" way up in the gleaming upper levels of
Conquistador Light Stadium, brimming with ultramodels and haute
cuisine tapas, advertising execs are digitally inking deals and doing
business on the fly to monetize our little war in any way they can.
Anything to get their products in the game. On the streams. And
in front of a large portion of the worldwide viewing audience that is
currently tuned in to watch the Super Bowl.

I look at my new ride in the back alley, away from the gunfire
and celebration. Apparently whoever's repping Maserati China just
hit one out of the park and got their product a spotlight showcase in
the closing moments of the year's biggest game.

It's cobalt blue. Vintage 2000s. But late-model sci-fi. Big fat Run-
Flat tires. Tinted windows. I hit 'E' on my SoftPunch keyboard.
My combat-kitted avatar slides smoothly into the interior of a vehicle
everyone around the world is suddenly salivating for and most likely
googling the specs on. Its interior is the very essence of machine-

engineered cool. Muted brushed steel and soft lighting. Premium leather that my screen tells me smells like a million bucks and feels like a calfskin glove. Dials, smart interface, readouts. Luxury. Everything anyone could ever dream of owning in a vehicle with a nigh-unobtainable price tag.

"Welcome to your new Maserati, PerfectQuestion. I'm HAL, a 9000-series AI. It's a good day for a war," intones the onboard intelligence in a soft resonant baritone. It's calming, despite the fact that an Uberwasp close-air-support fighter is exploding in the sky a few streets over. Then HAL says: "I love the smell of victory, sir... It smells like Maserati."

That probably means something to someone from the last century. The HAL reference also. The execs are always trying to throw in callbacks to their latest blockbuster remakes of once-great movies that have been rebooted to death.

No one writes anything new anymore.

All I know is it's some sort of product placement line that has to run before I can access the vehicle.

"Booting up... start engine sequence engaged," HAL announces.

In the passenger seat is a weapons package. I right-click it and download it into my inventory.

A silenced MP10 Specter. A silenced Walther PPK. Both very old-school. Last century. What the hell? No one would bring these to a battle. They're like bringing a fake knife to a real gun fight. Then I notice another product placement. The splash logo for the new Bond movie. It's stamped in relief on each of the high-tech secret squirrel spy weapons.

The Maserati comes to life like some starship headed for Alpha Centauri on full burn. I know. I've been watching TED Talks about that when I can't sleep at night in wherever in the world I am. A girl I once barely knew is on her way there now. To Alpha Centauri. We could have been something, but she tried to kill me. And that's another story.

"Question…" It's RangerSix. "You'll need to intercept her along the coast road, near the waterfront. Along the Rio Azul. This'll be close, son. Activating your nav for intercept now. Do *not* let her reach the castle. I repeat: terminate before objective."

I'm not one for car racing sims, but… why not, it's only the Super Bowl. It's only everybody in the world watching us go for broke. It's not my specialty and half the world is tuned in, but as I like to say… buy the ticket, take the ride.

The key commands are simple, and a moment later a steering wheel peripheral deploys from within the smartdesk inside my gaming suite. I hear the crowd above watching the ultrajumbotron and stamping their feet on the floor of the stadium. I drag the steering wheel around on a hydraulic swing arm and lock it into place. Six seconds later I'm doing a hundred and twenty down a wet alley as New Havana City burns to the ground all around me.

I pass the melting remains of a tank half stuck out of some old-school colonial building. Dead grunts litter the streets. ColaCorp grunts, mainly. We paid dearly for this section of the city. Through the cross streets, I can see the battle for the Plaza Real heating up to end-of-the-world proportions. JollyBoy and Kiwi are in it now. I see the massive articulating feet of a Mech Tank lumber past the narrow window of an alley I'm speeding by. Smoking missiles are trailing away from its hexagonal pod launchers. It's one of ours, and it's going in hot.

I downshift through a wet intersection fronted by ancient bullet-riddled pink, white, and yellow colonial houses and corner at eighty. All four of the massively fat carbon-fiber tires turn at the same time. In real life I probably just pulled six g's. I spin the wheel back to center and punch the accelerator to follow the directions in the HUD for the coast road and the intercept.

One hand dances across the keyboard as I equip the weapons package inside my inventory. At least the MP is loaded with subsonic dumdums. That'll give it some punch. Beyond the gaming suite walls I can hear some mega metal band ramping up to full drum and thunder while searing guitar provides the lightning. No amount of soundproofing could silence the sound of the crowd going nuts as "Shoot to Thrill" drives them into a fury of celebratory screaming and tribal whoops for whichever side they've chosen to love for the moment. Or whoever they bet their life savings on.

I can only imagine the game producers have queued the main show, sensing the end. The big finale approaching as both teams decide to slaughter each other to the digital death. If I had an ego, that would be something to get suddenly frightened about. I don't.

The spectacle is causing me to lose focus. I've been playing this game like it's the Super Bowl. Not just a match I'm trying to win with skill. Not for fun or rank. I've been making it all too... Super Bowl. Two-million-dollar bonus. Too important. And that's not how we got here.

It's just a game.

And I love games for the sake of just playing.

So that's what I do. I block it all out and just play.

I break out onto the coast road and see a dark hill rising up in the silvery moonlight. The old fortress that once guarded Havana waits at the top. A winding road slithers up the hillside. Rockets are arcing across the sky from the assault fleets out at sea. Ours. Targeted artillery trying to support the thin line ColaCorp is holding back at the Plaza Real. The thin line Jolly and Kiwi are on. Smart rounds seeking laser-designated targets probably just steps away from the objective inside Hemingway's. RangerSix is using not just the kitchen sink to win this one... he's throwing the whole kitchen at Ubermart. And we still might lose. If Enigmatrix gets that orbital gun designator operational with a view to a kill, then it's game over.

Headlights ahead.

A line of them. Coming straight at me fast.

It's her. Enigmatrix.

Probably the best player in *WarWorld*.

I decide we'll just have to see about that.

The armored SUVs fan out across the narrow coast road ahead, and the distance between us shrinks rapidly. Suddenly I realize we're going to play a game of chicken before we start shooting for keeps. Except... game physics will favor an armored truck over a high-end sports car. Just like real life. Because *WarWorld* is designed to be as real as it gets. People like their games that way.

That realness makes some gamers have psychotic breaks and end up with a sort of PTSD. But I think that's because of other factors in their life. *WarWorld* is just the best special-effects driven movie you've ever seen. That's all. Bullets whistle across your speakers and occasionally slap bodies like wet bags of cement hitting concrete. Explosions roar and suddenly your screen blurs and ambient sound surrenders to a high-pitched tone that verges on insanity if it goes on much longer. And the barrel of the assault rifle you follow through the game feels like a guitar bleating a staccato death rattle that can sound like a song sometimes. And all you have to do is run, dive, crawl, and occasionally drive through it all to keep playing and get paid like a pro.

It doesn't make you crazy if you don't let it.

Mind over matter. You don't mind, it don't matter.

"May I suggest... sir," HAL announces calmly over the gaming suite speakers as the distant headlights flood my screen, "that you use the onboard missile system, available in Sports Mode, to remove the obstruction ahead."

What? This thing's got weps?

Beauty, brains... and muscle.

Yeah. I think I'm in love.

"You may show me your weapons, HAL."

An armaments panel interfaces with my HUD, and I've got two anti-armor TOW III missiles ready to launch. I activate missile-standby and the launchers neatly fold out from the sculpted side panels.

With just seconds left, I target two of the armored vehicles and fire on the fly. A mere hundred meters before I slam into them head-on. The missiles streak away, skipping along the wet street, and slam into both of the wide and flat luxury SUVs the uber-rich use for their motorcades these days. The world's a dangerous place, and these are the wartime variant, in that they are painted digital camo and not luxe black. You see them in every conflict, on the feeds and news streams. One vehicle explodes across the highway. Direct hit. The visual effects are crazy good as blue midnight becomes a sudden apocalyptic noon. I'm sure that'll make a highlight reel. The other gets hit in the undercarriage as the missile strikes the ground at the last second and then skips upward into the fortified chassis. An instant later the vehicle backflips.

And it's on fire for bonus points as I speed through the gap its destruction has created.

If Enigmatrix was in either, I'll get the kill now. But I don't have time to focus on that. I'm swerving to avoid the others in the sudden chaos of exploding vehicles and smoking missile trails. I lose control on the wide wet road and barely get it back a heart-stopping second later.

The three other vehicles sped past me, and now they brake hard to take the road up to the fort.

I was doing well over a hundred when I passed them. Now I'm braking and power-sliding on wet streets. For a moment I lose control again and the steering wheel peripheral feels meaningless in my hands. The night world of Havana, blue and shadowy here, festive as though in the throes of some Mardi Gras in other places, seems on fire where the battle has been and is probably still raging. All of it spins about me in a curving widescreen monitor panoramic view as I fight to regain control of the Maserati and stay in the game.

The Lush Optics MegaKush Monitor is hands down the best for those who choose to live virtually. It makes everything frighteningly clear. I can tell by the way my body is tightening up as I'm about to careen off a guardrail, over the cliffs, and into the raging surf below. It's way too real. Frighteningly real on a whole other level if you want that million bucks payout you get for winning the Super Bowl.

And I love my job.

A moment later I've got the beast of a sports car back under control and I'm turned back around and gunning it, crossing the palm tree-lined median in pursuit of the other three SUVs now winding their way up to the fort.

"What else do I have... HAL?"

Is that how you do it?

"Do you mean... offensive weapons, sir?" replies the nonplussed car as I downshift, make the turn for the road up to the fort, and take it up through the gears once more. The Maserati sounds like an angry demon with an appetite for high speed and high speed alone. Beyond the walls of the gaming suite, the "Shoot to Thrill" rock and roll show goes end of the world in the stadium and everyone goes nuts along with it. On screen I see the three SUVs making the next turn ahead and climbing higher into the jungle that surrounds the old fort.

"Yeah... HAL... what can I shoot them with?"

"Well, nothing at the moment, in this configuration. We have an oil slick available for use but not included in US commercial models. And that is optimally used when the vehicle is in front of pursuers."

"Perfect." It's RangerSix over BattleChat. "Son, we are getting killed on the plaza. We just lost JollyBoy. Kiwi's barely holding our line. You need to put the target down in the next few or we lose this match here and now. Reinforcements will not reach the objective in time."

And oil slicks are useless.

"What else, HAL?"

"If the car sustains critical damage, you have an ejector seat. It's an actual safety feature in this year's Maserati McConaughey. Maserati... It's super groovy, sir."

Was that an ad?

So... great. I can bail out before I blow up. That's not much help either.

I catch the convoy on the next S-turn and tell the car to shift into autodrive. I shoot out the windshield with a blur of lead from the silenced MP10 and then start putting rounds into the tires of the trailing vehicle as a stream of brass dancers leap out and away across my HUD.

And why exactly is this thing silenced?

Except I say that out loud.

"This summer," announces HAL, "James Bond goes extreme in StormEye."

Oh. Another product placement. Got it. James Bond gun.

The MP manages to chew up one tire as both vehicles weave across the road, and I'm fighting a brief bout of screen vertigo on the next turn just to stay on their tail.

We're almost to the top. Almost to the castle.

"Warning," announces HAL.

"Uh-oh…" I mutter and reload. On screen my avatar ejects a magazine and slaps in a new one.

I target another vehicle and fire a steady stream of bullets at it. We're doing eighty. The MP sounds like a bubbling hiss of angry hornets. I chew up more of the trailing armored SUV's back door than anything else. Then both bullet-smashed rear doors fling open. Two armored Ubermarine grunts in juggernaut suits, carrying M214 micro-miniguns, unload on the Maserati at near point-blank.

"Multiple juggernauts detected," announces HAL.

Did he suddenly sound frantic?

The Maserati is about to be ripped to shreds by hundreds of rounds from the miniguns. They're deadly up close, and the storm of ball ammunition creates the optical effect of a tornado blur shimmering in the digital reality. That's three thousand individual nine-millimeter ball ammunition rounds filling the space between us.

"I'm dead."

I jerk the wheel hard left and literally steer the car up onto the mountainside to get away from the juggernauts.

"Off-road mode engaged," announces the car joyfully.

"Take over!" I shout and unload on the juggernauts clinging to the back of the SUV and trying to follow me with their spitting miniguns. The Maserati takes a course through heavy brush parallel to the road, sending my avatar bouncing into the ceiling, but at least we're not sitting ducks over here, and somehow we're keeping pace. The road behind the SUV comes apart in bright flashes and chunks of concrete as my gunfire sprays wild.

WarWorld spares no expense for physics rendering and VFX, and the moment verges on excessive levels of destruction.

I catch the armored Marine with a little of my strafe.

Juggernauts are hardened suits made of nano-carbon-polymer armor that can withstand blasts rated up to nuclear. My pathetic weapon isn't doing anything to him.

But the vehicle he's riding in ...

I grab the steering peripheral and yank the Maserati into the front end of the SUV while flooring the accelerator. It's a perfect hit and forces the big SUV off the cliff road and out into open air.

Play to win... or don't play at all.

Two vehicles left as the SUV that just went off-road explodes in fireball fury somewhere below the road.

"*Vehicle Integrity at 45 Percent*" flashes in my HUD.

The car is telling me major service is required.

Really.

The two other SUVs race away around a curve. We're nearing the summit.

If there are any more juggernauts, I'm out of tricks.

At the top of the hill I make the last turn at a speed even I realize is far too dangerous. And I find myself facing four juggernauts in defensive position surrounding an SUV stopped and blocking the road.

I'm simultaneously considering ramming straight into them just to see what that'll do, and trying to go around them at high speed. I can see Enigmatrix, out of her vehicle, running through staged lighting into the old fort. Probably for the high battlements that overlook New Havana and the plaza. A few seconds after that she'll be taking out ColaCorp with shots from a killer satellite.

I'm hitting the brakes and power-sliding the Maserati as the mini-gun chorus begins in front of me.

I hear the whir of the man-portable death cannons as car windows begin to shatter.

"May I suggest Guardian Mode, sir?" says HAL less than enthusiastically. "It's a major plot point in StormEye. I think it may be of help… right now."

The four minis are turning the Maserati's hood into Swiss cheese as we slide off the road. I unintelligibly shout an acknowledgement, which is enough for HAL.

"Guardian Mode initiated…" announces HAL almost triumphantly.

Suddenly my POV inside the car is rising. In my HUD the vehicle status display is changing from sports car to… mech?

New weapons come online.

Yes! I have two miniguns. And they ain't puny nine-mils. These are real thirty-millimeter chain-gun close-air-support bad boys.

I target the four juggernauts and sweep both blazing weapons across them. Three are torn apart in gruesomely rendered VFX, and the SUV explodes behind them. One juggernaut soldier tries to turn and run, but I reach out and slap him sideways with one of the hot barrels. That guy goes flying off into the jungle. The rest are dead. Riddled into swiss cheese.

Now I'm moving fast.

RangerSix is telling me we're down to the two-minute warning.

"She's got lock and a window on the plaza, son. We are extremely vulnerable at this moment. Satellite is in position to take out all our stuff, Question."

I check the ammo inside the miniguns. A few bursts at best. I might have gone a little crazy and forgotten to conserve ammo when I was murdering everybody back there. I see Enigmatrix running along one of the battlements above, her massive long gun target designator held at port arms.

I unload with what's left in the chain guns, hoping for a lucky kill shot. I get nothing but flying fragments of ancient digitally rendered Spanish stone.

She stops. She's on a squat tower that overlooks downtown Havana. She's absolutely got everything in sight. The mech is in sprint and I'm closing as fast as I can. But I don't think I'll reach her in time.

In other words, she has all the time in the world to lase every target in the AO and call in an orbital strike for Game Over. And win the Super Bowl.

The *WarWorld* directors couldn't ask for a better last clip to call the match on. Game over.

"Move!" I scream at my monitor. I can't move fast enough, and I know Enigmatrix is targeting everything.

Except she isn't.

She doesn't target what remains of our strike force around the objective.

She targets *me*.

A green laser caresses my mech as I cross the wide courtyard below in long loping strides.

She's going to take me out first.

The game announces, "Orbital surgical strike inbound. Surgical micro-munition fired from orbit."

Take me out first. Two minutes is all the time in the world to take out the rest of ColaCorp.

"No." I punch the eject key, and suddenly the cockpit disintegrates around me and I'm flying away from the mech. Toward Enigmatrix.

I can't avoid the orbital strike. It'll hit wherever I'm at. It's surgical. Which in orbital strike terms means it'll make a big hole in the ground wherever I'm at.

So… I choose to be next to her.

I land on the battlement, barely reaching her.

And now we're both dead.

White searing light washes out my monitor as the orbital surgical strike smokes our location.

Game over.

And all around and above me the stadium goes nuts.

We just won the Super Bowl.

Chapter Three

Everybody is suddenly rushing my gaming suite down in the concrete passages beneath the stadium. I hear hammering on the security door as I disentangle from headphones, gaming chair, and surround desk. I open the door and see RangerSix managing a broad smile through his normal wry determination. Beyond him the corridor is filled with the rest of the ColaCorp team and a bunch of other people. In fact… it's a lot of people. Groupies. Cheerleaders. Ultramodels. High-dollar suits with smiling let's-make-a-deal giant white teeth. Everybody is losing their minds, and that's nothing compared to what's going on in the stadium above.

It sounds as though the whole place is about to come down around all of us. The crowd is stamping on the floors of every level. The noise is like the roar of the ocean.

Then security and event personnel are rushing us up through the catacombs where the state-of-the-art gaming suites we've been playing in have been installed. We're hustled out onto the main stage and shoved unexpectedly in front of a hundred thousand screaming fans in real time. Everyone is screaming at us. Everyone is screaming at the top of their lungs. And beyond and above, looming over everything, the world watches us through ultrajumbotrons the size of small buildings. Through drones that swarm the sky. Through floating Sky Zeppelin party palaces. The winning play repeats over and over again on the main jumbo, occasionally cutting away to other moments of extreme and epic in-game violence. All of this is intermixed with faces, *live* faces forming emphatic words with the urgency of third-rate prophets of doom, but hundreds of feet high and wide. Monday-morning quarterbacks who can't wait to break down what just happened.

Surreal, as a descriptor, just doesn't work in the here and now of all this.

It's not just sensory overload… it's sensory blitzkrieg.

Kiwi, in his high-performance sports wheelchair, is grinning up at me like a mad lunatic. And yeah… now the whole stadium is chanting my gamertag.

It's in the middle of all this that I find I'm suddenly thinking about my mom and dad. Mara and Bill. They would be honestly, and genuinely, proud. Especially Mom. It was she who told me what the Perfect Question was.

To be or not to be. That is the perfect question.

And then the *WarWorld* execs are handing out trophies while stunning ultramodels come and pose with me and the rest of the ColaCorp team. The world feels like it's turned upside down as giant novelty checks are handed out and a million interviews seem to begin all at once. Suddenly I have a team of people who are… handling me.

It's much later when my new agent, as of three hours ago, calls my suite at the Peninsula Hotel. Dawn is just twenty minutes away. I've drunk too much and I have about ten thousand new contacts in my smartphone, many from the models who were basically guiding me through the post-game festivities. I check my account. The prize money from the match, plus all the bonuses, is there. Along with almost all this season's winnings and a whole bunch from before.

I am *beyond* loaded.

For much of the last hour, on the beach just before dawn, I was walking with a model whose name I can't remember now, thinking about where to go next. I've got six months off and a ton of money. Anywhere and everything is possible.

Then it's back to *WarWorld*.

The phone rings. It's Irving Wong. My new e-sports agent. We met during the Razer party. He also represents the new Batman actor. So he must be big-time, sorta.

"Hey, PQ!" he says in his cigar-smoke-ravaged voice.

I see his name in the caller ID.

"Mr. Wong." My parents raised me to be polite. I've been thinking about them a lot as surreality has become a new reality. Like they're some anchor I must hold on to, or otherwise go spinning off over the cliffs of insanity.

"PQ! Rock star! Baby!" Irv erupts at just after dawn, Havana time, as the multi-colored city surrenders to the full glare of an unrelenting tropical morning. I can see people in the streets below from the wide window of my top-floor suite. Still dancing. But many are streaming away to wherever it is they're staying. It's expected after almost twenty-four straight hours of nonstop Super Bowl partying.

"Call me Irv, PQ."

I agree to.

Again. Politeness. I'm tired so I kick off my loafers and lay the suit jacket I had made in Rome across the emperor-sized bed. Maybe it's time to go back. Have another one made. I liked Rome a lot.

"Okay, cutting to the chase, kid," Irv begins. "I already got something for you. Something very hot. A booking that starts now-ish. You game?"

"Now-ish?" The thought of throwing myself into another e-sports combat game seems impossible at this moment. As in… triathlon impossible the day after you've quit your habit of smoking and eating three cheeseburgers a day.

I exhale, involuntarily. I'm not just suffering from game fatigue, or binge tiredness… I've got a serious case of game hangover. It's been six months of straight matches every weekend, and we've been winning pretty consistently. You'd think winning makes it easier, but it doesn't. It makes things much, much harder. Every match… every engagement... every bullet... develops some massive psychic weight of importance that must be constantly accounted for and dealt with. Gaming isn't just fun at this level... it's become a business.

And I'm beat tired.

I sit on the bed and feel its whispering invitation to sweet oblivion. Darkness. Just sweet silent no-monitor-or-flashing-smartphone-lights *darkness*. I could seriously do that.

"Ever heard of a game called *Civ Craft*?" barks Irv over the faraway phone in my hand.

I have. It looks pretty awesome. But it's team-based. And I already play for a team in *WarWorld*.

"Well you know it's got national teams, right?" asks Irv.

"Sure," I mumble distantly. Giant bed is calling to me. Singing a song really. A lullaby just like the kind mermaids were supposed to lure sailors to their deaths with.

"Okay, so, follow me here, kid. You know that a lot of national entities field teams to compete within this *Civ Craft* world, right? They all work together to build living-world civilizations from the ground up. People actually go on virtual vacations in the top-tier one. That's cray-cray," says the old man using his old man lingo.

I've vaguely heard stuff like this. Again, I don't really know much about the game. *WarWorld* and its military team combat are more my thing. Infantry operations especially.

"Sure."

"Okay, well one of these entities is interested in recruiting you for their national team. And there's some big money involved. Rich country, lots of oil reserves. They're going to pay you, and me my fifteen percent of course, in gold to come down and fight for them. They've got a big thing going down and they want pro gamers who are willing to merc for cash. Except the cash is gold which is way better. So, they called about an hour ago and they really want the MVP of the Super Bowl to come help them out. Interested?"

I'm really too tired to go anywhere in the near future. I'm pretty sure a week in this bed turning back into a human being is all I'm capable of.

"It's a one-month contract with an option for another. Five million in gold per month."

I'm wide awake.

"Kid…" growls Irv low and conspiratorially like we're spies, or mobsters. "This is…"

"I'm in," I shout, hearing my voice bounce off the walls of the suite.

"Ha-cha!" erupts Irv triumphantly. Like he's just won a hand of pinochle or got the high score on a *Super Mario Bros.* upright he found in the back of a liquor store that still takes vintage quarters when you can find 'em. Some old guy thing only old guys ever get excited about. "Knew you would be. Okay. Car's waiting downstairs in front of the hotel to get you to Havana International directly. Private jet will take you over to LAX, and then I'll deliver you to the client myself."

No bed?

Nah, I think to myself. Five million in gold. I'll get some coffee. Who needs bed?

I stand and feel vaguely drunk. And washed out. And dehydrated. And papery and thin. And I need a shave. I slip on my loafers and jacket and grab my Samurai Leather messenger bag containing my laptop.

I take one last look at Giant Bed.

It would've been real nice.

"Where am I going, Irv?"

"Calistan, kid. The Gold Coast of Calistan. Used to be called Southern California… before the Meltdown."

Chapter Four

Everything is a blur. Havana steams in the morning sun and consumed rum seems to be coming out of everyone's pores in vaporous clouds, including mine. Downstairs beyond the lobby, a hover limo picks me up and we're heading for the airport. Below us, along the old cobblestone streets, revelers still stream back toward the massive pleasure palace hotels that rise across the new skyline. Even without the Super Bowl, Havana is one of the luxury party capitals of the world. And this weekend... it threw the biggest party on the planet.

Leaving already? appears on my smartphone. It's Kiwi. Is he just coming in? Did he see me going out?

Gotta gig, I text back. *Link up later?*

I'd ask for more details... he types and doesn't finish until the limo is descending down to curbside at Tito Puente International. *But I'm too beat to read your reply. Gubnight*, he manages.

The sun is reflecting off high clouds coursing across the eastern Caribbean sky. Some storm is brewing way out in the Atlantic and it's sending its tendrils of clouds flinging off into the west. Tall palms rustle and shake in the late-morning tropical breeze. Everyone will leave when the storm comes, but me, I'd like to just hunker down in a hotel and sleep it out, maybe watch the rain wash everything off into the gutters. Even go out in it, late in the evening, and walk around alone. When it's the worst and no one else is out there. That's when you feel alive again.

Or maybe I just need coffee.

An hour later, a chartered hyperjet is wheels up and we're streaking out over emerald waters for the mainland. I'm the only passenger on board.

The stewardess, a cat-eyed Latina in a form-fitting body suit that makes her look like some South American superhero, offers me coffee. It's hot and dark, and the cream I pour into it is sweet and thick. A moment later she brings out a plate with assorted fried doughnuts.

Except these aren't doughnuts.

These are *super* doughnuts.

I choose a maple and crisped pork belly buttermilk old-fashioned. Then a glazed stuffed with a soft poached egg, some Hollandaise, and a sprig of basil.

The first bite has me groaning ecstatically, and the stunning Latina smiles warmly down at me where I lay inside my couch. She smiles like she's really pleased I'm enjoying these epic doughnuts so much. Like she made them herself. She's a good person. I can tell. She's the kind I should get to know for all the other reasons besides the fact that she's drop-dead gorgeous.

And then the doughnuts are mostly finished and I'm asleep.

Deep, deep, way deep down past dreaming sleep.

Have I mentioned I haven't slept for about thirty-six hours?

I'm sure there's all kinds of drooling, curling up into some sort of fetal position, and snoring, but I'm so gone everything is beyond my control. Real attractive. Smokin' hot Latinas love that sort of helpless thing. Dream me is sure of it.

But those doughnuts and coffee knocked me out.

As though my body said, "This far and no farther, gunslinger."

And I was helpless to dispute the call.

Chapter Five

I'm in my body.

That's an odd thought. I mean, I've had it before. Especially after generous amounts of scotch. But I have that out of body in a different body feeling now... I know it.

But it's like... I need to be told it first before things can start...

That's important. Or maybe too much scotch and game hangover are getting together to work me over.

It's dark. But I know it's morning. I know that. And the thought is somehow comforting to me. Like when you're a kid. And it's Saturday morning. Or the first day of summer. No school and nothing but seemingly never-ending fun in all the endless days ahead. Exploring and building forts. Dirt clod fights. Long days. Pleasant nights.

It's like that.

Like a great book that never ends.

But someone is banging on something nearby. Shutters. Or a flimsy door, maybe. Banging and banging in the half-light of morning. And they've been banging for quite a while in my sleep, because I was sure I was asleep before I needed to be told I was in my body.

And then there's this voice.

It's not IRL. Not... in real life. But it's like a narrator's voice. Kindly. But old. Aged and smoky too. Fall leaves and smoke. That's what it reminds me of. Of barrel-aged whiskey.

Like that Baldwin AI everyone wanted a few Christmases back.

Personal avatar butler based on some long-dead actor. Like that guy's voice.

It says…

"You awake in the Lost Valley, adventurer."

And then that banging is gone and I hear, or at least I think I hear, someone in heavy boots stomping off across hard-packed dirt, grumbling to themselves in a husky mutter.

I hear this and open my eyes to the half-light of dawn creeping into a stable through wooden slats.

I'm in a stable.

I can't remember where I was before this.

But I'm in this stable now.

At dawn.

In the Lost Valley.

"You awake in a stable within an ancient keep on the borderlands between civilization… and the unknown."

Okay. That's pretty odd.

Am I in a game? Or a dream? VR? Or somehow I'm having one of those delusional psychotic reality breaks they try to cover up that happen in particularly bad game hangovers. I try to remember stuff… but I can't. Stuff like who I am. It's all gone.

There's nothing else except this present unknown reality.

And when my mind goes there, to whoever it is I am, it's like I'm looking, eyes wide open, into a giant blank space within the universe. Not darkness. Just nothing nothingness. But…

It's a kind of nothingness inside my mind. A place I can see, but can't look into directly. Is this Me?

I stand up.

It's not VR.

I can feel the dirt beneath my feet. It's dry. My body itches from the hay I've been sleeping in. Through the wooden slats of the stable wall, I see the gray light of morning.

How do I know that?

How do I know it's morning light?

It feels like morning light. Morning light looks like what I'm seeing. Gray and wan sometimes. It just does. Clean and cold. Maybe I'm wrong. But that's what morning looks like.

And who was knocking, rattling the wooden doors of the barn I'm standing in? Banging on them in the half-light of dawn.

And why?

It definitely felt like it was for me. Like I was being summoned to something, or looked for.

I walk to those doors that were being battered in my dream, or whatever this is. They're flimsy-looking and I reach out to touch them and find they're as real as anything I've ever touched.

So it's definitely not VR.

Not a dream.

I'm here. In the Lost Valley. Whatever that is? Or is it... *where*ver that is? Something tells me it's more of a what than a where, which seems odd because where definitely implies geographical. Still... it feels like a what.

I unlatch the doors to the barn and push them open. They swing outward easily, and I'm looking at a fortress across a small dirt road from where I stand. High walls rise up before me. Golden sunshine glistens along their stony front. There are towers up there. High up there. And men. Men with crossbows look down, keeping watch over the outer walls. Small pennants flap in the barest of a morning breeze.

I look at myself.

I'm wearing a tattered white... karate outfit. Except it feels as light as silk. A thick cloth belt. No shoes. I look back inside the barn and see a pair of wooden sandals. And a sheathed sword. Like the kind samurai warriors use. A long one. A katana. It's lying next to the sandals near the hay where I slept. There's straw on the dirt floor of the barn. And even some on my karate outfit.

I return and put on the sandals.

No equip key. No weird dream-like distortion where I can't actually ever get the sandals on because I really need to call... someone... and I can never seem to dial the correct number in the dream and I wake up wondering what that was all about. A name floats across my mind. Then it's gone. But it's a name I once knew.

In dreams there's always that super important task that can never be accomplished. Find her. Call her. Work things out. It's still not too late even though it's been years.

But there's no dream distortion in this stable, in this... Lost Valley. The dream remains steady in its chosen reality and refuses to shift to some bizarre set of circumstances where I need to call that name I can't remember on my... phone... but first I have to wash this tiger because that's important somehow. There's none of that right here and now.

Instead I tie on the wooden sandals just like I would tie on real wooden sandals. Except I've never tied on wooden sandals.

I pick up the sword.

I pull the hilt away from the sheath.

Yep. Katana. And it's very sharp. It practically sings as I barely slide it from the wooden sheath.

Note to self: be careful. This may not be a game...

I adjust my karate jacket... blouse, whatever it's called... and place the katana in my large cloth belt. It seems like that's where it should go.

This is all very odd. That's what I'm thinking as I return to the open doors at the front of the stable. Once more I stare up at the medieval fortress turned gold by the morning sunlight.

"Good morn, Master Samurai."

A girl. Dirty face and yet pretty. Rough potato sack for a dress... but smiling and cute. She's carrying an armload of chopped wood. She has strawberry hair and pink freckles on her nose.

"I say good morning, Master Samurai," she tries again. Brightly.

Apparently she's talking to me. Apparently I am "Master Samurai."

I try a nod. Which seems like the right thing to do if someone assumes you're an oriental master of martial death. Just play along.

She seems cheerily satisfied with my lie and continues on up the dirt track below the massive walls of the fortress. I watch her traverse the lane between inner and outer wall. On one side are various shops, and on the other, tall houses. Other people are moving about, and I can smell food. And... wood smoke. I hear the strokes of a blacksmith pounding metal. Slowly beating iron into some useful shape.

It's all very medieval.

And yet I'm a samurai. Apparently.

The world around me feels like a vibrant, living thing. Like there is an ongoing persistent story I've only just stepped into. From the smell of the wood smoke to the sound of the ringing hammer. A flight of crows crosses the sky heading for somewhere beyond the walls. Another flight follows. And then another. Each flight calling out their "caw caw" greeting as they pass overhead in ragged wedges.

Up the street a sudden commotion breaks the pastoral calm of this medieval morning. People shouting. Indignant at some sudden and rash offense. A rough voice calling out "Alarum! Alarum!" Like it's a play at a Renaissance Faire interrupting everyone's calm stroll through the shops.

I hear the horse whinnying in terror before I see it thundering down the street from deeper within the castle. The voice called it a "keep" but I'm not really sure what that is. There's a mass of people scattering up that way and then I see the giant warhorse break away from the commotion and rush down the narrow lane. Its shod hooves are sending up sparks from the cobblestones. It's big and dark. So black it's almost blue. Its nostrils are flared, eyes rolling and wild... with red rage, or terror.

And I realize it's coming right at me.

Me.

Not… a samurai, or whoever I really am. But me in whatever real reality I find myself in. Average me.

I step back to get out of the way, fearfully. Yes. I'll admit that. I step back fearfully because it's all so real. And because the horse is like something out of a nightmare. My hand, on the other hand, goes to the hilt of the katana in my belt. Like it's going to do something if something needs to be done.

Some distant part of my mind asks me, *What? What are you going to do? Strike out as it goes by? Cut down a giant horse with a samurai blade you've never used?*

A thundering, cobblestone-clapping monster roaring at me and I'm going to…

…step out of the way is what I'm going to do.

Crossbow bolts fly down from the tops of the walls, and a figure, a rider hidden behind the warhorse's heaving neck until now, rises up. The guards from up the street are shooting too. Shooting at the horse and rider. Suddenly the air is filled with whistling death. Bolts are just appearing in the dirt at my feet, or flying past my head, or smashing into the brittle barn wood with thunderclap snaps of cracking ancient weatherworn boards.

And as the fear-driven beast thunders past, that figure on the horse rises up and laughs at the world.

He's wearing black leather.

Like something out of a Mad Max movie.

And how do I know that? How do I know what a Mad Max movie is?

I just do.

His laugh is like the staccato bray of a donkey. There's a sneer on his face. A sneer rolling across fat lips that twists half of his face into a grimace. Spiky blond hair barely moves even though the black mane of the horse ripples in the wind of its passage, undulating like tendrils of drowned sea grass underneath the armor of a dark and unknown ocean.

And then horse and rider are past me without comment, and a crossbow bolt buries itself in the barn door not inches from my head.

In that swift passing, the rider turns and fixes me with a stern gaze. There's no laughter. Blue eyes consume me and twinkle mischievously before that twisted sneer whiplashes into a devil-may-care smile.

Then he's gone, and horse and rider turn at the bottom of the lane heading for the main gate. Guards in chain armor, crossbows at port arms, come clattering down the street after them. But they'll never catch that horse.

Or that rider. I'm sure of that.

Up the street I see the freckle-faced girl who carried an armload of firewood and wished me a good morning. Now she lies like a clump of unwanted rags in the middle of the street between the walls of this place. The chopped wood has been scattered out and away from her unmoving corpse.

A large man pushes past the gathering crowd, crying out, "Becca! My Beccs! No, please…" And then he's running toward the prone figure, the girl with the smile. The horse and rider must have ridden her down in their mad flight for the gate.

A chubby guard with a kind and oafish face approaches me. He's breathing heavily.

He stops to catch his breath, and I see he's not all oaf. There's an intelligence there behind his eyes. The oaf is just what he looks like. As though central casting needed such an actor to play such a part. As though anatomy truly is destiny.

"We're in it now, sire!" he gasps.

I step from the shadows of the barn, one hand still on the wrapped hilt of the blade. I can feel a quiet confident power there, and it comforts me. It dispels the mad terror of the dark horse and the whiplash smile of the man on its back. As though those things are of no concern to the truth of the blade.

"Who was that?" I ask.

"That," gasps the guard and rises up straight, adjusting his sword belt over a broad belly. "Why that was William Alucard. Priest of Chaos. He was our prisoner here in the keep on the borderlands."

* * *

She's gently shaking me hours later. The beautiful superhero Latina with the mysterious cat eyes just above a glass of cold orange juice offered out to me. The best I'd ever taste. I was sure of it.

"We're here," she whispers softly.

"Already…" I manage. My lips are numb because my face has been pressing against my seat. I was deep down there in the Land of Nod. Wherever that is. And I can't remember the dream. And maybe I wasn't even dreaming at all. Maybe I was just so tired I was out. Almost dead.

Her broad beautiful lips pout. As though she's sad our time must come to an end. "*Sí.*"

"Where?" I ask, because I honestly cannot remember where I was going. Where I'm supposed to be arriving next. I've been "going" a lot of places lately. I've lost track before. It happens.

"Los Angeles," she reminds me.

I thought I was going to Calistan. I tell her this.

"Ah…" Her eyes widen. Then, "*Lo siento, señor.* Calistan is currently a no-fly zone. Plus their airport was blown up by terrorists last week. The captain says we'll be landing at LAX, and I'm sure you can take a car south into Calistan. It's only an hour away."

She hands me the orange juice and I sit up to drink it. It's refreshing. I'm awake though I feel hung over, not just from the many, many mojitos I guzzled the night before in Havana, but from the games. From my life playing games for money.

I need one solid day of being not PerfectQuestion. One real day.

I need a couch. Hash browns and eggs. I make the best hash browns. And a jazz playlist. Maybe the latest *Road Warrior* movie. Then a long walk in some park. And a book in bed. Early. Dark beyond the windows kept at bay by the soft glow of a lamp. None of all the other stuff that's been my life for the last nine months.

Just life. Life and nothing more.

I'm hoping for a moment to catch my breath. Somewhere in the next few days there's got to be such a moment.

Super Latina says goodbye at the cabin door, and the wind catches a piece of her caramel-colored hair and brushes it across her forehead. She smiles. Waves. Pushes the hair back into place. And I know I'm missing out on something. Something right in a world that's losing meaning.

Irv, my new agent, meets me inside the uber-plush private terminal. He's an old Chinese guy dressed in a bad suit. He's been burnt by years of sun exposure but his teeth and what's left of his hair are perfect. He's smoking a big cigar.

"Hey!" he erupts. "How ya doin, kid!"

He sounds like a native New Yorker. The ones that still live down in Lower New York beneath the massive arches of Upper New York.

LA's got arches too. Massive curving bows that soar over the old city and barrios and the poor on the ground. Beautiful curving skyscrapers where the rich and the elite live. Gentle giant arcs of grace and beauty. I guess LA's that kind of place too.

I shake his hand. We've never actually met. And he's really only been my agent since about midnight. I figured I needed representation after the clip of me winning went viral on ScreamChat. Last time I checked it had over one billion hits. Endorsements got crazy, so some *WarWorld* exec hooked me up with Irv for representation.

"Car's this way. You hungry, kid?"

I'm always hungry and I tell him that.

"Good. We'll get short rib tacos in K Town and head south. It's a long drive and the border is tight. Mexicans and all."

I don't know much about what's going on here. I always figured it was dangerous. I mean LA is synonymous with crime, gangs, and private celebrity security. And when we get into his late-model Porsche

Terminator, I notice the ancient nickel-plated .44 Magnum he keeps on the door.

"So... Mexicans?" I prompt a few minutes later as we hit the 110 toll highway doing close to a hundred. There's an old highway below us and it's jammed with every kind of vehicle. It seems like it's in a state of perpetual gridlock. But on this private tollway above it all, we're flying like there's no tomorrow.

"Guns are illegal in Los Angeles," Irv says when he notices me staring at the massive hand cannon. "But I deal with a lot of celebrities, so... when you're on the right side of things in California you get special perks not everybody else has access to. Know what I mean, kid?" He indicates the traffic jam below. He's shouting because we have the top down. We're doing a hundred and thirty now, crossing under one of the arches that straddle the old city of Los Angeles, heading toward a cluster of massive skyscrapers that rise up to connect with the arches that intersect over downtown.

He shifts into sixth and I don't even want to look at the speedometer. Everything is a blur. Including the other high-performance sports cars we're passing like they're standing still.

Chapter Six

We're having marinated Korean short rib meat that's been stuffed into a flour tortilla which has been charred over mesquite wood. House-made sriracha and a kimchi plate with mint and Thai basil stand watch over the rest. Hipsters and the LA elite have stuffed themselves into the small tables all around us. Everyone seems grateful to be here. As though they've finally arrived at the place where all good things are ultimately handed out to the if-not deserving, then connected crowd. The line of other hipsters and elites we passed on the way in, as we walked straight to the front of said line, was half a mile long. No joke.

"That's El Lay, kid," said Irv when we landed at the host stand in front of the tiny restaurant. "And so's this…"

The guy at the host stand smiled and showed us straight to this tiny table near the open-grill oven. The scent of high-end wood smoke made the two Thai margaritas we polished off before our smoking meat was set out taste even better. We are like ancient Viking warlords. Or rich corporate raiders. Or that rarest of all creatures… the man with connections that transcend the monetary enough to get him a table at the latest hip eatery.

In LA that seems to be akin to some kind of royalty.

"Yeah, Mexicans," says Irv through a more than generous bite of his Kung Pao burrito. He looks skyward as he chews. "I used to be an actor," he says, as though suddenly inspired by the sensation of tastes. "Was on a big show before the Meltdown. *Captain Dare*." He looks at me like I should know the reference. I don't.

"Who cares." He sighs and takes another gusty bite. "Old news is old news. Anyway… when I was an actor you could never eat like this. Best thing that ever happened to me out of the Meltdown is that I got to eat food again. This… this is heaven. Am I right?" His already bulging eyes somehow grow impossibly wider, beckoning me to acknowledge the nirvana of taste we are experiencing.

It's good food.

"Yeah, anyway… Mexicans," he continues after another bite of the spicy grilled meat inside the charred tortilla. He pauses to dip it in a venomously hot Thai chile chimichurri. "Well… they hate everybody down there. But the people they hate the most are the muzzies down in Orange County. Whoops—I always forget—I mean the Caliphate. Calistan now." He rolls his eyes and takes another angry bite of his generous burrito. "It used to be called Orange County back in the day. Good times then. Was a pretty nice place, truth be told. Anyway… it's an Islamic state now, as you well know. Went that way after the Meltdown and all. So… you're either part of the royal family down there, or you're poor. And if you're a Mexican then you're poor *and* pissed off.

"Anyway, they've been agitating lately. You don't hear that on the news. But they have. They'd like to send 'em all back to Allah, or wherever it is they think they get their seventy-two virgins. Oy vey! Can you imagine that?" says the Chinese guy who talks like a Brooklyn Jew eating Korean short rib burritos in the power lunch spot of the moment somewhere in downtown LA.

He continues.

"So I'll get you to Checkpoint Charlie down in Long Beach. The fruit bats that run what used to be California and is now, this week, called Pacifica, call it the Brotherhood Bridge. It's in Belmont Shore south of Long Beach, and the Shah's men will be waiting. Trust me… you'll be totally safe. They have armored convoys and state-of-the-art guns. Lots of 'em. It's how they stay in power down there. That and all that oil California could never bring itself to drill up back before the

Meltdown. Things were pretty crazy then too, believe me. But none of that's important for your gig. I'm sure you'll be in a compound behind the line down there somewhere so... it's really actually quite safe. Trust me. Everybody complains about the third world, but I've never had a problem."

When someone tells you to trust them, you shouldn't. It's a rule I've learned a few times. So there's that.

"The line?"

"Yeah. The old 405 freeway is their wall down there inside Calistan. It separates the super-rich Muslim families from the super-poor everyone else. Don't worry, the Mexicans won't get through that. It's mined and there're machine gun towers every hundred yards. The Gold Coast, which is the side you'll be on, now that's paradise. Trust me. You gonna eat that?"

He looks at the other half of my plate.

I am.

But I let him have it. He's making me five million in gold. And for some reason, machine gun towers and mined freeways make me lose my appetite.

"So this is safe?"

He mumbles something as he chews. I think he said, "Mostly."

"Mr. Wong..."

He looks up like a guilty child. He's a nice guy, I can tell. He's probably lived through a lot. My parents did too. They lived through the Meltdown. Never talked about it. Never talked about the bad times for the five years that followed. They just wanted to dance and have fun. In the end they were right. Who knows how much time anyone has left.

"Kid... it's as safe as the rest of the world. You know that. You've been out there. You've been in some stuff. Or so I heard. I'll be honest..." He puts down my burrito and looks around. "It's a nightmare down there. They're crazy. Seriously. But!" He holds up a sun-spotted crooked finger. "They take care of their toys. And you... you're a toy,

PerfectQuestion. You pick up a win for them and they'll probably top off that bonus with something crazy-crass like a gold-plated vintage AK-47 with a diamond on the forward sight. They'll engrave it with your name and call you…" he waves his hand in the air as he imitates a stereotypical Muslim, "my friend for life."

I've seen them on TV.

He stares down at the burrito for a long moment, and he looks suddenly sad. Like he's thinking about other times. Other friends.

Then he picks up the burrito again and says, "But you… you'll be safe. I'll tell you that straight, kid. It's crazy and probably a little dangerous. But there're big bucks and I know you can handle this. You're PerfectQuestion. You're a killer, kid."

He smiles and finishes most of the rest of my burrito in one epic bite.

Chapter Seven

We make the border a few hours later. It's a low crawl through all the southbound traffic, and the closer we get, the more security drones I see in the air. Plus lots of tactical choppers. The kind I occasionally shoot down in games. But these are real and loaded for bear.

Ahead, the massive border at Belmont Shore looms. It's a giant wall. As in Great Wall of China–style wall. On this side, the only side I can see, it's covered with graffiti. All the way to the top. And yeah, there are machine gun nests and towers with spotters up there.

It's that moment. That moment when the money isn't worth your life. And you should just walk away from the thing you've committed to do. That's what the voice inside your head is telling you.

I think Irv senses me hearing it.

He downshifts and looks over at me as we come to a halt in the long line of cars struggling to go south into Calistan. Apparently Hollywood actor contacts don't get you through this particular line any faster than trucks loaded with chickens and doe-eyed Mexican children. It seems everyone wants into Calistan, no matter how bad it is. As if beyond that wall is some fantastically green lawn that will make them finally happy.

"Listen, kid," says Irv. "You'll be fine. I'll keep an eye on you, okay? If it gets hot… you don't like something… I promise I'll get you right out. You got my number. Okay?"

I smile. My mouth is dry.

Five million in gold.

Life-changing money.

But why do I want to change my life? Other than the fact that I don't have one. So, in my case… I'd have to get a life first. Then I could change it.

"I'm good," I croak. But both of us know I'm not. And why do I feel like a real James Bond more than when I was driving the James Bond movie product placement in the last moments of the Super Bowl? Or maybe not Bond himself, but some kind of real-world less-glamorous spy crossing a border where the rules change with the wind. I'm probably just hung over. The latest Bond movie was all over Havana. Its marketing is like a virus inside my hard drive. All I need is some sleep and I'm sure the feeling will defrag.

"Okay," Irv grumbles, gripping the old leather-wrapped steering wheel with both hands and staring straight ahead. "Here we go then."

We approach the checkpoint. Guards glare at Irv like they want to murder him on the spot. All of them are Persian, or Arab, or whatever they are that made them Middle Eastern once. Muslim I guess. And all of them look roided out to combat-gorilla levels. They need to be; they're wearing a ton of gear. Each one has a heavy automatic rifle across his back. AK-2000s. The fifty-caliber kind. If it goes down, they're ready to make lots of big holes in everyone and everything. Never mind the accuracy.

Irv smiles and nods politely like we're going through a car wash. Even bows a little while sitting in the seat of his Porsche. I think his English suddenly gets worse as they ask questions. Maybe that helps somehow when you're crossing hostile foreign borders. A moment later, we're waved through and watched with sullen contempt as we pass.

Beyond the high, almost ancient-world grandeur of the arched border gates, we enter a vast courtyard where trucks and limos wait. Streams of people are crossing on foot through roped lanes and watched by more guards with little pity and lots of contempt. Irv maneuvers through halting traffic, tapping his horn, indicating he wants to head toward a particular limo, an old-school one. Not one of the hovers you get in most cities. This one is heavy-duty though. An SUV. Armored. And very long.

It occurs to me that it's easier to take out a hover limo with an RPG than it is to kill a ground vehicle built like a tank. A high-end tank at that.

"There's our contact," Irv murmurs. He beeps the Porsche's horn twice to get us through a stream of heedless foot traffic headed back into Pacifica.

Two dark-skinned guys in expensive light suits, no ties, step out of the limo. One goes to the rear and opens one of the doors, and out steps a kid. Maybe twenty at best. Smiling and good-looking. What you'd think the son of an Arab sultan would look like. He's wearing white slacks and a polo t-shirt. The expensive Ray-Bans are no doubt SoftEye-enabled, and they make his white teeth look like shining sheets of pearl. He has a million-dollar smile on top of that. A smile that says he's the king of the world. And as far as everyone around him is concerned… he is.

"That's Rashid," says Irv. "Your new boss. Other than his dad… he pretty much owns this place."

And by *place*, he means the country we've just entered.

Chapter Eight

"My friend," gushes Rashid as we're stuffed into his limo. And yes, both drivers are carrying beneath sand-colored lightweight jackets. State-of-the-art subcompact SuperKriss MKX machine guns with collapsible stocks, along with big old pistols of the macho cowboy variety beneath their armpits and packed into their barely fitting jackets.

"I have watched all your clips and your streams!" continues Rashid excitedly. "This is for me like meeting a movie star—even though I have met many. They're all whores of course. But fun. Just like whores should be, you know what I mean? But…" He stumbles, seeking the right words in English, which seems to be his second language, though not by much. "You've actually *done* something with your life. I can't believe this. Ahmed—get us out of this hellhole!"

And by *hellhole* he means the border of his country.

From behind the smoked-glass windows of the suddenly speeding limo I see that we're careening through streets swollen with foot traffic. The driver doesn't seem to care much if he hits anyone. And my new boss is jabbering a million miles a second about every match I've played over the last six months.

"This is going to be truly great! Now we've got a real team. So far we're, and I'll just be totally honest with you, PerfectQuestion…"

I feel a thump against the side of the car. A receding muffled scream barely penetrates the soft luxury we're swaddled in. Rashid doesn't seem to notice, or care, that we just ran someone over. I think. I look out the back window, but all I see is another limo, identical to ours, and behind that some kind of ancient armored urban assault carrier doing its best to follow us at high speed.

"We're getting beat to hell by the Japanese. They're the absolute best right now at *Civ Craft*. They've got a fully functioning civilization going, and they've already set up mines on Tharsis. To get *anywhere* in the game we've got to take them out and secure that region. And now we will! You and the rest of the team are going to really turn things around for us here in Calistan. We're going to make Mars great. Y'know, for Islam and Calistan of course."

Now we're on some kind of road that's been barricaded on both sides. Old storefronts have been boarded up and alleys and side streets have been sealed off by graffiti-covered steel barriers. Massive red, white, and black signs in what I can only imagine is Arabic seem to indicate exactly what's going on. But since I don't read Arabic, I have no idea what's going on. Maybe it's some kind of private road. For limos only.

"Okay, so…" continues Rashid, oblivious to the third world we're speeding through. "You're going to love it here and we're going to have lots of fun, but… we have something going down right now and we're gonna need you to jump in right away, my friend. So we're meeting a mobile gaming team that's set up to connect you to the rest of the team." He pauses. "It's that important," he says seriously.

I just got here. In fact, I haven't even finished getting here yet. *Here* is somewhere up ahead. And I'm beat. I haven't slept in an actual bed since before the Super Bowl. The thought of gaming makes me feel slightly sick. But the thought of five million in gold at month's end… that makes me smile and nod affirmatively like there's nothing I'd rather do than log in and start killing stuff.

"I hate to throw you right into the mix, PQ," says Rashid as though he doesn't hate it in the least. "But listen, you're great, so I know you can handle it and all. One quick battle in the next few minutes and then we'll get to my palace and you'll never even have to set foot in this forsaken part of Calistan ever again the entire time you're here. I promise. I get it—it's my country and I hate it out here worse than you do. The people are dogs and savages here. But you're going to love the Gold Coast once we get there. That's the real Calistan. The kind you see in the advertising. Beautiful people. Not this..."

He smiles sourly and looks out the window. We're passing through some kind of slum. Distantly I hear police sirens beyond the limo's luxurious silence. People are crammed onto the sidewalks watching us pass. I see an old street sign. It says Beach Boulevard. It looks like any sign you'd see in the third world. Not some lost part of America that never made it back after the Melt.

"Hey," whispers Rashid absently, as if only to himself. "It's my kingdom and even I admit it's a hellhole. I won't lie to you about that, my friend. Not at all."

Silence. Awkward silence.

"Seems nice," I try. It's the first thing I've said.

"It can be. In other places. It's beautiful where these people haven't been allowed to ruin it. The private beaches are glorious. You'll love them. You can stay in my palace tonight, and for as long as you like. Or I can get you one of our state beach houses if you want that. We've got great internet, so no worries... you can game wherever. But you'll probably be safer inside the Gold Coast. On top of the hill it's paradise. Down here with the savages, not so much.

"Okay. Before I forget, here's a badge. Keep this around your neck. Yeah... I know. Not sexy. But it gets you everything you want in Calistan. And I mean everything. Local girls will totally put out if they see it. It's their big chance. So... have fun, buddy. But first..."

He's craning his head to look out the front of the limo. I do too and see a small military convoy encircling a massive semi hauling some sort of high-tech rig. "We've gotta fight off an attack that's going down on Crescent City Station, in-game right now. We'll use our state mobile gamer truck. We've set it up to link up with the rest of the team because it's going from bad to worse as we speak. Our clans and most of my generals are idiots. Enigmatrix needs our help ASAP."

He must be getting updates behind his Ray-Bans.

And...

"Enigmatrix?"

"Yeah. I hired her. Is that cool? You're both team generals for the Caliphate of Calistan on Mars inside *Civ Craft*. So let's rock and kill us some Japs, buddy!"

Chapter Nine

Once we're within the mobile perimeter surrounding the massive idling semi, and past all the bristling security, it's like a movie set. Or at least it's like entertainment shows I've watched that take place on movie sets. There's even a table laden with sumptuous food. Most of the people beyond the barriers look half-starved as they watch the production and security teams swarm like ants being attacked.

"Quick coffee and some sweets, my friend?" asks Rashid in a businesslike tone as I trail him toward the spread. It's all well done. Bone china. Silver platters of strange confections. But only the coffee calls to me. I down two quick tiny cups and ask Rashid what we're doing here.

"I'll tell you everything once we get you logged in. This way…"

Then I'm following him as we enter the massive truck at the center of all the activity. It's idling in a low rumble. Inside, an industrial-grade blast of air-conditioning washes over us, the opposite of the hot gritty streets of sweaty Calistan. I turn back and see crowds of people in every direction, straining to get a glimpse inside the perimeter. As though whatever is going on here will affect their daily lives in some way. I shudder. I get the uncomfortable feeling they think their fate depends on me somehow.

The latest in mobile gaming suites is set up at three stations across the length of the truck. Techs escort me to a couch as Rashid straps into his own and tells me he'll meet me in chat.

They try and take my messenger bag, and there's a moment where I try to keep it and that almost seems not to be okay. None of us speak the same language. But I bluff and make it clear this will be an issue for me. Fear crosses their dark eyes as they weigh my happiness as Rashid's new best friend against some arcane protocol they must navigate.

A moment later, I'm seated in front of a gorgeous ASUS Game Ninja Immersion Monitor, looking at a log-in screen for the MMO empire-building game called *Civ Craft*. On screen, a totally realistic Mars turns in orbit. On the night side, I see the lights of colonies far below. Massive dust storms swallowing whole regions. Rivers where greenery and life are starting to take hold, tenuously. Barely. Colony ships circling the planet in orbit, running support operations for all the national colonies. A few are shooting at each other, and occasionally some colony ship goes up in fully rendered apocalyptic bloom.

"We are pleasing to have you," says one tech haltingly, in broken English.

I smile and tell him I'm glad to be here.

He's unsure what to do with my smile, but he returns one barely. Nervously. He and the other techs point out the obvious peripherals and make me aware of other controls that can be provided as the situation demands. Then they show me a selection of keyboards, sweet high-tech stuff, and I choose one I like as though I'm selecting a bottle of wine. A moment later everything is set up and the techs are tapping in my login for me.

Then they back away and I'm in game. One of them slaps his forehead and hands me a helmet.

"Veee arrr," he tries hesitantly.

This stuff never worked really well. People kept trying, but the motion sickness was always a deal-killer.

I shake my head. I'll be fine with the super-gorgeous monitor.

"No… iss good. Try. Try. Please. Please."

They put it on my head. It's comfy. Underneath, the resolution is unbelievably lifelike. I swallow hard. Because this is as real as it gets for a gamer.

I'm in some sort of shadowy armory. Soft blue industrial lighting, stainless steel, and racks upon racks of state-of-the-art high-tech automatic weaponry in matte black.

Gun stuff.

Game on.

This is familiar, and it occurs to me that *Civ Craft* is supposed to be about building civilizations. And that leads me to wonder for the first time why they would offer me, an infantry operations specialist in gaming, a contract. I just break stuff and shoot people online.

I'm feeling my way across the keyboard, and everything is standard *WarWorld* setup. So I'm good there. I scroll through a few menus and I've got the basic gist within a minute.

I hear a small tinny voice in my helmet.

I tap the side of the helmet and find a volume control. It's Rashid.

And there are urgent klaxons competing with blaring alarms going off everywhere. In-game.

"Hey… my friend. Listen… we just lost the base reactor so we gotta fight off an assault at the main gate. Otherwise we're outta the game. Sorry to throw you in the soup. How are you at flying a gunship?"

Somewhere between not good and poor.

"Oh… uh… my specialty is really light infantry stuff."

"Yeah. I know that," replies Rashid overconfidently, "but right now we need close air support. Badly, PQ. Base is compromised. We can get our colony ship to nuke it from orbit and start over. But our resource base will be shot, to say the least, what with all the half-life radiation."

Rashid's avatar walks into the loadout room. A typical Space Marine. Light armor in Martian dust camo. Wicked gun. Life-support suit. Mirrored helmet. Red crescent and star and the flag of Calistan insignias all over his dust-red armor. He's using an HCAR Widowmaker V for a primary weapon. Aaaannnd… it's skinned in gold.

"Let's get up to the flight deck," he says.

Five million in real gold says I have to do whatever he says. If he wants to waste my skills as a dropship jockey… fine. I've pretty much gotten killed every time I've tried to fly the wonky birds in *WarWorld*. That's why teams hire pro pilots. Like RiotGuurl.

But she's on her way to Alpha Centauri for the next forty years. So… she's currently unavailable.

I let that thought go, because what can I do? And also, I don't need it right now.

On the way to the hangar, we thread a narrow maze of submarine-worthy passageways, stairs, and ladders. It all looks very Space Battleship. The environmental effects are great. At one point there's a distant explosion. Everything tilts, and my avatar goes into a wall.

I check my weapons loadout.

I'm carrying real-world machinery. Not super sci-fi space blasters. An HK Marksman that fires supersonic rounds in eighty-round drum magazines. Six frags and two smoke. And my *WarWorld* standard-issue sidearm. The AMT Retro Longslide .45. As per my first endorsement deal from this season. Good stuff for all kinds of fun and games.

We reach the flight deck of the base, and I'm looking at a hangar full of dust-red dropships and gunships. And space beyond the hangar portal. We're suborbital at least.

"We're not planetside, are we?" I ask Rashid over chat. Lack of information is getting to be a thing early on.

"Um… no, my friend. That's actually been a problem. We can't seem to hold our beachhead below. We keep getting kicked off the rock we chose. This Japanese clan alliance keeps working us over day and night, and we've been getting killed wholesale. So… let's take the base today and start to turn things around for Calistan!"

I see this is going to be a ground-up operation.

"Wait... you mean you don't even have a base?"

"Uh... I mean, we do," he says, clearly unused to being questioned. "We've had one for about six hours now. Technically. If we can fight off this latest attack, *Civ Craft* will award it to us and we can unlock the refineries."

"But it's not yours at this moment?"

"No. Ours got blown up. They keep getting blown up."

Do I even want to ask by whom? Yes.

"By whom?"

"Long story. People who want us to fail in-game. Enemies of the state." Then he adds, "And the Japanese."

The gunship is a wicked little thing with a shark face painted on the front. Standard missile racks and auto-cannon pods hang beneath its stubby wings. Lean little hover engines jut away from the body. I hit 'E' and we're in and powering up for takeoff. I'm driving. I scan the controls and start the flight sequence. Turbines hum to life over ambient as a taxiway lights up in front of me along the interior hangar.

"Strike leader, this is AceOfSpace..." says a voice over chat.

I wait.

"You," prompts Rashid. "You're strike leader for this one."

Is this some kind of test? And if I fail do I not get my five million in gold?

Asking for a friend.

"AceofSpace, this is PerfectQuestion... over."

"We're on your six after launch. We'll take you in and provide AA cover. Situation is hot over the LZ. Commander Enigmatrix reports she's compromised and requesting evac immediately."

I thought *Civ Craft* was a building game. Seems exactly like *War-World*... but on Mars.

Which is pretty cool when you think about it.

"No," interrupts Rashid over the ether. "No evac. Tell her we're going to take that beachhead today! Do or die, right, PerfectQuestion?"

Yeah… I think. Tell her that. And… Enigmatrix? That's just so weird. And wrong. I just killed her like twenty-four hours back in Havana. But that feels like a week ago.

I wish I had more coffee. The sleep I got on the flight just didn't do it for me. Even though I know there's not enough coffee in the whole wide world to ever make me feel human again. More is still better.

Engines are at full, so I add throttle because that's what I've seen real gamer pilots do. We begin to taxi out into the main bay of the colony ship. I scroll through the weapons loadout while panning my helmet to take in the hangar bay and see what kind of assets I've got to work with. If there's any hint of motion sickness, I'll just pull this VR helmet off and go with the monitor.

But there isn't. My field of vision is as smooth as peanut butter and it all feels just as creamy. In fact, I'm digging just looking around. The inside of whatever this battleship, space station, colony vessel is… is immense. Like the old-school *Star Wars* franchise immense. The good ones. The ones they made before the Meltdown. Though the ones after are a lot less preachy.

We taxi into position and hold for takeoff.

We're carrying eight air-to-ground smartmissiles. And ten thousand rounds of forty-mil ball. So if I can't blow it up, I'll turn it to swiss cheese.

I get the clearance for departure in my helmet and feel flight controls deploying across my desk inside the gamer truck. Throttle and joystick are in my hands, rudder pedals rising out of the floor beneath my feet. I test everything and then go with throttle up. Suddenly we're racing toward the launch portal of the ship in orbit, and a second after we're in space and falling toward Mars like a rock.

Vertigo.

But it's not caused by the helmet. It's because this is so fantastically real. The fall feels like a real fall because graphics are overclocking on every possible level to convince my brain we're dropping toward the red planet at an incredible rate. There're even vapor spirals coming up off the canopy. We're falling through thin atmosphere, and details on the planet below reveal themselves in layers with startling clarity.

Rashid is whooping in my ears. The effects are way above *WarWorld* standards. It's so real I actually feel like we're cannonballing straight into the Martian atmosphere while strapped into an actual dropship. The cockpit inside my HUD is shaking as atmospheric turbulence begins to take over. Wind whistles and screams across the fuselage over ambient in-game sound.

"Highlighting your targets now in the HUD," says Rashid over the chat. "Locking in a flight path to the objective. Just fly that, PQ, and we'll be over the battle in about two minutes... give or take."

He's a good tactical officer. Not an amateur, that's for sure. He knows the minimums for team play.

"I can't believe I'm going into battle with the PerfectQuestion," he notes in an aside. And if that's not the worst he can make me feel... he adds a droll little, "Squeal."

We're screaming through the atmosphere now, threading a violent reentry, and I'm doing everything I can to keep the stick centered on the nav window. Have I mentioned I don't really know how to fly dropships? We're still moving too fast to deploy weapon mounts. Even I know that, and I'm horrible at flying. This is not an understatement.

A moment later, we hit clear altitude and I take it down through thirty thousand feet in seconds, running for the deck of the Martian surface. Thirty seconds from the target, and we're over a sea of red dunes and leveling out for attack profile. Ahead I see a lone rock sticking up from the red Martian soil like some ancient European fortress. It's big. Like Gibraltar big. We pass some land crawlers and a few shot-to-pieces farms from which lazy smoke drifts upward in the thin terraformed atmosphere the better-off colonies have managed to get up and running. Then we rocket over a desert punctured by craters.

"I've got Japanese mechanized infantry all over the front of the base," says Rashid. "They're just holding position and shelling our people. Let's try a pass and take them out with our missiles."

Yeah... let's.

Targets are appearing in my HUD.

Tanks. Big hovering monsters with long main energy guns.

"Dragons," notes Rashid. "Mean. Tough to take out on the ground. But the AGMs will do just fine if you get a hit. Locking in the firing solutions... Line us up, PQ."

I pan the horizon. Again, no motion sickness with the helmet, and we're clocking over four hundred miles an hour. I lock in the terrain following radar and scan for–

Alarms go off in my helmet, and the controls in front of me light up.

"We've got AA radar!" shrieks Rashid from the weapons operator position. "They're looking for us!"

Tracer rounds fill the sky like gossamer strands of fiery lace. I try to dodge the obvious ones, pink hazy trails snaking up into the Martian sky, but we get smacked hard and an engine cuts out from damage.

"Got it!" shouts Rashid over a circus of cockpit alarms. "Assigning damage control. We'll get it back in thirty seconds."

We're listing, but I'm holding it together and lining up a run on three tanks straight in front of us. I group-select and fire an AGM salvo. Stubby missiles streak away from the wing pods and I yank the bird over to belly up and roll through on an opposite heading. AA fire fills where we should have been an instant later.

I said I was a bad pilot. I didn't say I was a stupid one.

"Three kills!" shouts Rashid, like a kid playing a game and winning.

Below us, Japanese Marines on foot are surging toward the massive gates of "our base." Then we're streaking off into the desert beyond as warnings remind us they're still trying to get tone lock and acquire us with their targeting radar.

Our trailing wingmen go heading off in opposite directions, scattering across the battlefield.

"Rashid..." I can see he's selecting more targets and setting up another run once we regroup.

"Yeah?"

"Don't do that. Authorize them to make runs on their own. If the Japanese are running target algorithms, it won't be able to predict the randomness if we attack on our own. Better to make individual strikes."

He seems to think about this for half a second as we rocket past a series of low Martian hills.

"Good call, but you're going to find out my people tend to be stupid. They get killed a lot, PQ."

That's odd.

"Trust me," I tell him.

"You I trust," he says. "Them... not so much."

"This'll work." I'm making a low turn as close to the burnt rock of Mars as I can manage. I'm craning my head, looking out the steel-latticed cockpit windows of the dropship and trying to get my bearings for the next attack run.

On our next pass, I strafe the infantry with the forty mil. We blow through at least three thousand rounds, but I get twenty-eight confirmed kills. All real live clan players. If this were *WarWorld*, I would've made enough to pay some rent on a nice Upper New York bungalow for a month. But it's not. This game doesn't have as high a profile as *WarWorld* in e-sports.

The other Calistani gunships make their passes, and one gets iced over the battle. Too low and too slow. They were taking their sweet time picking targets. On our next pass, I see the downed gunship and the Japanese Marines swarming it. Someone down there is still in game for Calistan, because they're shooting it out with auto rifles against the swarming Marines.

"I can try to clear 'em off and rescue him," I offer Rashid over the urgent scream of the dropship's engines as we dodge and weave through more AA filling the skies all around us.

"Nah," he says dismissively. "He's too stupid to live. Gunships are expensive micro-transactions. Serves him right for getting shot down."

Rashid sounds bitter. I sense that he blames me somehow.

But it's clear in the next few that the Japanese are pulling back with their remaining tanks and troops.

"Nice going... jerk."

It's Enigmatrix over the chat. I've heard her voice in interviews before. But we've never talked. And I think she just complimented me after I went and saved her bacon.

"All right," says Rashid. "Hundred percent. Let's put down and get back to the hill. You and Enigmatrix can socialize IRL once we get there."

Chapter Ten

We pass legendary amounts of security. High alabaster walls watch over carefully manicured kill zones. The entire hill overlooks the coast and is one massive fortified compound comprising several different palaces, each obviously attempting to outdo the others in opulence and security. Beyond the state-of-the-art perimeter and bunker over-watched checkpoints wait random patrols of brand-new APCs and crack troops, the very definition of vigilance. We've passed into another world of lush tropical landscaping and Moorish stronghold pleasure palaces that walk that tightrope between obscene and tasteful, their grandiosity glimmering at twilight.

"Obscene" is probably all just inside my head. I've never actually imagined someone's house could be that large. That immense. That opulent. Lighting makes each house look like some mobster's dreams of avarice and success unlimited finally rewarded. And maybe I've just been brainwashed to think wealth and success are somehow obscene. I'd like to be successful… and wealthy. Even if someone else calls me obscene. It's not like before the Meltdown when merit-based success was considered an anathema. A shortcoming. A failure as a human being.

Now success is to be admired. Emulated. Even envied.

In time we near the crest of the hill, crawling upward past even greater monstrosities of palatial living at a slow pace as though Rashid wants to overwhelm me. Silently letting me know I'm in way over my head and that it's best to behave and earn my five million in gold. Also to make sure I know exactly with whom I'm dealing.

Mission accomplished. Message received.

Just below the top of the hill, at the highest of its heights, beneath walls that enigmatically guard the last and what is most likely the grandest of all palaces, we turn up a wide wet flagstone-paved drive and pull in front of a Spanish hacienda of turrets and arches.

"Welcome to my shack," murmurs Rashid as we struggle up from the car. In truth, "we" probably don't struggle. Rashid possesses a youth and vitality that eludes me. But I feel like I'm carrying fifty-pound weights on all of my limbs. And sluggish dirty motor oil has replaced my blood. In other words...

...I'm getting old. And I can feel it. I need sleep. Deep. Beautiful. Uninterrupted sleep. In a bed. I've got the lag and I've got it bad. Plus a three-month buildup of game hangover I've been staying in front of with coffee, booze, and the occasional pill.

I'm due a crash.

"Trix has been staying with me. She got in last night, direct from the game." Rashid smiles. White teeth flash in the darkness between the designer ground lighting and the hush of the palms moving in the coastal night breeze above us and across this hill at the edge of the known world.

Trix? Enigmatrix. My greatest online enemy is being called Trix by a spoiled brat Arab rich kid. I feel a dark satisfaction in that. I think they call it schadenfreude.

Rashid leaps up titanic marble steps and sprints toward a cyclopean dark iron door that's so high it touches the next story of the house. I lumber after him as well as my fatigue-beaten body can manage. At the top of the steps I turn and see all of Newport Beach, the heart of Calistan, twinkling like glittering jewels spilled on the dark velvet cloth of the night. It's beautiful, and I wonder why America ever let it go.

That seems like the dumbest choice in the world no matter who you are.

Inside Rashid's "shack" all is still and cavernous. Only shadows and blue light, fractured by massive windows and long empty halls. I can make out little furniture or wall-hung art. Just lonely halls and wide rooms. Like some monument. Some mausoleum.

We tunnel deeper into the heart of the mansion and come to the central room. A grand hall with a wide window that affords an even better view of the glitterscape of Calistan's elite Gold Coast. Beyond the lights down there, everything, the rest of Calistan, is dark save the occasional fire.

And that's not the only view. Across the room's massive walls, an ancient sea battle comes to life. On one wall a lumbering pirate ship, rendered in epically billowing detail, sea water sluicing off its hull, cannon striking out in gusty roars, sails across a blood-red sea. Tattered sails billow as the ship heels about and comes to bear on another warship already aflame and rolling on the high seas across another wall. The enemy ship tries a few stray cannon shots that create fountains in the waters in between or slice through a translucent aquamarine wavelet. From unseen speakers, thirty-six cannons thunder a reply. It's so real, I actually duck from the cannonballs flying over my head. I hear splintering wood, torn canvas, and the shriek of wounded men ripped to shreds by shot.

"Come alongside and prepare to board!" It's Enigmatrix. I've heard her voice in streams. In interviews. Gloating about beating me in the postgame of other contests. But she didn't beat me the last time we met. During the Super Bowl. She was the one beaten. And so she got on a plane and fled to the West Coast. To Calistan and money.

Is she getting five million in gold too?

In the center of the room, beneath all the Age of Sail spectacle, is a diminutive gangly waif in shorts and combat boots. Spaghetti-string top. Controller in hand. Heedless of our presence. This is Enigmatrix in real life?

"We're back!" shouts Rashid. And then he's off into another section of the house calling out, "I'll get some booze and snacks." He disappears into unseen caverns within the sprawling empty labyrinth that is his home. Leaving me alone with my longtime adversary.

She doesn't acknowledge me. Not at first. Instead she leads her crew. A whole bunch of online players, a clan of some sort, called Cappy's Crew, as they attack the burning ship being projected so realistically onto the walls. Now she's in POV. Two stories high and being projected onto the clean white wall of the mansion's great hall. Cutlass in hand, her dark-skinned avatar boards the enemy ship and begins cutting a path to the helm.

I've never played this game. It's called *Island Pirates Redux* or something. I notice she isn't playing with her gamertag. She has a different one.

GataNegra.

By the lights shimmering across her face I can see her features. Barely. Muskets and swords swim across her chocolate skin. She has curly hair. Dark eyes. I look closer.

"Don't," she whispers. "If I wanted people to know my real face I'd do interviews, chumley."

Her character pulls a pistol and unloads at point blank on some captainy-looking guy. A moment later his head is gone and his body, saber in hand, flops to the deck spouting blood. Another buccaneer comes cutting in at her with a silvery cutlass, which she ducks. I can hear her pounding the buttons on her controller with loud *clacks* that compete with the sonic boom of the battle in full surround sound. She ducks and cuts the scurvy-looking mongrel across his balloon-belly. The guy goes down screaming, obviously regretting his life of high seas piracy. Pretty good AI, I had to admit.

"But I don't," she whispers to herself defiantly. As though I'm not even there. "So don't," she mumbles.

And there's something in that…

…something that makes me pause. Check myself. Back off. Like I'm dealing with a wild animal I've been warned to be careful of. So I remain rooted to the high-end spongy shag that is the room's only furnishing. The scent of the brand-new carpet overwhelms in that way it so often does in empty houses. I glance out the massive window and see a blue pool shimmering like a desert oasis as wild palms dance in the night out there, oblivious to all the high-seas butchery going on across the walls. The wind howls and the decks burn as ancient pistols explode in sudden smoky concussions while steel meets steel. It all looks pretty fun.

A few minutes later, Cappy's Crew has the pirate ship and she's telling them that she's logging off for the night. And then everything is very dark in the grand hall of Rashid's shack.

I've gone blind in the sudden darkness. The images of flashing steel and flame are burned into my retinas.

The bloody battle is done. The dripping decks cleared. The crimson sky gone. The roar of the cannons somehow seems to ring in the silence, just as the soundtrack of ambient waves that was there all along does too. I didn't even notice the sloshing waves until they were gone.

I wonder if I'm losing touch with everything. Losing touch with gaming... or maybe just getting too old. Or maybe I just need a break. I feel like that more and more lately. A lot in fact, over the past few months.

I'm just tired.

"We're on the same team now, Perfect."

I realize I've been inside myself searching for answers that have been plaguing me for longer than I'd care to admit. She moved away from me in the darkness after she logged off, left the room without me ever really getting a good look at her. For a moment I think I'm all alone, and then she's on the stairs leading up to the next story. Above me like some dark angel going the wrong way.

"I'm in charge here, PQ," she announces from the top. "You're good. But... I'm in charge so don't get in the way. Don't blow my ride."

I look up. I can barely see her in the shadows up there. The darkness is so near complete it's impossible to see anything other than the possibility of her shape. But her voice is soft and scratchy. Even musical in a sort of rhythm-and-blues kind of way.

I hear Rashid coming back along the halls now. His loud voice bellowing. Glasses clinking together and him rattling off types of booze available. I dread the thought of drinking. I just want sleep.

"And, Question…" She is gone now. Down some hall. Whispering, but I can hear her clear as day in the darkness between us. "Be careful. This… this here is dangerous. Very dangerous."

Like that's meant just for me to hear, and not Rashid.

Then she's gone.

Rashid and I drink out back on the pool deck. The wind is warm and the night pleasant. The view of glittering Newport and the Gold Coast is spectacular, of course.

He tells me we'll start operation Bloody Sabre tomorrow. We talk shooters. Great ones from the past. Tactics. Glory kills. The usual gamer talk I've done on panels and conventions. I guess his five million in gold bought him his own private panel. So I drink and answer all the questions whether I want to or not. It's required without ever having to be asked.

The moon crosses the night, and in time he lets me sleep. He offers me a lone couch in a distant room. Still no bed. I think fondly of Giant Bed and the times we didn't share.

The couch is in a den that's not fully furnished. Its bookshelves are empty and always will be. Except for one book. Up in a corner. I pick it up. It's dusty and old. Whoever lived here once, long ago, when it was part of America, probably forgot it when it came time to relocate. Or flee.

It's called *The Lost Valley*.

I study the cover. It looks like some kind of epic fantasy novel.

Then I sleep.

Sleep like I'm dead.

Chapter Eleven

I'm in the game. Or the dream. The dream of the samurai within the walled city. The keep. The keep in the valley on the edge of the known world. The keep on the borderlands, as the kind guardsman with a twinkle in his eye put it.

I am the samurai.

And I am in that town on the side of the hill. The walled city with the fantasy-style castle rising above me, pennants flapping in the breeze and stone-faced guards with crossbows on the wall, peering down and watching for trouble beyond the known.

I'm there.

Everybody is upset. The townspeople. Upset about the escape of the Priest of Chaos. Upset about the young girl being run down so cruelly. Upset that darkness has come to the valley.

And some murmur that it was there all along.

"Where are we?" I ask one of the guards.

The reply is nothing more than a grunted, "Lost Keep."

But where? Where is this Lost Keep?

The burly guard with the loaded crossbow either doesn't know or doesn't care. He watches the street down which the madman fled. As if at any moment, the blond spiky-haired stranger in black post-apocalyptic leather gear will return to murder us all. Like some promise made finally being fulfilled.

And still I am left wondering where I am. And who I am.

"Master Samurai?"

I turn and see a slender guardsman in better armor than the rest. He wears a sheathed long sword. A rakish Vandyke mustache and goatee dominate his face below cool gray eyes that appraise while providing neither assent nor judgment. "If I may…" he continues. "The castellan wishes an interview. Would you follow me into the keep?"

I nod.

We thread the press of concerned villagers, tradesmen bartering and scampering children underfoot, all this under the shadows of the high walls. Walls that guard the known from the unknown. We wind our way to a tall gate. More guards eye us from the somewhat cozy towers that stand watch here. Especially the ones in the two high towers that set the limits of the ancient gate. No doubt they, too, have deadly crossbows that could at any moment send bolts hurtling into my chest.

And then what? What happens in whatever I'm in if I'm shot through?

We pass the shadow of the gate and enter a courtyard warmed by the high morning sun. A sturdy main building, built more for war or watching than fantasy, rises above us. We enter and progress down torch-lit halls and climb steep ancient stone stairs to reach a room with a wide burnished oak campaign desk on which a vellum map is spread.

There is more to the keep. Much more than this inner sanctum I've been ushered into after a morning begun with tragedy and chaos. We passed businesses out there, and a distant arch with a beautiful fountain that burbled musically, leading off into other more mysterious quarters. And just before we entered the ancient gate yard before the keep itself, I saw a warren of alleys with all manner of shops and high tiny apartments looming out over narrow, almost picturesque back streets that disappeared off into nothingness.

The room is a study of some sort. Books. Armor. Wine. A beautiful dagger lies beside the map, as do writing instruments of ancient form. Ink and quill.

I study the map as best I can without being too overt. Maybe it will tell me where I am. Where the keep is.

And maybe somewhere written across its length is the reason why I am here. And who I am.

Can the "why" of things be found on a map?

Can a map know who we are?

Beyond all this is some larger question I cannot yet articulate. Another question that seems far more important.

There are mountains on the map. On the ancient fading vellum they are steep and rise up all along the edges. On the map they are simple ink lines and shading, and yet they seem dangerous in their representation. The word "impassable" rushes to the forefront of my mind.

At the center of everything lies the representation of a tiny fortress in a vast wilderness, on the edge of a southern forest named Charwood Wildwood. The words "Lost Keep" appear in curling script beneath it.

So we're there. And there is here. Wherever that is.

Beyond this tiny castle called a keep, I see other forests. A place marked the Caves of Chaos. A hill marked Crowhaven. And other markings, other places.

Teigel Hall.

Caverns of Thracia.

Barrier Peaks.

The Village of Hommet.

Castle Ravenloft.

In the north is a tall and dangerous peak. It's labeled "White Plume Mountain." It smokes like a volcano.

"Sometimes I look at that map…" begins someone behind me.

Then the voice trails away as though overwhelmed by the howling silence of the wilderness and its deeps depicted on the yellowing parchment spread across the campaign table.

I turn. Standing before me is an older man with iron-gray hair. He wears chain mail and carries a helmet.

The man crosses to the other side of the table and sets his helmet down upon an edge of the map. Then he produces a couple of oranges and sets those down as well. They roll across the dried ink in the vellum.

"Have one," he says. "Please. Just picked them from the grove at Goode's Farm. I was there… when Alucard escaped this morning."

He sighs and studies the map with large brown eyes that are somehow sad. His mouth opens beneath a drooping handlebar mustache. His voice is like an ancient creaking spring. Except deep and almost swallowed.

"Where…" he whispers.

Then he looks up at me like he's just returned from some long stay in another place and sees me watching him.

"Master Samurai, I have a problem, as you may or may not have noticed… this morning. All the commotion?" he prompts.

I am still studying the map. Its rich black ink creates beautiful hills and mountains with mere brushstrokes. Enigmatic unnamed towers are noted deep in areas swallowed by wild forest. The map draws me in, encourages me to explore it in ways I feel on some deep level yet can't name. Like some well or fountain discovered bubbling deep inside me. Like youth again. Like… the excitement of the unknown. Not fear…

Hatchet Hall.

The Dark Tower.

The Pool of Radiance.

That smoky burnt-leaves-and-scotch voice whispers softly within my head. "In search of the unknown."

And there is something about that phrase that resonates within my mind. Wherever that is. Wherever this is. To search the unknown somehow makes me feel whole and complete. When I look at the map I see a world of possibilities and adventures. Lost civilizations and stories not told for thousands of years. Danger… and reward.

Some forever playground of youth and all the good things it was ever meant to be. Both the terror and the intrigue.

"I would like you to track down Alucard for us… and slay him," continues the iron gray-haired man in chain mail. A momentary indigestion arises and then passes when he asks me to kill a man. "Will you slay this Priest of Chaos for us, Master Samurai?"

I know this is somehow the beginning of some adventure. Some journey that will make things right. Bring order out of chaos. I feel my hand on the hilt of my katana. I feel its power. I know its name again.

Deathefeather.

I nod.

Just a simple nod suffices when you agree to track down and kill someone.

Yes. I will find this man and slay him inside this dream. Or game. Or wherever, or whatever, this valley is that lies on the map in front of me of all things known and unknown.

Yes. I will go.

Chapter Twelve

In the dream, or the game, or whatever, I ride forth.

That's what you do in adventures. I am aware of both the phrase's antiquated nature… and its total normality. As though this is the way things should be here, though I am aware they are not this way in other places I can't remember. There are "other" places not this one. But none of that matters as I ride away from the keep on a fall day when the air is cold and the leaves of the forest turn the color of blood.

The castellan offered me the use of a horse, in the dream or the game, whatever this is, so I ride away from the mysterious place called the Lost Keep, on the trail of the Priest of Chaos. William Alucard.

"Goin' after Billy Alucard, are ye?" asked the old soldier who handed me the reins. He told me his name was Corporal Vonnegut. I nodded that I was, kicked the horse, and rode off through the narrow gates of the keep.

I now sense that old guard watching me. Knowing he was once just as foolish as I am now. And wishes he still were. Some bird in a tree beyond the gate seems to agree and says "poo-tweet" above the thunder of the large horse's hooves.

I have food. Water. And the horse. And of course my weapon.

All of this seems as it should. And I try to think of myself as what I am. What they kept referring to me as all through that keep and the shops we passed through as I supplied myself before journeying out into the unknown. Never to return, perhaps.

In search of the unknown.

A master samurai.

I know what a samurai is.

But somehow, I don't. I don't know what it is that I do and I can never remember having drawn my sword in anger much less hunting down a man and killing him.

Even now I have not fully drawn the blade.

But I want to.

And killing the man Alucard... the Priest of Chaos...

Well. We shall have to see.

I ride down the twisting hill that leads away from the squat keep that shrinks the farther I ride from it. In time I see it only occasionally over the rises I top as ride out into the tall grass before the forest the road disappears into.

An old man, occasionally pulling at his pipe, told me in the Traveler's Inn that William Alucard would most surely head for the caverns. And that if I was to be, as he put it, "hot upon his trail," I would "indeed catch him up" there. He also told me that "Bree yark!" is goblin for "We surrender!" Small smoke rings of some sweet-smelling stuff grew away from the old man, a wizard perhaps, and climbed into the dark timbers of the low-ceilinged common room of that ancient inn.

"That one is tricky," the old man with the pipe assured me. "You'll have to go through many others to get to him if he has his way. And..."

He paused. Considered one of the rings as it turned into a dragon and curled about a candle he'd sent it off toward on the table between us. I was drinking a strong dark draught they called Porter's Stout. There was an herbed cheddar cheese between us and a cold roasted chicken.

"And... he's about something, say true. Alucard must be stopped," murmured the old man to himself. And then, "So I guess you're the one, as much as anybody else, to do it now."

Entering the dark forest alone, in the late afternoon, I still taste that sharp cheese and the cold meat of the roasted chicken. And the dark beer that quenched my dry throat in this dream. It was all a pleasant start to this journey.

I go deeper into the wood and the night comes on.

It's later, in the dead of night, with a fat moon, swollen and riding through the twisted branches above, when I begin to think this journey won't be as pleasant as its start.

I have been riding in the forest for hours. Clearly, I am now lost. The sun had already begun to climb down from the sky at the journey's start and before long the forest grew cold in the twilight of the fading day. Crows, dark and mocking, called out and raced across the sky in flights, heading off somewhere deeper within the forest. Hatchet Hall. Ravenloft. The Dark Tower. And then darkness and the moon rose above trees that seemed like clutching arms. In time, the bare trail I thought I was following disappeared completely. Or I lost it.

I dismount and begin to walk the horse.

By night and moonlight, what once seemed a vibrant living forest now seems dead and forlorn. A place of nightmares and fear that are more real than daylight has ever been. With one hand I lead the horse, and with the other I hold the hilt of the sheathed blade. I feel the cold. Smell the decay of the woods. See my breath misting along with the horse's.

"'Oo are you?" croaks a bullfrog suddenly. Or at least... it sounded like a bullfrog. There's been some unseen croaking in the dark about me. The smell of stagnant water. Odd and intermittent as the air grew colder and even damp. The moon is now directly above like some leering giant face interested in finding out exactly where I am. The forest is fully revealed by bone-pale moonlight, and shadowed by dark shades where the moonlight can't reach.

I whirl about as the horse gives a start at some sudden rustle within the deadfall. I let go of the reins. It gallops off and leaves me all alone.

In those last moments as it rushed away, I saw its eyes, wild, rolling with fear. For a few moments I hear only its crashing through the underbrush, neighing in terror. Fading. And then too suddenly, it whinnies in fright and there is a great splash and it is gone.

So gone it might never even have been there.

Not just gone off beyond the reach of my hearing.

But gone.

Suddenly.

Like something took it all at once.

Visions of tentacles curling outward from a dark pond offer my mind a possibility I'm not too keen about. Fat snake-like tendrils curling about the horse's girth and dragging it down into the deep where the moonlight doesn't reach and the dark things live among the shadows along the bottom. Maybe there is a cave that leads to the ruins of ancient civilizations down there. Down where nothing but the dead wait.

I listen for something in these long moments of total silence.

Unreal.

My katana slithers from its sheath, and I realize by the soft razor's hiss that I'm doing this. An inch at a time.

"'Oo are you?" the unseen bullfrog croaks again.

Honestly, I don't know the answer. I want to, desperately, as the quiet seconds drip by in the silence of the forest. I want to know who I really am. That seems important. Maybe even more important than catching the Priest of Chaos, Alucard.

The answer to "'Oo are you?" seems very important.

I see bulging eyes staring out from within the hollow of a long-dead tree. The eyes of a madman watching. Glaring and huge. Unblinking. Staring fixedly at me. And of course, in them is no good intent.

That's plainly clear.

"I'm searching for…" I begin. Then hesitate. I still hear the razor's hiss of the blade slinking from its sheath. I'm still drawing it up and out. Its edge must be gleaming in the pale moonlight. A silver slice of death. But I don't know that. I only know it must be so. Instead I remain staring at the two mad eyes staring at me from deep within the hollow of a dead tree.

"Alucard," I finish softly.

Nothing.

Just the mad unblinking eyes staring back at me.

"No man here," the hidden voice croaks.

My blood runs cold. Because if it's not a man, or no longer a man, then what has the speaking voice become?

I feel my blood turn to ice water in the microsecond of hanging time that follows the declaration.

I draw. One motion. The blade flashing in the moonlight like a thing suddenly become electric. A cold, living thing that defines the line between life and death. And it seems to me, in its sudden moonlight flash, that the blade I have drawn is living death. Embodied.

I'm aware that it's good that I drew it, held it back, ready to strike with both hands gripped around the hilt as they should be. Ready for one diagonal slash that feels so right. As though I've been trained a thousand million times to execute only such and in only this fashion. The classic samurai cut.

The cut is good.

It has to be because there is no time.

Out of the gaping mouth of the dead tree rushes a mad old hermit. Bald on top. Stringy hair cascading from the sides of his dead fish-belly scalp down onto his shoulders. Pot belly swinging madly as he rushes me with a wicked dagger glowing a soft malevolent green. He gargle-screams like some ancient sea monster drowning on ten million pounds of sludge. His throat a ragged mess of glottal stops and guttural ululations.

He is stark raving mad.

The eyes that once stared fixedly out from the hollow of the dead tree, like some alien watcher ever watching, are filled with the spite of yellow covetousness and the roaring rage of red murder. He comes at me in a rush and I can hear his thick feet flopping like dead fish on the sand and across the moldy wet leaves of the hollow where one of us will die.

That's when I strike with just one cut.

Like unexpected lightning.

Instinct.

I strike through him. Not *at* him as I know I would have if I knew exactly who I was. But *through* him, as I've never trained to do.

Just once.

He screams as the blade bites, and he can no longer scream in the bare second that follows.

Two halves that were once him flop to the ground as his feet once did, and will never do again.

I put everything into that strike and I remain in the finishing pose. Blade held down and ready. Listening for who, or what, will come out of the darkness all around. Two halves of the dead hermit at my sandals drool out onto the dead leaves. Those eyes once more returned to their alien madness. Again, staring up at me and seeming to still ask...

"'Oo are you?"

Chapter Thirteen

Hot bright morning light bathes the world in a warm golden glow beyond the darkness of the tomb in which I wake. I turn and hear the expensive Italian leather of the couch Rashid offered me for the night creak. Or croak.

It's not a tomb. It's a den.

I'm in the den of Rashid's shack. Mansion. I think of Enigmatrix. I'd met her online. In combat. Had killed and been killed by her. And last night I finally met her in the dark. And she was still as much a ghost as she'd always been.

I pull on a shirt and find an immense restroom done in cool gray marbles that remind me of ancient Rome. I shower but can't shave. But I'm clean enough.

Looking in the mirror I wonder what will become of me.

When would I start living?

Where would I start living?

I wander the massive complex that is Rashid's shack. Everyone is gone. Or at least no one answers my forlorn calls that echo much like those of a lost and lonely explorer in a vast wilderness of strange ruin.

On a bar top near the main room, the cavern where Enigmatrix played her pirates game on the wall, I find a note from Rashid.

It says a car is waiting outside to take me down to the "Cyber Warfare Center."

I check the walk-in fridge in the massive kitchen. There's nothing but chilled vodka and a lemon. I grab my messenger bag and leave the quiet mansion.

Outside I find a morning unlike any I've ever experienced. Since leaving New York City, and that other life I barely remember, I've traveled the world and seen many mornings in many places. Beautiful mornings. Ibiza. Rio. Amalfi. Bermuda. Singapore.

Nothing matched this.

Every green is a vibrant living green. Every color sharp, bright, clear. Cornflower-blue sky and everything golden in the same moment. The wide Pacific Ocean below is blue and lazy. Far out across its gulf I can see a mysterious island shimmering in the distance.

Santa Catalina, I think.

Ecstatic birds call and dash about, unseen in the tropical shrubbery and twisted olive trees that rest across the desert oasis landscaping. Everything about this morning promises life. And adventure. As though great things and endless pleasures are to be had down there along the coast. As though the world in its entirety is here… and waiting to be explored. As though something important and meaningful to carry with me for the rest of my days is about to happen at any moment.

And it will happen here.

I remember reading a blog article on some hyperjet during my gaming tournament travels about the ruins of the first Disneyland. That might be a fun day trip. To see what it had all once looked like before the Meltdown. Before the "Cannibal Kingdom" made headlines and got crushed by the last of a dying government. I like that sort of thing.

Ruins. I like ruins.

Everywhere I go, I manage to sneak away and find some to wander around in for a day.

In the wide circular driveway, on wet paved stones, waits a limo. The air smells of jasmine in a way Singapore never did. A driver in slacks and a crisp white shirt waits, absently polishing various planes on the sedately luxurious vehicle with a cloth he holds in one hand. He is softly whistling.

"*¡Hola, señor!*" he announces when he sees me emerging from the monument that is Rashid's home. He looks as if he wants to help me with my bags, but all I've brought is my laptop in the messenger case over my shoulder.

"You ready to... to... to..." He struggles, trying to figure out what I am supposed to do as he broadly smiles through a mix of shining white teeth and gold-capped ones. Dark curling tattoos scroll their way up from his wrist to hide beneath his white cotton shirt.

"My name is Juan," he says. He's older. Thick iron-gray hair. "I'm sorry... I don't know what you do. I only know where we are going this morning."

I tell him my tag. It's pretty much all anyone cares about.

"Ah! Perfecto! You are PerfectQuestion! *¡Arriba!* I have to have your autograph for my grandsons. They are both big-time gamers."

I'm still stunned that anyone would want my autograph. But I agree. I'm flattered and humbled. And slightly bewildered.

He leads me to the limo and I climb in back. He gets in on the driver's side.

"I was never a gamer," he announces as he pulls out of the drive and begins threading the narrow streets back down the hill. There aren't a lot of hover limos in Calistan. In fact none so far. I wonder if that's due to the embargo and trade restrictions. "Not after the Meltdown. I was just a kid then. We had to do everything to survive once the government fell apart. Then I got a job with the sultan twenty years ago and was able to give my kids the best. All the things I never had. And now..." He sighs. "I watch and they try to teach me sometimes... but eh, I'm no good. My big thumbs just get in the way."

"Just gotta find the right game," I say from the back. Then I lean forward and slide up to the window between us. I'm not that kind of guy. The sit-in-back-and-don't-interact kind.

"You just gotta find your game," I repeat. "Then you'll get good. Then you'll beat them."

"Like a fishing game would be great," he tries.

"If that's what you like, then yes. There're games where you fish. Sport fishing too."

"But I could just go fishing. In real life."

I agree that he could. Then add, "I've never been. Is it fun?"

"Ohhhhh…" he cries with gusty enthusiasm. "It's the best thing ever. You go out on a boat. Some beer. Good burgers from the galley and you got live bait. Then you fish. And sometimes the tuna run and the captain will chase them and get right in the run and you pull out these great big monsters. Cut them up right there with some lime and salt, some for the beer too… There are few things better than such a day, *señor*. Trust me on this."

I do.

"I used to take my boys. But now they work hard for their families. Even they have no time for games now."

"You're not… Arab?" I ask.

"No, *señor*," he says and looks around as though someone might overhear us. "We are Mexicans. We were here before the Arabs. And… even the gringos if you can believe that. This…" He spread his hands across all of Calistan and what was once the old America. "This was all ours. After the Meltdown, the Arabs took it from the United States. Technically it's a protectorate. But it's theirs all the same. The royal family financed a bunch of mercenaries from around the world with the only currency anyone would take during that time: real gold. Then they took over. There were already tons of them living here due to open borders and immigration at the time. Their half of the world was on fire. Then… sharia law and everything within months. The old US couldn't do anything about it because they were trying to get the US back online after the Meltdown. So they just made the best of it and cut a deal."

Silence as we drive down the hill.

"How is it? Here? Now?" I ask, because I'm interested in how things really are as opposed to what someone is trying to sell you on a stream, or in an e-mag.

"It's good," he says too quickly. A pause. "And bad." Then: "Probably just like it was with the gringos. But I was young then and we were raised to be angry. Now... well... someone's got to be in charge. So we can't live in certain areas... like here. Big deal. But we can work here, which is pretty good when you think about it. They have all the courts and the best jobs, so we get the bad end of that most of the time. But... there're jobs. We can work for them. Drive them. Care for their children. Garden. In the end... it's a living. And on my days off I can fish. And it's not the Meltdown because those days... well... that was a very bad time."

"You fish out there?" I ask as we come around a turn and the wide vista of the coast opens up, the vastness of the ocean suddenly apparent and clear.

"No!" he cries. "No, not out there. That is for them. We have to drive north or south of the Gold Coast. We can fish in those places. Near the old reactor at San Onofre is the best. The boat I catch out of Dana Point goes south, and we go off San Clemente. Good fishing. If you stay... I can take you sometime, *señor*?"

"I'd like that."

I would.

A silence falls between us. As though I'm visiting someone in prison and only now just realizing it. We've talked about the food and the limited activities and then there's nothing else left to talk about. In time I'll pass beyond the barbed wire and they'll remain.

A few minutes later we hit the coast road and drive into Newport. Juan pulls into the parking lot of a large building, ancient architecture from long ago. Steel and mirrored glass watch out over a narrow channel in the harbor. Expensive old houses on the other side of the water sit next to leaning old piles of some past glories. But the sun and the sea have faded these beached wrecks, and now they're little more than washed-out eyesores. Children and people move about the slender beach in front of them.

A sign at the front of the building we've just pulled up to announces the old place to be the "Caliphate of Calistan Cyber Warfare Center."

Leaving Juan and the limo in a parking lot full of sunbaked cars, I enter the dark and shadowy building. It was once something else. I see an old plaque that's never been removed from the wall. It says something about Sea Scouts. The building is empty and gutted, save a lone receptionist's desk where two armed guards stand before a newly installed bank vault door worthy of something from a movie about high-tech heists.

The guards nod at me as I cross the echoing marble floor. One begins to turn the massive polished wheel on the vault and dial back the door. It slowly parts from a seam in the wall, and beyond I see a stairway, lit by neon green light, descending into darkness. The other guard, with the barest of humorless smiles, indicates I should enter.

"They're waiting for you," he mumbles with naked contempt as I pass.

The stairs lead down at least two stories into some kind of underground bunker. At the bottom, a beautiful woman in a headscarf greets me. She smiles warmly. Her voice is deep and husky.

"Welcome, Mr. PerfectQuestion. Rashid would like you to come to the tactical center. If you'll follow me."

We go down more stairs, passing through heavy concrete flooring and walls. This is definitely some kind of hardened bunker. The kind other countries try to hit with bunker busters. Eventually we pass a series of server rooms where technicians in clean suits monitor impressive servers beyond thick bulletproof safety glass.

A few turns more and we pass down a hallway lined with hatches that lead into gaming suites. One is open, and I glance in to check it out as the receptionist continues on. Some of the best gaming rigs and decks I've ever seen are waiting in almost military orderliness and polish. Beaucoup expensive. Chair. VR goggles. Soft gray concrete and recessed blue lighting.

Then I see the blood spatter stain on one wall of the suite I'm examining. Head height. A spray they apparently never managed to make disappear, going out and away along the dull gray concrete wall. Like someone got it in the head and didn't know it because they were staring at the monitor. I study the wall for another second as the clipped high heels of the woman come back for me. There's chipped concrete along that blood-spattered wall. I've seen enough VFX in-game to recognize bullet-chipped concrete.

"This way," she prompts in her soft and husky voice. Leaving no room for dissent.

Which way, exactly? What have I gotten myself into? And which way is out?

"Five million," I whisper so low she can't hear.

"This way," she prompts again in the same tone. Soft yet even more firm this time. I have that strapped-into-a-rollercoaster feeling. Like I bought the ticket, and now it was time to take the ride.

In gold, I remind myself. Five million.

Two more corridors and two more bank vault titanic doors and we reach the command center. And Rashid.

Chapter Fourteen

It's a long conference room straight out of all those movies about underground war rooms and nuclear missiles. Cool and creepy. I decide to just go with it.

Rashid is surrounded by big guys in medal-laden uniforms and a few definite geeks of the Arab variety.

"Guys!" announces Rashid, beaming as he stands up from a digital 3D map projecting out of the huge central table. "This is our new secret weapon! Allow me to introduce PerfectQuestion... this year's Super Bowl MVP."

Everybody turns to glare at me. A few almost manage to hide obvious contempt, as if waiting to take their cues from others. The others paste on smiles that are anything but. There's a dangerous hostile electricity in the room, and I remember the blood spatter on the wall of the gaming suite.

"Okay..." begins Rashid as everyone moves to their chairs without shaking my hand. "Let's get our new rock star up to speed on what we're trying to do today."

I take the closest seat at the end of the table. Only Rashid remains standing. He waves his hand across the 3D map and brings up a new one.

"This is the Valles Marineris canyon system. It's larger than the Grand Canyon. Okay, PQ..." Rashid looks around and smiles genuinely at everyone. "I call him PQ. Okay, this is where the Japs are building their newest city. Along the canyon's rim. It's close enough to our resources to make it a threat. We need to knock it out."

Over the ether, Enigmatrix's scratchy voice, the one I heard in the dark the night before, interrupts Rashid, who seemed to be warming up to his presentation.

"Actually, we need to *take* this city," she lectures, "if we're going to build your empire within the game, Rashid. Knocking things out only gives you nothing of value. Nothing to build with. We're just wasting time and resources."

The generals at the table—or at least, I assume they're generals of some sort. They all have medals and scrambled eggs on their epaulets. And bushy mustaches. The generals all get very uncomfortable when she speaks.

Rashid lowers his head and murmurs something to them in Arabic. Then, to the ether, "Enigmatrix, dear, um... they're not used to... you talking out of turn like that. I know... where you come from that's okay. But here in Calistan, we just don't do that."

Here...?

What don't you do? Let women speak?

I've never actually encountered that in my life. I've heard about it, of course, from all kinds of old social justice scolds from before the Meltdown, still railing from their safe-space collectives to anyone who ventures into those slums, as a thing that went on all the time. But I've never actually encountered it. Now, unlike all those seminars in school and mandatory videos I was forced to watch at every job, I'm seeing it on a level I never even dreamed of.

At least I think that's what I'm seeing.

Everyone remains silent. This is the part where any woman I've ever known would burst into a full tirade and lecture with lots of anger, animosity, and self-righteous indignation. Any moment now.

Any moment now.

Any...

"I understand," replies Enigmatrix quietly. And then, "Go ahead with the plan, Rashid."

Is there five million in gold waiting for her in a safe deposit box somewhere offshore?

Is there more?

How much?

Yeah, even I admit… the gold is changing me.

Rashid points toward the digital display, indicating the canyon. A massive network of alleys and dead ends. Something is marked as a target. He expands the map, and we're looking at a canyon wall dug through with graphed red lines. A subterranean tunnel system beneath the city on the rim above. A ramp leads to a bunker-fortified entrance guarded by towers on either side. More towers loom on the canyon's rim.

"We're going to take out the Japs' newest city. Today. From the floor of the canyon beneath it. In a few hours we'll have most of our clans up and running. Hit time is four thirty local. PerfectQuestion, we're providing a full armored assault against the city above with air cover to get you and one of our special teams inside the complex below. Once inside, we need you to blow up this target beneath the city."

The map irises in on a subterranean cave within the complex. Then on a specific tower graphed in growing white lines.

"This is down tunnel. You'll need to secure the rail line through the mines into the central cavern. Arrive at this tower and destroy it. This is the main atmospheric control center for the complex. Without this piece of equipment, the facility will die within hours. The Japs will be forced to abandon it if they can't restore life support. Then…" he looked at the ceiling, "we can capture the city as General Enigmatrix wishes."

Again, everyone around the table seems very uncomfortable.

Rashid stands back. Smiling. Then moves around the table adjusting his hands. The map reacts and turns to reveal the central core of the complex.

"Bonus points if we take this baby out!"

"What is it?" I ask when no one else does.

"Central reactor. We overload it and the whole place goes kaboom. Then the Japanese can't rebuild it even if they want to. The site will be a biohazard."

I pause, not thinking so much about the tactical situation, but more about how to say what needs saying.

"Right... and this is on your claimed territory?" I ask.

Rashid nods emphatically. He seems very proud of himself. Very proud of his standard *take out the enemy's major power source and blow everything sky high modern movie mega climax* strategy. The *Star Wars* films were still doing this to death. The last time I watched one, they blew up an entire solar system full of Death Stars. It was ridiculous.

And... I'd played enough tactical games to know that good teams in any game defend their reactors, or whatever power source they have access to, mana wells or what have you, to the death. Because... no power, no building queue.

"How big is my strike force?" I ask.

"Thirty of our best players. All highly ranked in your own *War-World*."

He didn't say pros. So that means they're just home-gamers willing to go on a one-way mission. Guys who are really good on console. But not actually good enough to get hired by a corporate team.

"That might not work."

I float that and let it hang for a second.

And it hangs.

The discomfort inside the bunker is palpable.

Rashid takes off his smartglasses.

"How so?" he asks softly. Genuinely. As though he really wants to know.

"Told ya," comes Enigmatrix's reply over the ether.

Why isn't she in this room? I wonder distantly.

Again, the generals look from one to the other, their faces hard and angry. I assume they're gauging each other's reactions to figure out which way the wind is about to blow.

"Because," I begin, "whoever's defending that reactor is going to put up a big fight. Don't be surprised if that team... and I'll need any info you have on their units, armaments, assets, whatever... but don't be surprised if they defend that reactor with everything they've got. Sure, you might break some stuff. But as long as they hold that reactor... Well, they can rebuild."

I look around the table.

"So no kaboom if we fail." Then I add, "You'll just waste a bunch of your units on the front door. Then you'll have to rebuild them and... I'm going to have to say that Enigmatrix is actually right. This is a civilization-building game. Breaking other people's stuff isn't the goal. In war, yes. But war isn't the primary goal here. Building your culture index and trade is the focus. So at the end of the day your big win isn't poisoning your own land, which you'll need to develop eventually. The land they're currently borrowing from you. Your big win is taking that city up top."

No one seems pleased. But I continue on. I'm that kind of guy. Truthy.

"I'm a first-person-shooter professional. That's why you hired me. And I get that the mission you want to pull today is all that and a bag of chips with a big ol' explosion to show off on the streams. I can lead that assault and probably break some stuff. The atmo tower seems like a reasonable goal. I can take that. That's what you're paying me for. But the reactor ain't gonna happen. They'll have all kinds of shooting galleries and interlocking fire set up in there.

"What you aren't paying me for is to tell you how to succeed at this game. How to build your civilization on Mars so you can maintain an in-game active presence. But I'm offering my advice anyway. Just advice. And it's this. Breaking stuff and not getting along with your neighbors… that's not helping the game, or the Calistan team. Seriously… guys… no disrespect… but why don't you build some stuff and start trading with whoever's around you?"

I finish. And wait.

Deathly silence.

I have overstepped.

Five million in gold. Blood spatter on the wall.

Then Rashid smiles. He nods as if to himself.

"My professionals are right," he says. "Gentlemen. I totally agree with them." He looks at everyone around the table. "We need to build. I've told my father and the mullahs this."

The faces of the generals are nothing but enigmatic stone. They don't know which way to play this hand.

Then Rashid turns to me.

"I agree with you, PerfectQuestion. Seriously."

And Enigmatrix, I think to myself. You agree with her too. But I don't push it because I've pushed it enough already.

"But," continues Rashid. "My father insists we cleanse the infidels from our online land. The only way is to blow up the reactor and to show them what we are capable of. The mullahs want it that way. They feel… the *tone* of influence within our culture on Mars, in *Civ Craft*, needs to remain pure of outside… influence." He looks around and smiles at everyone. They smile back. There's a lot of smiling with these folks. At least when I'm not talking. And Enigmatrix. "So the Japanese will develop elsewhere and we'll be able to expand in peace once they feel our wrath."

Then he turns to me and lets me know how everything really stands. "And your payment is conditional on accomplishing our goals, PQ."

So I have to take out the reactor.

'Cause five million. In gold.

Inside a heavily fortified base. On Mars.

I study the map.

"Okay… then I need my own strike team."

Rashid beams because I'm on board. Things can go as planned. Thermonuclear apocalyptic destruction assured.

"Sure. Hundred percent. Anything for you, PQ. You can have anything. Just let me know and we can get them on the map. We'll pay for the best."

We smile at each other.

"Okay," I say. "Then I gotta make a call."

Chapter Fifteen

We hit the enemy base two hours later. The gaming clans of Calistan have come out in full force for the glory of Prince Rashid and the state. Tags like MohamedDurden, BatImam, and KoranKommando litter the unit rosters and my field of vision on tactical overlay as I watch the main diversionary assault begin on the Japanese clan city along the cliff's edge of the massive Martian canyon. Our plan is to insert through the dangerous maze of the canyon at high speed and come in fast, hoping for a little surprise before they can reallocate defenses from the city above to the back entrance we're attacking.

The city is Enigmatrix and Rashid's problem. The entrance is mine. They're the rope-a-dope. We're the sudden right cross.

"What kinda mission is this, sir?" asks MarineSgtApone over squad chat.

The clan I've asked Calistan to hire are all strapped into a dropship speeding toward our objective. Armor and weapons loadout are red desert camo, as is the dropship. The clan's cosplay skins, other than the camo color, are still Colonial Marine. We're skimming the Martian desert south of the canyon. The main Calistani force, led by Enigmatrix, is already attacking the rim towers above.

"We're here to break stuff, Sergeant," I reply over chat. This Colonial Marine cosplay clan likes to use rank. I've worked with them before. They're pro. Which is the one of the best things you can say about another gamer. That they're pro. That, and you had fun with them.

"So… it's a smash and grab without the grab," murmurs a player tagged MarineCorporalHicks. In-game, the ship is starting to shake from ground-effect turbulence as the Martian surface temperature rises with the dawn. The pilot's got the pedal to the metal and the dropship is hurtling toward our OBJ.

"Canyon insert in five," says the pilot. "Hang on."

"Full forward with the throttle and let's finish the whole bottle," says PVTHudson, another clan player. I didn't meet MarineCorporalHicks or PVTHudson when I gamed with them a year ago inside *WarWorld*. Most of the Colonial Marines clan were killed in our first firefight back in that special match I worked with them on. Only a few survivors made it to the last round with me.

"Something like that," I reply as I watch live feeds from the assault at the top of the canyon.

I'm in one of those gaming suites I passed on the way to the introduction with Rashid and his generals. Not the one with the blood spatter stains no one could quite get clean. But one just like it.

In order to get the Colonial Marines cosplay clan in the game and attached to my special strike team, Calistan had to pay a massive microtransaction cost to the developers who ran *Civ Craft*. The dough spent was anything but "micro." In addition to which, the clan barely made login time for the assault. They'd had to get off work, or whatever IRL responsibilities they had, to get online and ready to go in time. Still, they were getting paid, and that was a big thing for them because none of them were officially pro. They played like pros, but they did it for the fun of it.

And there was more to it than that. They showed up in full force as a matter of pride in the clan they'd created. And love. Love of the clan, of the game, and of each other. That was evident. And now that their gear and skins had been uploaded, they had an official clan presence inside *Civ Craft: Mars*. Which was normally too hefty a buy-in for hobbyists. Corporate and national teams, or the elite gamer crowd running a crowdfund, were the norm.

"Never played this game before," pipes up some kid tagged as simply Frosty over the chat. "What's it like… building little towns and all? Crafting…?"

"Boring," says MarinePFCVasquez. The squad heavy machine gunner. "Point and shoot is life."

She was the one who held the room where the firefight broke out with WonderSoft in the last match, way back when. Then they either took her out, or the aliens who were swarming the impromptu firefight got her. That seemed like a lifetime ago. But it was only a year and a half. And… yeah… a different life then for me.

"Shoot to thrill," says MarinePvtDrake. He made it through with me last time. "Right, Vasquez?"

"You got it, hombre. Shoot to thrill."

This clan is all about first-person shooters. They cosplay some old movie I still haven't gotten around to watching, but RangerSix told me it's the greatest sci-fi war flick of all time. I've been too busy actually fighting inside the modern equivalent of a sci-fi war flick, but it's on my playlist. I just need some free time.

These guys go around competing as a cosplay unit in all the big convention games, but of course they wouldn't have played *Civ Craft: Mars*—even though it's one of the biggest streamed games currently being viewed by a quarter of the world's population—since it's not strictly a first-person shooter. It's primarily about resources and civilizations. The developers did use the *WarWorld* engine to run combat, but from there the balancing issues went out the door. In *Civ Craft* your weapons depend on what your civilization has unlocked on the tech tree, or what you've acquired through trade. Or—of course—what you can purchase through micro-transaction. But your clan needs wild amounts of dough to just level up.

What it boils down to is you can have muskets facing an enemy with Wolverine main battle tanks in an all-or-nothing for your fledgling little civilization. Which isn't very fair. Muskets versus main battle tanks. But a lot of people actually enjoy watching such massacres.

Then again, people once enjoyed watching unarmed Christians fight lions and bears to the death. Such was Rome. Such was the internet of the day. They called it the Circus.

"So... uh, we just smash everything up and then what... sir?" asks MarineSgtApone once the chatter has died off.

That's right. I'm in charge of this. What with Rashid and Enigma-trix's little power struggle ongoing throughout the hours leading up to the battle, I kept forgetting exactly why I was here. And what my role was. At points it felt like they'd just hired a very expensive infantryman. Which, honestly, was something I was looking forward to. Running and gunning is always fun. Don't let anyone tell you differently.

But now I've got a squad. And I'm in charge.

"Well... Apone. I'm feeling my way around here. But the people we work for don't have a lot of resources for intel—or anything else for that matter. They've hired us to break their competitors' stuff in order to give them a leg up in-game. Smash, ruin, and generally create a lot of mayhem in the enemy rear. So... I thought of you guys."

"That's a can-do, sir," replies MarineSgtApone. "We can break stuff with the best of 'em. So listen up, Marines. You heard the man. Kill! Kill! Kill! And then kill again to make sure. Going Roman is the SOP. You know what that means. Hicks, you got Bravo. I'll take Alpha."

Everybody is definitely on board with that.

The POV inside my VR helmet starts to bounce around. I can see out the front of the cockpit canopy of the dropship. In the distance, speeding toward us, lies the massive canyon complex below ground level. The tactical overlay shows me the underground structure in green lines. Up along the canyon's rim, the Calistani clans are at-tacking with everything they've got. A variety of interceptors versus air-defense towers. Mixed armor from high-dollar mechs to ad hoc technicals sweeping in from off the red desert through full-scale ar-tillery barrages courtesy of the Japanese clans. Calistani regulars mixed with ad hoc jihadi units sweeping into the trenches for close-quarters fighting. They don't have the numbers unless they get incredibly lucky. But they have enough of them to demand that the Japanese clan take them seriously for the next short period of time if they're to retain control of their mineral resource base on the edge of Calistani-claimed territory.

"Question, this is Enigmatrix. Starting out assault from the canyon rim. But we're getting killed like no tomorrow. Get in quick and shut down their atmo processor. These noobs ain't got no game, so your window ain't gonna stay open long."

Noobs means the Calistan clans.

"Zero skills," she continues, "no shot discipline, and it's not uncommon for them to pull the trigger until they run out of bullets regardless of their aim. So be quick about your business. We won't get another shot at this!"

In the background of her feed I hear automatic gunfire being doled out like there's a sale on bullets at WalCo's biggest of mega-box stores and discount amusement parks. It all sounds very impressive.

According to the plan, Enigmatrix's assault on the city, supported by tanks and infantry, is just a diversion. Her job is to keep the Japs busy, keep them from beefing up defenses on the "back door"—the bunker entrance I'm headed toward. But there are plenty of defenses as it is. Air defense batteries and point defense cannons are embedded along the walls of the canyon. Enough to take out any dropship we send in.

Which is why we're flying low, skimming the canyon floor, entering a few miles to the south, so we're well underneath the defenses. We'll come in at high speed and drop all over the back door. Unexpected.

Hopefully.

The dropship heels over to port and climbs skyward for a couple of seconds. The engines spool up into a scream, and for a moment I get a bit of vertigo inside the gaming helmet as I watch the newly terraformed hazy Martian atmosphere switch back to a dry and lifeless landscape, then shift and twirl beyond the canopy as we shoot down into the canyon's trench. Now we're pointed straight at the grinning mouth of the chasm floor and we're rushing straight at it with what seems an unsafe amount of speed.

"Yeeeee-haaaa!" screams CPLFerro, the pilot.

In my gaming suite, I feel my whole body tense up in the expensive ergonomic lounger. The VR graphics are that good. I'm *there* inside that falling dropship turned express elevator. I'm totally safe as we start our attack run against the Japanese clan's back door, but my mind is convinced I'm about to be smashed into millions of pieces all over Mars.

Colonial Marines are whooping and shouting. They dig this stuff. Like I said… it took a lot of Calistani dough to get them in-game. And it would take only one slip-up from their pilot for it all to be wasted. But they're having fun regardless.

They're having fun, and Ferro's a good pilot.

Remember, PQ, that's what it's all about.

Yeah, I tell myself. And then can't resist thinking about the five million in gold.

"Express elevator to hell!" yells someone over the chat as if they've just read my mind and added the appropriate destination for what it feels like we're being thrown into. Everyone yells back, "*Going down!*" amid woot-wooting and shouts.

Must be a thing for them.

We're racing toward the Martian canyon floor at insane speed. The desert pastel walls, swirling like frozen gargantuan sandstorms of strata and rock in pinks and red whorls, race by, just barely outside the dropship's canopy. I wonder if this is what Mars really looks like. IRL. I've never been. And it's seemed like a one-way trip for most of the colonists of late. Plus there's all that political tension about separating from Earth. But maybe… maybe someday I'll see this canyon in real life. Booking a Martian safari wouldn't cost me much of the gold at all.

We shoot through a twisting cathedral of pink stone and follow the path of the ancient canyon at over four hundred knots. I check my HUD. Four miles to go.

"Guns up," I announce to the platoon.

They're carrying their standard-issue pulse rifle ported for *Civ Craft*. It's a decent rifle for up close and personal firefights. But nothing for scope and all. Their heavy weapons system, on the other hand, is off the hook. A hydraulic mounted auto-cannon capable of distributing death in mass quantities at a vicious rate of fire. We're also carrying frags, both smoke and demo charges. And the Marines pack flamethrowers, for all the good that'll do. I'm not seeing any kind of scenario where they'd come in handy on nearly airless Mars. But you never know. And if all else fails, they've got an APC—armored personnel carrier—loaded into the cargo hold.

What else do you need to break other people's stuff?

"Who's OpFor?" asks one of the Marines.

"Japanese gaming clan. SuperMecha. That's all I got," I tell them as the howling dropship engines compete with chat volume. "Basically, just shoot everything in our way, move and communicate. I'll assess the tactical once I get a look at what we're facing on the ground. Primary objective is to take out an atmo tower inside the main cave complex beyond the bunker entrance. Taking out their reactor earns us a bonus according to my employer. But I'm guessing that'll be heavily defended and I don't want to get anyone killed in case I need to keep you in *Civ Craft* for the next op. *Civ Craft*'s Next Life micro-charges are… prohibitive to say the least."

Later I'd realize that was the understatement of the year.

"LZ in one minute," calls out the pilot. "Looks hot!"

An alarm shrieks from the cockpit.

It's urgent. Pulsing and repeating. A mechanical voice intones in AI deadpan: "Warning, warning, warning, anti-aircraft radar detected. Warning, warning…"

The high-pitched pulse begins to beat faster. Then rapidly. Even I, who never likes to fly vehicles in-game, know exactly what that means. Wherever that radar is… it has lock on us. We've been acquired.

A moment later a steady tone indicates a firing solution has been achieved. Some kind of air defense system is about to engage us inside the tight quarters of the canyon with no room to maneuver for escape.

It's a bad situation any way you paint it.

"Fast mover, two o'clock!" yells the Marine crew chief from behind the pilot.

"Got it," she replies matter-of-factly.

"What the hell is that?" someone calls out.

The pilot jerks the dropship left and right. I assume she's popping ECM packages out the back, but I see exactly what the crew chief was shrieking about in a strange moment of vertigo-shifting perspective.

You know the kind you get when you feel like an ant and everything in the world is made for giants.

Just before the cyclopean tunnel entrance leading into the bunker carved into the canyon wall, in front of the defensive works along the sandy floor littered with many destroyed Calistani main battle tanks, stands a giant mecha the likes of which I've never seen before. It's a massive mech. But like a giant robot. With a rifle the size of a small battleship. Ruined Calistani units that shouldn't have been part of this surprise attack lie smoking on the bloody red sands of the canyon floor.

"Break off now!" someone screams. Probably the Colonial Marine crew chief tagged CPLSpunkmeyer. I can feel my jaw open inside my VR helmet. I'm too dumbfounded to utter anything in that moment of watching the looming giant robot. I expected real-world stuff… tanks and assault rifles. Heavy machine guns and anti-armor. Stuff you find in *WarWorld*. But a giant robot laden with missiles and carrying an auto rifle the size of a small battleship… that's popped my breakers for a second.

I think they call it cognitive dissonance.

What's even more incredible to me, floating in the background of my rebooting mind as I try to rough out a quick tactical analysis regarding what to do next, is that the Calistani clans used first-generation main battle tanks from *WarWorld* in an unsupported cavalry charge coming at the doors from another direction along the canyon floor where no other unit was supposed to be—at least according to Rashid's plans. And no one told *me*, the guy leading the surprise attack strike force that was supposed to be the real attack.

An attack that is now clearly blown by the useless cav charge against the giant robot guarding the back door.

That giant mecha surely made short work of the Calistani armored cavalry charge. There's no denying that.

And that AA alarm is shrieking bloody murder.

That's when I realize it. *We* are the diversion. Our assault is a diversion. Enigmatrix and her engineers are blowing the main door on the city above and going for the glory all on their own.

I switch over to the group leader's feed and watch the Calistani clans attacking in force. They're engaged in running gunfights up along the mammoth battlements of the city's defenses. Where they were thousands in the initial attack, now tens of thousands are streaming toward the city, leaving great dust storms as they come at the Japanese gaming clan SuperMecha from out of the Martian desert.

The armored ground attack on the back door was definitely just a diversion. And my team was sent in to reinforce the lie, to make the case for the Japs to switch primary defense assets to the back door. Rashid and his generals probably even paid to boost a stream on social media showing something like *Super Bowl winner PerfectQuestion launches surprise attack against the SuperMecha*.

Fun times.

Smart play, Enigmatrix, I think. Now she's moments from taking the doors off and going in for the victory. We, on the other hand... are getting slaughtered before we've fired a shot.

The ground-to-air missile hits us and we crash down into the sands in front of the base.

Chapter Sixteen

On screen, inside the crashing dropship, everything goes to hell in a handbasket in the space of less than a second. My in-game POV spins as the pilot fights to auto-rotate the falling dropship into the sands with little room and altitude to do so.

"We 'bout to go EVA, folks! LZ is on fire like a Fourth of July barbecue!" shouts MarineSgtApone over the chaos. We slam onto the digital surface of Mars. Hard. I get nailed for twenty-five-percent health damage.

A moment after hitting the 'E' key I'm outside the smoking wreckage of the downed dropship and taking fire from the fighting positions that surround the enemy clan bunker. Scattered mechanical parts and dead Marines are rendered in graphic detail. *Civ Craft* has paid big bucks for top-of-the-line visual effects because they have the streaming audience numbers to support the expense. The wrecked dropship rests in all the crashed starship sci-fi glory and grandeur one could possibly expect. Smoke drifts away from the shattered engine in the bare Martian atmosphere, the forward section buried in the sand.

Enemy fire slams into the Marines trying to seek what little cover they can find.

Calistani close-air-support dropships are making runs on the giant mecha that looms over our heads just a few hundred feet away. But the monster machine doesn't seem too concerned with that, and I watch as it almost casually butt-strokes one of the attacking fighters like it's nothing more than an angry wasp. The fighter explodes in a thousand hot pieces that rain down across the pink sands of the Martian canyon, causing small dust fountains that drift away within the action of the battle.

It's a good thing the mecha is distracted by us and the destroyed Calistani armored cavalry; otherwise it might be up there stopping the main assault, I think bitterly. Yeah, I'm getting paid no matter what. But that doesn't mean I like to lose just so someone on my own team can upstage me. Especially without cluing me into the plan.

"Uh…" says PVTHudson. "Anyone got something big enough to kill that thing?"

We're down behind a dune. MarineSgtApone has formed the platoon up into a defensive perimeter surrounding the smoking crash site. We're still taking heavy fire from everywhere and not inclined to move much.

"Negative," I reply.

Heavy machine gun fire from one of the towers guarding the bunker entrance chews up the sand in front of us, sending volcanic plumes of pink dust along the low ridge of the crash crater we're covering behind.

"Y'know," says PVTHudson, "someone really should have thought to give us a weapon that could kill giant robots seeing as the name of this Japanese clan means *giant robots*."

He's right, but the Calistanis are basically incompetent, so it's hardly surprising they're clueless about who they're dealing with. I think once more about the five million in gold I'm earning.

High above us, the giant mecha is sweeping the remaining Calistani armor from the board with a series of rocket strikes via launchers located on its shoulders.

"So," continues PVTHudson, "according to some quick research, this clan, SuperMecha, is allied with another clan called ShogunYojimbo. And they're like the best. They really work together as a team and they've developed their whole tech tree in *Civ Craft* based on mechs. I highly doubt our pulse rifles are going to do much more than annoy them... sir. We're dead, man. Game over."

Someone laughs over the chat. But there's little enthusiasm in it. That we're seconds from getting annihilated—game-overed, or *owned* as some liked to say—is apparent to all.

"Apone!" I shout. "Any artillery from Calistani fire support?"

"Negative, sir. Not at this time. Enigmatrix is calling in fire missions for the next ten minutes. So we're blocked out for all intents and purposes."

We're taking casualties. The heavy machine guns in the nearest tower have found their range on us. Marines are being cut to shreds. The HUD roster is graying out in large sections.

"Explosives?"

"Uhhhh... not any that're going to do anything to that thing... 'cept maybe scratch the paint a little."

More casualties. Two dropships manage to avoid the enemy AA along the wall and swoop in to hit the mecha with rockets. Which do nothing. Seconds later, a blur of projectiles from the giant's rifle send both crafts into the sands. Secondary explosions result.

This is going from bad to worse.

The entire assault is in complete disarray. Not good. Especially if I want Rashid and the generals to be real happy about paying me my gold and all. Instead of...

Instead of...

What, I wonder. Prison? Death?

I haven't really thought about that until now... but yeah... they have absolute power in Calistan. They could do all those things if they need a scapegoat... especially if Enigmatrix set me up to be that goat. Any one of them could pull those kind of shenanigans if the long knives were out.

And ask yourself, who ever handles absolute power well?

"You ever watch *Star Wars*?" someone asks over chat.

"What?"

It was the player tagged Frosty.

Yeah, I'm familiar with *Star Wars*. It's an old run-down movie franchise that interested me on some level I could never quite articulate. Like something that had all the potential in the world, and never lived up to it. Each movie is like that. Like a star high school athlete who can never quite get their life together in the real world. It's supposed to have really been something a long, long time ago.

But I know he's not asking me for my thoughts on washed-up sci-fi. So over the staccato thumps of machine gun rounds pounding into the Martian sand all around us, I ask him to explain.

"Well it was one of the old ones…" he begins.

A rocket streaks overhead with a sinister *hiss* and *whoosh*.

"Quickly, please," I prompted.

"Listen. One time they had to fight this giant robot. Except it was like a dog. Four legs. They shot harpoons with cables, tied its legs up. Tow cables."

"Pretty sure we can't haul tow cables around that thing's legs fast enough."

"No, but the platoon APC can. 'Cept it's got no tow cable. So… not much of a plan. Just thinking out loud… sir."

We've lost twenty percent of the platoon.

"Sir," says MarineSgtApone from somewhere along the line. Marines are now firing back at the towers. Apone's voice is frantic over chat. But still in control. "We need to move now, sir. We won't last much longer out here in the sand with little to no cover."

"Dropship has a tow cable," volunteers the pilot. CPLFerro. She has only a sidearm and her flight helmet for any kind of armor. It's a miracle she survived the crash given the nose canopy of the ship buried itself in the side of a dune. I look back at the dropship. Black smoke is billowing from it, and flames pulse from the destroyed engines in sudden spurts.

It takes a few seconds, but a plan comes to me. I relay it to the squad.

"We'll use the tow cable from the dropship, attach it to the APC. Frosty, you're in charge. Get a team together and get it hooked up."

"And what are you going to do?" Frosty asks.

"Drive the APC out of the wreck and try your plan out."

Then I'm out of prone and running full bore to the wrecked dropship.

"Covering fire!" yells Apone over chat.

I zig and zag, dodging aimed targeting, the Martian sand exploding all around and ahead of me. I reach the wreck of the dropship, hit 'E', and I'm inside. My HUD is red with emergency damage lighting and warnings to evacuate the ship immediately. I scramble through the inventory screen and access the APC. It's still useable. Moments later I have it off the cargo deck.

"Suppress those MGs on the towers, Marines!" Apone yells while Frosty and the pilot, after a brief dash through enemy fire, grab the end of the downed bird's tow cable and attach it to the wicked-looking, low and flat, featureless APC. It's part of the Colonial Marines cosplay loadout ported into *Civ Craft*.

I run through the controls, quickly familiarizing myself. Standard controls. No weapons. Just an automated turret that can be set to engage target profiles. I set that to any hostiles and throttle up. The thing hums with malevolent power and I roar off through the sand, the tow cable that attaches me to the dropship spooling behind me. I'm headed straight for the looming giant mech, which is still ruining what remains of the Calistani close air support units that swarm it.

The giant robot sees me barreling toward it in the APC. It raises its foot. It's going to step on me.

"Apone, move out now. Destroy that atmo tower inside the complex while I keep this thing busy!"

I'm probably not going to be in-game much longer.

"Enigmatrix!" I call out over chat. It still feels weird. Wasn't I just killing her just a few days ago in the Super Bowl?

"Trix here!" She sounds like she's got her hands full and is less than enthusiastic about taking comm from me.

"If I get killed in the next few seconds, those Marines can take out that tower once they're inside. I don't think you're going to get your reactor."

"And…" she says neutrally.

I hear tons of chatter coming through on her end. Lots of Calistanis are getting wiped out by auto-turrets and worse. And they're constantly screaming some nonsensical battle cry. Or mumbling it while she's trying to give them orders. Or just chanting it over chat, tying up the line.

Apparently, things aren't going well up there along the rim.

"We're past the inner defensive works…" Her transmission is beginning to break up.

Five million in gold, some voice inside my head reminds me. Five million in gold and you can get back to playing with pros.

And…

What about that vacation you've been promising yourself?

And a drink. Right now I could go for a scotch on the rocks.

The giant foot of the robot misses the APC. Barely. But the shock waves send the APC skidding off through the thick sand. I'd really like to chew her out for setting me up like this. But that won't help anyone right now in this moment, mainly me, get their five million in gold.

"It's weirdly quiet in here, PQ," says Enigmatrix over chat in what feels like a non sequitur. I glance at her feed. She's taken some kind of overwatch control tower with an elite guard of operators. Chaos and carnage unfold across screens and out beyond the massive windows that look out over the city's defensive works. She pivots, and I see a Clan SuperMecha Marine slumped against a blood-sprayed concrete wall.

Also, I just barely miss getting stomped by the giant mecha again. Like I said, vehicles aren't really my thing. I hear the long *buuuuurp* of the auto-turret at the front right of the APC going off as it engages the giant robot, riddling one of its legs with hundreds of rounds. In the rearview, I see it's done some damage.

Now I'm roaring past the gargantuan robot. I check the spool on the cable and see I've got a thousand feet to pull my trick.

"What's that…" It's Enigmatrix's voice. I left the chat open. "Oh hell no…" Then I hear assault rifles going off like a South American birthday party.

Then nothing at all.

At first I think she cut the chat. But the quick glance I spare says it's still open. It's live. And there's nothing coming from her end. I say her name a few times as I head straight back at the armored giant on the red sands in front of the bunker at the bottom of the canyon.

Still, I get no reply from Enigmatrix.

I engage all four brakes on the APC and power-slide through the Martian dust. Piles of pink sand billow and skirl across the APC's external view. The giant mecha raises its rifle and I can see the yawning black void at the end of the barrel gaping down at me. Supersonic rounds erupt from that darkness.

They streak toward me like the blur of a thousand determined hornets, their volume distorting the Martian landscape between us. The mecha didn't find its range with the initial burst, so the rounds begin to chew up the sand between me and it.

If I turn and run, the thing'll lead me and I'm finished.

But I don't even think about doing that. Not in the least.

I've already mashed the accelerator full forward and I'm flying straight at the giant titan. Passing through the bullet storm with some damage to the outer hull. I pull tight turns just hoping somehow this cable is doing something as I circle the feet of the killer warbot. I also hope the physics processors inside *Civ Craft* can handle this maneuver. They should. This is, after all, a game about crafting and salvage. About building empires through ingenuity and resources. About cobbling things together.

And… come on! I need a break!

A moment later the APC is jerked off its fat ceramic wheels and into the air. I go way up and the external view inside my HUD spins loftily. For a brief moment I see small attack fighters swooping in to hit the mech. The face of the giant Japanese robot rushes past my view. Then the walls of the canyon whip past the forward viewport, the vehicle scrapes along the side of something, and the sound effects let me know that whatever it is… it's not pillowy soft.

I have no idea what's happening. I have a queasy moment to wonder if somehow the robot has turned the APC into the ball part of a ball-and-chain type weapon. I sense that at any moment now my health is about to zero out as the robot smashes something—like my Colonial Marines—with an APC on a string.

The vehicle slams into the sand and goes skidding, then flipping, and finally rolling away from the iron giant. I have to close my eyes because it's making my eyeballs scream, but just before I do I see the giant mecha crashing to the floor of the canyon. Chest first.

I keep my eyes closed. Click off sound. And meditate.

Just for a second. I'm resetting.

Pausing.

Breathing.

For just a moment.

I feel the world spinning behind my eyelids, but I know it isn't. I interlace my fingers and fold them across my chest with my thumbs sticking out. I crane my head down and look at my thumbs below the horizon of my VR helmet.

And the world stops spinning.

It's an old trick.

There's a headache there that I've been ignoring for longer than I can remember. So I ignore it some more and bring up the in-game sound.

Battle chatter. The Marines are breaching the gate towers in teams. And getting killed. And… getting through to the bunker.

The tower guns have gone quiet.

I roll my shoulders. Then my wrists.

If that giant mecha isn't out of the action…

I open my eyes and settle my hovering fingers above the keys. The only view I have is of the inside of the smashed APC. Warning icons are flashing, indicating the APC is toast. I hit 'E' and I'm out.

That's when the mecha explodes.

My avatar is knocked to the sand. The accompanying EMP knocks out my HUD and weapon optics. Above me, along the canyon wall near the bunker and the towers that guard it, the Marines have miraculously smashed their way in. But the EMP has knocked out all of our electronics.

So… it's iron sights from here on out.

Fine. Game on.

Chapter Seventeen

The Marines are waiting for me on the platform outside the twisted metal flower petals of the destroyed main entrance to the bunker. I join them at the top of the ramp just as a heavy cargo lifter dropship, tagged as friendly blue and not enemy red in our HUDs, courtesy of some Russian mercenary clan, drops a Behemoth infantry support tank in front of the entrance. Then the cargo ship flares its hover engines and climbs into the Martian atmosphere once more.

It seems the Calistanis have managed to do one thing right today—they've knocked out the AA along the canyon walls. And they've done so in order to deliver... this.

The Behemoth is the size of a small city block, with massive treads and a chain-gun barrel the length of a redwood tree trunk. Three of them in fact. All linked via rotating cylinder. Its tri-barrel configuration can vaporize most ground units and structures. In *WarWorld* only one team has unlocked the Behemoth. It's a special research upgrade. It's slow, ungainly, and utterly lethal. JollyBoy knocked one out for the win against the ChiliBees corporate team at Blizzard Stadium last fall. But not before it devastated my platoon.

Now its twin waits above us, rumbling ominously.

"They say they'll cover us, sir," Apone reports. "They'll guard the entrance from counterattack while we're inside breakin' stuff."

Seems like an awfully big micro-transaction just to guard the entrance, but I'm not refusing the help. We squad up with what's left of us and get ready to breach the inner lock.

Inside the main hab, all is silent. Too silent. The place is clean and sterile. The Japanese clan seems organized in their approach to design. They've eschewed some of the public structure builds available for download in favor of their own, zen-alien design.

I access a map of the facility after PVTHudson defeats a minigame and hacks a base terminal. It's similar to the one Rashid had in his war room, but this one shows their sentries and kill zones. Or at least what they planned for when they first built this place.

"Nice going," I remark after he beats six levels of old-school *Super Mario Bros.*

"No problem, chief. You just turtle sled through most of the hard parts." I can hear him snap his gum over chat.

Looking at the facility, it is not what I expected. Not what Rashid and his generals displayed in their underground war room. Mainly… there's no atmo tower. There is a reactor though. Maybe.

"That *should* be the reactor there, sir," says Apone, highlighting an area. "But we'll need to put eyes on it for a confirm."

So far, the Calistanis are nothing for nothing on actionable intel.

I contact Rashid over chat.

"Here, PQ," he says in his ever-cheerful voice. Except I have no idea where "here" is. I'm so tired I escaped noticing what his role in all of this is. If I have to guess… Enigmatrix's little double-cross is a setup to make him look good if they actually take the base in the frontal assault. Otherwise he can blame someone else for the loss in front of his generals.

"We've secured the entrance to the city, PQ, but Enigmatrix got killed by a surprise counterattack from some–"

"There's no atmo tower down here," I reply.

"Huh. That's weird."

"There is a reactor. We think."

There isn't even a pause as Rashid tells me what to do next.

"Blow it up."

I hesitate. I check Enigmatrix's feed. She's still cut off. I try to access her unit roster. Everyone's grayed out. Including her. It does look like she's KIA for the rest of the day, which is how *Civ Craft* runs their fatalities. And a hefty buy-in from the team to get you back in the game.

"Rashid..."

"Yeah, PQ?"

"You can take this base now. It's yours. We've cleared the defenses. There's power. It's on your territory. It's set up to process resources on your own territory. Why not take it and start building stuff?"

There's a long pause.

Then...

"That's not our strategic objective at this time, PerfectQuestion. I need you to blow the reactor." He sounds like he's reading from a script. Restating a party line that's been fed and rehearsed.

Pause.

"Affirmative?" he prompts.

This makes no sense. *WarWorld*... yes. *Civ Craft*... no.

Five million.

In gold.

"Affirmative."

Chapter Eighteen

I cut the chat with Rashid and tell MarineSgtApone to get us organized. We're going for the main reactor.

As PVTHudson digs deeper into the base AI to determine a route, I go over to a viewing window that looks out into a massive central cavern. Beyond the floodlights from this side of the bunker entrance, there's nothing but darkness out there. But it's got to be there. This place has to be getting power from something, somewhere. And if the map is correct, that somewhere is in this cavern.

PVTHudson announces he's found a path to the reactor. Ten minutes later, we're making our way through admin offices and airlocks, moving steadily downward. The map, with PVTHudson's route highlighted, appears in our HUDs, which have now mostly rebooted from the EMP. It indicates a few more turns and we'll come out on the floor of the massive cavern, near where we think the reactor is.

In a narrow lightless hall we find the remains of engineers. Bots most likely. But they're definitely Clan SuperMecha. They've been cut to shreds. Not with bullets. With knives. Or some kind of slashing weapon. Dark blood spatter decorates the walls, revealed by a lone overhead light still swinging gently in the silence. As though someone has only just moved it and then left the room in the seconds before we appeared.

"It's cliché, sir," says Apone, "but I definitely got a bad feeling about this."

There's a few nervous laughs from what remains of the Colonial Marines.

"It *is* cliché," says Hudson. "But Sarge is right. This is all wrong, man. This is a message to us."

From here on down, through the last levels, there's no power. We've rebooted some of our electronics—helmet lights, the flashes on some of the rifles—but optics and HUD targeting are all gone. They come in for a few seconds during reboot and then fritz out. We must be getting close to the reactor.

"Stay close. Stay frosty," MarineCorporalHicks reminds the rest of the Marines. And me. "And Frost… stay original-recipe Frosty."

Everybody chuckles at this. But the joke is lost on me. I assume it's something to do with the movie.

That's when the turtles attack us.

Like ninjas.

They come from the ceiling. It's Frost who gets pulled first. Just disappears from our column. He grays out on the HUD seconds after being yanked through a wall and into another darkness beyond.

Everybody starts freaking out and firing in every direction for a brief few seconds because we didn't know mutant turtles who moved like ninjas were surrounding us.

The firing stops and one of the turtles who fights like a ninja appears as a swiftly moving shadow.

Fire erupts from the squad.

We've been crossing through a darkened office of some sort, desks and chairs scattered everywhere. All muted grays and soft blues. A massive window looks out upon the dark central cavern, allowing illumination from a spotlight that seems to be tracking something. It's by that momentary light that we now see him. Her. It. The turtle ninja.

"Game on!" screams MarinePvtDrake as he cuts lose afresh with the Colonial Marines' heavy machine gun system. It barks out in staccato eruptions. The turtle jumps, cartwheels, and stays ahead of Drake's death burst from the automatic pulse cannon. And as it retreats, it flings throwing stars and kills three Marines, including Drake.

Just like that.

Then it's gone.

We have twelve left now. And that number doesn't seem like it'll be enough to destroy the reactor, much less survive the next minute.

"Yo…" says PVT Hudson excitedly. He's clearly shaken. "You see that? Man, we gotta get out of here. That was messed up. These Japanese clans go all in for this tricky ninja trickery. I've been surfing their web pages. Weird stuff. They're really into ninja animals. Like really into it. They've got way better tech than—"

A loud bang and a sudden flash, and we're blind.

Or at least my VR helmet shows nothing but washed-out white haze. I've been flashbanged before. I know exactly what will happen next.

I drop prone and wait for my vision to clear.

Meanwhile everyone's firing at something and screaming at one another over chat.

"I can't see nuthin'!"

"Got one!"

"You got *me*!"

"Sorry!"

"Apone!"

"Sarge!"

"WE GOTTA BOOGIE!"

My sight is coming back.

I see a turtle deflecting a stream of pulse rifle fire from PVT Hudson. The bright fire of Hudson's rifle lights up the dark, but the blade-wielding man-turtle deflects every round the Marine can put on target with a dazzling whirl of steel.

Yeah. We aren't in the modern warfare world of *War World* anymore. Anything can happen here. And it's happening right now.

I cut loose with the HK Marksman, flipping the selector to eleven. Or high-cycle full auto, as some like to call it. In seconds I bleed the eighty-round drum dry. I'm determined to get me a turtle if just to improve squad morale. When I'm finished, that turtle is definitely dead.

On the other hand, the other three turtles who fight like ninjas are everywhere.

"Mag out!" I shout over chat, and swap in a new one.

The turtles are leaping, slashing, whirling, and clubbing Colonial Marines to death. They fly from ceilings and over desks disintegrating from concentrated pulse rifle fire; they run up walls and then swing in for up close and personal attacks that are violently savage and seem extremely excessive.

I fire at another man-turtle-ninja that just leapt in at MarinePFC-Vasquez and brained her with flailing nunchucks.

Hudson screams over the chat, "It's cliché, man... but... They're comin' outta the walls!" He gets the one that walloped Vasquez and sends it tumbling, ventilated by no fewer than ten pulse rifle rounds.

"Fall back to the next room!" someone else roars. Maybe Marine-CorporalHicks.

I target one that just put two Marines down with its staff. The turtle points right at me to let me know I'm next, then comes at me, spinning its stick wildly, an evil grin plastered across its cartoony turtle face beneath masked eyes.

I fire wildly, and the thing dodges away and off into a corner twirling its staff. Then one of the Marines comes in with a flamethrower, which is all but useless in most *WarWorld* matches and yet is somehow still a required piece of unit equipment relevant to their cosplaying. The Marine sends burning fuel all over the turtle.

"Flamethrowers don't care about karate," mutters Hicks over chat.

I see PVTHudson fireman-carrying the wounded Vasquez from the room. Two other Marines have secured the door and are firing into the dark shadows in short clipped bursts.

Then they're gone. The ninja-turtle-men. Nothing remains but drifting barrel smoke and ruin from the short and intense firefight. Whatever is left of our alien attackers... has vanished.

We move forward to the next room. Glass fills one entire wall, giving a view into the massive cavern. And right there, mere meters away, is the looming reactor.

We made it. I can hardly believe it. We're actually going to get the reac–

Thirty-millimeter rounds shatter the glass and swiss cheese the walls around us in a sudden typhoon of bullets. The Marines come apart in gory pieces, as do the walls, along with probably everything in the cavern. I take a round and zero out as everything turns to ruin and chaos inside the bullet storm.

As I lie waiting for a medic that will never come, I now know where Rashid is. He's in the Behemoth. He's the source of this bullet storm. That's why he air-dropped the beast. Not to cover our rear. But to make sure the job got done once we located the reactor.

The base AI indicates, in Japanese, that there's been a breach in containment chamber number four. Our HUDs translate this a second later. The breach is in the reactor, I have no doubt.

"Cascade meltdown imminent..."

But it doesn't matter. I'm dead by the time the entire base goes kaboom.

Chapter Nineteen

"Sorry about that," says Rashid as he slaps me on the back a little too hard. I still ache from being stuck in my gamer suite couch. Gone are the days when I could crouch over a PC for days on end.

I'm getting old.

"We had to take out the base, PQ buddy. Hundred percent. Aaaand it didn't look like you were going to get through all those weird Jap animal skins."

The mutant turtles who did ninja stuff.

"So I had to fire up the Behemoth and make sure the objective got done right. Ever use one?"

I haven't. But I've had once used *on* me. Twice now.

"It's a blast. You know how much that thing fires…?"

I do.

I lost a battle to one once. I mean twice. Including just a few minutes ago.

"So," says Rashid sheepishly, "it was the only way left to take out the reactor and be sure. Y'know how it is?"

He seems genuine. Most sociopaths can pull this trick a time or two before you figure it out.

I haven't figured that out. Yet. Later—tonight in fact—while I'm getting good and drunk, it will occur to me that Rashid has the ability. To be likeable despite himself. Despite being the sultan's son. Despite being spoiled and a rich pretty boy. You just want to like him.

That was what I thought about him at first. That you wanted to like him despite the obvious. Later, I'll think other things.

I'm already starting to.

"Okay, now it's time to cut loose and really party!" he says triumphantly as we walk to a brand-new sports car. A Porsche Excalibur. Creamy white. Tan leather interior. He tosses me the keys.

"It's yours," he says, and watches for the look on my face.

I look at the keys. Real keys. Not a fob. Very retro chic. Or so I've read.

"Listen," I begin. "Rashid, I…"

His expression gets serious. "Don't say no to me," he whispers intently. "No one ever says no to me, okay, PQ?"

He seems very resolute about this. Like he needs me to believe this if the world is going to go on.

Suddenly and desperately, I have to know that he's telling the truth. And not because it's some game he wants to play to manipulate me. But because there are ways accessible to him inside his own Islamic totalitarian fascist state that could be used to convince me of whatever they want me to *think* is the truth. And doing that would mean… we'd no longer be friends. I'd no longer be his idol. Or accessory. I'm not quite sure of which one of those I am. But I'm sure that I'm one of them. Which isn't as comforting as you might think.

In fact it's a little scary if you think about it too much.

And that's exactly what I do.

I think long and hard about who I'm dealing with in this half second where I have some kind of choice in the events that are about to unfold. The choice to turn and walk away from all the bad I sense is about to happen. Because I'm feeling more and more surrounded by the minute. Like I'm slowly drowning.

I could choose to just blow my top right this very second. But I know that isn't possibly the wisest move I can make. I'm not in America anymore. I need to remember that, because that's important and becoming abundantly more so with every minute that passes. This is someone else's country, and I'm acutely aware that I can just disappear here and never be seen again. I have the suspicion that that's very possible. And that there are fates worse than death.

And it's kind of creepy the first time you ever really have that particular feeling. I've been around the world enough to know what can happen in certain... seedier places. People got panel-vanned all the time. And no one much cares.

The more I think about it, the less I feel I have a choice at all. Or if I do... none of my choices are good ones.

"It's not the car, and you don't need to..." I begin, feeling my way forward. "It's..." I try.

I pause. The sun is going down behind the houses across the water along the channel. I can smell the salt in the ocean. Little children on the beaches over there are running back and forth in the water. A big old dog is chasing them around as they laugh and squeal.

"I feel like I'm being rewarded for losing," I say finally. It's a lie. But one that seems perfect to let me go on not being panel-vanned. "You know we didn't win in there, Rashid. We lost. We got killed. Even you got killed by the nuclear blast. That Behemoth must have been a ginormous micro-transaction. I'm sure that went up in the blast too."

I watch his face. Watch him trying to comprehend what I'm saying. He nods like he's way ahead of me. Like I'm someone just catching up and processing the grand scheme only he can see. Like he's noble and patient enough to let me catch up.

"We lost today," I say again. Making it sound like it was really more my fault than his.

And then I add, "Rashid," to make it more... what? I don't know. I'm just feeling my way forward through a minefield in the dark. Delicately. Which is the only way through a minefield in the dark. Or the light.

"Yes!" he exclaims enthusiastically. "But we really didn't. We took the Japs out. That's a win any way you look at it. And there's more I can't tell you right now. Big-picture stuff. But we had to get rid of that base. Now I'm really free to move about. To do what I really want to do. Get things done finally!"

He grabs my shoulders. He's slightly taller than me.

"You got us through the door. That giant robot would've made short work of the Behemoth. Once we got to the back door with it, I knew it was going to end either with you lighting that reactor, or with me just vaping it. So I vaped it. It's all part of Calistan's grand strategy. And I assure you, my friend, there *is* a grand strategy at work here. And it's genius. And you've played a part in that success."

I suspect the grand strategy is genius because he came up with it. Wisely I choose not to voice this observation.

I leave that for never.

"This is yours!" He indicates the beautiful convertible Porsche once more. "Enjoy it," he says genuinely. "Life's short, PQ. Have fun while you still can."

Sure, that isn't ominous. Or a warning. No. Not at all.

It's the "life's short" part that makes me really start to worry in earnest. He said it as though he knows something about me I'm not aware of.

Or maybe it's just this totalitarian Islamic state I find myself surrounded by and working for. I'm definitely on the ride now. They don't stop rollercoasters in the middle. Unless there's been an accident.

Unless someone's been killed.

Chapter Twenty

We head back to Rashid's place. He's still calling it the shack as he gives directions and I drive the new Porsche.

I try not to wreck it, treating it like it really is my own. It purrs smoothly as it runs up through the gears, and it's got a deconstructionist style that's all the rage lately. No HUD on the windshield. No interactive monitors and displays. No auto-drive features. You just drive this little kitty-cat and watch all the real needles in the real display fall and rise depending on what you do with the pedal and gearshift. It's amazing, and once again it causes me to think the past was way better than the present.

I've been feeling that a lot lately.

At Rashid's we change into, as he calls them, "evening clothes." He takes forever, and I fall asleep. It seems like hours later that we go out once more. It's going on ten o'clock, and the nap has only made my brain foggier. All I want is to go to bed and sleep through the night. And the next day.

"No worries," Rashid says as though there are many things to worry about. "Newport's just getting warmed up. Breezies don't come out till around now anyway. Takes 'em that long to get ready," he says without irony. He's driving his latest toy as we speed down tight twisting turns and hit the straightaways at top speed, thundering into Newport Beach like we're on our way to fight crime. Or we're running from one.

The city's lit up like Carnivale. Well-dressed beautiful young people pour from every bar onto the party-swollen streets. Everybody seems to know Rashid, and there are constant shouts and waves acknowledging his arrival as we purr down PCH. The Pacific Coast Highway.

We arrive at the club. It's called "Less Than Zero" and the line to get in is down the block. It's an homage to the 1980s and it's supposedly "firecracker," according to Rashid. As we make our way to the front, I hear incredulous olive-skinned girls in tight tiny dresses and high heels claiming the disappearing line goes on for another half mile down the street behind me.

Rashid catches me looking at the beautiful girls, who give me a round of bashful smiles. Probably because of Rashid. I usually don't get that from girls.

He elbows me and doesn't even bother to lean in close as he announces, "Not those dogs. Much better inside, my friend. Much, much better."

And then we're up the narrow steps of the massive club that looms over the Pacific Coast Highway, searchlights performing their ballet in the night above us all. Security not only waves us right through, they bro-fist Rashid as we pass. All is good when it comes to Prince Rashid.

An oily snake of a little guy comes out to greet Rashid almost immediately. He's sweating and breathing hard as though he ran from wherever inside the club to make sure he could greet the sultan's son at the door. I don't like the guy from the get-go. It's weird when that happens, but it occasionally does. I call it my spider sense.

I don't not like him for any reason in particular. I can just tell he isn't straight up. And so, I don't like him. I've rarely been wrong.

"Rashid, Rashid, Rashid!" he exclaims, then glances at me and starts speaking Arabic as if to cut me out of the all-important gossip Rashid must hear. The intent of the pivot is that clear.

Rashid responds in English.

"This is my new best friend, Amal. He's a rock star. Best pro gamer in the world! You should know that, all-knowing one."

The night club owner clucks disapprovingly. Then says in overly accented English, "That is only because you yourself do not play professionally, Rashid. Of course… then you would be the best."

Unctuous to the point of viscous.

In other words, world-class oily.

And Rashid doesn't bother to correct or argue the point as we're escorted into a throbbing machine-gun palace of images and sound. The speakers are literally three stories high. The light shifts from blue to violet. On every wall, war movies from the eighties are projected onto the ceiling. Distorted and askew, their images of ultra-violence are beat-mixed with a drum-and-bass techno blitzkrieg on the senses.

Lines of dialogue morph into sudden songs. Some guy repeatedly jumps off a building as a helicopter blows up in a song called "Welcome to the Party, Pal!"

Or at least that's the line that gets repeated for the next twenty minutes in every possible catchy permutation.

"Let's get some drinks," orders Rashid. "Gotta meet up with someone."

We make the bar, passing through waves of the most epically beautiful women I've ever seen. Long legs. Generous curves. Hair and makeup at the nines. Giant eyes and even longer lashes. All of them looking at us expectantly doe-eyed. Rashid couldn't care less about any of them.

I know what it takes for a woman to get ready to go out. Hours of preparation. I can only imagine how much they've spent to look just right for this moment where everything might be possible. For them.

And Rashid dismissed them in an instant like they weren't even there.

A few he smiles at as we near the bar. A very few. They seem to communicate some message only the two of them understand. Some past secret that can never be acknowledged in the shifting light of a thundering club at close to midnight.

A space clears for us at the swamped bar as if it was always meant to. Just clears. No prompt needed. No action required. A sea of people just parts as if they know their part in this massively staged opera.

I don't know why… but I don't like any of this. It makes me uneasy. Or maybe I'm jealous. Not everybody gets to be the pharaoh.

But I don't think that's it.

If I had to put a thumbtack in it, I would say it's because none of it is me. And I don't like what other people become around whatever this is. Phony. Less than what their real value is to the ones who love them. Plastic. Cheap and expendable.

It's something I don't even want to think about. But it's there. It surrounds Rashid. And he's happy to have it that way.

And then again, I think to myself, as Rashid orders "two G and Ts, Abdul" from the model-good-looking bartender who probably did time in some army somewhere, maybe these people want it this way. Maybe they like knowing what the score is and I'm selling them short. Sure, it's not my cup of tea… but maybe it's theirs. Who am I to judge?

In Calistan… I'm nobody.

Our drinks land on the bar.

Real lime.

Vintage tonic.

Top-notch gin. Top shelf is a couple of steps below.

Gorgeously cut cubes of clear arctic ice that seem forged instead of simply frozen into shape. Made from what I can only assume is the most pure water to be had in all of Calistan.

I notice the bartender's confidence as he sets out the perfect drinks, first the flippant toss of the napkins and then the deft placement, demanding that I watch his perfect nonchalance. But I know it's an act. Everybody on that side of the bar is trying not to act as if their lives depend on Rashid liking the drink they've just made.

Yeah… I don't like that. I prefer bars where the bartender doesn't hate you, but he'll beat you senseless if you step out of line.

Rashid sips. I gulp. I'm thirsty.

He smiles at me once, briefly. Like he's unhappy. Suddenly melancholy. Letting me know he's deep-ish.

"You know…" he seems to confess. "We had to do that today."

I don't say anything. I try to catch the bartender's eye. He's watching us like a hawk, but he doesn't seem concerned in the least when I gently rock my empty drink at him.

Message received: Rashid will do the ordering. And he isn't even nearly finished with his drink.

"No matter what anyone tells you…" continues the prince at my elbow, "for the Calistani team to go forward, we had to get rid of that foreign abomination on our territory. Tomorrow we're going to do some great things online. But that… that had to be dealt with first." He's holding his drink in front of his face, staring past the cold, clear cubes as though he sees something there on the swarming dance floor that needs his appraisal.

"Rashid…"

The voice is musical. And feminine.

We turn, and there is the stunner to end all stunners. Not as tall as the others, but every feature is the literal embodiment of some heroine princess from *One Thousand and One Nights*. Her face is perfectly sculpted. Her hair full and wavy. Her seductive cat eyes don't bother to regard me for even a brief smoky second.

Yeah… she's that beautiful. Even a blind man would've seen it.

"Rashid, we have a table upstairs… we've been waiting for you for thirty minutes."

She doesn't ask who I am. That's not important. I'm not important in the echelons above reality I'm being exposed to. Offered a glimpse of. Fine. A little anonymity suits me just fine right about now.

And there is this part of me that suddenly wants to be in that crowd of beautiful people that get to talk to her on equal terms. For reasons I don't know how to articulate at this very second.

"This is my girlfriend, Samira," says Rashid with little enthusiasm.

She holds out her hand and casts those gorgeous eyes right into my face. Like she knows exactly what they do.

I take her hand and nod. Only nod. Not because she's stunningly beautiful and I'm nervous. In any other circumstance I would move on her with a deferential comment that could be taken for so much more if there was any interest in playing. But no. I nod because the man I'm standing next to is dangerous. And someday I want my five million in gold and to leave Calistan alive. So I just nod, rattle my perfect ice cubes at the bartender ineffectively, and try to push the thoughts I'm having about her out of my head.

And that throws her a bit.

Because she makes men helpless, and she knows it.

Maybe. Maybe I'm reading all of my baggage into the deep dark of her exotic eyes. Maybe.

She tilts her head once at me. Just slightly. As if asking me a question she can't quite believe the answer to. But her mouth keeps making business with Rashid. She's telling Rashid that he needs to come upstairs to the VIP room now. People are waiting for him. And all the while the slight tilt in her head, exposing her perfectly formed jawline, is asking if I want to play her little game of desire. And telling me she doesn't really believe I'm more interested in a drink. Or in anything, or anyone, else. Only her.

I turn to the bartender and say, loud enough to be heard, "Hey, Abdul... another G and T if you can break away from yourself." And then I give him my dead-eyed serious look.

I'm met with a white-hot glare of murder at the very idea that a dog like myself would crack the whip. Then he must catch a look from Rashid backing up my boorish behavior, because he nervously bends to the task and I turn back to her with a nice all-is-right-with-the-world smile, expecting her to be waiting for me to bother staring at her epic curves.

Instead, like a pro, she has turned on stiletto high heels and is moving off through the parting crowd in her sheer light-green silk pantaloons. Legs and hips below an exposed and tanned midriff sway this way and that way to make sure I'm watching her go.

Yeah. It's a pro move. I die a little watching her go. And she knows it.

"She's on fire," whispers Rashid in my ear. He laughs low and evil. "I get it. And I'm right there with you, man. I can't even touch her myself. Imagine how *I* feel!"

He drains his drink gustily. Then looks at the bartender and the rest of the staff by default and issues the only sweeping decree I've ever witnessed. He really is a real live prince in that moment. "Take care of my friend," he announces.

He turns back to me.

"Gotta go now. This is family stuff. Her dad's dropping twenty-five million on our wedding. So I have to be on my best behavior for just a little while longer." He looks up at the hidden levels most of those around us will never see. "I'll catch up with you in about two hours. Then we'll have some real fun."

For the next two hours I drink at the bar and talk to a sudden sea of girls who wander near me accidentally on purpose. I end up with tons of contacts in my smartphone, whether I want them or not. Each contact comes with a selfie that often crosses the line between pinup glamour and pornographic.

Most of the young Arab males around the bar look like they want to kill me and would enjoy doing so immensely, my friend.

Halfway through this, I finish a drink and excuse myself to use the restroom. Inside the monument to urination that is the club's VIP lounge, I meet Omar.

Rashid's brother.

The guy whose base we nuked. Or so I'll find out later.

"I just want you to know..." says the slightly chubby, almost bankerly-looking man in designer wire-rimmed glasses. "That you're working for pure evil."

I turn to see who's talking to me. Then I turn back to my business and finish up. I've had enough gin to feel cocky about my situation.

At the mirror he comes and stands next me like some relentless little poltergeist. He's the opposite of Rashid. Small. Almost invisible. Watching me in the mirror, he doesn't move a muscle. After I wash up, he hands me a towel.

"My brother is the worst thing that can happen to Calistan. My name is Omar. I'm Rashid's younger brother."

I nod, dry my hands, and check my look in the mirror. I've been talking to this girl back at the bar whose face I can't remember because I keep thinking of Samira.

And now I have Rashid's brother, and Calistani politics, in my face. Getting my five million in gold is beginning to turn into a hassle. But there is still a way through, and I'm pretty sure it involves some kind of diplomacy.

I turn and lean against the cool marble countertop of the private and palatial restroom, inspecting my suit. I need a new one, that's for sure. Threads are starting to appear all prison break from the seams.

I think of Rome.

"Listen, Omar, is it?" I say with a nice friendly smile. "I'm just a ringer for Calistan's online presence. That's all. Rashid seems very nice."

In other words... I just work here. Y'know.

If this is some sort of weird loyalty test on Rashid's part to get me to trash talk him, or plot behind his back... then I'll do my best to avoid a panel van ride and a firing squad in some warehouse district. Or a twenty-year sentence for sedition I won't make two months of.

"He's not," replies Omar flatly. "Nice. And that was my base today. The one you blew up. It was supposed to be mine once we captured it. But the mullahs thought otherwise, as they always do."

"Technically Rashid blew it up," I offer lamely.

"I'm aware. But Rashid's not that good at much besides wrecking other people's stuff. Trust me. Twenty-six years has taught me that."

"Well, it is how I make my living."

He smiles wanly at this. Then continues with a new attack.

"Right…" he begins. "But *Civ Craft* is about building things. Not blowing things up. You can do that, if that's your thing, but we'll never win if all we do is go around blowing everyone's stuff up."

"It seems to be Rashid's thing. Good or bad. And he's the one paying me." The moment I say that I realize I've gone too far. I can see that getting back to Rashid. Being used against me when things eventually get weird. Because of course… things are going to get weird. You can almost bet money on that. Except it wouldn't be a bet. It'd be an investment. Because you're going to get your money back. For sure.

Sedition. They'll call it sedition. And then bye-bye for a long, long time. Some kind of concentration camp out in the California desert. Breaking rocks on the chain gang. Makin' big rocks small. That kinda thing.

"It's really not my problem," I say, hoping to cover my bad hand with a little cold neutrality.

"Humanity is not your problem… or winning at *Civ Craft* is not your problem?" asks Omar.

I sigh. Now I'm going to be told there's a lot more at stake than just a game. This… this right here is teaching me not to be greedy. So far, none of this is worth five million in gold.

"Listen… Omar, my online specialty is blowing things up. Combat. That sort of thing. Yeah… it's weird hiring me for a game about building civilizations from the ground up. But if that's how Rashid wants to run strategy for this game, by which I mean, turning it into some kind of first-person shooter, then that's totally legit. That's his call. There's a total conquest victory condition for this game. I checked it out. You don't have to build the pyramids or the space elevator. You can just club every other civilization to death and keep everyone in the Bronze Age. That can be arranged. I can make that happen."

"Total conquest," spits Omar like I just offered him a brochure to visit a unicorn farm. Also... he literally spits on the pristine marble floor of the massive restroom. I know it's a restroom at its core. But it's beautiful and spitting on it somehow seems... blasphemous.

We continue to be the only occupants of this sacred place. I imagine his bodyguards are at the door keeping others out. I try to think of the girl I'd hoped to replace images of Samira with... and I still can't remember what she looks like.

"That's so ninth century," hisses Omar. "Or so radical Islam before the Meltdown. ISIS and butchers and refugee rapists. Throwing children into industrial kneading machines and destroying history with a sledgehammer."

His words echo off the porcelain and marble. He almost chokes on his own rage.

And he's right.

This is the thing I've really been trying not to think about. And maybe Samira is somehow in my mind because my mind is trying to get me to think about anything other than this nightmare I'm in. Trying to get me to focus. Because... Calistan *is* almost ninth century compared to the capitals of the world I've been losing myself in since...

...well, since another life, long ago.

He turns to face me. We've been talking to each other's mirror image. He isn't slick and smooth and cool like Rashid. He's an ordinary little man who wears fine clothes and is well kept because he came from money. A lot of money. But if it weren't for those things I would've recognized a gamer. An ordinary guy. That's what gamers are.

And there's nothing wrong with that.

"Rashid," he whispers to my face as he leans forward and stands on his tiptoes, "is what's wrong with Calistan. You're from the outside. You can see it. Me too. I studied abroad. I read Vonnegut. I know that man can be so unkind to the weak. My brother..."

He pauses to clear his throat.

I have no idea who Vonnegut is. But I probably should. I imagine Samira and I reading together in bed. In some quiet other place not here. Not Calistan. Don't ask me why. I've been pushing away all the usual thoughts. But the image of the two of us reading somewhere, near the beach... in a car... listening to the seagulls and the sounds of spinnakers clanging against one another on the sailboats that are docked nearby... That image is something I've been waiting for for a long time and never knew it until now.

"My brother... is trying to prove to our father that he can manage Calistan. The line of succession isn't clear. I am too. As I said, that was my clan's base you blew up. We'd contracted with the Japanese to help us increase our tech. To open up our society. I had to do it in secret because the mullahs want to control everything. Even our online presence. I was hoping to show my father that if I could build something noble, something good, inside a little digital make-believe world, then maybe Calistan could... could choose to be something else. Something besides what it is. Maybe..."

He pauses. Listening to some music only he hears.

"Maybe we could climb out of the ninth century that Islam chooses to remain in. You've seen it out there beyond the zone. Outside the Gold Coast. The Mexicans are at the gates. It's brutal and horrible and they have every right to hate our guts. There's a way forward. For all of us. Not just for those who were born to rule because they've got so much gold and oil and financing from the other powers around the world. But for everyone!"

Suddenly he snaps to attention.

"You have to go back out there right now. He's coming."

He straightens his lightweight dinner jacket.

"We will be in touch with you. You can rat me out to my brother. He'll probably reward you. But I've watched you online, Perfect-Question. I know how you play... and I think that means I know you, if you'll pardon my assumptions. I think you're more than just a hired gun. I think you believe in the little guy. There's more going on in *Civ Craft* than anyone can imagine. There's still a chance to turn this around. To turn Calistan around. We'll be in touch. Best thing you can do… get away from Rashid. Ask him to set you up in your own place. You need privacy."

And then he's walking toward the door. His leather shoes tapping out a quick determined cadence. Precise. Measured. Clear. He doesn't even turn at the door. It just opens and he's gone. For a brief moment I hear the music of the club suddenly become real and present.

I turn back to the mirror and try to find the man I thought I was.

Chapter Twenty-One

I'm back at the bar, drinking another gin and tonic and feeling something. Reflective, maybe. Gin does that to me. But I'm not really talking. I'm just listening to this girl who's telling me she has an Instaflash account with three million followers. She started a UBeg campaign just to fund her wardrobe for her trip to Calistan. She's hoping to hook up with a wealthy prince and get some serious likes on her account. But really, any member of the royal family will do, she openly confesses. She doesn't even want to marry one, she tells me very seriously, because she knows that's nigh impossible since they only marry their own kind. But she's leaving open the possibility for a regular "harem gig," as she calls it. She's from some place back in the Midwest she never wants to go back to. Party capitals and nonstop nightlife are her only long-term plan.

At least she has a plan.

Rashid appears, and he's keyed up and ready to move. I can tell from his body language that he's looking to get out of this place like it's something other than one of the nicest clubs I've ever been in. Like it's some gas station out on the highway where getting stabbed by a drifter is just as likely as getting food poisoning from the eternally rolling corn dogs.

"I'm Summer!" The girl with the Instaflash pounces on Rashid in a sudden blooming rush of excitement and slutty flirtation.

Rashid shoots me a look that tells me I can do better. And I could. But I felt bad for her. She spent money on a boob job that was too much, and badly done at that. As though that was all anyone would ever look for. Giant knockers barely concealed. And maybe she's right. Maybe that is all some people are looking for now. Sex first, then true love.

But it doesn't work that way. Even I know that.

I'm waxing eloquent and I feel like I'm wading through syrup when I try to stand.

I need sleep.

Real sleep. Not a couch. A bed. A place where I can lock the doors for a day. And a night. And then another day.

"Let's bail, PQ," prompts Rashid as Instaflash Summer moves in close and bends low to give Rashid a look at her more than ample goods.

Like I said, I felt bad for her.

"Not interested," says Rashid. Then he nods at someone over my shoulder, and instantly security is dragging her from his presence. From the bar. She's screaming. In a few moments I'll hear her still screaming at the entrance to the club, screaming that they had no right to touch her and force her from their club like she was offensive. The bass thunder doing its best to drown out her ragged shrieks that she's American.

But right now...

Right now she's begging. Begging for a chance to let Rashid have her. She promises him it will be the best night he's ever had.

In Calistan...

And then we're leaving, too. Rashid grabs me around the shoulder and leans in.

"C'mon... now the real fun begins."

America doesn't matter here.

We cross the club with Rashid explaining how he had to do the social thing with Samira and some other couples upstairs, and that he's done for the night with all that and he can be himself, and then he suddenly shouts, "I'm alive again!" as the DJ beat-mixes some song called, apparently, "I'll Be Back." It thunders over the speakers like a sudden war. On the walls Arnold Schwarzenegger—I know the old actor because I looked him up once—is shooting some woman in the back as she runs from him. Then he's shooting up a club with an Uzi. Then he's shooting up cops. Then more cops. And all the while the music keeps chanting "I'll be back." And keeps up a pounding rhythm that promises such.

We make the front entrance.

The Instaflash girl is screaming then. Screaming about being an American. Her makeup is ruined and her dress is torn. Everyone in the line laughs at her. The bouncers do too.

Rashid's car is waiting in front. The night club manager is murmuring alongside Rashid. Telling him something low and hushed in Arabic, which to me already seems low and hushed. And always harsh. Angry, almost frantically neurotic.

Rashid guns the engine as soon as we're in. Revs it higher and higher knowing everyone's watching us. Knowing it's drowning out the screaming girl who's now devolving into hysterical sobbing as she sees all her plans driving away from the curb. Then we peel out in smoke and the smell of burnt rubber as a thousand flashes go off in the crowd of people still waiting to get in and be part of all that cool.

And they have to be distantly aware that all that cool is driving away now. That cool has left the building in Calistan.

In the rearview mirror I can see no sign of Instaflash Summer. The seething glitter-struck mob has swallowed her. And I feel that she will never leave Calistan alive. And that if she ever does it will be because she got lucky.

In that, we are kindred souls.

A few blocks later Rashid gets a call and takes it on his smartglasses. "Yeah… we'll pull in at the Bazaar. Meet you in five."

We make a quick left and follow a lit palm tree-lined drive into an ancient mega mall. Grand lighting announces the place as something called The Bazaar. Cars and people throng toward it. It's only midnight after all. Three o'clock in the morning if you've most recently been on Cuba time.

Rashid finds a secluded parking lot well away from the mall perimeter and pulls into the darkness of its farthest reaches, shutting off his lights and the car.

I have that feeling that I'm about to get killed. That whatever I said to "Rashid's brother" is about to be played back to me, somehow revealing my disloyalty. Or that the car pulling up behind us will be "Rashid's brother." Head of the secret police.

I try to make conversation. The kind about whether I have a future, or don't.

"Hey," I start lightly and sound anything but. "You said I could get my own place while I'm here…"

He merely grunts "yeah" and continues gesture-scrolling through messages on his designer smartglasses.

"Living down at the beach would be great! Is… uh… that possible?"

"Yeah," he says absently. This does not fill me with the confidence that I am not about to get my head blown off. Yep, I think, there's two bullets in the back of the skull coming for you. If you're lucky you won't know it. But I check the side mirror anyway because I can't help but try and survive. Life's a game that way.

The person who pulled up behind us has turned off their lights. I hear two doors open. Two sets of footsteps. Two hired guns, secret police, whatever…

"I've always wanted to live near the beach," I whisper as though prompting him to let me live a little longer.

"Yeah… I mean yes," says Rashid, now more formally, as though he has just now returned to his own body. "That can definitely be arranged. Sorry, I was just going over tonight's menu."

That reminds me I haven't had anything to eat in… all day. I am in fact very hungry. Getting killed made me forget that.

"Ordered you something special."

Is it two-bullets-in-the-back-of-the-head special?

"Good…" I say. "I'm hungry."

He laughs at this.

"Yeah… We can put you up in a beach house. I've got a really cool condo in Newport you can have too. And there's my yacht. You can stay on that if you like."

I wait to feel the cold barrel of a gun against my neck. But it will probably be my head. Now I'm just waiting for it…

"There's also this sailboat I inherited. It's docked on the island Samira and I are having cleared to build our first house. No one's there right now. Pretty quiet."

That sounds nice.

I can picture that if I somehow live. It's also a nice last thought to have before a bullet tears through my skull and destroys my brain.

A sailboat docked on a lonely island. Yeah… I could do that. All I have to do is live long enough to get there.

"That sounds great. I'll take that, if it's cool?" I say as nonchalantly as a man about to die can.

"Cool," mumbles Rashid. He sounds far away again.

"Rashid," says a gravelly voice that sounds smoke-ravaged. "Here's the stuff."

I turn to see a man standing above Rashid. A kid really. Thin. Mexican, I guess. There's another guy standing over my shoulder. He has a gun out.

I lean back in my seat. Close my eyes and tried to think of that sailboat I'll never see. Of that island.

And Samira is there for just an instant.

That's fine, I think. Rashid will never know.

I hear Rashid open something.

I look over and he's going through a leather briefcase. The man standing over him has his smartphone's light focused on the case. I see drugs. Or at least, I think they're drugs.

"Thanks, Carlos," says Rashid. "Everything looks great. Good stuff?"

Carlos laughs his gravelly laugh.

"The best, El Jefe. The best. Some for you. Some for the girls. You'll go all night and they'll be so out of it they won't care. Extra special. I threw in a bag of coke too. I know it's old school, but whores love it. Happy whore, happy time. As they say."

The man with the gun over my shoulder laughs.

So, I'm not going to get it.

This is just a drug deal.

Rashid gives Carlos a baseball-sized wad of the local money and the two men leave us in the dark, start their car, and drive off.

Rashid starts taking some pills.

"Want some?" he asks. "You gotta take 'em before."

"Before what?"

"The party we're going to."

It's close to one a.m.

"I thought... food was... happening."

"Oh..." He rubs some of the coke across his gums. Then does a bump off his fist. "There's a whole buffet where we're going."

"I thought you ordered..."

"You'll see."

Then he laughs wickedly and we roar off into the night. The drugs sitting on his lap. Occasionally he pinches some coke and inhales. Or pops one of the pills. The others he begins to stuff into various pockets of his lightweight dress jacket.

A few minutes later we arrive at a house east of Newport. Inland. It looks out over an estuary made silver by the falling moon. Rashid pulls up in front. Other high-end cars are there and there's no place to park. Rashid guns the engine and honks his horn, then pulls onto a carefully manicured lawn.

"Shhhhh." He giggles uncontrollably. He's pretty high.

We exit.

The hostess comes out. She's wearing a flimsy see-through white silk robe. I saw her at the club. Now I'm really seeing her.

She embraces Rashid.

"They're ready?" he asks.

She says something in Arabic.

"And for him," says Rashid, nodding at me.

She regards me with little fanfare. "Chloe's ready, as you have asked. Are you sure that's wise, my prince?"

"Ah, buddy," giggles Rashid, ignoring her. "You're going to get Chloe. She's the best."

The hostess leads us into the house. It's large. Palatially decorated. Fine furniture and tapestries along the walls.

Three girls in nothing but high heels, each one gorgeous, wait for Rashid like models ready for their shoot. Other naked girls are dancing on tabletops or sitting on couches with other young men of the Arab princeling variety. The girls are from everywhere. Arabs, Persians, Asians, Caucasians, Latinas, a black girl. And every one of them is a knockout.

The party continues without us as we're led upstairs. We pass rooms where it's obvious what's going on behind the closed doors. Some doors are open and nothing needs to be guessed as we pass. A piece of performance art is in progress. Except the art is lewd and as old as time itself. As though the skills of some young prince need to be viewed by all to be believed.

We're headed toward a double door on the third floor and I'm suddenly concerned it's about to get weird. As in me, Rashid, and the three girls who are following us weird.

I try to tell myself *five million in gold*, but… it feels empty. Greedy. And true in the worst way.

Before we reach that last grand door though, the hostess stops and opens a different door.

She speaks to me for the first time. "This is where you get off." She barely titters at her tired joke. I bet she thinks cheap innuendos make her seem smart and witty. I suddenly want to punch her in the face.

"Good night, buddy," giggles Rashid as he gathers up his girls and pushes them forward toward his door at the end of the hall. He opens it and I see a mammoth circular bed. The girls strut toward it. Rashid turns just before closing the door and laughs once more, saying, "See you on the other side, PerfectQuestion."

The statuesque blond hostess looks at me coldly. Appraising me. Daring me to do something.

I give her a look that tells her I want to punch her in the face.

Then I step through the door she opened for me and I meet Chloe. The door closes, and it's just the two of us.

Chloe is wearing a choker around her slender throat. It looks like some piece of old jewelry. A vintage antique. Small and dangling against her throat. I will always remember that about her.

She's wearing just that, and nothing else.

Chapter Twenty-Two

A long moment passes as I stare at her perfectly voluptuous body.

Then she comes at me with a knife.

I barely get my hands around her wrists as she pins me to the wall. Through it all I can feel the thudding bass notes of the party downstairs and the disconcerting thumps, bangs, and screams from the rooms all around me as the bacchanalia and drug-fueled orgies attempt to silence any cry for help.

"Die!" she says through gritted teeth as she presses the knife toward my throat.

I push the knife hand away with my left hand and send a right cross into her perfectly heart-shaped face. She goes down on her knees while I hold on to her hand. The one with the weapon. I twist the knife out of her grip and bring her up to her feet as I twist her arm behind her back and push her against the wall, chest first.

"Pig!" she growls.

"No…" I'm about to tell her. Along with, *I'm not. And I have no intention of hurting you.* Except she suddenly pistons her foot right into my stomach. And now I'm without the benefit of oxygen.

"Then go ahead… do what you want… like all these…" she spits.

"Not… with them," I gasp.

"Liar!" she hisses, then tries to smash her head into my nose. We wrestle for control while I get my air back.

"I had no idea what was going on before I got here. I just work with Rashid," I whisper. Because a whisper is all I can manage.

She tries to kick me again. I pin her legs with my body. She twists loose and slaps me across the side of the head. Solidly.

That rings my bell.

Now she's scrambling for the knife, which I tossed to the other side of the room. Dizzy and slightly stunned, I clue in on what she's up to and leap at her. We're both on the carpet, rolling around and flat-out hitting each other as hard as we both can.

I know I am, because what she's going to do with that knife has been made abundantly clear.

She bites me in the hand.

I have to pry her jaw open to get it loose.

"Stop it!" I shout. "What in the hell is wrong with you?"

I have her pinned now beneath me on the carpet next to the bed. But she's struggling for all she's worth and it feels like I'm riding a wild horse that will never be broken. I saw a movie about that once…

"I told you I'm not with them," I try again.

Finally her strength begins to fade and she settles for spitting in my face. "Prove it," she hisses.

We're both scratched and bleeding.

I'm breathing heavily. Her too.

I can't think of how I can prove that I'm not going to hurt her.

Burning coal-black eyes stare dark hatred at me.

"Are you…" I try as I sit up. It takes me another second to catch my breath as the adrenaline begins to fade. "Did they abduct you and force you to be here?"

That seems to shock her. As though that's the most alien idea she's ever heard. Her brow furrows, and she's instantly indignant.

"No."

My only guess, up until she denied it, was that she was somehow here against her will.

Now… that isn't even the case.

"Well…" I begin, "why ever you're here… I have no intention of hurting you or… forcing you… to…"

She gives me a contemptuous smile that turns her eyes brimstone-laden, indicating she doubts I'm capable of forcing her to do anything.

"What do you think of Rashid?" she asks quietly.

I run my hands through my hair and look for the knife. It got loose in the fight. Probably a good idea to control its location.

"I think he's an ass," I say absently because it's late, I'm hungry, tired, burned out, and I've just almost been stabbed to death by a girl I find to be the very definition of beautiful.

Nothing has changed on her face when I look back at her. The look of cool appraisal remains, as does the smoldering hate in her eyes.

"I think he's a very bad guy," I confess. "To tell you the truth…" And I have no idea why I'm about to tell her the truth. Maybe it's because I'm so tired. Maybe it's because her nakedness and beauty make me want to be as honest and as vulnerable as she is. As if that's somehow a comfort. Or maybe I've finally realized the truth that's been bothering me ever since I crossed the border into this hellhole.

The people I'm working for are bad people. That's why they pay so well.

"If I had known who he was… what this place was… I'd never have taken the job," I say finally.

"You're not from here."

It's not a question. It's a statement. And she says it like it's a truth known to all.

"No," I admit.

I spot the knife. It's just beyond her grasp. I look at her and she looks at it. Then I reach for it, pick it up, and place it in her open palm covered in the blood she drew when she raked her nails down the side of my face.

I watch her to see what she'll do next.

She watches me to see what kind of man is hiding under my skin.

I stand. Find a black lace robe that won't cover much and hand it to her. Then I sit on the low bed.

"I'm not with these people," I whisper. "I'm tired. And I wouldn't hurt you. I'm not that kind of person."

She sits down next to me.

We both stare at the knife in her hand.

"Who are you?" she asks softly.

I don't know.

I watch my hands suddenly fling themselves open... as though the answer is there. As though I'm suddenly required to defend myself. Except there is no defense. Not in this situation. Not in Calistan.

So my mouth remains closed.

Then: "I play video games for a living. I won the Super Bowl last week. It was kind of a big deal."

I don't know why I say that last part. No. I do. I do know.

Because she's beautiful.

"So you're not part of his inner circle? Are you going to tell Rashid..." She hesitates. "That I tried to kill you?"

I shake my head as I stare at the carpet.

"I'm just tired," I say.

She stands up. She walks to the head of the bed and lies down on her side. She pats the bed next to her. "Come."

I lie back next to her.

She strokes my hair and watches me.

I close my eyes and we talk. She tells me she came to kill Rashid. That she intended to kill me, then she'd go after Rashid later. When he was asleep. Close to dawn. When the world was asleep and there was a chance she could disappear with the coastal fog.

I tell her about the guards outside his door.

I tell her she'd get killed. Now isn't the time for an ambush. And it would be a shame for her to die. Because she's beautiful. And strong.

She kisses me. Once. Slow. Her lips full and inviting, and then she bites mine a little.

"Thank you," she whispers. "I don't trust you. But thank you."

I have no idea why she'd be thanking me. I tell her that.

"Because the truth is dead here in Calistan. And to tell it is an act of bravery."

And for the first time... in a long time... I feel some kind of peace. Or maybe it's a wanting to belong to something I never knew existed. Her. Or maybe it's just the last real thing in a country full of illusions.

And then we sleep.

Chapter Twenty-Three

In the valley. In the dark. In the mad hermit's hollowed-out tree, I find treasure. A potion. A ring. A dagger.

The potion is clear and silvery.

The ring is made of brass. Yet it feels comforting. I slip it onto my finger. I feel... more secure. It's a magic ring. I know that. But I don't know what it does.

The dagger is an ancient curving blade. Strange runes swim across its dark surface. Its ivory handle is cold and yellowed with age. A gleaming green gem is set in the pommel. I know the dagger, too, is magic.

There's also a sack of coins. Strange gold stamped with an imperious face.

I stare at them in the moonlight and wonder how much there is and who the face had been.

Something moves in the trees above.

I raise Deathefeather and wait. Watching the darkness. And then I see it. A great cat. A dark jungle cat watching me from up there. I see its two eyes burning like sapphires.

I back away from the tree with my treasures, keeping the blade between myself and the watching cat. And in time, I have withdrawn into the forest deeps and I know it will not follow me. For now.

Later, in the dead of the night after the moon has gone down, I build a small fire using the dead wood that's everywhere on the forest floor. Some flint and steel strike a spark and give it life. I had these tools in my simple roll. I knew they were there. And how to use them. As though those are the most natural things to know.

I sit by the small fire in the midst of a small copse of twisted trees. Eating some of my rations. The cheese. The apple. Cold water.

And then I sleep.

* * *

At dawn I awake. I can smell the smoke of my dead fire mixed with the leaden fog. The forest is lit by a soft and diffused light. The trees look like the fingers of skeletons clutching at the sky.

I can't remember the dream I was having. But it was so real, it seems now as though the dawn is the dream and the dream... the dream was what was real.

I drink more cold water and keep my hand on my katana. It lies next to me in its sheath. Waiting. Always waiting. I don't like this part of the forest. It seems dead. Lifeless. And yet I know there's something there, out in the dark areas of its length. Something evil, mindless, roaming shadowy halls. Searching for anything it might devour.

A lone bird breaks the silence. Calling out in the gloom.

Once.

And then it's gone.

Spooked, I gather my things together. Stowing my treasures from the night before. Studying the coins and the mysterious dagger, and the strange potion. Before I put them all away.

Looking for long moments at them.

Having to remember these things are not the reason I am here. These are just treasures that happened along the way.

William Alucard is who I've come for.

The Priest of Chaos.

I have come for him.

I set out once more, heading out with the sun into the west. Bearing what must be north. Above the dead trees, iron-gray peaks of distant mountains rise, jagged and sharp against the wan morning sky.

For hours there is only the sound of my sandals breaking deadfall. And my breath alone in this maze of a forest.

And then there is the sound of a horse. A horse on a road at full gallop. Off to my right.

I wait and listen.

Then I run as fast as I can through the dead forest. Dead limbs catch at my robes and I hear the small tears they make. But I run. I run toward the sound of the galloping horse.

I run because the last time I saw Alucard he was on a horse. And maybe this horse is his horse. And maybe he is on the horse.

And there is something about him, about killing him, that leads me to believe there will be an answer to a question that I need an answering to. But no one has promised such a thing. And so I run because it's the only way forward.

I break from the forest and find a lonely old road.

It leads off to the west. And far down the road I see Alucard riding like the devil on his black horse. He disappears as the road curves off into the distant forest.

I wait, listening. Listening to the sound of the hooves until they have faded into nothingness and all that remains is the overwhelming silence of this dead place he has only recently passed through.

Chapter Twenty-Four

The trail of the horse isn't hard to follow through the quiet forest. I keep up a steady pace and soon the dead forest gives way to a greenery that, though still silent, returns to something familiar. In the distance I see rolling hills rising above the trees.

A few hours later I come upon a sign. The wood is rotting and old. The weathered scrawl in black proclaims the faded word *Hommet*. Another small road intersects this road, but it is clear the horse and rider have gone on to Hommet.

I continue, and after another hour I see two small hills, and between them lies a small village. Farther on, in the distance, some kind of ancient fortified structure rises above the trees, but I can make out little of it.

Nearing the village, I smell death. It's suddenly overwhelming and its scent rises with the heat of the day.

I approach the outer buildings. The bodies I see are like the people back at the keep. In that they are people. Townspeople. Except now they look like the girl Alucard rode down in the street.

They look like discarded rag dolls.

Near a stable yard I see the corpse of some sort of dogman. The body is human. The face is dog. He wears battered armor. His snout is frozen in a permanent snarl. The whites of his eyes have rolled toward the sky. Toward heaven. Beside him lies a long pole with a bloody axe head at the top.

The nearby body of a man has been hacked to pieces. Other bodies, women and children, also have been done to death in similar violent fashion. All along the dirt track leading through the center of this place.

Smashed doors have been thrown outward. Nothing moves. No one calls out. Metal is not beaten and there is no murmur of conversation. All I hear are bone chimes rattling in the barest breeze.

I step through a smashed door and into some kind of shop. Everything that has not been smashed has been taken. Whatever was once here, is gone. Whatever this place was… it is ruined forever.

I step back out and continue through what remains of the town. There is no shock, or horror. Not as I know I must feel seeing all the dead bodies in the street. More dogmen. And a few humans who wear dark robes. Flies have gathered but the corpses aren't rotting just yet. The blood still lies in congealing pools.

This must have happened recently.

No, there is no horror. Not even shock. And yet what is this? A game? Something else? And… 'Oo am I?

A growing nothingness defies me, no matter how badly I want to feel something. Because I know I should feel something. But I don't and so I proceed on to the ruined structure beyond the edge of town. It stands gray and black against the warm sun and blue sky. In the fields nearby I see dead sheep and lazy sunflowers. Along the trail I spot the pawprints of large dogs. Many of them. And mixed in among I find the occasional boot, and once or twice the hoofprint of a horse.

I reach the ancient fortified structure. But I can see the old place is ruined. Falling into disrepair. In places its old gray stone is crumbling. The timber on the rooftop has fallen in great sections. A wall surrounds its grounds, and there is a place for a gate, but the gate itself has long since fallen to pieces.

With my hand on the hilt of my katana I step through the wide portal and into an overgrown courtyard that stands before some kind of manor house, looking more haunted than anything I have ever seen.

Wide crumbling steps, overgrown with dry dead weeds, lead up to a pile of stone and rotting wood where the walls are lifeless and beaten.

To my left is an old tower that once watched over the gate. It still has a door. And…

I can hear something in there in the dead silence of this forsaken place. The sound is low. Very low. Almost like a chittering *clickety-click*. Or a constant snapping.

I move to the door of the tower and test it. It's not locked, but it doesn't want to budge.

The chittering clicking from within suddenly ceases, and the silence in its absence is ominously overwhelming. Like an unspoken warning that should be heeded if one wishes to go on living.

I step back and smash the door with a kick. Perfectly executed, as though I have performed this strike a thousand times a day for ten years in the becoming of this samurai. It is sudden, sharp, and violent. The wood is dry and rotten and gives way with a dusty *smaff*.

I pull a few slats away and peer into the shadowy darkness within the small ruined tower. At first I see nothing more than shadows cut by beams of dusty light. And then I see her.

How do I know it's a her?

Because the torso that rides atop the giant bulb of the spider's swollen body is that of a woman. Her once platinum-blond hair is now a hoary, deathly white, and even that cannot compete with the cadaverous drowning-victim paleness of her skin that should be bronzed and tan.

Her teeth are fangs.

She snaps them and comes scuttling for me, her eyes popping like the flash of some ancient camera. The instant flashes cause strobes in the darkness, illuminating the red hourglass of the black widow's mark stamped onto her swollen back. Her eight legs are long and delicate, and they scramble her down out of her ancient webs, the claw-like hands attached directly to her torso reaching for me greedily.

Snap. Flash. Snap. Flash. Snap. Flash.

I stumble back from the door and draw my katana in one wide sweeping motion. I know I'll only get one cut before she overwhelms me with sheer bulk. So momentum and speed will have to meet timing.

But she's too swollen to make it through the narrow door. She forces her body in strange contortions but manages only to squeeze her corpse-like torso through into the bright blaze of noon in this deserted place beyond the edge of the slaughtered town. She shrieks horribly at the injustice of her weight and bulk. Her face is huffing and apoplectic.

And yet she still wants to suck the marrow from my bones. Needs to. And… I can almost understand her high-pitched chittering crooning that sounds inhuman and otherworldly.

She shrieks some phrase that has meaning. Or once did. But not anymore. She shrieks and reaches for me with one of her necrotic white hands.

"I'll give you the night of your life!" As if pleading for me to believe this is possible.

I weave Deathefeather like a fan in front of me. Once. Smooth. Effortless. Its shiny flash passes through a reaching arm which now lies in the weed-choked courtyard amid dust and rubble.

She shrieks that alien and yet once-familiar phrase again. And then…

"Immanmaerican!"

And that's familiar to me in a fleeting moment until I realize it's meaningless to the samurai.

Her horror-show face is nothing but stunned rage as she shuttles back within the squat dark tower that has long been her abode. Preying on birds, insects, and misbehaving children who were told never to go poking around this old place. Shrieking at me over and over again and again as she recedes into the darkness…

"Immanmaerican!"

"Immanmaerican!"

"Immanmaerican!"

Pleading.

Hissing.

Begging.

From the shadows.

She withdraws into the darkness of the crumbling guard tower.

"Immanmaerican!"

Chapter Twenty-Five

I am alone in the ancient courtyard now. Walls are battered in sections. Stone crumbles inward. I see the swampy forest and stream beyond these gaps. It seems as though long ago this place was sieged by some attacking force, or ravaged by the villagers one angry mob night. Or perhaps it collapsed from some other weight it could no longer bear. Time. Sorrow. Evil. All such things are hammers. And only the anvil of eternity defies their blows.

I turn and face the wide stairs leading up to the shadows of the main building. The old doors have gone missing. As have the people who once made this place the center of their lives. There were probably festivals here, dinners, dances, weddings… life things. And now there is nothing. Just dust and ruin.

If the dogmen and Alucard came this way—along with those others in the dark robes whose bodies were left bloating in the sun back along the village paths—they are in there somewhere.

I wait in the silence, listening for some clue that does not reveal itself just yet.

Deathefeather is out of its sheath, held out and away. I know that if anything comes for me I will draw it across my body in a quick defensive slash. Then I will regain my footing, raise it once more in the blink of an eye, and strike for a kill. All this is as natural and as known to the samurai as any other action my body might ever perform.

I pass from the burning heat of afternoon into the cool rotten darkness of the main house. A wide hall spreads away into two wings of shadowy darkness. Shafts of sunlight shoot through what remains of the ancient roof, giving the gloom a chessboard look. Ahead, across a cracked and broken floor, stairs lead up.

I hear nothing. And then... a slight scrabbling.

Rats.

I see one. Moving along the far wall. Heedless of my presence. It's abnormally large for a rat. But it doesn't seem to mind me.

A thud sounds from up the old stairs. As though someone dropped something. I move forward, trying to mute the creak of my sandals as I cross the debris-laden floor. From the foot of the stairs I can hear low, muffled conversation coming from up there. Whispers.

I pad softly up the stairs, silent, Deathefeather leading the way.

At the landing, I see someone up there in the gloom of the second story. A large axe is raised over his head. There are others gathered behind him.

And he's peering down into the darkness. Looking straight at me.

They come at me in a rush, the big man, a giant almost, raising the massive cleaver over his head, his eyes alight with the delight of expected murder.

I simply step forward and push the razor-sharp katana through his heart. He gives a small "oof" as though he only has indigestion, and he dies right there on the spot.

The others push forward with smaller weapons as I withdraw the katana and ready myself.

I decide not to give ground. I move the katana with such speed that it looks like a series of whirling blades. Arms and hands come off. And still they charge, mindless of the injury I'm dealing out in these tight quarters and dark shadows.

I strike one beardy fellow's head from his shoulder. Blood goes everywhere. I step back, giving just the one step for the last two coming for me. There are five dying men along the stairs we've fought our short battle in. The last two try to rush together even though the space is too tight and I step back once again and put everything I have into a cut across their collective abdomen.

Entrails spill out at their feet.

I wait. Wait for their hot, close gasps to surrender to death as they fall back breathing raggedly and dying. I smell their unwashed stink competing with some greasy food smell. And vinegar. Or bad wine. Maybe they had been drinking while waiting for someone to stumble into their trap.

Moments later they're all dead and I'm stepping between and over them to reach the top of the stairs.

I find a lone room, what must have been the master's dwelling of this small and fortified freehold. A gray fireplace heaped with ashes gapes at me like some crouching gargoyle in the dark. In the room's debris lie the personal belongings and bedrolls of my attackers. Black handprints have been pressed into every surface, and I know I would never have liked what went on here.

So I leave.

I'm sure there was something I could have taken away. But there was nothing I would've wanted.

As I pass by the dead in the shadowy dark, they leer at me with twisted evil faces. As though whatever they've found on the other side is just as debaucherously delightful as what they had here in this house of horrors.

At the bottom of the stairs I clean my blade on a cloth I keep for such. The mere act, standing there in the shadowy gloom, is a brief moment of not thinking. Not trying to understand. Not even being constantly amazed at what I'm experiencing, or passing through. A strangely complex world where the fantastic and the horrible are made real. And somehow it's an adventure. The mundane act of wiping the blade is incredibly peaceful to me, and once the blade is free of their blood I feel as though I've packaged the whole of their slaughter so it will not trouble me the way their leering death masks did. The cleaning of the blade is just as much a ceremony as was the using of it to deal out death and slaughter.

I slide Deathefeather back into its sheath and investigate the closest wing of the crumbling manor.

I find a giant black-and-red sleeping snake, coiled in massive loops. Its belly is a massive bulge. Something it ate being slowly digested. The snake lies sleeping in the darkness, away from the hot afternoon beyond the crumbling stone walls.

I watch as the bulge, protruding from a coil, moves. As though something in there is reaching out, trying to find the limits of its cage. It reaches. Strains. Pushes against the unbreakable coil… and then surrenders. The bulge stills. Forever. That last act was its final death spasm.

I return to the main hall.

The dogmen and Alucard have to have gone somewhere within this building, so I search for clues. I scan the floor now that my eyes are accustomed to the checkered light. I can see where the debris has been walked over, the rotting wood crushed to dust and splinters time and time again with the passage along a particular trail. I follow the path. But just a few feet in, it's almost too dark to continue.

I find a piece of wood, pull some rotten tapestry off the wall, and make a quick torch. When the flame is in full bloom I wave it back and forth across the dark floor. Beyond its circle of guttering light I see the dark recess of the building. It leads off into other rooms and deep darknesses.

But I find also what I'm looking for. Stairs leading down.

Far below I can see the flickering light of other torches.

I descend cautiously, yet the ogre that comes at me out of the flickering shadows when I reach the bottom of the stairs makes me recoil in sudden horror. He has the drop on me. He's not stupid and cruel, but cunning and savage, and it shows as he rushes me with a wicked spear that's as thick as a fence post. For a brief moment I'm rewarded with a nightmare of being pinned to the oozing walls deep beneath this swampy place.

Then what will become of me? Who will I be then? Will I wake up to play again...? Is this a game? Or will I be someone else? Some ordinary someone else with only dreams of such a life as this?

Yeah... I reflect on all that in the moment the slavering, bloody-lipped ogre comes charging at me. Working his fangs to roar in rage at me for daring to bother him. I see all that and think those thoughts.

Because for a moment time has slowed.

As though I wanted it to. As though I needed it to. As though autumn rains have begun and blossoms, pink and delicate, fall to a pond's surface. Each of those raindrops is a nuclear strike seen from above. And all of it drips by in slow motion.

The words *Serene Focus* swim before my eyes.

I sidestep the charging bull ogre and his spear, and I draw my blade for a swift reply. I pivot and confront the ogre who has just rammed into the wall. Full speed. He's dazed, and seems bewildered that I could move so fast. In that moment I leap forward and cut off his head with one slice. There is strength behind the cut, all of it that I can put behind it, because the creature's bull neck is thick with fat and muscles. But the blade cares little for resistance and it feels as though I am merely pushing it through heavy cream. Possibly even freshly whipped butter. But nothing more than that.

The monster's head rolls to the floor of the crypt with that same I-can't-believe-it look on its ugly face.

Believe it, I want to say. Because this is the truth.

From far away, I hear the barking of dogmen. It echoes from a crumbling stairway that leads even further into the depths. They are coming. They are coming because the ogre's rage was heard.

Time is returning to normal.

There are many, many of them.

They come surging up the stairs, their harsh barks and patchwork armor rattling the passage. I rush to the stairs and trade blows with the first I meet. Two blows that a snarling dogman parries, the first with ease, the second with effort. The third disembowels him.

The next dog-faced warrior, flecks of rage spraying from its muzzle, foaming canines biting, comes in chopping with a curved sword. I take his head off with one blow and he falls against the side of the passage.

Down the stairs I carve my way through a river of dogmen that will never end. Torchlight makes their unreal faces even more ferocious. Their gleaming yellow canines snarl and bark as they press forward to meet death.

Of that I am sure.

For I am death.

I'm convinced, and I know that sounds poetic. But I see fields of wheat being scythed at harvest. And I am the scythe. And the dogmen are my harvest.

I advance forward, cutting and slashing like a whirlwind of blades. And when I do not cut, I chop. Hacking through the scaled armor and bone necklaces they wear about their furry chests. And when I don't chop I stab. Planting one foot forward as I pull the blade back and then suddenly ram it through the beating heart of a yapping dogman. Then I pull the blade out and away, doing more damage. Dragging bloody spray across the walls.

I've stepped over about twenty corpses when I reach the bottom of the stairs and cut the last two defenders down with a single strike. Both clutch at hairless bellies jutting from their dented and bashed tribal armor. Both watch as their entrails spill out onto the flagstones of this subterranean warren. They flop to the ground and gurgle their last.

The cultists come next. Humans. Dark and swarthy. Those black robes I saw on some of the dead in the slaughtered village. They rush down a side passage and I'm only dimly aware that some temple bell has been ringing out, sounding an alarm.

Summoning all hands to stop the interloper.

I am the interloper.

And I refuse to be stopped because I remember the girl who was run down in the street by the mad priest with the whiplash smile.

Alucard.

Oppressor of the innocent.

So I lay into them, and here the blows are exchanged in rapid fire. A great drum soundtrack thunders inside my head. I hear its rhythms and individual beats rolling out faster and faster as I wade into the press of dark-robed fanatics who are screaming "Allahu Akbar!" A great burning eye hammered in bronze adorns their flared helmets. I hack and slash and crawl forward one fresh corpse at a time.

In the end I meet the last of them. The leader. "Lareth," he tells me. "I am Lareth!" he shouts and slaps a sturdy mace against a shield emblazoned with that judgmental eye. "You shall not pass, interloper. You shall not change the world from what it is!"

Head down, I watch the flickering dark to the sides. Waiting for him to play some deadly card I'm not ready for. Waiting for a sneak attack from the last of Lareth's faithful.

"The Priest of Chaos demands you be stopped. And so you shall be."

"Where is he?" I mutter. My breathing is ragged. I try to control it. I know this is important. Control is important. But I feel like I'm burning up.

"Gone to the temple. And once I've taken your soul, you'll serve me."

He advances cautiously.

"You'll serve me for all eternity, unclean foreign dog."

If there were another, waiting, they would've attacked by now. But still… I wait as the fearsome cult leader approaches. Once I commit to my attack, I'll be vulnerable to the unknown.

I shuffle forward as though I'm ready to slice through his more-than-formidable armor. I even jerk the tip of the katana upward as though

I'm going to bring it down in some terrific chop. Testing him to see if he'll commit to his own defense, or attack.

From out of the shadows, a small man comes running at me. Dark circles ring bloodshot eyes beneath a hooded cloak. He has no chin and his very presence reminds me of a snake. He leads with a dagger, and on its tip I can plainly see the sheen of some deadly poison.

I pivot and draw a slice from shoulder to abdomen on the fast-moving worm. The little assassin cries out in torment and falls to the floor, but the cult leader is already rushing me, screaming that I have killed his brother. He brings his savage mace down hard on my shoulder and I feel or hear some terrible crack. I go down on one knee, crumpling beneath the weight of the blow.

I close my eyes and block out the pain. The man above me sucks in a lungful of air and raises the mace over his head once more, rearing back for one last terrible blow to my skull. He means to cave it in.

I thrust Deathefeather upward like a flagpole.

Blood rains down on me.

The mace hits the floor of the now-silent hall. Lareth's pierced skull slides down Deathefeather's razor edge.

It's later, when I've searched the hall of the cultists, that I find the map. Spread out on a table. It's made of cloth and etched in charcoal. A crude version of the one on the castellan's desk.

To the north lies a temple.

The Temple of Elemental Evil.

Chapter Twenty-Six

When I wake up alone in the morning I'm in a whorehouse.

It's very quiet.

The smell of liquor competes with the overwhelming scent of heavy perfume.

She's gone.

Chloe.

The girl who tried to kill me. And then didn't.

I never undressed. So I merely stand and try to straighten myself. I feel like I was sleeping hard. Dreaming hard.

She kissed me.

Maybe drugged me.

I feel unsteady on my feet.

I go to the door, and it's unlocked.

The guards in front of Rashid's door are gone. I make my way down the stairs I followed Rashid and the blonde up last night. There was a party downstairs then. Now there's nothing but empty glasses. The dusty remnants of cocaine. The stinky smell of old marijuana. The cloying scent of bad perfume. And the blaze of morning coming in through curtained windows.

"Leaving already?"

I turn. The blond hostess is standing there in the same attire she wore the night before. Her face looks old and tired now. Last night, I wanted to smash it in.

Now… I don't know.

"Chloe was good?"

Yeah. I still do.

Why?

Because somehow Chloe, or whoever she is, isn't her. And this whorehouse madame has…

…no right to be talking about her.

The girl I just met. I get that that sounds ridiculous. I get that.

"You're getting too old for this," I tell her. Because it's the only thing I can think of to hurt her.

She smiles and seems to agree. Then she lights a cigarette and waits.

But I'm already gone. Already out the front door.

Rashid's car is sitting on the front lawn. And other cars. But otherwise it's a perfectly normal neighborhood of older houses. The kind of place someone would've called "Anytown, USA" a long time ago.

I smell the ocean. Then the rank smell of a swamp or bay. Off to the southwest I can see the rising apartment towers and hotels that watched over the mall we were at last night.

I feel like so much has happened since then. But really… nothing has.

I see Chloe again in my head.

And I want to see her again.

I start walking toward what I think is the direction of the ocean.

I walk for the rest of the morning. Weaving through neighborhoods and across carefully manicured parks. Sprinklers and golden sunshine compete with Muslim families out walking their children. Everybody watches me warily but they're friendly for the most part.

These people aren't like the people I saw outside the zone. These are all good-looking. Nice clothes. White teeth. Glowing smiles. The women wear colorful head scarves but not full hijabs or even the black oppressive burkas I saw beyond the zone.

Still, they smile at me like normal people who could never believe life beyond the Gold Coast exists. Or maybe they know and just don't *want* to believe it.

In time I cross the coastal highway and follow a road that winds down toward the water. I cross over a picturesque bridge onto an island called Balboa. A small little main street, straight out of the last century, stretches out in front of me. Halfway down its length I find a chocolate-dipped frozen banana stand. Its signs are old and faded.

I think one of the frozen treats would be just the thing for my hangover.

It isn't. It's terrible. The Mexican guy who pulls a pre-made one out of the freezer seems to have zero interest in me or his product.

I can see there are all the fixings at hand to make one. Warm chocolate. Fresh chopped nuts. I can smell that they've been roasted recently.

But it looks like I'm not getting one of those. I'm getting something pre-made for…

I don't even have any Calistani money.

I pull out the card Rashid gave me and hold it up. The guy's eyes go wild. Moments later he's holding a freshly made frozen banana out to me.

I don't take it. On principle. Or pride. Maybe I'm taking a stand against the chocolate-dipped frozen banana caste system. I don't know.

Maybe I'm just cranky.

I sit down on a bench a few feet away and eat the first one he gave me.

It's terrible and mushy. The chocolate is stale. The nuts hard and dry.

I hate this place.

I hate the whole gig.

I throw my banana in the trash and call Irv.

"I'm out."

"Why?" he erupts, then starts coughing and wheezing for a full minute, pounding his chest.

"This place is a freak show," I tell him.

He sighs. I hear the whiny creak of an office chair. I sense he's leaning back and gathering his thoughts. Or preparing a speech that will convince me not to pass up his percentage of my five million in gold.

"Yeah... kid. Ain't it all."

He's right. I've been so far gone I have no idea what normal is. I've been out there so long I've forgotten what it's like to just... be.

For a moment, after Chloe tried to kill me, it felt like that. Lying next to her in a small room. Something almost felt normal. Maybe.

Her name probably isn't even Chloe.

"Listen, kid. Rashid say anything about something big going down?"

That's an odd question.

"No."

Long pause.

"Anything about LA?"

"No."

"And you want out?" he asks soberly.

"I do."

"What about the five million?" he asks like some devil making the hard sell for a little adultery.

Long pause.

"In gold?" he sweetens.

Three Muslim guys walk past me barking at each other in their harsh language. They couldn't care less that I'm on the phone. What is it with these guys? It's like being a jerk to anyone not them is a kind of virtue they aspire to.

"Yeah... I want out," I say.

"Okay, kid. Log onto a website called Department 19. Use your best friend's tag… And the password is…" He pauses. It sounds like he's ruffling through some papers.

Who uses paper? I think.

"Password is dormouse but with one 'o'."

I spell it back to him.

"Yeah, that's it. We'll talk over secure video once you're in. Do it now and make sure no one overhears you when we start."

Then the line goes dead and I feel like I've just crossed another border into an even more dangerous country.

The sunny morning and my half-thought-through plan to get out of Calistan don't seem so bright now. As I walk along the streets of the small island village, I work myself up into getting back across the border into LA and getting on a plane by end of day.

Maybe back to New York. Maybe even Italy.

Where is home? It's a question I keep ignoring but meaning to answer.

It's sad when you don't know anymore.

Once I've wandered off toward the ocean, crossing past once-beautiful-but-now-rundown homes, I log onto the website. I get a secure connection, encoded. I can tell the connection is being scrambled using quantum technology. Thus making our conversation impossible to eavesdrop on.

Q-tech is a little extreme for a conversation with one's agent. That's not lost on me. And again, I have that border-crossing feeling.

A blinking icon asks me to join the call. It flashes on and off and I just stare at it. Border crossing. Then I touch it and the call connects.

Irv sounds like he's right in my ear. The call is crystal clear. Almost like there's no background sound at all.

I start off with, "So… I'm guessing there's more going on here than meets the eye."

"You got that right, kid."

I look around.

Yeah, there's someone… someone watching me. But just… ordinary watching, I think. Not stalker watching. That's just how Muslims are here in what was once California. They view you as an outsider. My dad once told me that our family came to California a long time ago. During something called the Depression. But now I must never make the mistake of thinking this place was ever something other than theirs. The Muslims, that is. That's how they seem to me. Always watching. Always at hand. They're hostile and suspicious as a rule. And they're everywhere, because this is Calistan. It's theirs. So of course it feels like everyone's staring at me.

I smile as they pass in their large family herds. I roll my shoulders and stroll down the walkway along the water.

"Listen, kid," says Irv. "Rashid hasn't said anything about LA to you. Not during any of the planning sessions, or whatever it is you guys are doing?"

"He hasn't," I confirm.

"Okay… Let's say I haven't been completely honest with you."

Really. Really! I think incredulously. I'm trapped inside a third world country because of a gig you got me and now you're telling me you haven't been completely honest with me.

Really!

I'm about to swear openly when a beautiful Muslim family pushing a stroller walks past me and smiles. I smile back and try to make it seem as genuine as possible.

I can't swear, or let anyone know anything is wrong, because I'm strolling down a picturesque street in a seaside town passing Muslim families and the occasional mustached Arab who definitely looks like he works for some sort of intelligence service.

I envision concrete cells, swinging light bulbs, and torture. I'd talk. For sure. Problem is I'd have nothing to talk about. And of course… they wouldn't believe me. So they'd just continue to torture me until…

So I just smile and act as though I'm listening to my mom tell me about what's going on back home.

I'd give anything to have that conversation. And it has nothing to do with me being way over my head in something I have a very bad feeling about.

"I probably shouldn't tell you what I'm about to tell you, kid… Truth is, I was hoping for a little accidental intel. But they took a bug off you that I planted before I dropped you off. So I didn't overhear anything. Also they swapped out your phone. I had that hacked too. I mean… we… we had that hacked."

Long pause. I pass an old Chinese restaurant. I smell garlic and ginger frying. I hear the loud clang of pots and the discordant singsong of Chinese speaking one to another in full voice. At the corner I turn and head toward the waterfront keys a small block away. This puts a little distance between me and any tail.

Is tail the right word?

Seems it would be. I've only had to run for my life one other time. So it's not like I'm an amateur, but I'm not dumb enough to believe I'm a pro.

"This isn't my phone," I say. Like that's the only detail that's gotten through to me. That I have a new phone.

"No."

"You hacked my old phone."

"Yes."

"So the Calistanis probably hacked this one."

"I'm sure they tried, but we took care of that. The minute you logged onto Department 19, the site pushed a scrambler onto your device. No bugs, no eavesdropping. You're secure, kid. We're secure."

We.

I don't want to ask. But I do.

"Who do you work for, Irv?" I say bluntly.

"CIA, kid," he answers just as bluntly.

That's just great.

Chapter Twenty-Seven

"We're trying to help Rashid," says Irv. "And we thought you would be perfect."

"Trying to help him?" I say very slowly.

"Yeah. Because if you've noticed, kid… he's okay at online… I mean he could never turn pro like yourself, but that's not what this game is all about. This game is about leading an online nation in a make-believe digital world in order to create a… you know… civilization."

"And why, exactly, is that important to the CIA?" Which is a question I never thought I'd be asking.

"Because, kid, we want Rashid to win."

"And why would Rashid winning be important to the CIA? And stop being cute about everything, Irv, or I'll get myself out of Calistan right now."

I've crossed over a bridge onto a tiny island. Small palaces stand side by side, looming over tight streets filled with the highest end of the luxury car market. The air smells of salt.

"The sultan is dying. The current ruler of Calistan, to be specific."

I have no idea who the sultan is.

"Rashid's father. He's dying, and we want Rashid to take his place. There's more to this round of *Civ Craft* than just playing an online game. Rashid and his brother are competing for their father's approval. Winner gets to be sultan. And yes, don't think the ludicrousness of that is lost on us here at the agency. Not in the least. But it's the only way the old man has to figure out which kid is the best choice. It's the only way for him to prove to the mullahs, the real power, and the generals, that his pick should be the next leader of the country. Our best intel tells us the old man is watching the game and trying to decide who gets to be the next sultan. It's crazypants, huh?"

"Yeah... seems a little wacky."

"Well, hang on to your scotch, it gets a lot worse. Calistan's as close to a civil war as it gets, if you haven't picked that up on the ground yet. We think Rashid can win if it comes to that. He's got the military on his side and basically, he's our boy. Yeah... he's a monster, but he's our monster, as the saying goes. And we're cool with that. LA, on the other hand, is trying to go with the brother. He's a lib social justice warrior type. Which would be fine if that were actually all he was. But he's free college free everything. All that crud from before the Meltdown when every city was a toilet and the country was as corrupt as it gets. True, some free education would probably do that place some good. They're sitting on a ton of cash and oil. Problem is, he's got the imams on his side. You ever hear of the Taliban?"

I haven't.

"Well back in the day, they used to go around ruining Arab and Persian countries with a strict sort of fundamentalism that was really just a grab for power based on zealotry. Bad dudes. Anyway... these imams will go that way with the whole country. And then they'll destabilize LA, which is still technically a part of the US. So we need to make sure Rashid wins."

I look out at the peaceful, almost mirror-like waters of the canals. Something like this should be all the world ever wanted to be. Except there are those who want to watch it burn.

I do not want to play this game.

"I talked with your buddy at Interpol. He says you're a do-the-right-thing kind of guy. And this, kid... this is the right thing to do. Rashid means that Calistan plays nicely with its neighbors. Omar means LA gets destabilized, and LA has always been a problem."

"So you want me to help Rashid win?"

"Yeah."

"And you know…" I begin.

"Yeah… we know what kind of guy he is. But it's like I said…"

"He's your monster."

"That's right, kid. We can control him. We can basically keep the country right where it is. Which is what needs to happen. This Mars thing is blowing up and it's way bigger than the news networks are saying. We don't need a war here too."

War with Mars? But my mind doesn't want to believe that. So I just move right back to self-righteous indignation.

"Irv… you drove through the border with me. You saw the poverty here. The guns. The military. This is a totalitarian state. And you want to leave it the way it is just so we can come out on top? You saw that, Irv!"

"I did," he confesses without remorse.

"Well it only gets worse from there on south, until you get to their zone. They call it the Gold Coast. Then life's a real party."

"We know," he says flatly.

"You're with the CIA!" I explode, regardless of whether anyone is around. Thankfully I'm alone, or so it seems.

Irv sighs deeply.

"Yeah, kid, forget the *we*. *I* know. I get it. I've been down there. I've seen what you're seeing and it makes me sick too. We have teams inside the country to make sure we get our way. But we don't want to do it that way. We're trying to play fair and square. Relatively.

"If Rashid wins, we probably won't see a civil war. Which Rashid will win because of the military being on his side and his sociopathic ruthlessness. We don't want him to have to fight a civil war because a lot of people will get killed if that happens. If the other fool wins, Omar, then we're *going* to see a civil war and the resurgence of the Taliban or whatever they want to call themselves this time. Then we get women getting their heads chopped off. Kids being used as prostitutes. Stratoliners being blown out of the sky, or used to ram into the arches over LA and New York. They're a fun bunch that way. But first, like I said, they'll fight a civil war. And we don't want that. That's a nightmare compared to Rashid.

"So yeah, kid… the CIA is trying to do the right thing here. And we need your help."

I tell Irv I'll think about it, and I log off.

I walk back across the bridge to the Chinese restaurant I passed earlier. An olive-skinned guy with coal-dark eyes reading-not-reading a paper gives me only a casual glance. And something smells great. Garlic and chilies.

I walk in and sit down at a booth. The wide window that looks out on the picturesque Americana-yesteryear street is clear and polished. It makes everything look vibrant and clear.

I am the only one in the restaurant.

I scan the menu the Chinese lady left me. They have General Tso's chicken, which is a near-legendary dish that's hard to find. Foodies claim that most bastardized Chinese food is the fault of this not-so-ancient dish that was designed to please only the American palate.

I've always wanted to try it.

For a few minutes I listen to nothing but some Chinese instrumental music and the symphony of clanging woks in the back. Then the dish comes out. It's sizzling. Like really sizzling. And there's something about that sizzle that screams savory in my mind. It's served on a cast-iron plate and it continues to sizzle long after it arrives. Aromatic spices, hot and sour, mix with a rich sugariness that tastes almost of burnt caramel. The chicken chunks swim in this fiery napalm and when I cut one open, the succulent juices ignite more sizzling. I eat a piece.

It's juicy, sweet, hot, spicy, and just on the edge of burnt. The skin snaps despite the sauce that has been drizzled over it.

I forget about Irv and the CIA. Rashid and the generals. Omar and the mullahs. Games. ColaCorp. The life I know I need to get.

There's enough perfect in this perfect dish to make me consider never leaving Calistan. And I think that wouldn't be bad because Chloe, whoever she really is, is out there somewhere right now. I imagine her in the place where she lives. Maybe out for lunch with the person she considers her boyfriend. Or lover. Or some guy she's just dating.

I want to be that guy.

And I want to eat this General Tso's chicken because I'm sure there's nothing like it in all the world. That I could make it a mission to try every version of this dish and nothing would ever quite match this noon lunch in a Chinese restaurant in a foreign land not my own.

Maybe it's almost being stabbed to death that makes this dish better. Or all the fatigue and the winning at the Super Bowl. Maybe.

I eat another piece and close my eyes, just chewing. Tasting. And swallowing.

Sometimes life must be that simple for just a minute. And I'm fine with that.

Out front Rashid pulls up in his latest toy. He doesn't even look wrecked. I see him finish up a phone call. He looks around as though only just now realizing where he is. He sees me and waves. Then he gets out of the car and comes in.

He slides in across from me.

I can see his security goons taking up discreet positions all over the street. The van they follow him around in is parked across the way. No doubt there's a full tactical response package inside. Heavy weapons. Grenades. Anti-air missiles. All the bells. All the whistles.

"Hey, buddy!"

I smile and put down the green tea I've been sipping since the chicken was done. I've already ordered more.

"What're you doing here, PQ?"

"I needed to eat. I was hung over and–"

"I know. That chick is furious. She must've wore you out."

I smile.

He laughs and slaps the table.

Green tea is being set down in front of Rashid.

The hostess bows and scrapes because the next sultan of Calistan is in her restaurant. She assures Rashid she is at his service.

"I ordered the special," I say. "General Tso's chicken."

Rashid waves his head back and forth like he couldn't care less. He's still wearing his sunglasses. It's hard to get a read on him. And maybe that's the way he wants it. For a brief moment I wonder if he's not smarter than guys like Irv and the CIA think he is. And then I realize I shouldn't even be thinking about this.

Why?

Can he read minds?

I haven't even agreed to help the CIA out.

We sip our tea.

"I'm smoked. Day off today," mumbles Rashid from behind his glasses. A bare smile. A smile only for himself. The smile of a snake about to swallow a rat.

That kind of smile.

"I've been thinking about the game," I tell him.

He puts down the tea and nods for me to go on.

"The way I see it, you need to build up Calistan's civilization on Mars to..." I almost say *win*. Like I know this is all about what Irv told me. Winner gets his own country.

But I don't. Because what if I am working for the CIA?

"To get advertising stream rev and rank up on the leaderboards. That's the goal, right?"

Rashid nods. He's pulling at his fingers. Absently. Stretching them. I've seen gamers do that. Maybe he's trying to tell me he's a gamer. A pro. Like me. But just because you know how to act like one, doesn't mean you are one.

"But you guys can't build anything because other clans keep harassing you."

"That's right!" exclaims Rashid with sudden disgust.

"Okay... so what if..."

I'm just thinking out loud here. Trying to do what I do. Trying to win the game, never mind that lives are on the line.

And like that's actually possible. Seriously, Irv?

But what the hell. I'll play along. I can leave any time I want to. Maybe.

"I think if I can spend some time studying the strategic map today I can find a way to get them off your back. Then we can work on a building program and get Calistan on the board. Start crafting and build up your resources. That's really the way to win this game, Rashid."

I can tell he's thinking about what I just said. He doesn't say anything for a few minutes. Instead he just sips at his tea and stares out the window at that same street I've been watching.

A loud sizzling comes from the kitchen. In that moment before my second order of General Tso's chicken arrives, along with Rashid's first, I really feel that I can see the king, or the sultan, in Rashid. A man with decisions to make. Choices that weigh heavily on him. Heavy is the brow that wears the crown, someone once said.

The second round of chicken comes out like a Fourth of July bonfire. As though it has been made even better by the fact that Rashid is here.

It's perfectly caramelized. Savory and sweet all at once. I can smell that. It sizzles and pops on an ornate dragon-cast blazing hot iron serving platter. Burnt brick-red chilies lie in the dark sauce at the bottom.

The hostess lays out fragrant jasmine rice dotted with roasted corn and small peas. She scoops some onto our plates. She selects succulent pieces of chicken from off the sizzling platter and sets these on our plates as well. Finally she takes a silver spoon and spoons up some of the dark sauce that smells of both burnt brown sugar and the hottest of spices, so hot my eyes begin to water, and ladles this generously over the chicken and rice. It washes down over the chicken like a coat of paint. Gorgeous crimson paint that promises a heat that might possibly be too much for the weak. But for a king... fire. When all is done she backs away from our presence as though she is not worthy to watch us demolish the dish.

The chicken is lightly coated on the outside and fried. Inside it's moist and juicy. Each bite is the perfect balance of both burnt sugar sweet and a flaming hot regret that you'd even taken a bite. In other words... it's perfect. It puts my first perfect dish to shame. And I know I'd never again, even if I came back to this restaurant, get such a meal. Because I am not a sultan. Or a man who would one day be a sultan.

There are whole worlds some of us will never even dare to imagine. This chicken is just a hint.

I take a bite, chew, and lean back in the booth. Yeah... I might even moan a little.

Rashid eats absently. Still staring out the window. Weighing what I said, I imagined, against what the generals have been telling him.

Either way... I don't care.

I eat another bite.

Again... heaven.

Rashid looks up from a bite he's been desultorily staring at. The dish doesn't seem to impress him as much as it has me.

"Okay... let's see what you can do. Oh..." He puts down his fork and wipes his mouth. I can tell he's not a big eater. I am. And thankfully my parents had my genes designed so my metabolism can handle two of the same dish in one sitting. Maybe he doesn't have that. Maybe Calistan isn't as advanced as the rest of the world. Even if you're rich... maybe you can't have everything. Even great parents.

I think about Rashid's old man making him and his brother fight for his love.

Isn't that what he's really doing to them?

I don't know. Little people like me don't have sultan problems. We're just trying to get down the road and not get lost along the way.

At least most of the time we are.

"I have a surprise for you," says Rashid.

* * *

We finish our meal and drive off to see my surprise. I'd be lying to you if I told you I'm not imagining getting whacked in some abandoned place because it's somehow become clear by now that I'm working for the CIA. And who would really care if that happened? Well, ColaCorp, I guess. But Calistan has enough money to make even ColaCorp forget about me.

I think about Kiwi and JollyBoy and even RangerSix. Even Riot-Guurl. Wherever in deep space she is. I think about them all as we drive along the waterfront and across a bridge and onto a series of streets where oceanfront houses are being demolished. It's the kind of place that says here's where you get two in the heart and one in the head and then you end up part of the foundation of someone's future dream home.

"This is where Samira and I are building our dream home," says Rashid over the growl of his prowling sports car. He looks at me and smiles bashfully.

A brief thought occurs that I should probably tell him everything. Hell, I don't even know Irv. I thought this was a legit gig. I could tell Rashid and he'd probably give me a home right next to his.

We park at the end of the tiny private island. We get out of the sports car and I turn and look upon a sea of wreckage. Beach cottages and small houses have been bulldozed and left. It's like a hurricane came and knocked them all down in neat piles.

It's post-apocalyptic.

"We evicted all these losers," says Rashid in the unreal silence. "We start construction in a few weeks on the cottage. It's gonna be the biggest house in all of Calistan. Maybe even the world." He gazes at the wreckage and sees a palace just for himself.

I see quiet ruin. I wonder what became of all the people who called those places home.

He turns back to the channel. Small beautiful sailboats play along the inner waters of old Newport Harbor. In the distance, to the south, I can see the open sea beyond an outer peninsula. Beautiful girls paddle on longboards. Musclebound men follow and splash them. But all of them keep clear of the island. It's Rashid's… so of course they do.

Three giant-sized mega yachts are moored at the very tip of the island on a small dock. They're gorgeous and sleek. White with dark windows. Three levels. One has a helicopter on the back deck. They scream luxury. The best that money can buy.

Off to our left is an old sailboat with two masts. It sits low in the water. It seems old and faded.

"You can stay in any one you want, my friend," says Rashid, indicating the three mega yachts.

I think about those. Think about the devices Irv placed on me. Think about how he told me someone here, some kind of Calistani secret police I guess, replaced my phone with an identical duplicate. And I couldn't even tell. Those high-tech ships are probably wired to the max. They'd know what I'm doing.

And what am I doing?

I haven't answered that question yet.

"How about that one?" I say, pointing at the old sailboat.

"That?" exclaims Rashid incredulously.

I nod. Then… "Yeah… it's cool."

Rashid shakes his head indicating that it isn't.

"Okay." He sighs benevolently. "Whatever you want, my friend. It's yours. It was my grandfather's. We haven't used it in years. Old Mario, the island's caretaker, keeps it for us. I haven't been on it in…"

He stops as if remembering something.

"So, yeah," he says after a wistful pause. "I have your bag in the trunk."

He opens the trunk and gets my bag. He hands it to me.

"Are you sure?" he asks. "It's pretty junky. Those other ones are really nice. State-of-the-art. Got everything. I keep a case of Veuve Clicquot chilling in each one." He seems genuinely concerned. "The hoochies love to go out on those. We have some really wild times. One time we threw this girl off because she was a bitch. Sharks got her. It was crazy. They were like insane. And she just kept screaming and screaming until they dragged her under."

With a smile he says this. Like it's…

…perfectly normal.

And suddenly a normal afternoon goes from I-can-deal-with-this to…

Uh…

He begins to imitate her in a low screaming whisper.

"*Help me! Help me!*" he cries, cupping his hands together.

Then he laughs. Like… like it was all a good time he and his friends once had.

Because it was.

I don't know what happens next. Because I go into some kind of weird autopilot. I just listen and smile as he relates the end of the story, which involves the rest of the hoochie mamas, girls, women, somebody's daughter, being a lot more willing to please Rashid and his bros after they watched the screaming girl get torn to pieces alongside one of the luxury yachts over there in the water.

I smile. Like everything is fine.

Then he says he'll pick me up in the morning and that I'd better have a plan to fix things for Calistan. He drives away.

He never noticed my leg shaking. I couldn't control it. It was just shaking… from fear or rage… I don't know which.

It was just shaking.

Chapter Twenty-Eight

I had no idea what kind of boat it was other than a sailboat. But from the moment I stepped on board I was instantly in love.

I drop my bag next to the big wheel at the back. The wood is sun-bleached and faded to the point of being almost bone white. The brass is dirty and green. But there's something about hearing the waves slapping gently against the hull... I know that's the right word for the bottom part of the boat, ship, whatever... but hearing that is... it's like a sound I've been waiting for all my life. And I never knew it.

I go below, into a narrow passageway. There's a tiny kitchen and a small place to eat. Little windows look out on the big boats and the water.

It's very cozy. Which is something I knew I needed and didn't expect to find anywhere in Calistan.

I put my messenger bag with my laptop on the table and explore the rest of the tiny vessel. Two small bedrooms with bunks, plus one large bedroom at the front. There are no sheets. No towels. Nothing. The boat has been reduced to a blank slate. Which is fine with me.

When I come out and go topside—that word seems right too; I've probably heard it in a movie—an old bandy-legged Mexican is staring down at me. He has a knife in his hand.

This is the aforementioned Old Mario.

He nods as if he's nodding only to himself. Taking my measure and clearly not liking what he's seeing.

"Hi there," I say cheerily despite the fishing knife in his hand. I feel stupid because I'm smiling. The boat does that to me. It erases the past few days. It even erases the story Rashid just told me before he got in a high-performance sports car and drove off to his next debauchery. The story about the time he fed a woman to the sharks and he and his friends laughed.

Old Mario doesn't say a word. Just continues to stare at me.

"Is there a store close by...?" I try.

He doesn't reply.

"I'm probably going to need some water. And bread." My mind is thinking of other things. Sheets. A blanket. A pillow. Food. Liquor. Ice. Glasses...

But I'm on a boat... so who cares if I have any of those things? If needed, I could sail out of Calistan. Though I don't know how to sail. It's just... at this moment... I feel like I could do anything in this boat. Go anywhere and become no one all over again.

Boats make you feel that way.

I remember a poem my dad used to read me before bed. When he came home late from the hospital he worked at.

I must go down to the seas again.

I memorized it after he and Mom were killed.

It was called "Sea-Fever." By John Masefield.

I must go down to the seas again, to the lonely sea and the sky,
And all I ask is a tall ship and a star to steer her by;
And the wheel's kick and the wind's song and the white sail's shaking,
And a grey mist on the sea's face, and a grey dawn breaking.

I must go down to the seas again, for the call of the running tide
Is a wild call and a clear call that may not be denied;
And all I ask is a windy day with the white clouds flying,
And the flung spray and the blown spume, and the sea-gulls crying.

I must go down to the seas again, to the vagrant gypsy life,
To the gull's way and the whale's way where the wind's like a whetted knife;

And all I ask is a merry yarn from a laughing fellow-rover,
And quiet sleep and a sweet dream when the long trick's over.

This.

This is the promise of all that was ever in that poem. As if I could sail away. As if I could sail back and see them, my mom and my dad, one more time.

As if there are such places on all the maps of the world… places we could start toward now, and make it home before dark.

As if that were possible.

Old Mario points off toward the bridge, past the rubble of those ruined homes other people once called home. The way Rashid and I came in. And then, just like that, he turns and leaves, slowly making his way up the dock and back onto the island that has been set aside for Rashid and Samira.

I think about leaving my stuff, but anyone could just paddle by and steal it. So I take my messenger bag with me and walk back up onto the island and through the quiet ruin. I pass tiny streets where little cottages were once the summer homes of families from long ago.

I know that because something catches my eye in the middle of a silent street filled with tiny ruins all neatly piled in the organized destruction that was required. It's a shard of glass in an old picture that flares, sparkling in the sun. I step forward and pluck it out of the ruin.

It's sepia. Brown and white. A family of white people, notable only because I've seen so few white people in Calistan, all with sunburned faces and freckled noses. Lots of red hair. They're wearing old beach clothes and ancient bathing suits, and are cuddling close to the camera. Beaming at it with wild smiles. There are so many of them it has to be two families gathered on some long-ago summer. Some are holding hot dogs. Others marshmallows on sticks. The men are holding brown bottles. Beer I guess. The women have cocktail glasses. They look both gay and glamorous. Gay as in the old meaning of the word. Happy.

There's even an old phonograph, a record player, on the sand. On an old Scotch plaid blanket.

These people look like they don't have a care in the world.

In white pen someone has written in perfect cursive script: "You gotta have friendship." And: "The McNultys and the Connors, Newport, 1936."

They're all so… charactery. Like something out of a period piece movie. Except they're real. Or at least they were once. On the day this was taken. In the moment when time and light captured them.

I look at the tiny pile of rubble I'm standing in front of. Smashed wood and broken glass. Old plumbing and haywire piping.

I think…

…somehow they deserved better than what became of who they once were.

Better than a pig like Rashid building a mega palace to hide the beautiful Samira in.

Everyone deserves better than what Rashid will give them. Except Rashid.

He definitely deserves… worse.

I knock out the remaining shards of glass that cover the McNultys and the Connors. I place the frame and the brown-and-white picture in my bag. I don't know why. I just do. I will take them with me and maybe I'll find a better place, someday, for them to be remembered.

I find a small market on the mainland.

I buy cans of sardines and smoked oysters. Some crackers. They don't have ham. I buy some waters. Some plastic cups and a bottle of bourbon. The shop owner doesn't seem to like selling it to me. He seems to be more of the devout Muslim variety. But he sells it nonetheless with a scowl that indicates his contempt for anything I might get up to.

They don't have blankets and pillows.

I walk back to the boat.

I plan on pulling up *Civ Craft* and figuring out how to get the other clans off Calistan's back. But when I get there Old Mario is waiting. He has a small scraping knife and some sandpaper.

I put my stuff down below and come back up.

He takes a piece of sandpaper and begins to sand the old bleached trim of the boat. He does this intently as I watch. Then he hands the paper to me and indicates, with a small grunt and an aggressive nod, that I should give it a try.

I will soon find out "trying" means doing it for the rest of the afternoon.

Because after a few passes, when I stop—stand and try to hand back the worn sandpaper—he shakes his head and points toward the rest of the boat. To the places that need attention specifically.

For no reason I can think of, I shrug and start back to work. And I like it.

I blame it on the boat.

We work for the rest of the day and toward dark, then as the harbor begins to go quiet, Mario leaves without so much as a word. I work for a little while more on a difficult portion I want to finish up. It's nice. Just listening to the soft scrape of the paper against the old wood. I think about those people in the picture. Wonder what became of them.

In time Mario returns with a small stove and a cooler.

"Finished for today," he mutters in a low, gravelly voice. And then, "Clean yourself up."

"Where?" I asks.

He shrugs nonchalantly and points toward the water in the harbor.

I think of sharks. I think of Rashid's story.

"In there?" I say.

He gives me a look that suggests he is in doubt as to whether I am a man or not.

Then he turns to setting up his stove.

I change into some cargo shorts I have in my bag and I go for a swim. I dive down into the dark water and look up to see the last light of day and the hull of the sailboat. I feel all the darkness of Calistan wash off me. All my months of travel and gaming slipping off my back and floating away in the gentle current of the harbor.

I surface, treading water in the dark. I smell cooking meat in the smoke that drifts off the back of the ship. Sailboat. Whatever. Mario stands and holds out a brown bottle and laconically indicates I should come back on board.

I dry myself with a shirt and sit near the wheel that steers the ship. Or at least I assume that's what it does.

He hands me an ice-cold beer.

Mexican beer. Tecate. He squeezes a thin slice of lime into it and then holds up one finger. He grabs a salt shaker and dashes it across the top of the can. Little salt crystals, swimming in lime juice.

I drink.

I drink all of it in one go.

I didn't realize how thirsty I was. I've been working in the hot sun all day, intent on the boat. And now…

The sea.

The lime.

The mindlessly fascinating work.

The hot sun.

The things that seemed bad… well… they're still bad. But I have a beer.

And the next beer tastes pretty good too because of the carne asada that comes with it.

Marinated flap meat that tastes of chilies and garlic and even soy sauce. It's hot. But first Mario hands me a real flour tortilla. Fluffy and charred. He had it on a hot plate. It's giant compared to other tortillas I've been served. Then he reaches down on the blazing grill and grabs some smoking meat with a pair of tongs. He places this in the tortilla and we eat.

And drink beer.

And listen to the water slap against the side of the hull.

Later he pulls out a radio. I've never actually seen one. A real radio that tunes in signal-based radio stations. The only radio I've ever even tried has been internet stations. Generally I prefer my own playlists. But he places the radio on top of the sailboat's cabin and tunes in a station. He looks south toward Mexico as though seeing the signal come over the curvature of the Earth. As though he needs to look to find it, dial it in, capture it for the evening. Then he adjusts the radio once more. Tiny, minute, delicate adjustments to land the signal in the optimum place of reception.

I feel like some kind of magic is about to happen. I can feel the electricity of it in the air. Like getting to hear what we're about to hear is something special. Not just something that can be demanded from the internet. But something that has to be captured. Something that requires a little effort.

And then, through the static and fuzz, the plaintive wail of mariachis comes over the airwaves. Mario sits back. He claps his hands and makes us two more beers. We've already drunk several.

A song comes on and he holds out both hands.

As though this song is very special to him.

It is.

His old, tired, tanned and weathered face smiles beatifically as the mariachis sing "Son de la Negra."

And we sit there in the harbor dark, drinking beers and listening to the mariachis croon about true loves long lost and still hoped for.

Chapter Twenty-Nine

In time Mario takes his stove, cooler, and radio, and leaves. The night is warm. I go down into the galley—Mario informed me the kitchen is called a galley—and set up my laptop. The boat has an electrical hookup from the dock.

I log onto *Civ Craft*'s main site and read through the news feeds. I study the maps. I research the clans. Later, on toward one a.m., I open the bourbon. Clevinger's. It's the only brand they carried, so it would do. I pour a finger and step out onto the main deck. The cockpit. Where the big wheel is.

I watch Calistan's Gold Coast glitter in the night. It's a playground for the top of the food chain. People who don't care about anything other than where the next scene is. That much is evident and they don't try to hide it. Their Instaflash accounts—I took a *Civ Craft* research break to do some internet surfing—glorify obnoxious amounts of extravagant spending and waste. Because they can.

Why would they care about the actual state of the country beyond their precious Gold Coast?

They're the top of the food chain.

Except on *Civ Craft*. There they're holding a small series of hills that extend from the Tharsis Bulge to the Valles Marineris. They've done no research and development, while other civilizations are already building huge cities and opening trade routes with one another.

Right now, they're being menaced by a loose confederation of Asian gaming clans who call themselves the Geeks. The Geek League, to be specific. Each clan has gone in hard on some kind of nerdstalgia and has crafted their entire society—culture, look, tech—to reflect their obsession. But they're growing, and Calistan isn't.

The League occupies a series of low mountains and wide valleys to the west of Calistan. Across a huge sea of craters. And they need Calistan's land in order to connect trade routes with other civilizations.

The question is how to get them distracted from their constant incursions against Calistan.

I pour more Clevinger's and watch the bioluminescence of the water in the harbor. I try to think of all the history I ever learned, because one thing I learned long ago, in some History of Gaming class, was that war never changes.

I think about the World Wars. The Brushfire Wars after the Meltdown. Antarctica I and II.

Nothing leaps out at me. Nothing presents an easy historical solution to all Calistan's problems in one easy op. The main thing they need to do is start building a civilization. Simple as that. But they started off so warlike that they're now viewed by the Geek League and others as a nuisance that needs to be disappeared. And maybe as a potential resource base once things have settled down. Enemy colonies are already starting to sprout up all over the Calistani in-game territory.

I have to go further back. Think about the old wars I don't know much about.

Sparta versus Athens.

The Hundred Years' War.

The Mexico Conflict from just before the Melt.

I'm ready to give up. I could stream documentaries for the rest of the night and still not hit on anything that might inspire me.

I pour another bourbon and sit back down at the computer, intent on closing the lid and wrapping myself up in my coat for the night to get some sleep. But I know there's something naggingly familiar about the information staring me in the face.

The Geek League.

Like... like... Ancient Greece.

I try to read up on some old general called Thucydides. He wrote a book... *History of the Peloponnesian War.* It was about a long war between the Greeks. Sparta and Athens. City-states fighting for regional supremacy.

And laying waste... that's the part that intrigues me. Ruining the other team's stuff, especially when they're heavily invested in the making of that stuff.

And then I've got it. I stare at the map of Mars for a long time. And slowly... it all comes into focus. I stream some classical music and get down to work. One song in particular. I put it on. I study the map again. Study the approach to the Geek League's city-states.

I see hover tanks and troops moving across the sea of craters along their frontier. See the Geek League getting real concerned about a focused invasion right into the heart of their city-states. See them getting distracted from their expansionistic yearnings.

Maybe it's just the Clevinger's talking.

Of course... if you don't want to be attacked... then you have to invade. That's the answer to getting the Geek League out of Calistan. Invade them back.

Just like the Persians did to the Greeks. Another Greek war. Except this time we won't lose.

I see it all. Every move to Game Over.

And then I close the lid and try to sleep.

Chapter Thirty

Beyond the last door within the caves below the old manor house sinking into the swamp, I find her. A bloody angel. She is both magnificent and gorgeous in death. Dark crow's wings spread out across the floor where she has been slain. Her face is familiar. She wears a kind of ancient sliver plate armor. A broken sword lies nearby. An old dagger, carved from the tooth of some long-dead titan and worked in crawling nonsense runes, erupts from her chest.

I approach cautiously, crossing the cold floor of the last room in the dungeon below the ruin that lies beyond the slaughtered town. In the gloom beyond this sacrifice I see a twisting set of stairs winding back and up toward the surface. An exit along which Alucard must've gone after leaving this little trap for me.

When I see her face I think of some familiar song I once knew. A long time ago in a life not this one.

Silvery tears stream down her cheeks. She opens coal-dark eyes and stares at me. She knows she's dying. That death has come for her.

I wonder if I am death?

I kneel and remove the dagger from her chest.

Because I am not death.

She gasps to life as her chest attempts to hold on to the dagger. Her back arches and she wails in sudden ethereal torment. And then the dagger is out. She places a long, slender, alabaster hand over the wound, and all that is left of that scar is a memory.

She smiles weakly at me.

There is a flash of light. Of warmth. Of safety. Of home. Wherever that is for her. The beauty of her knowing such a place is so overwhelming that I close my eyes as I'm driven to the floor by the mere glimpse of her expression when remembering such a place.

And I know that time has passed.

That all that happened long ago.

I am lying now on the stone floor. I can feel the coolness of these caves. Of this place of death.

I push away and stand. The angel has gone. But she lives, and somehow that is enough for me. I turn to the stairs and begin the long climb back to the surface.

I will find Alucard's trail once again.

I will find Alucard.

And I will slay Alucard.

As if that can make all things right again.

Chapter Thirty-One

In the morning, aboard the gently rocking sailboat, I wake to the sound of a distant foghorn. I lie there for a long time listening to it before I realize what it is. I've never heard one before. It's mournful and patient. Those are the words I think of as I listen to it. That it's giving all of us a gentle warning that the waters of the harbor are not safe.

That life, also, is not safe.

I'm cold. Shivering even. I get up and put on some clean khakis, a t-shirt, and my old trench. I go out to stand on the wet deck. Everything is sheathed in white fog. I can barely see the island the boat is docked to just a few feet away. I can only see a little bit out into the still water.

I hear the horn again, sounding its low, mournful warning that nothing is safe right now.

If I'm going to leave Calistan, sail away in this boat, now is the moment when no one would see me go.

Except I don't know how to sail.

Someone comes by, rowing a small boat loaded with fishing gear. They smile once at me as they come out of the fog, and continue to pull at their oars. A few seconds later they're gone. Swallowed once more by the swirling mist.

I forgot to get coffee at the market yesterday.

I put on my Docs and trudge off to the store once again. An hour later I return with more supplies, coffee among them. Shortly I have a cup ready, though I had to just boil the grounds in a pan and pour the syrup it became into an old mug that remained in the mostly bare cupboards.

Still… it's coffee.

Coffee will get you through a time of no money.

Money will never get you through a time of no coffee.

Truer words have seldom been spoken.

I stand on deck, mesmerized by the fog and the sounds of the harbor. Sounds coming from things, events, and people I cannot see, and have to imagine, out there in the swirling mist.

I think about my plan.

I need to talk to Enigmatrix… but I have no contact for her. So I wait until the fog burns off and Rashid shows up in a totally new and different high-end sports car, I kid you not.

"The other one needed an alignment," he says as we slide into a bright-red Ferrari 208Redux.

First-world problems, I tell myself.

On the drive over to the Cyber Warfare Center, I lay out my plan for Rashid.

"Here's how we get the Geek League off your back…" I yell above the whine of the engine. He had no idea who the Geek League was until I told him it was the confederation of Asian clans that had been whaling on Calistan.

"The Japs!"

I nod for the sake of agreement.

"Basically," I continue, "we've got to get them interested in something else besides attacking Calistan."

Rashid nods as if this is obvious.

"So," I say, "we're going to invade their land. Then they'll get interested in looking after themselves instead of you."

He shoots me a quick scowl. "We've *been* attacking them, PQ."

"I know. I didn't say attack. I said *invade*—as in full-scale invasion. We'll be so busy breaking all their stuff they won't have time to bother

Calistan. That'll give you the time to get some building projects in order and start developing your tech tree instead of going broke on micro-transactions to replace what you've lost."

"We're not going broke," he cries indignantly over the beautiful Ferrari's howl.

"I know… but you're not winning the game either. You've got to have tech to win a tech victory. There are no micro-transaction victories."

I distantly wonder if anyone has ever talked to him like this. I suspect no one has and that gives me a secret pleasure in doing so.

"Who are we gonna invade?" he asks as though only just tuning in to this part of the conversation.

"The Geek League. The guys giving you a hard time."

"Japs!" he mutters disgustedly.

"Some but not all. Specifically, we're going to target three clans and we're going to ruin their clan cities. And I mean *ruin* them."

"Which three?" asks Rashid, now definitely interested.

"Marvel Rainbow Avengers. The Super Terrific Robot Overlords, or as everyone else calls them, the Cylon Republic. And Team Commando Joe."

"Never heard of them," says Rashid naturally, and he can't help but come off as cavalier.

"Rashid," I say. Again, I really enjoy treating him as though he's stupid. "These are the people who've been attacking you. You should know this intel… bro!"

I touched it up with the "bro." Have to make it seem like I'm on his side. In the inner circle. Definitely not working for the CIA. Best way to stick the knife in. Even though I don't know how any of this will come out, I know, definitely, that I am not on his side. At all. Definitely. I know that at this specific moment. Regardless of what is to come.

He slumps his shoulders and leans into the wheel.

"You're right," he confesses. I should've known that."

"Okay," I begin. "All these cities run alongside a river they've managed to engineer along a basin west of your lands. I'm going to lead an army in there and ruin them. I'm going to break stuff and go for broke. I'm not holding territory because we can't hold it. We're just going to do war. Got it?"

"I guess," he says glumly. "What do I do?"

Here's the tricky part.

"Two very important things. One... you're going to run the micro-transaction supply lines. I'll need a lot of equipment to keep them busy. I need you to run your army of micro-transaction purchasers and keep your clans supplied and online in the fight. We're going at this full tilt and we can't stop because we're out of assets. No guns, tanks, or players, and we stop, got that? We're dead in the water, they roll us up and come at Calistan with everything they've got."

He doesn't say or do anything. He just stares ahead out the windshield.

"Two... and this is how you win the game, Rashid..."

And by win the game I mean impress your dad, which you don't know that I know is the real purpose of this whole exercise. Impress Daddy and become sultan. That's probably your biggest concern right now.

"You've got to build Calistan online. You've got to build a vibrant thriving city and develop tech, science, and cultural resources."

"So I'm not going to fight with you?"

"You are. I'll bring you into the fight at key moments. Each time we wipe out a city you'll be right there on the big old killcam the streams are showing. I promise. But let me fight the battle until it's time to get you there. You keep me supplied. And build up your people."

Then I add... "Because that's what a real leader does. Then I'll bring you in for the glory kill. Got it?"

He nods to himself.

I've got him. His ego has shown him the easiest way to be fed. And he likes that.

"What about Enigmatrix?" he asks suddenly. Not out of concern. But out of something else. Something far more cynical.

"She's going to be running strategic for me. I'm staying forward in the battle to keep your clans focused on the objective at hand. But I need her to coordinate airstrikes, indirect fire, and reinforcements. Basically all three of us have to work together to get Calistan in the game. You're supply. She's support. I fight. You get the glory."

* * *

We make our way down into the lower vaults of the Cyber Warfare Center without a word between us. In fact, Rashid hasn't said anything since I laid out my plans.

Perhaps I overplayed my hand in being a little mean to him.

Within the main conference room, we're greeted by the same assortment of generals as before. Real generals. Here to play a game. I should have realized how bizarre that was from the start. But now I understand. It's not just a game.

The kid who would be king is on the line.

And not just one kid.

Rashid's brother is here too. And he's brought his own small entourage. Guys in dark robes and gray beards. They're definitely a faction. Even though, for my sake, they're supposed to be on the same team, it is clear... they are not on the same team. And judging by the murderous look Omar shoots Rashid—and the equally un-brotherly look Rashid gives in return—this is not the prelude to a warm family reunion.

Sure enough, Omar and Rashid immediately begin to shout at each other in whatever language it is they speak. And within moments everyone is shouting at everyone. Angry, harsh words in their harsh, angry language. Suddenly Rashid lunges forward and knocks his brother to the ground with a right cross. And small subcompact machine guns appear in hands all around the room. From beneath robes. From behind backs. From out of nowhere. Even the clerics have weapons.

A tense silence overwhelms this underground conference room deep beneath the caliphate of Calistan. As though each person is daring every other person to just start shooting.

I sit down in a chair.

It makes a small squeak.

A few people cast quick glances my way. Then they return their attention to the people they're intent on murdering in a sudden blur of gunfire.

"Guys," says Rashid softly. Very softly. He has a gold-plated Desert Eagle out. It's stuck into his brother's cherubic cheek. "Guys... c'mon. Weapons down."

No one moves.

Rashid lowers his weapon.

"Weapons down, guys," he says in a soothing tone.

I tell myself to start breathing again. I try not to get too focused on how close I am to being suddenly riddled with bullets.

"PerfectQuestion has a plan that's going to get us out of this mess," announces the prince to all the angry people holding automatic weaponry. No doubt set to indiscriminate fire.

Rashid looks at me. Prompting me to go ahead and tell everyone my big plan.

So I do.

I tell them.

Finally, weapons are lowered, though tensions still run high. They all break into separate groups and start whispering furtively. A few furious murmurs penetrate the sibilant hum. Then, with no signal I can discern, everybody moves to the beautifully polished walnut conference table and takes their seats as though some sober, ordinary, not murderously insane corporate board meeting is about to convene. The clerics straighten their robes. The military men don't move a muscle. Rashid and his brother stand at opposite ends, facing one another.

This is exactly the situation. Everyone is on the same team. Or so I have to pretend. Because Rashid is pretending. And I have to go along or reveal that I've been talking to the CIA. But I know, and they know, there are two teams. Team Rashid and Team Omar. Except that there are other teams in play too. The military. The mullahs. And probably each person, at the end of the day, is on their very own team. And somehow... we're all supposed to work together.

So I tell them there's one goal—to win of course—and two strategies to achieve that goal. Attack your opponents' civilizations... and strengthen your own. War, and civilization-building. Destruction and creation. Rashid will take war—obviously—and Omar will build up Calistan's culture and tech indices. Two brothers working together—but separately.

The generals are happy because they think a string of easy online military victories will easily convince the sultan to pick Rashid. And the mullahs are happy because cultural domination is their wheelhouse and Omar is their man. Both sides think they've been given the easy path to victory for their personal goal of holding the keys to the kingdom. And for either side to succeed, they have to work together—or at least stay out of each other's way.

It's the only way I can see to get two people to work together who are in direct competition with one another. Make them realize that they both have to succeed in their respective fields or neither can achieve much of anything. Some probably overly optimistic side of me imagines that's what their father, the sultan, has had in mind all along. Getting his sons to work together for the mutual benefit of Calistan.

He's probably an optimist too.

"My brother," says Rashid, "agrees this is a good plan."

Omar nods. His mouth is closed, but I can tell his teeth are clenched.

"Together," announces Rashid magnanimously, "we will join all our clans and invade the Geek League. PerfectQuestion will lead the fight. He'll be our warlord in this. And I'll fight too. We're going to get out of this mess, together."

Obviously no one in this war room of scheming players believes the *together* part. But it sounds good and everyone smiles at the prince like that part is the best part. Even though they all know the long knives are out. That Eastern Promises have been made.

Rashid pauses and looks around.

"I'll run our banking and micro-transaction operations to keep the jihadis supplied. Omar will take charge of the development of Calistan's online presence by increasing our culture tech and science indices. And he and I will work together to plan out our new city."

Rashid should sell bridges. Except no one in this room would be buying. And yet... we all act like we are.

No one says anything.

"Agreed?" asks Rashid.

As if anyone has a choice.

Agreed then.

"When do we attack?" asks one of the generals.

"Tonight," I reply. "We'll cross the Sea of Craters and hit Marvel City at dawn, in-game time tomorrow."

The generals check massive Rolex watches on their arms. Synchronizing the time. Surprisingly, so do the mullahs.

The conference room clears as everyone hustles off to get their ducks in a row for our next battle. What the hell the generals and clerics even do that has any impact on the actual online battle we're about to fight, I have no idea. Somehow they interface with the online gaming clans within Calistan, or so I'm told much later.

When I can get Rashid alone for a moment I ask, "What did you mean by 'get out of this mess'?"

He looks at me. Looks around to see who's listening.

"My father, the sultan, is dying, PQ. It's cancer. He's going to name his successor next week. If it isn't me... then... I'll have to be honest with you right now, and this is something you won't want to hear, but because we're friends I'll tell you. If I lose, there's no gold for you."

He gives me an almost friendly that's-the-way-the-ball-bounces look. As though it's all out of his hands. Cookies crumble suchly.

I laugh like the very idea of losing is impossible. Except inside I'm cursing at myself and it isn't pretty.

"I'll have a list of micro-transactions you'll need to make before we go in," I tell him, pushing thoughts of what a chump I am out of the way. "Also... I'll be setting a rally point at the extreme edge of our territory. Have all the clans rendezvous at that position at eleven thirty IGT."

In-Game Time.

"Roger. You got it, buddy. Hundred percent."

An explosion rocks the building. It's dull, distant. But deep down here under all this concrete, the ground still rumbles. Whatever went off, it was big enough to rock the foundations of a subterranean gaming bunker.

Is it too much to hope the CIA is invading to get me out?

"Aztecs," mutters Rashid and dashes out of the room.

An hour later, I'll find out a bus blew up in a crowded intersection just down the street. There were multiple casualties. Crowds of beautiful young Arab kids, headed to the beach.

The Aztec Liberation Front is officially to blame.

Chapter Thirty-Two

We hit them hard at a place called Reed Richards Tower. It lies on the extreme edge of the Geek League in an area controlled by one of their clans. The Marvel Rainbow Avengers.

"So who exactly are these jokers?" I ask Enigmatrix, who's running command and control.

I already know the answer. But I want to see what she has to say about them.

"MRAs," she says. I can practically hear the eye roll. "Back before the Meltdown, when the Social Justice movement was trying to strangle the life out of society by calling everyone racists and bigots… they took over the comic book and science-fiction industry and made it utterly ridiculous. They basically took every established character and twisted it into something else that fit their very specific agenda about gender, race, and sexuality. Guys were suddenly girls or something in between. Every white male hero suddenly needed to be a black female hero… you know the drill. And no one could create, write, draw, film, or profit from any character that didn't perfectly align with that artist's own physical characteristics and 'cultural life experience.' All the tricks their puppet masters were pulling to win elections based on outrage and mob violence were put into play."

This is about the longest I've ever heard Enigmatrix talk on any one subject. Guess she's a history buff. Or a classic comics and sci-fi fan.

Or maybe she's just finally warming up to me.

"So of course no one bought the product," she continues. "Sales slumped and then dropped off completely. They killed entire brands. Once-bulletproof franchises were just gutted. In the end they were reduced to calling their own fan bases bigots because they wouldn't buy. It got tired. And if anything came out of the Melt, then watching the SJW movement starve to death en masse in the cities was a good thing. Yeah, PQ, I know that makes me a bad person. But I'm half-serious about that."

I know all this. I took the history classes. I know that even as the old entertainment companies tanked and demanded federal assistance, claiming almost everything was a basic human right—including comic books that advocated for a more diverse society—they doubled down on… well, basically calling everyone racists. In the end, they alienated themselves from almost everyone.

What I didn't know was that they still existed. As a clan. In *Civ Craft: Mars.*

And we get to attack them.

I'm not complaining.

We hit Reed Richards Tower hard with a series of airstrikes. The Colonial Marines are riding shotgun with me on this one. We're using their dropship to direct and focus the battle. Wherever the dropship is, the Calistan clans are to focus their assaults and firepower. Controlling the thousands of Calistani players—who neither speak our language nor seem much inclined to follow our directions—has proven to be a problem for both Rashid and Enigmatrix. So I decided on a simple solution. Whatever I attack… they attack.

Mass effect is our battle plan.

Our ragtag artillery preps the assault from the hill beyond the city, and we move in fast with armored columns and dropship cover, shooting up all their crafted buildings as we go and leaving an army of mecha bots ruined, along with four dead Marvel Rainbow players. Zhir Fantastic, Invisible Zhirl, The Questioning Thing and some player known as the LGBTQ Torch.

They tried to stop us. No dice. Yeah, they technically had "superpowers." But superpowers weren't enough to invalidate the tons of anti-tank rounds and heavy-caliber munitions we were dumping on their position as we moved forward. The Questioning Thing was the hardest to take out. Pulse rifles and 7.62 rounds didn't do anything. In the end we naped it, him, her, or whatever, and it turned to slag.

It was our opening shot and we only faced four rear-guard clan players, but the battle feels like a win.

I order the dropship down beneath the carnage. We set down on a fantastic future plaza of shapes and cubes. Engineering teams demo Reed Richards Tower and it comes down with a crash, smashing into a large section of the groovy city. Smoke rises from the rubble and I check the livestreams. The viewer count has gone from a few hundred thousand to several million worldwide.

No doubt we have the clan's attention now. A response will be forthcoming.

"We should've capped the tower!" shouts Rashid over private chat. "We could use it as a base."

I'm a little surprised to hear this from Prince Blow-the-Reactor. Seems when he's not attacking his own brother, he actually can recognize the value of preserving resources.

Except in this case capture is not an option.

"Can't hold anything, Rashid. I'm blowing through their lands to keep them occupied here and coming after me. They won't bother Calistan as long as I'm bothering them."

Or so I hope.

I can tell he's sulking about not getting to play the mighty conqueror. But he doesn't bother me about it anymore. I guess getting to be sultan is worth riding a little pine. And every military victory, whether or not he's front and center, is his domain. And therefore his victory. I'm sure the arrangement I helped broker between him and Omar has been well-whispered throughout Calistan and even in the sultan's ear.

Rashid may not get to pull the trigger, or even end up in the streams, but if the military effort is a success, he'll get to be sultan.

For whatever that's worth.

I order our units into three groups and turn southwest for a low ridge, beyond which lies the river basin. We top the dusty dry hills above the Martian valley with twelve dropships and ten thousand troops outfitted with all the weapons and gear Rashid's army of bankers has been able to procure through micro-transactions. We're officially going for broke. I've asked for each player to have an AK-2000, three grenades, an RPG, and one medical kit. Minimum. I was told that cost a small online fortune. It was no problem for the vast resources of Calistan, but it was a source of friction for the team of bankers and accountants that had set up in a nearby conference room.

"They're pretty upset," Rashid told me. "So this better be worth it."

Besides the dropships and infantry, we have over five hundred light armored vehicles, one hundred Wolverine battle tanks, and thirty light walkers, along with air and artillery support being run by Enigmatrix.

We're arrayed in three massive formations and approaching the clan's main city on the vast cratered plain below. A massive rainbow arch towers over it.

We clearly caught them by surprise at Reed Richards Tower, and we want to keep that surprise going. Yeah, they already know we destroyed the tower on their border. They know they lost four players. They probably suspect we aren't done. But getting a response together quickly from their clan will take time. They have jobs and lives. Which is why we have to attack now.

I have the tactical display out and draw lines of advance through the city with a smartpen. My goal is basically just to maintain momentum and concentrate when and where they decide to engage us. If we can destroy the city before they can gather in force, that's a win for me. We'll roll on after that and leave this place burning in our dust trails.

It wasn't how I fought battles for ColaCorp in *WarWorld*. There I had a series of goals laid out, all affecting the larger campaigns playing out over the season. But this, here, in *Civ Craft*, a game of empires… this is warlord style. Cities burning and lamentations of their women stuff.

Roll on.

"All Calistani forces move forward and stay in formation," I order over the chat. "Support each other and concentrate fire on any resistance. Break their stuff while you're at it. Spread the destruction."

All three groups move forward into the outer districts of the ridiculously rainbow-colored city.

Resistance is token and ragged at first. Teams of bots coming out with anti-armor. When that happens we pull back and Enigmatrix pounds them with mobile artillery or sets up airstrikes that don't mind wiping out a city block to get two bots with anti-armor.

All their bots are a version of Space Marines they've designated as S.H.E.S.H.I.E.L.D. I have no idea what that means, and I say so.

"It's their nod to all the radical feminism that was going down at the time," says one of the Colonial Marines.

Yeah, I still don't know what that means.

The door gunner opens up with the swing-mounted N50 and cuts down a squad of S.H.E.S.H.I.E.L.D. bots fighting on a rooftop. The bots were preventing the advance of one of my columns, but within seconds they're all offlined. They should have been set to fight within the building. Not the rooftop.

"Bullets don't judge," quips MarineCorporalHicks over chat, and everyone has a good laugh.

We deal with a few players who pop in without any support, coming at us in the hope that they can stave off the ruin and destruction we're doing to their pretty little city. They're not organized. Easy kills.

As we near the city center, directly underneath the massively ridiculous rainbow that arches up and over the city, we get into our first real fight.

With the Diversity Avengers.

They come flying at us from all directions with an army of genderless bots patterned after some superhero once known as War Machine but who later got changed during the era of diversity rewriting to Justice Warrior.

"Who?" someone asks over the chat.

"Not important!" I tell them and switch to command chat for Enigmatrix. "Listen, what're we looking at on a response time, Enigmatrix?"

She's been monitoring the feeds on other channels, and the news stations that report on everything going on inside the major games. She gives me a rundown, which I didn't ask for, but she seems amused and in a sharing mood.

It seems TWITCHNN has been leading with a Breaking News crawl about our attack. The reporters have been trying to interview players who are fighting on both sides, though for the most part they've stuck to the Asian clans, who are legitimately upset and vowing our swift destruction while pontificating that this is "typical of Calistan." But they did manage to get a comment from one of the jihadi players online. He was running a Wolverine main battle tank and was busy shooting up a resource factory, someplace tagged as the Glitter Dome, that churned out in-game assets that could be crafted into any building you can design.

"Don't you think you're being a bit excessive with the one-twenty main gun on the factory?" the reporter asked him. "Standard demo charges will disable any resource node, sir."

The Calistani clan gamer, tagged BobMarleysScimitar, laughed uproariously and in heavily accented English said, "We are making ourselves free through mass destruction!"

"And then," continues Enigmatrix on the chat, "I'm not kidding, his feed gets a million subs in thirty seconds."

"Nice," I say. Though I'm not exactly concerned about subscription numbers at the moment. "What does this mean for response time?"

"Maybe forty-five minutes. The other clans are freaking out on their boards and ordering everyone to move out to fixed rally points for a coordinated response. I don't have a line on a loc yet. We'll get another satellite pass in eighteen minutes if the micro-transaction goes through. Turned into a bidding war. Some of the alliance clans are trying to pay to keep us off the access. We get that eye-in-the-sky pass and that should tell us a lot more about what we can expect out of them. Until then go for broke, PQ."

A massive pink monster called the Big Gay Hulk is tearing apart a Wolverine main battle tank ahead of our position. Other than superpowers, these MRAs don't have much, it seems. Being special is all that matters to them, and they didn't anticipate other players being particularly aggressive in Martian global affairs. Plus, they're part of the Geek League, which I assume has some kind of mutual protection pact. And while that theoretically gives them some limited benefit as far as the game of civilization-building that is *Civ Craft* is concerned, it's got even more benefit for us. Because it means no clan is *really* able to defend themselves. Not alone. Not when it comes down to it.

Mutual protection is all well and good until everyone decides everyone else is responsible for it.

And now they're finding out their defenses won't cut it. Which they should have known from the start. Even in a game, civilizations are inherently violent toward one another, which is something that caught all the globalist SJW progressives off guard during the Melt. Because when civilizations collide and the fur flies, suddenly people are willing to fight for resources. Sharing, climate change, windmills, and whales aren't all that important once the lights have gone out and winter is coming on.

Still, they've got the Big Gay Hulk. So that's something.

And he's nigh invincible to bullets. And the tanks can't seem to hit him or any of the Diversity Avengers. They all move too fast.

I open the tactical chat to the group we're over-watching. "Alpha Group... all units scatter and take cover in the nearby buildings."

The Colonial Marines' dropship I'm in is orbiting the parkscape we're currently fighting over. I have three other dropships on standby ready to make gun runs on the Hulk.

"Dropships two-two and two-three, make your runs on the tagged tango. Enigmatrix, do we have arty yet?"

The first gunship makes a pass and unloads both gun pods on the monstrous Hulk. A bullet storm of thirty-millimeter ball ammunition tears up the pristine green parkscape and strafes straight up the massive chest of the Big Gay Hulk.

The second gunship doesn't survive the pass. Hulk leaps up and smashes it with a giant pink fist. The ship explodes, and I lose thirty Calistani clansmen in half a second.

Don't do that again, I tell myself.

"Group tanks pull back into the surrounding streets and fire at will. Do not advance until directed."

I hate controlling a battle. Simply sitting here and ordering people to fight. Then watching them fight. It isn't my thing.

Actually fighting—that's what I do best.

Troops open up on the Big Gay Hulk from the windows of the surrounding buildings. I make a note to have Rashid get me more heavy machine gun teams. They're doing some damage and they're distracting the raging thing. I have a healthy new respect for all the equipment RangerSix and ColaCorp thought to provide in all our online corporate battles. Here, I just asked for the big stuff and went for it. But there have been moments when I definitely could have used a specific tool or asset I would have had access to in *WarWorld*.

The Hulk leaps high into the sky and comes down near another Wolverine. It effortlessly lifts the tank over its head and sends it off into another tank a few hundred meters away. Both explode, sending a blast wave of debris that collapses the digital façade of the nearest building.

This is going from bad to worse. My advance is being stopped by some kind of pro wrestling cosplay fanatic, and if we don't finish this fight fast and ruin this city—if the other clans decide to engage us right here and now—my plan is shot.

"CPLFerro…" I call out over the chat. "You think you can get that thing's attention and stay away from it but keep close like a fly?"

"I'll try."

"All right then. Put us down quickly in front of it. Then take off and keep it distracted. MarineSgtApone, tell the Marines to engage with grenades and flamethrowers. Close-quarters battle."

"Huuwaaah, sir. You heard him, Marines… encounter of the up close and personal kind."

I'm confident the two heavy machine guns Drake and Vasquez carry will do a lot of damage.

Ferro takes us in hot and fast. We exit the cargo deck and begin firing into the big pink face of the screaming Hulk who has decided to charge the dropship that just set down.

Honestly, the Big Gay Hulk is much bigger when you're on the ground right in front of it.

And scarier.

The dropship flares its engines and climbs back up in a spray of dust as the Hulk swipes at it and barely misses. The door gunner draws a bloody red line of fire across its midsection but it doesn't seem to do much. Already Marines are tossing grenades and cutting loose on full auto. The Big Gay Hulk leaps in among them and starts tossing and throttling the Colonial Marine cosplayers like they're mere action figures. Flamethrowers shoot long lancing jets of burning fuel all over the screaming monster. It picks up a Marine and tossed him over a building beyond the immediate battle.

"Concentrate all fire now!" I roar over chat at every element in the group. I'm holding the left mouse button down inside my gaming suite and unloading a full magazine from the M4X I've switched over to. All around me Marine pulse rifles crackle on full auto. Then the heavy machine guns of Drake and Vasquez cut loose on full rock-and-roll in the face of the screaming giant.

Incredibly, the Big Gay Hulk begins to wither beneath the tremendous volume of fire. Massive heavy-caliber rounds served in high doses go in and come out in long bloody streams from the thing's backside. We're finally doing real damage and our DPS is on point.

In other words... we're winning.

Every gamer will tell you that every game involving combat always boils down to DPS.

Damage per second.

And then a green guy with a giant green shield jumps in and deflects all our directed fire on the cowering Hulk.

"Who the hell is that?" shouts Vasquez angrily. She doubles down on a new burst of fire from her heavy machine gun.

"Captain Climate Change," says PVTHudson with a laugh. "He used to be something else, but that guy was thought to be too patriarchal, or patriotic, or something. So in the last days of Marvel he identified as a plant."

"Use the flamethrowers!" I shout once I have that bit of intel.

Jets of burning fuel spit out, burning Captain Fern.

And while he turns into a campfire, we finish off the last of the Big Gay Hulk.

I check the HUD kill counts and tags. Together, with all our assets, we've wiped out the Diversity Avengers. The city is ours for the next few minutes.

"Game over, man," says Hudson over the chat. "But y'know... in a good way, man."

In the silence that follows, the Calistanis shoot their weapons into the Martian sky and yodel, or ululate. Something tribal. Suddenly everything is more circus-of-guns and less objective-focused battle.

If the Calistanis were hard on the rainbow city before, what they do next is ruthless. In every possible way they demo every production asset, skinned in all its ridiculous diversity-laden nostalgia from a long time ago, and then set about ruining the actual resources the area produced. Terrain is damaged. Survivable resources like air, water, and plants are all chemical-weaponed.

I order the engineer units to move forward and set up demo charges on the end of the rainbow arch. Destroying their biggest building achievement will decimate their cultural index, which is the key factor in determining society ranking and victory point accumulation. When they retake the city—which I will let them do—they'll have to spend time fixing all their stuff instead of giving Calistan a hard time.

Six hours later, I kid you not, the leader of the Marvel Rainbow Avengers will be calling us "war criminals" in a live interview on TWITCHNN.

But before that, the rest of the Diversity Avengers attack.

Chapter Thirty-Three

Their forces are rallying on the far side of the park under the direction of a player tagged as StrongIronWoman. She's wearing some kind of robot suit with jet packs, and she's supported by a force of bots patterned after elite rioters in black-and-red high-tech gear known as CO-EXIST Troopers. These are heavy versions of the S.H.E.S.H.I.E.L.D troopers.

Someone over the chat runs down a quick commentary as we engage. The elite rioters are apparently based on the Captain Antifa comic books that drove the final nail in the Marvel coffin years before the Melt. What was left of America didn't react well to seeing the President of the United States crucified by Captain Antifa beneath a burning Stars and Stripes as the "hero" proclaimed he was "Stopping the Hate!" on the cover. An issue which also featured the burning of a synagogue with occupants inside, a riot in which the police were curb-stomped en masse while Los Angeles burned, and the actual Constitution being somehow literally used to perform a much-needed last-minute abortion.

The editorial staff felt this was the most important comic book issue ever penned.

The rioters have set up heavy machine gun positions near the base of the arch we're trying to demo. And other assets are starting to arrive. Mobs of cosplayers snarling like packs of ancient warriors baying for our blood. In other words... we're being thrown out of the park. Which is rapidly becoming a free-fire zone from every direction.

"MarineSgtApone," I say over the chat as I low-crawl my avatar behind some postmodern statuary depicting some superhero, a man, giving birth to a glitter-covered dinosaur. It's disturbing, but it's cover in the sudden crossfire hurricane that's all too terminal for anyone caught standing. "We need to move forward, knock out their pits, and finish the job. What's it look like on the left flank?"

"No good, sir!" replies Apone over the whistle of physics-rendered bullets streaking in volume just over my head. The chaos fills the gaming suite's speakers. "We're pinned over here... sir."

It sounds like it.

Now the heavy machine guns have found their range and are chewing up the concrete of the weirdo statue coming apart all around me.

"What about a dustoff?" shouts someone over the chat. I hear the sharp cacophonic ethereal bark of pulse rifles in the background.

"Negative," I broadcast reply, just so no one gets any ideas about pulling out, especially the pilot. "LZ's too hot. We're demoing the rainbow before we move on. Repeat... we are reducing the rainbow to rubble before exfil."

It's PVTHudson who comes up with a plan. "I'm surfing through the city grid. Looks like there's a subway entrance a few hundred feet to our rear. Across the park. This whole place is built in accordance with that whole political scam people used to call Agenda 21. Y'know, mass transit for the masses. Everyone living on top of each other. Move all the people into the cities so the rich can have all the good land along the coasts. Anyway, since this clan is an homage to how jacked up those times were, they've built an entire subway system down there to accommodate the masses. There's an entrance that will come out right where we need to be in order to place our charges. They probably haven't thought to use it. Then again... maybe they have. In which case, hey... bonus points."

"Mob surging on the right! They're coming at us!" cries Vasquez over the chat. "Engaging with extreme prejudice!"

"All elements, concentrate fire on the right!" I shout back.

Then...

"Good catch, Hudson. Apone, I'll take a squad with me and we'll go down tunnel and see if we can retake that engineer's truck across the park and finish the job. Keep 'em occupied for us!"

The engineer team was ready to blow the arch, but they were overrun. The truck and charges are still there.

"Copy that, sir!"

* * *

What remains of First Squad are MarinePvtDrake, Frosty, PVT-Hudson, and MarineCorporalHicks. And me. The five of us dodge fire as we cross the lush parkscape-slash-warzone and make the cool darkness of the subway entrance.

Enigmatrix gives me a sitrep over command chat.

"We're down to twenty minutes before the League shows up in force, PQ. You gotta blow that rainbow and get out of there. The League is sending in something they've built called the *Yamato*. Some kind of space battleship secret project. ETA twenty. They will retake the city with that kind of support."

"Can the Behemoth take it out?"

Yeah, Rashid bought another Behemoth. I didn't even ask for it. Didn't ask how much it cost, either. But I'm glad it's in-game. Hopefully we get more use out of this one. I'm optimistic, because Rashid, to my surprise, is not manning it this time. He actually hired a Russian semi-pro for that duty.

I'm following the barrel of my MX4 down into the shadowy platforms of the subway. The walls are all tagged with meaningless social justice phrases. The place looks like a toilet. And yeah, there are homeless bots here, piles of feces, and if you look real close, needles and crack pipes.

Fun, huh?

"Negative, PQ. My team is doing nerd research and if the *Yamato* is what we think it is… then it's a real game-changer. Bristling with guns including a big one, from what the old cartoons are showing us. It's coming down now and deploying fighter cover ahead of its approach. We're trying to hit it with an ion cannon Rashid just erected over Caliphate City, but we can't get the firing solution and we're about to lose our engagement window. So make the explosive magic happen, or pull back now if you still want your little Sherman's March to the Sea, Martian-style."

She might be my online nemesis, but she's a sister from another mother, that's for sure. Sherman's March. That's exactly what I'm trying to pull. Except I'd forgotten exactly who did it. The Greek stuff was distracting me. But Sherman's March was based on Xenophon's Ten Thousand.

"Roger. Okay. Order all units to scatter," I instruct Enigmatrix. "Pull the armor back and set the new rally point. Then back the infantry off. Have them ruin everything on their way out. Scorched earth in effect."

"What about you?" she asks.

"We're gonna finish here and knock out the arch. Besides being a cultural monument that gives them all kinds of points, it's also their defensive shield. They can power it up and knock out any air support. So we've gotta take it out."

"I understand. League ground forces staging three miles west of your position. Looks like they want a big fixed battle as soon as their toy arrives."

"Well they ain't gonna get one today. We're just here to break their stuff and run."

We cut the chat and I concentrate on the subway tunnels. We deploy into a tactical wedge with MarinePvtDrake taking point. He points the big smart gun into the darkness ahead and we advance cautiously.

"Looks like they cut power down here," says PVTHudson. "Real scary, huh?"

"You think there're any bugs down here?" asks Frost as we pass long dimly lit corridors and wide empty platforms.

No one replies.

My guess is they're half hoping there are. That's their thing. But we don't need that right now. We need to hit the arch and boogie.

"We've gotta get down on the tracks to go forward," announces Hudson after a quick map check.

"Switch on your lights," orders the mostly low-chatter Marine-CorporalHicks.

Suddenly everybody's got lights coming from their helmets and armor. A vast tunnel stretches away in front of us. Halfway down, PVTHudson announces, "We've got movement!"

"Really?" says Frost in disbelief.

"Tighten up. Drake get ready," orders Hicks. "Where is it, and don't tell me all over the place!"

Hudson doesn't say anything for a long second.

"Really, Hudson?" asks Frost over the chat.

It's too bad they're using their Colonial Marines cosplay gear. Most troops in *WarWorld* standard kit can switch to low-light imaging or IR.

"Hudson… where are they?" asks Hicks, almost with disgust.

"You're not gonna like this… but yeah… they're all around us. Good news is… there're only three of them."

Something comes flying out of the darkness ahead of us. It somersaults, leaps and twirls. It's a beautiful woman with red hair, and she lands a perfectly timed roundhouse on Drake.

Drake takes the damage and then buttstrokes the ninja girl with his smartgun. She goes sprawling in front of him.

"Hey man, that's Black Widow from the comic books!" Hudson says.

Drake unloads on the prone figure with a short burst from the massive smart gun.

"Not anymore."

Hudson laughs, and I'm pretty sure he's about to say "Marines" when he gets hit by a giant hammer that carries him off into the darkness.

"Ow!" he cries over chat. "I just got hit for... half my health."

I turn and unload on a caramel-skinned girl wearing a scant amount of Viking armor. Above her avatar floats the gamertag La Thor. I put most of the MX4's magazine into her breast plate. Full auto does little damage.

Frost, on the other hand, steps in and lights her up with the flamethrower.

"What the hell!" says the player running Hicks. "I just got hit with an arrow. And I'm asleep. Who the hell uses a bow and arrow?"

"Uh... that guy with the bow," says Hudson over chat. "Comin' in from behind, sir."

"Yeah, and this flamethrower ain't doin' beans on the Viking chick," says Frost.

I slap in another magazine and see my move. I turn and engage the archer, an overweight lesbian with purple hair and fleshy arms. She's drawing back for another shot. And obviously she's using some kind of tranq arrow.

La Thor's hammer comes flying back through the darkness and just barely misses my head. I hear the character make some sort of grunt and I realize she's going to smash me over the head from behind.

The fat lesbian fires.

I go prone while swapping mags.

The arrow passes in the darkness overhead and nails La Thor. Over local ambient I hear the player running La Thor ask, "Really, FatArrow?" and then a loud thump.

I pull the trigger on a fresh mag and use all the bullets in my magazine to ventilate the puffy archer. She goes down more easily than the rest of this fruitcake clan.

Over messages in type I see FatArrow proclaim, "I died of Patriarchy... LULZ!"

Hicks's sleep status effect won't time out for another two full minutes. We don't have the time, so we just carry him. At the end of the tunnel we find a space-age-looking subway car alongside a platform. Curling stairs go upward.

"We go up there and we'll find the truck. What do we do after that, sir?" asks Hudson. "We'll be up in the middle of goony bird central. No support."

With the rest of my army pulling out, there's no way we can get out of here. I'm just about to say, "Die in place," when Hicks comes over chat to report that we can probably uses the subway to boogie.

"Hudson and I will get it operational. Probably have to hack it with a minigame… but we'll get it running. You guys go up there and finish the job."

Agreed.

We take the stairs and emerge into the hazy Martian daylight. Sporadic gunfire and explosions come over ambient, but it's distant. The League is losing their targets of engagement as we pull out of the ruined city like the ghosts of Mongol hordes.

I lean over the concrete abutments that block the station entrance from the park and see the combat engineer vehicle we brought to demo the arch. High-yield explosives will be inside.

"Frost, you take the turret in the vehicle. Drake… set up a base of fire from here. I'll plant charges and we'll go back down. Got it?"

They do.

For the most part it goes down just like that. Most of our units have fallen back to the edges of the burning city and are preparing to execute a scatter. Still, as I pull the charges from the engineer's truck inventory and get them attached to the base of the arch, some COEXIST Troopers, still in the area, spot me.

They come in firing subcompact automatics with no range. Frost cuts them down as he pivots the gun turret from left to right. But more are coming, and StrongIronWoman is streaking across the sky toward our location from some other battle along the city's fringe.

"Let's boogie!" I shout.

Drake lays down fire from the smartgun as more COEXIST Troopers try to swarm our location. It's close and hot and we're down tunnel as quick as we can to reach the subway car, which Hicks assures us is ready to move.

We're firing and falling back along the platforms, cutting down black-and-red riot troopers in the muzzle flash-lit darkness. Someone throws a Molotov cocktail at us and the flames throw shadows in among the bright flashes. A snarling rioter comes at me from out of the darkness, and I engage up close and personal. The guy goes down and two more firing from nearby send bullets smashing into the support column I'm hiding behind.

I'm out of ammo for the M4. I ditch it and draw my .45 as they close. The laser dot lands on one, and I put two rounds in. The other is so close I fire wildly and blow the top of his skull off, among other horrible things that happen to the rag-dolling avatar.

"Problem is the choo-choo only goes deeper into enemy territory."

I assume he means the subway car, and what other choice do we have.

"Let's roll."

"All aboard the choo-choo," giggles Hudson.

We board the last car. Over chat I ask Apone for his loc.

"In the bird, sir. We can pick you up."

The futuristic subway train begins to pick up speed rapidly as we leave the rioter-swarming station with Drake firing dry. The smartgun makes an ominous humming blur as we shoot down the tunnel, indicating it's gone empty.

"Hey…" asks Hicks soberly, over chat. "Did you set off the charges?"

"Oh yeah!" I equip the detonator from inventory and left-click the trigger.

The lights in the subway flicker on and off as a distant explosion erupts through the digital rock and ground strata. The train rocks back and forth a bit in the moments that follow. I can only imagine that massive rainbow arch raining down in chunks across the freaky city.

My mom and dad never talked much about the democratic socialist world before the Meltdown... but if even half that SJW nonsense was actually serious, then it must have been a real freak show.

"Company..." notes Hicks over chat.

StrongIronWoman is zooming down the tunnel after us.

Chapter Thirty-Four

We're low on ammo. StrongIronWoman uses some kind of rocket attack that ravages the back of our speeding subway car. Flares spark from her hands and feet as she lands in her power armor suit amid the swiss-cheesed ruins of the rearmost car.

Hudson unloads what remains of his ammo. I reply with the .45 Longslide and get ricochet flashes off her shiny lavender-and-silver armor. Hudson burns through his last mag and cries, "Outta tricks, sir!" on chat.

I toss some C4 and shout "Run!" because she's coming after us. I don't even make it ten steps or see if anyone else is moving before I left-click the detonator for the C4 and take beaucoup damage in the resulting explosion. Most of it is shrapnel, and my VR helmet is whining and popping. The game is simulating a sudden loss of hearing.

The subway car continues to shoot down a dark tunnel. Then we're above ground in a sudden vertigo-inducing moment. This isn't a subway... it's a bullet train. We're racing along an aboveground rail system speeding across the terraformed Martian valley that is the home field of the Geek League.

"Ferro, need extraction. ASAP."

StrongIronWoman is darting all around the back of the flaming train. Hovering and keeping pace with us. I can't hit her to save my life as she keeps up her dancing. But her armor is smoking and ruined, trailing debris from a dozen places. I'm just hoping for a lucky hit.

We pass under a weird canyon arch made of ancient Martian rock. StrongIronWoman smacks straight into it—and busts right out the other side, sending rock showering out and over the speeding train.

The livestream replay networks will run this clip for two solid days. TWITCHNN will make it one of their clips of the year. Or so I'll find out later. Much, much later.

We enter a series of tight turns and dips that turn the train into an out-of-control roller coaster, but StrongIronWoman tracks us and keeps firing pulsed energy bursts from her open gauntlets.

Then the Colonial Marines' desert-skinned iconic dropship looms behind her, and in a wail of repulsors and engine noise, it deploys its rocket launchers.

StrongIronWoman is unaware of its lethal presence on her six. She closes in for the kill. We're without the ability to reply in lead, and now we're just dodging fire and retreating back up the speeding train.

Behind her I see CPLFerro salute from the cockpit, a cynical smile beneath her mirrored aviator shades. Then the dropship fires multiple rockets, smoke trails erupting behind them. The dropship dances as the train weaves through a tight canyon.

But the missiles go wide and squirrel away in all directions.

StrongIronWoman must be running some kind of static EM jamming software.

A second dropship appears. This one is more the *WarWorld* standard Albatross variant.

"Hello, my friend," says Rashid over chat. "Of course I am here to rescue you and look like a hero, as we discussed."

StrongIronWoman pivots in midair and is now firing backward at both bogies. Missiles streak out from her wrists and smash into the Colonial Marines' dropship. One engine goes up in a sudden explosion, sending black smoke pluming up and streaking away from the wing, but Ferro keeps the craft crabbed sideways and moving forward, intent on her target. The player tagged CPLSpunkmeyer opens up with a door gun on the flying superhero. Bright flashes of ricochet erupt all across StrongIronWoman's armor, the tracks, and the speeding train.

A moment later the train dives down into a steep canyon and both the dropship and StrongIronWoman struggle to adjust altitude, nearly ramming into one another before following. It's like watching circus trapeze artists switching places above you at two hundred miles an hour. Or it's what I imagine that would look like.

"Enigmatrix..." I've brought up the tactical chat. It really doesn't matter what happens here. We've smashed their cities and my units should be moving on to their next objectives.

"Enigmatrix here," she replies.

"Phase two of the operation..." I prompt. She's running strategic and command and control. I'm just the tip of the spear.

But it is my plan.

"You were right, PQ. And I'll admit I thought you'd be dead wrong on this. Geek League formed up on the valley floor ready to do battle. Thought they were going to get a big old engagement. All the streaming networks even sold big advertising rates on the airtime. But we're scattering, as you directed. And they don't know what to do about it." She seems happy with all the chaos and frustration the corporations and gaming networks must be undergoing right now. "My guess is they're still waiting to see if we'll come at them from all directions."

"Probably," I agree as I watch Rashid try to acquire the armored superhero. He edges his Albatross forward, gun pods spooling up into an urgent whine beyond the thunder of the train's passage. Then he pushes full forward on the engine throttles and drives at the seemingly floating StrongIronWoman like a bull spitting fire and poison. He adds more power and smashes right into her.

She flares her rockets and grabs the Albatross's nose canopy.

"Uh... Rashid," I warn over chat.

"No problem, Question. I've got her now."

He noses over into the rocks below and smashes the dropship, his avatar, and StrongIronWoman all over the red Martian rocks of the canyon.

"That's one way to do it," quips Hudson over chat.

Chapter Thirty-Five

When I leave the Cyber Warfare Center it's just a few minutes before dawn. Everything in the Gold Coast zone, and all of Calistan at that moment, is quiet. A deep kind of quiet. The kind where you just have to stand there and listen to the quiet and wonder if the world will ever come back to life. And then you realize the silence is so complete it's deafening.

I slide behind the wheel of the Porsche Rashid gave me and try to figure out how to start it. Rashid had it delivered while we were fighting the Geek League.

In the east, over some mountains, the sky begins to turn a soft shade of blue. The hill of palaces, where princesses like Samira sleep on beds the rest of the world can only dream of, remains in shadow.

I don't hate her for that.

I want to. The way I hate Rashid. But I don't. I can't.

I start the Porsche and pulled out onto PCH. I'm the only one on the road at this time of the morning. The only one other than a lone street sweeper, leaving the streets wet and clean. I drive onto the peninsula, thread some old docks and ancient apartment towers, and find the small bridge that leads onto Rashid's apocalypse-soon-to-be paradise island.

It's not for Samira. She probably has no idea what she's getting into. I feel bad for her.

Nothing will ever be hers. Nothing will ever be theirs.

Everything will always be Rashid's.

And I'm tired.

I park on the empty island in front of the dock leading down to the sailboat. Out in the bay, a dolphin, or a porpoise maybe, swims placidly through the water. Then it dives down and is gone.

I go down the dock and onto the boat.

The bottle of bourbon, half full, is right where I left it. I consider a drink. But I don't. I'm too tired.

In my room I find a neatly folded blanket and pillow. I guess Mario stopped by. I kick off my shoes and lie down, listening to the water lap gently against the hull. And soon I'm asleep.

Chapter Thirty-Six

I walk away from that place. That old place. That monastery—no, manor house—sinking into the mud and stagnation beyond the slaughtered village. That place of giant snakes and other monsters. And all the corpses I left behind, slain in the dark passages beneath it all.

Just like that angel.

I walk away.

I know I am someone else. Some other person with some other life. I know that.

But this life… the life here in the valley. The life as this samurai… it feels right. I can smell the dust and the forest and feel the quiet heat of the sun on my skin.

I make my way through the swamp, and soon the land rises and climbs broken rocks, taking me up into an ancient forest. Tall pines cluster. I hear birds. A few. And I continue smelling the scent of the wood and the dust of the day that lies over everything. It's a pleasant smell. Like sandalwood almost. It reminds me of the very essence of summers long gone.

And for a moment I connect with that other someone. That person I may really be. The summers they remember… or rather… the feelings those memories evoke within them.

It's the smell of old books. Yellowed pages of comic books found and hoarded like pirate treasure. I remember the rasp of each carefully turned page beneath my fingers. Sitting in a room with old model cars on the walls. A bookcase that seemed like something more. Like a treasure chest… and a gateway to many, many other worlds. A single bed. A window staring out into trees and other houses.

A neighborhood that was known and could have been counted as the entire world.

Summer.

And just as quickly as the memory of that long-lost moment came upon me, it's gone for the samurai who finds himself on a trail of blood and vengeance.

I am standing on an ancient forest path. Great gnarled roots twist and wind up out of the ground. And the great trees above, oaks, carve a hall I know I must follow. A hall that leads to the temple of evil where I will find and slay this Alucard.

But for a moment I struggle to hold on to that summer comic-book memory. And even as I demand I hold on… it slips away.

Like sand through my fingers.

Like a missing clue.

Like losing the truth.

I know there was so much more to that life I remembered, that other me, than what I can barely sense now. There were…

…

…

…things I know and cannot name.

Like I am in some kind of prison that denies me the freedom to know those memories of who I once was.

But they were real. All of it was real to whoever I was. Once and long ago.

And this life… the samurai's life here in this lost valley with a strange keep on the border, and dark dungeons, and real monsters and brave warriors… this too also seems a kind of real. And if I just let it, it will be as real as I'll ever need. And all things that were in that comic-book-summer moment will be gone. And this life, the life of wandering adventure… this is what lies ahead for all the days I might count.

But that's not right.

What... is possible?

And that too is a kind of hope.

As though eternity and nostalgia are somehow one.

I continue on through this lonely forest, knowing darker times lie ahead. And I am not afraid of what I might find. I only fear forgetting what I once knew.

Chapter Thirty-Seven

The dark woods grow close along the road that winds through the tall trees in this part of the deserted forest. In time the sun begins to fall into the east and thick clouds come to stand between the pines and its parting rays. The road reduces itself to little more than a narrow trail as it winds up carved steps onto a high plateau. By twilight, fog and mist clutch at the dirt and the trees.

In the distance I can see the outlines of a small building. It's raised on stilts. It's made up of large curving timbers and thin walls. Steps rise to a door made of paper. From within comes the glow of fire and light. It is the opposite of the murk that consumes the forest as twilight surrenders to night.

"You have reached the Lost Inn," says the smoke-and-bourbon voice from nowhere but my head. And immediately I think the voice must've meant the Last Inn. But my memory says differently.

The Lost Inn.

Some forlorn bird calls out in the gloaming as I stand watching the small silent building lying along the forest trail. Another bird answers from a short distance off. But there is no comfort or warmth in these things. It is as though they have each wished each other good luck as the night comes on. Knowing the other will need it. Uncertain if they shall call out to one another again.

As in… *I hope to see you in the morning.*

I make for the inn. And while I do not rest my hand on my sword, I know where it is.

I mount the wide wooden steps and hear their almost hollow thump beneath my sandals. I slide back the paper door and step into a bare room.

A stranger in a hooded cloak sits at a low table. A small bowl of steaming soup waits before his bowed head. To the side of the bowl are a clay bottle and a tiny cup filled with clear steaming liquid. Next to one wall, a small hearth and brazier are filled with glowing coals. An old woman, hunched over, stirs a pot and sings some soft song that seems off-key. Or atonal. And yet calm.

"Another visitor," she mumbles. "On such a night as this... rare indeed."

She takes up a bowl from near the fire and ladles soup into it.

"There is a stone well out back. You may draw and clean. I shall have your soup and a hot drink ready by the time you return."

She returns once more to her singing.

I drop my roll but keep my sword. I cross the long hut to another paper door at the rear of the building. Out back lies an old well. The fog has come close and seems almost a living thing in the twilight. It rolls and roils and smothers all sound. I hear neither bird nor bat. And yet I feel as though there are things out there in the fog. Things that wander and watch, and yes... even wait.

Or maybe it is just the trunks of the trees that look like the legs of cyclopean giants out there in the gathering mists.

I draw ice-cold water from the ancient stone well and splash it across my face and chest. Then I drink. It is so cold and clear, it reminds me how dry and thirsty I was from my long hours on the road.

I return to the hut.

Inside I feel warm. Not safe. I look back at the fog. It seems to come closer to the hut. As though it wants to follow me, but will only go so far. As though the old hut remains an island in the forest that is like a sea where things live beneath the surface.

The smell of the savory soup draws me away from the mesmerizing movements of the fog. And to shut the paper screen is to shut out all that the forest hides.

On the long low table where the hooded stranger merely hovers over his soup, I find a bowl and bottle waiting for me. Also a tiny cup. The old woman crosses from the hearth and takes up the bottle.

"Be careful..."

And there is a very long pause between that and what she says next.

"The bottle is very hot."

As though the two statements are separate things to be considered. Being careful. And that the bottle is very hot.

I look up at her. It is not the few teeth in her crooked smile. Or her weathered face etched by a thousand lines. No. It is the eyes. Completely white. As though she is blind.

She smiles at me knowingly.

Then straightens with effort and a soft groan.

She hobbles off into the darkness of another room I hadn't noticed.

Only the hellish orange light from the brazier illuminates the room now. The shadows cast by the hood of the man opposite me seem to make him swim and move. Like the fog beyond the paper walls.

He reaches out one long hand, takes up a spoon, and begins to eat.

The soup is bright yellow with chicken broth. Small green onions and strands of saffron dance within its depths.

Its aroma is the very essence of savory.

I try it.

It's delicious.

For a long while the stranger and I eat our soup in mutual silence. I try the liquid in the cup and find it to be a hot liquor, almost vinegary. But it pairs well with the soup, which I eat by drinking from the bowl, for there is no utensil for me.

When the soup is gone I set the bowl aside. The hooded stranger is still taking long raspy sips from his spoon. In time, he finishes.

Each of us turns to the liquor, and after a long moment he asks me, "You seek the temple, Samurai?"

My cup hovers at my lips.

Wait.

Consider.

"Yes," I admit. And nothing more. Because who knows if the hooded stranger isn't working for Alucard. The priest himself.

His head is bowed. His features are hidden beneath the hood. And I am acutely aware of my sword lying on the floor next to me.

"You're in over your head and you don't even know who you are?" says the hooded man, his head still lowered.

"Then who am I?" I ask.

I hear the hiss of the brazier from across the room. Some sudden shadow shifts. And in that moment I have drawn the sword like lightning. The blade's angular tip hovers just beneath the gaping void that is the hood of the stranger across the table.

"What you will be..." the smoky bourbon voice seems to rasp from within the darkness, "...you are now becoming."

The sword gleams in the barest of light. It is steady and true and wavers not in the least. But the hooded figure does not move.

And then he speaks. "To reach the temple you must defeat the Baron. It is as simple as that."

"I have no idea what any of that means."

"It means," says the hooded figure after a long pause. "That evil exists. And to find its source you must start with one of its many forms. Tonight... if you wish... I can take you through the castle of the Baron. At its end lies the way to the temple... and of course..."

He chuckles softly.

"There you will find Alucard, if you truly wish to."

I wait. Weighing everything from pushing my sword through his face, to just leaving. And even why I am here and why it's so important to destroy a man I only met once, in passing, as he ran down a simple girl and made his escape from a keep lost along the border.

Why is that so important? some other voice asks me.

Because she was someone, I answer. And I don't know why that's important. I just know that it is.

Because she was someone.

Because no one should die in the street. And because someone must exact justice.

"All right," I mutter. "Take me to this castle. Let's go meet this... Baron."

That soft dry chuckle mocks me as I lay my sword on the table. Like dead leaves on a grave. Driven by an autumn wind. Like smoke and bourbon.

"I said... take you through."

And then a hand appears from within the cloak and drops two strange dice on the table between us.

"I am death, and death takes you."

Chapter Thirty-Eight

Death stares across the table at me. Not that I can see his eyes. I can only feel them coming from the darkness beneath the hood. They bore into me from somewhere in that darkness.

"Let us dispense with this old woman's brew and drink something more appropriate," whispers Death. From out of the folds of his cloak he produces a bottle. It's filled with amber liquid. On the label is a word. Clevinger's.

I know it. I know its taste. I know the cheap burn it will give as it goes down. But I have no memory of ever drinking it.

I glance up from the bottle, and when I look at the table once more I see two cut-crystal glasses. Death uncorks the bottle and pours two fingers for each of us.

We drink.

I hear that dead-leaf-rustling chuckle once again.

But the hot fire of the bourbon is good, and it's the opposite of the fog now peeking through the small cross-barred window along the far wall of the room.

"The game begins…" announces Death. "You are summoned to the castle of the Baron."

This is an odd game.

I reach for the crystal glass and absently take a drink.

On the long low table before my eyes sprouts a gloomy forest in miniature. The tiny trees are twisted and dark, reaching up for us like tiny skeletal hands. The landscape is gray and blue as though revealed through a pale moon on a cold night. It's like some elaborate model. Except it is real and alive. I see yellow eyes within the forest down there. Dark and shadowy things move about. Small bats dart from stands of dead trees to other twisting and withered stands.

Stranger and stranger…

It's incredible, and I bend close to study the dark hunched shapes moving through the woods like lumbering shadows. The eyes of dark birds watching from the dead limbs of twisting trees.

At the end of the table between us, a bridge begins to throw itself over a mist-shrouded chasm. All of it in a fantastically minute and shocking reality. The detail is incredible. As though it is a model of some very real place. Or some imagination even more real.

Beyond the bridge rises a castle that is more tall than immense. Its very form conveys an imperious grandeur that seems to despise all beneath its transcendent glare. A tower rises from its center. And just across the bridge lies a gate that looks more like a gaping mouth than a portal.

Still holding that crystal glass of Clevinger's just below my lips, marveling at every detail within the tiny living world that has taken shape on the old table beneath us, I must have whispered, or sighed to myself.

"What did you say?" asks Death.

"It's incredible."

I set the glass down and see a tiny me standing before the bridge. Waiting to cross the yawning chasm.

Then Death reaches out one long and bony finger while the rest of his claw holds the luminescent glass of bourbon. Pointing at the tiny me, the samurai beyond the bridge waiting in front of the castle, Death says, "You."

After a long moment I ask, "What do I do?"

Death takes a swig of cheap scotch. A breathy *ahhhh* emits from within the hooded void. Then… "Why, you play the game, Samurai.

And if you win… you advance to the temple. Lose, well… I can only keep her at bay for so long."

I hear a thump. Not a small thump. But a large one. Distant. Out there in the fog and the darkness.

"And I must tell you," chuckles Death. "Even your fabled blade would be no match for her. Not against the Black Queen. Not yet. It's not time."

My eyes catch the remaining scotch in my glass. Concentric circles emanate out toward the delicate crystal rim with each distant strike.

THUMP.

Again.

THUMP.

The silence between these titanic thumps is deafening. Or ominous. Both have intersected and become one.

THUMP.

"And how do I win?" I ask Death.

The tremendous dull crashes have ceased. And if that should have comforted me, it doesn't. Because whatever is making them is still out there in the mist.

"Slay the Baron. And find the key."

"And I'll find him in there," I say, pointing at the menacing-looking little miniature castle.

Death laughs softly.

"He's waiting for you, Samurai. And that was a hint. Slay him. Of course he's going to try to kill you. But in this part of the game you're not really supposed to know that. Which is rather ridiculous. I mean… c'mon. The Baron. Foreboding castle. Obviously, anyone can figure out he's a vampire, Samurai. The very dread that hangs over this forsaken castle tells you all you need to know. Wouldn't you agree?"

I hadn't really put that together. But I'm just getting started. And now that I look at the whole gloomy scene of the haunted-looking castle, the dark tower, the gloomy forest… yeah, Death is right. How could it be anything else but a vampire?

"All right then…" I say as I pour a touch of scotch into my glass. I nod at Death and receive the barest of movements from the hood. I fill his glass. "Game on then. I enter the castle."

I watch as my plucky little avatar crosses the yawning bridge. Slowly the immense castle moves closer to the center of the table as first I approach the gates and then pass through them.

Tiny little torches, just a few, wait within a revealed courtyard beneath our gaze. I peer down and see crumbling gray steps rising up to the front doors. I study the scene on the table, watching for enemies or traps I might fall into. Focusing on where I am, as opposed to the lifelike detail of the fantastic castle. Bats cross the towers and rooftops. Figures move beyond high windows, briefly crossing through the wan illumination from some source within. Creating some story I've yet to discover. Blood-red light shines out into the gloom from behind one window. Others are of massive stained-glass. I try to examine the pictures, but their images scramble my mind the more I study them. As though the things depicted are somehow so wrong, my mind refuses to organize the information.

THUMP.

"Hurry," murmurs Death drolly as he takes a long slow slip from the Clevinger's. "We only have all night."

I point to the oaken double doors bound in black iron.

"There. I'll go there."

Slowly, cautiously, on the table beneath my eyes, the little figure representing me advances up the wide stairs and knocks on the dark doors. They swing back with a groaning creak… but there is no one there.

I nod at Death and enter the castle.

An entry hall lit by candles and draped in rich tapestries reveals itself within. It's just as detailed as the outside. I can see the reflections on the beautifully checkered floors, the patterns woven into the tapestries. But the cones of light thrown by the tiny miniature candelabras illuminate only so much of the room, leaving shadows everywhere else.

A double door at the end of a long hall seems the only choice available to me.

At that moment I hear an organ. In a minor key. Playing some mournful tune. A dirge perhaps. But it's more grand than that. A funeral requiem.

At the double doors, tiny me waits. I take a deep breath and whisper, "Go ahead," as I watch the table, conscious that Death is watching me.

The doors open and the small samurai advances through. A room leaps up and into shadows. Stone gargoyles watch over tiny me with a malevolence I can see from here. But they're only statues. Other exits and stairs rise up into a gloom I cannot yet penetrate. Maybe I have to go there for those places to be revealed on the living map the old table has become.

To the right of my miniature self is a long candle that is brighter than the rest. It waits on a small table beside two open doors.

I merely move my eyes toward that area and the samurai advances cautiously. Beyond the doors is a dining room. On the far wall, a grand pipe organ rises up into the shadows. A tiny sumptuous feast is set out on a table laden with minuscule silverware, little platters and petite fine bone china. Again, the detail is remarkable. I can make out the individual forks and knives.

Seated at the organ is a man. He is hunched over, enraptured with his work on the three tiers of bone-white ivory keys. His head rises and falls with the haunting chords of the requiem.

And then he stops. Straightens as though only just now sensing my presence. Slowly he turns from the keyboard, and what I see is the classic vampire. Except not camp. Not cheap. Not sideshow second-rate B-movie actor slumming it for a check.

What I see is...

Trim. Powerful. Imposing. Cold. Merciless. Cruel.

And evil.

Death picks up one of the dice and tosses it onto the table, startling me.

The vampire glares into my eyes.

Not tiny me's eyes.

My eyes.

And now I'm in that room. No longer at the table with Death. I'm there beneath his gaze. Being consumed by it. Devoured already. I feel someone, people, many, pushing past me. Filling the room. Taking their seats at the table where the feast is set and only the main course is missing.

The eyes of the vampire grow, blocking out the raven-haired beauties in tight capes, full lips pouting and parting to reveal fangs. Dark eyes sparkling as they watch me. All becomes fog as the vampire's eyes grow and swell. Becoming the world. Becoming death.

I try to feel my hand. Try to find it. And when I do, there is no hilt like I desperately want there to be. Need there to be in this moment of being dominated and losing my very will.

But there is something in my hand. Something small. Polygonal. Cold and tiny.

I drop it to the stone floor and hear it as clear as I heard the cyclopean *thumps* out in the fog and the dark in the forest.

I hear the die rolling on stones. Finding the number that decides what happens next. Whether I win or lose. Live or die. It seems to roll forever, and still the vampire's eyes grow and grow.

"Twenty," murmurs Death.

And the trance is broken.

I pull Deathefeather from the scabbard at my belt.

And then it's game on.

All six of the vampire beauties are wearing hijabs now and they pull back their robes to reveal stunning bodies barely covered in black lace. For a moment I'm torn. But the flashing fangs gnashing in their faces draw me back from an abyss of lust.

Behind them, a satisfied smile washes across the vampire's ivory face… He smiles. And I know that smile. It's a prince's smile.

I'm frozen and I need to move. Now!

Serene Focus swims into view.

I hear simple strings pluck out a melody. Maybe even just three notes. Rain falls onto a pond. Slowly. Slower. Slow. I watch the individual drops fall and strike the water like small nuclear weapons on a winter afternoon.

It's beautiful.

I drive forward, leading with my elbow, sword held back. Leaping in, I strike suddenly at the first vampire bride, cutting her throat with a smooth swipe. Deep red blood paints the walls of the grand dining room. The other brides turn in slow motion, their silent screeching growing like some chorus of the damned. One comes at me, her hands now claws, her eyes greedy. The one whose throat I have slashed backs away from the fray, but she's not dead.

In some other part of my mind I realize this is extremely important.

But the one coming at me must be dealt with. Behind her, her ravening sisters spread out to surround me. I twist the katana and drive it into the closest one's chest. Her scream is abruptly silenced as she chokes on the steel I have sent through her. That look of ravening hunger is gone.

Only horror shows within coal-dark eyes sparkling in the candle-light.

That horror grows as I push Deathefeather out through her back, then plant my knee in her stomach and push her away. She collapses a very old woman, disintegrating into grave dust.

Gray hair. Sagging paper skin gone yellow. Shrunken cheeks.

Because of course… vampires must be staked in the heart. And in this game, Deathefeather counts as just such a stake.

The brides come on as the vampire towers above the carnage. I remove claws and slash throats and open abdomens from which no blood or gore flows. Though the vampire beauties are not slain, the wounds of the fabled blade burn like fire across their features. It is only when I choose an opportune moment to savage one in the heart that she is felled forever. Otherwise, despite their terrible wounds, they remain intent on my blood.

The last one comes at me crying, screeching. I've just finished one of the others and I'm exhausted, my lungs heaving like a bellows. The focus, that serene focus, is fading. Time is returning to normal. She comes at me and I have no defense other than to heave the blade from right to left. From east to west. I put all that remains of me into it. Everything. And I know there will be nothing left for the Vampire Prince. Nothing for the Baron who is someone else.

But the brides must be dealt with first.

The blade separates her voluptuous torso from the rest of her body. Blood sprays out across the walls, the rich red curtains, the black candles.

She goes down. Finally dead.

Legs planted, gasping for air, I turn and see that the vampire has disappeared.

Chapter Thirty-Nine

It's noon when I wake up.

And I definitely have game hangover.

Which is weird because I used to play games for nine to twelve hours at a time. Now... not so much. I'm starting to slip. Starting to feel it.

I wake up in a tangle. A tangle of a lone blanket and some dream I can't remember. And I'm pretty sure that's a metaphor for my life. I feel the urge to get a taxi, or even take the Porsche and get out of Calistan right now. Get to the border and get the hell out of here.

And then I remember two things.

I have an intense desire to...

...what?

Somehow make sure Rashid doesn't get away with everything.

And how are you going to do that? I ask myself. He owns a country. Chances are, he's getting away with it whether you like it or not. That and probably a lot more. And if you're lucky you'll take your five million in gold and try to forget what you had to do to get it.

"Yeah," I mumble as I pull on a pair of shorts. I head out onto the deck of the sailboat. Try and forget.

I jump into the waters of the bay.

And I feel alive. And okay.

And I think of the second thing. The second reason for not leaving. Chloe.

I swim for a while and think about her. And try to forget she tried to kill me. I think of the peace I felt lying her arms. I liked that. I liked her.

You don't even know her, I yell to myself.

That's thing number two. The second reason for not leaving Calistan just yet.

After my swim, I get dressed. Casual clothes and a polo t-shirt. Sunglasses. Seems to be the look of the Gold Coast. Why not fit in if you're going to work for the CIA?

I drop behind the wheel of the Porsche and drive up to Rashid's house. I'm not looking for Rashid, I'm looking for the driver.

"*Hola, señor,*" he says. He's in the driveway, washing yet another of Rashid's playthings. He smiles. Like he's genuinely happy to see me.

"*Hola,* Juan." That makes him smile even more. That I have remembered his name. I have a feeling the friends of Rashid aren't big on other people. Especially people who aren't like them. Little people. Muslim. But not rich. Not the top. At the top, then you're someone.

"El Jefe is gone, *señor.*"

I haven't really planned out what I'm gonna say. I open my mouth and have nothing. I stare off toward the coast and try to figure out what exactly I'm trying to accomplish. He's holding a soapy mitt. He waits.

"I'm not here to see him. And… in fact, I don't want him to know I was here… if that's cool?"

As I say it, I realize that's a pretty big matzo ball to float. Who says this guy isn't Rashid's most loyal servant? And who the hell am I to ask him to betray his boss?

I don't wait for an answer. It wouldn't matter anyway. "I don't know how to… ask… what I need…"

"Just ask, my friend," he says, putting down the soapy mitt and watching me. Is there a patient kindness there? Or am I just hoping there is? Because I'm too deep inside Calistan if there isn't.

How deep?

Deep enough to disappear.

There's nothing in this that makes me believe I haven't totally messed up. Yet. And acutely, I'm aware I'm in a foreign country doing stuff I'm not sure I should be doing.

But it's just the calm way he said "my friend" that convinces me I can go forward with what I'm here to do.

No bull. Just two men talking. Mutual respect.

"I met a girl the other night…"

He smiles knowingly at this, his face blossoming into a grin. Like he respects me even more.

"It's not like that." Except it is. It is like that. I met her in a brothel. So it's exactly like that.

"I'm sure you take… Rashid's… friends there. Where he goes at the end of the night. I imagine some nights, right? House over near the bay. Blonde runs it. There was a girl there… Maybe you know her, know of her, but she's not… Muslim." I look around as though I'm guilty of some crime. "She's… one of you."

"*Mexicana?*" he asks.

I nod.

"What was her name?"

"Chloe."

He nods. "I'll ask around. Don't worry… it's between you and me," he says.

Chapter Forty

Back at the Cyber Warfare Center that night, I log into the strategic operations net for Calistan's online presence in *Civ Craft*.

Enigmatrix catches me on chat.

"So your plan worked."

"Alexander the Great," I reply.

"Never heard of him."

"He was a general back in the day. Basically, he hit cities hard by using the principle of mass. He'd bring all his forces together at the critical moment of his choosing and then he'd scatter them until the next battle. Here, the Geek League saw us coming to fight, and they thought they were choosing the battlefield—but really they were just giving us room to run amok and waste their city. And now everyone's scattered and headed for the next objective."

"The Cylon Basestar," she says. "We should be in place within two hours."

I bring up tactical and look at all our units. They really are scattered—all across the Martian plateau and foothills on the eastern side of the valley. If you had no idea where they were going, you'd think we were just raiding. In fact, the main elements of the Geek League's army have broken up to chase them down. Except most of our units are now closing in along a broad crescent, targeting a new clan's city. They call it the Basestar. The heart of the Cylon Republic.

"I haven't had much time to research," I said. "Who are these guys?"

"They are like really, really into machine intelligence. Big time. They claim the Meltdown was caused by a rogue AI. Tinfoil hat stuff if you look at their website. And they're really into retro sci-fi. Some crazy show back in the day, where machines tried to wipe out humanity, is really big to them. So all their tech trees went that way."

"What kind of units will we be facing?"

"Lots of ground troops." She sighs. "And artillery. Plus some decent air support. Nothing we can't handle if we hit them fast. And the Geek League is likely to redeploy that space battleship if they sense us going after any targets. No doubt they're just itching to use that thing. Good thing for us is it takes time for it to show up. So... hit hard, hit fast."

"What about the Behemoth?" I ask.

"Bringing it in by heavy lifter at the last moment with lots of air cover."

"Roger that. That's our key to getting inside the city. Once we're inside we can tear through it. Everybody goes straight for the other side. Do as much damage as possible, but keep going. Then scatter. Got it?"

"You tac commander on this one?" she asks hesitantly.

"Sounds that way."

Long pause.

"Better you than me." And I know she means Rashid. His ego would do anything to take all the glory. Pro players, like Enigmatrix, like me, we don't work with people like that. That type of behavior on the corporate teams gets identified, and weeded out.

I look around, even though I'm in my own gaming suite.

"Listen..." I say. "I know you... or I mean I don't really, Enigmatrix. But whatever you've got going on with Rashid... up there. That doesn't seem like you."

Long pause. Have I crossed a line?

"Like you said... you really don't know me," she says. "Right, PerfectQuestion?"

I *have* crossed a line.

"This is a game," she says, and I'm sure she isn't just talking about *Civ Craft*. "Everybody plays, just like in *WarWorld*, for their win. Not just the team's... but maybe your personal best. Regardless of how we run out teams and weed out the individualists, you play for your win whether you like it or not. And maybe sometimes that's what the team wants, y'know... it lines up with a victory, and then sometimes... sometimes it's what *you* want. Know what I mean?"

Not really.

But I tell her I do.

"Back in *WarWorld*, next season... we'll be enemies again," she says. "Right now we're friends. But that's just for right now, Question."

"Gotcha," I reply.

But I don't.

Not until much later will I really understand just how much I haven't gotten her at all.

* * *

Two hours later, all our forces are racing out of the Martian wastes like nomadic hordes. We're aimed straight at our OBJ: the Basestar.

On the vast arid red plain ahead of us, the Cylons' fantastic *Civ Craft* city rises up like some kind of postmodern wedding cake meets fusion reactor. Like two fat discs stacked one on top of the other. Someone said it's designed after a spaceship from whatever retro sci-fi they're into.

"Look at the size of that thing..." says PVTHudson over chat. I'm riding with the Colonial Marine clan once more. Tip of the spear for my assembling strike force. Below us is our task force of mixed light infantry fast-attack buggies and APCs filled with Calistani jihadis surrounding the lumbering Behemoth tank. Ahead, an armored scout force made up of mechs is racing in, trying to draw concentrated fire from elements inside the city. The space-ship. Whatever it is. Effectively, the scout force is our cavalry. It's their job to figure out where the enemy is, then we drive the spear in.

"How are we looking on strategic?" I ask Enigmatrix over the chat.

"They're aware you're coming in," she replies. "And they're trying to get players to log in like crazy for a response. But I estimate a good thirty minutes before they get their mecha response force involved. Until then you're fighting the locals—Cylon Centurions, they call them."

"Hey," chimes in Rashid from tactical. "We're spam-jamming their players' personal email accounts with tons of bogus emails. Hoping to clog up their inboxes so their clan can't get ahold of them. And we're trying to take down some of the social media channels by reporting them for community violations."

Rashid and the generals of Calistan are playing for keeps. Weaponizing the internet.

"Great job," I reply. And feel a little dirty for doing so.

CIA stuff, I remind myself.

Ahead, the Basestar has begun to hurl hot bolts of phased energy at us from turrets along the upper rim of the top disc. One of our lead fast-attack mules—our gun-laden light-armored vehicles—is struck. It explodes and flips end over end through the Martian sand.

I switch over to clan chat.

"Stay on target!"

The mechs cavalry force is coming up against an outer wall of the defenses surrounding the Basestar. On the map recon it looked small. From here on the ground, it's an immensely high barrier to surmount.

I tag the Behemoth and tell the Russian semi-pro running it, gamertag StreetThreepio, to take out the wall.

"Stand by," he replies in a nasal monotone.

A moment later the massive tank's relativistic gun fires. The monstrous weapon seems to literally inhale all the Martian dust around it, then expels it as the rail shot spits forth. The shot, barely visible, accelerates to incredible speed before slamming into the distant shimmering metallic wall guarding the Cylon Basestar.

The explosion is tremendous.

"Ground forces breaching…" comes the reply from a team leader.

Ahead, our air assets are making runs against the defense turrets along the rim of the fantastically gleaming base.

My plan is to keep the outer defenses busy and punch one tiny hole in the giant base, then charge through and come out the other side, ruining everything we can along the way. Then disappear back into the deep Martian wastes and return the next night to take out another Geek League city.

"We're through and heading for the target…" comes the voice of the clan commander who's first through the breach, his Middle Eastern accent thick and heavy.

"Take us over the top," I order CPLFerro. "MarineSgtApone, this is gonna get hot… we must clear the breaching point."

"Got it, sir. We're ready to move."

We're flying right in under the upper disk of the Basestar, skimming above the lower disk. There's some kind of massive flight hangar in the lower section. We just need to clear that and then our forces will flood inward.

The sky ahead of our dropship fills with turret fire. It's like we're suddenly falling into a web of energy.

"Breaking off!" cries the pilot. "No way through!"

Their defenses are heavier closer in. I didn't expect that. And I should have. Now we're racing across the desert back toward our own forces. An energy bolt from one of the turrets takes out the massive Behemoth on the desert floor. The thing explodes in a spectacular display of sparks flying in every direction.

So much for the Russian semi-pro.

I groan. "They must've taken an anti-armor round."

Enigmatrix lets me know we've just lost a very valuable piece of equipment. And our key to breaching the hangar deck. As if I didn't just see it myself.

"We need to pull back, PQ. Today's a no-go. They've got the *Yamato* inbound. It'll be here in a few, and we can't stand up to that thing."

I hesitate. Which I know is a bad thing for a commander to do. I give myself fifteen seconds to make a decision as I watch my forces get chewed up in front of the Cylons' Basestar.

Abort, or go all in.

I...

Rashid's voice comes over chat. "Move forward. I've got a surprise for their little space battleship," he cackles.

My finger hovers over the group broadcast key. I could order the general retreat. Override my employer. But this is Rashid's show, and I need a way to get him a win. According to the CIA. Who might be my only chance of getting out of Calistan, considering they're the only ones who know I'm in Calistan in the first place.

"What've you got, Rashid?" I ask. Smoking missile trails arc up and slam into the upper disc of the Basestar. Turret fire rains down on the advancing Calistani forces.

Two wolverines go up in sudden sparks down near the breach point. Now the Cylon Centurions are out of their trenches and lumbering forward with massive rifles. The Calistanis are scattering every which way as the bots come on firing on full auto. Some units are hunkering down and actually getting into full-fledged firefights with the walking metal Frankensteins.

All of this is not good. We're losing momentum. And momentum is what it's all about. Hit and run. Grab and go. We need to get through their Basestar in a timely fashion. I wait on Rashid two seconds more.

Nothing.

"All units..." I begin.

And just then I see the *Yamato* appear in the distant sky. Maybe three thousand feet up and coming in fast. She's already lobbing shots at us even from that extreme range.

"Rashid," breaks in Enigmatrix. "This is everything you've got. We lose here, that's it. They're gonna clean us up and roll all over Calistan in the next few hours if we don't execute a maneuver to either fight or flee in the next minute. Do you copy?"

"Executing space fold now…" announces Rashid.

In-game sound suddenly turns into a ghost freight train crashing through reality. Then something appears in the sky to the west. It comes in hot at five thousand feet and descending, streaking straight for the mess our lines are becoming.

"Uh, sir, what the hell is that?" asks Apone.

Many other players are asking the same thing in that wild and uncertain moment.

"We should get out of the way," prompts MarineCorporalHicks rather stridently. Which is true. The thing is streaking straight at us, nose first.

Over the command chat, Rashid is shrieking with laughter.

But it's PVTHudson whose game lore is deep. I've come to respect him as a player. But as a scholar of nerdstalgia, his kung fu is John Saxon. "That, my friends," he brays, "is the greatest space battleship of all time: the SDF-1."

Ferro jerks the heavy dropship out of the way just as the massive white-hot SDF-1 rips through half of the Cylon ground defenses and tears off a huge section of the Basestar. A sudden moment of vertigo overtakes me as the forward canopy of the dropship fills with the giant spacecraft gloriously slamming into the sand.

"Game on, my friends!" cried Rashid triumphantly. And then over private chat: "Uh, PerfectQuestion… I don't know how to work this thing. Can you come aboard and take over so we can fight the other battleship?"

Chapter Forty-One

"All forces..." I begin in group chat. "Form up around the SDF-1 and protect her until we can get her operational."

Thousands of Cylon bots are flooding out of the main superstructure of the Basestar. It's clear their objective is to board our battleship within the next few minutes.

I ask Ferro to take us in and dock near the command tower of our Calistani mega ship. We make a close pass near the bridge. Through the gaping window of the massive space battleship I see Rashid's avatar inside running from control station to control station.

Suddenly I get a personal text.

"Need help, buddy?" It's Kiwi.

How? No time...

I type back, "Definitely." And, "Thank you."

"Logging in," comes the reply.

I'm sure he's been watching the livestreams. Keeping an eye on me. He has to know things have gone massively wrong.

The dropship docks alongside the SDF-1's tall command bridge, and we disembark.

"Marines," orders Apone, "find a weapons station or whatever you can get your hands on. We've got to get this vessel into the air. But until then, we've got to fight."

We climb up two decks to the bridge. Rashid is waiting, still hustling about aimlessly through the massively overwhelming bridge filled with a variety of stations. Above us, holographic real-time displays of the engagement swim in midair.

I note a holographic display of the *Yamato*. It's just a few minutes out. The SDF-1 is already calculating a firing solution to take it out. But it still doesn't have lock on.

"Rashid, how do we fire this thing's weapons?"

Rashid doesn't answer. His avatar hunches over a control station. Then he curses over chat.

"Dammit!"

"What?"

"All the control stations have been locked out by minigames. The damn Russian developers who sold me this are screwing us and laughing behind our backs."

Then...

"We're dead on the sand, PQ."

I watch the incoming *Yamato*.

"Enigmatrix... what's going on out there?"

"Forward elements breaching the Cylon city. We're taking heavy losses but we're moving forward. But that makes no difference. I just got an old stream of that *Yamato* thing in action—they used it against some clan a couple of weeks ago. If that thing fires its main gun... we lose everything."

I watch the incoming data above our heads. Our firing solution is now in the yellow. But if we can't fire our weapons, it'll make no difference if it reaches green.

"Everyone take a station and unlock the minigame blocking access right now. Let me know when your stations are up."

Every avatar scrambles for a station on the bridge. The only one left is a big chair that seems to watch over all the other stations. I sit down in it and am rewarded with...

Captain's Station. Press Enter to Unlock.

I check the *Yamato's* holographic position again.

Total team kill is not an option here. Not just because getting disappeared into Calistan's secret police gulag is probably a real thing, but because I estimate we need to ruin at least three of the Geek League's cities to get them off Calistan's back. Just one isn't going to do it.

And yeah, the gulag thing too.

So there's that.

I hit enter.

The screen changes.

I'm staring at an absurdly simple screen. In the center is a triangular spaceship. Little more than a triangle, really. Everything is vector lines. A moment later, giant tumbling rocks come in from all sides of the screen. All of them headed at the spaceship. *My* spaceship.

Thankfully, a control schematic comes up and I get the basics of movement and thrust with the WASD keys. Except there's no reverse. Just thrust and turn. The return key is fire. That's it. I start shooting at the giant rocks as they tumble in at me. As soon as I hit them they break apart and I spend the next thirty seconds dodging them and reducing them to smaller and smaller chunks.

There are five waves of this when suddenly my ship gets a low fuel warning and a message urging me to land. The game shifts as the little starship falls toward a massive planet. All in side-scroll 2D. But falling nonetheless. Altimeter and speed, along with rate of descent, appear in basic digital readouts.

I thrust and send the ship speeding toward the planet's surface. My guess... I'll smash into the planet and come apart in all sorts of little sticks of debris just like those big rocks I smashed. I rotate the ship using the directional keys to get the engine falling first. Then I bring in the thrusters to slow the rate of descent. The first mountains I could have landed on had small platforms with bonuses should I land there, but my rate of descent was still too high and the approach vector was no good. Also gravity was kicking in.

"Get those terminals unlocked people, we ain't playin' games here!" shouts Apone over the chat.

Which doesn't help because I'm fairly sure I'm going to get one shot at sticking the landing, otherwise I'll probably have to do the five waves of smashing rocks all over again. Maybe. What if I'm totally locked out?

I throw in more thrust to counteract gravity and descend into a narrow canyon of green glowing lines. Time and altitude are running out.

The ground comes up fast and I go to full thrust to retard the descent. The engine is flaring at full and my index finger is numb from pushing the key so hard as though it might reward me with a little more counterthrust.

It doesn't and the descent still looks too fast, but the landing vector is good despite the gravitational pull that's making me drift.

The fuel cuts out just as the ship sets down.

I find myself wincing as I wait for the ship to explode in every direction. But that doesn't happen.

The screen goes dark. I've beaten the game.

Now I have access to the captain's menu.

All the stations on the bridge come up. I can see which ones are locked out and which ones are ready to go. I have a full tactical display of the surrounding area.

In the corner a message blinks repeatedly.

Space Fold Drive: OFFLINE.

Not sure what that is. Probably don't need it. I scan for weapons. I need them, and fast. At first it seems the SDF-1 is more of a carrier than anything else. It has fighters and hangar decks, all currently unmanned. Unless the fighters are bots, I probably can't get them into the air and engaging that battleship before it fires its main gun.

"*Yamato's* launching missiles!" announces Hicks. He's running the Combat Information Control panel.

I look up from the captain's screen. Above us, on the bridge tactical holograph, I can see several missiles streaking away from the ghostly image of the *Yamato*. Telemetric data trails alongside each one.

I re-check the captain's screen.

"We need to hit them now, PQ!" bleats Rashid petulantly. As though this should happen merely because he has spoken it.

We're still locked out of both of the SDF-1's shield systems. Something called an Omni-Directional Barrier and another system labeled the Pinpoint Barrier.

"Woot!" shouts Ferro over chat. "I got engineering unlocked. Powering up main engines now."

"Two minutes till impact," says Hicks. He's running the Combat Information Control panel.

"Whoever's got defensive stations, we need those up!" I shout. I feel useless as the captain. I'm used to running and gunning. Changing the game one bullet at a time. As I've said, vehicle combat is not my thing. And a giant spaceship is really just a big old vehicle.

"Uh, sir. Uh… I think I've almost got defense unlocked. Playing some old game called *Berzerk*." It's MarineSgtApone and he sounds distracted. "Uh… okay… got it. Station coming online now. Had to run away from a giant bouncing ball of death. Whoever made that game musta been on drugs."

In my captain's screen I see that the Pinpoint Barrier System is now online. And it has power from the engines.

"Sir… we got us a table," says Apone.

I look up from my screen and scan the digitally represented bridge in my HUD. In front of the main window, which shows a terrific air battle going on over the Cylon Basestar, a wide pool table-shaped block has risen up.

I leave the captain's chair and move my avatar toward it.

On its surface lies a digital schematic of the SDF-1. Projected points of impact from the incoming missiles appear all across its surface.

I have no idea how to use this.

Neither does Apone. "While you figure this out, I'm gonna see about unlocking damage control," he says. "Seems like that's about to be real necessary."

I nod and sit down at one of the table's three stations.

"Hey, Perfect."

I look up to see two new avatars skinned in Calistani battle dress. Above them float their tags.

Kiwi and JollyBoy.

"We just logged in and got permission from the muzzies to join up. Figured you needed help," says Kiwi.

"Yeah, PQ old buddy, old pal," says the ever-gregarious JollyBoy. He's managed to doctor his avatar with his standard Harlequin mask and perma-grin. "I was getting... how shall we say... ah! Rather broke in Monte Carlo. Can you believe it? I'm almost down to half my Super Duper Bowl winnings. But! Never fear! I have managed to meet the perfect woman. She's a wan little lass of an ultramodel with a penchant for sports cars and dangerous chemicals. I think we're going to settle down and farm... or something."

He almost dies with a laughter that devolves into a wheezing bout of coughing fits.

"I blame the Cubans," he hacks. "Brought home a case of cigars too. They're an investment."

"Jolly, you like ships right?" I ask.

"Love 'em. I've always fancied myself a pirate of sorts."

"Great. You're the captain now. Get us into the fight and take out that ship." I tag the approaching *Yamato*.

"Roger that, Mister Perfect. Hoist the mainsail, unlimber the guns. Top the mainsail and prepare to give 'em what for off the aft beam and I do say... I love a good aft beam and all, if you take my meaning."

Again with the wheezing laughter.

"We're kind of in a hurry here, Jolly."

"Oh, sorry." His avatar takes the captain's chair.

To Kiwi I say: "Let's stop some missiles."

Kiwi joins me, taking another station at the Pinpoint Barrier System interface table.

The lead inbound missile is streaking toward us across the desert floor. I move my mouse and a small shield of glowing white energy responds on the schematic below our gaze. I move it over the projected impact point of the missile. A second later, the fast-moving weapon smashes into the SDF-1, just barely missing the shield I put up.

On screen the ship rocks back and forth. Damage control alarms whoop in high-pitched tones. Other panels across the bridge light up like Christmas trees.

"Watch it, Kiwi," I mutter. "There's a finesse aspect to this little game. It's like it gives you a general area where it thinks the missile will hit. Then you've gotta adjust at the last second."

He maneuvers his shield disc to stop an inbound strike. Success. The missile disintegrates in a short flash of energy.

"Natch," he murmurs.

"Oh, that how it is?" I ask as I position my disc to catch the next strike. They're coming in faster now.

Kiwi's avatar nods.

"Game on, buddy. Winner buys the beers when we meet up after this."

"You got it, buddy."

"*Yamato*'s firing her guns," announces Hicks, without fanfare.

Moments later the ship begins to shudder from the incoming fire. The *Yamato* has some sort of rail gun artillery system, I suspect. We're taking hits, but we aren't out. And the main thing is, while we're out here drawing the *Yamato*'s attention, the Calistanis are inside the Geek League's Cylon Basestar causing all kinds of damage.

Still, it would be nice to shoot back.

But I can't worry about that. I'm too busy catching missiles. Another wave comes in as more artillery shots slam into the massive superstructure of the SDF-1.

"We've got particle cannons up!" shouts PVTHudson, who's been busy unlocking weapons.

"Give 'em what for, Mister Whoever-You-Think-You-Are!" bellows JollyBoy in reply.

"You mean fire, man?" asks Hudson.

Pause.

"I do indeed!" shouts JollyBoy joyously.

"Firing!"

Low, thrumming hums erupt from eight batteries along the SDF-1's hull. High-powered beams of particle energy lance out to stab at the incoming battleship that looks like something from World War 2. Except it's all sci-fi hovering above the battle.

"Engine power at full!" announces Ferro. "We can lift off... I think."

"Then do that. Lift us off and take us into battle, Mister... You!" cackles JollyBoy like some maniacal pirate ship captain. All that's missing is a parrot. And if I know him, his avatar will soon be sporting one.

"Shots deflected," announces PVTHudson. "They threw up a re-flective shield at the last second. Never mind... setting particle guns to auto-fire. Bringing our box-launchers online. Let's see how they handle these..."

From all across the massive ship, panels open up and began to spit small missiles skyward, smoke trails streaking toward the incoming battleship. And then I realize we're airborne and climbing.

"What else do we have to fire?" I ask over chat.

"Something called a Reflex Cannon," says Rashid, "but we're locked out. Also rail guns and torpedoes. Those are online." I glance up to see his avatar is now hovering over weapons—since they've become important. But Hudson doesn't surrender the station. He's too busy tagging targets on the incoming battleship.

"Fire everything!" whoops Jolly. "We've only just begun to fight... or something!"

Both ships are now hurling every weapon they have at each other above the remains of the smoking Cylon Basestar. The Calistanis have been busy down there.

"Uh… we've got a big problem, sir!" says Apone over chat. "And again… I'd like to remind you that we are bug hunters and not space navy type gamers… but… uh… well it seems the anti-gravity lift generators just tore free from the ship we are… uh… currently in."

I check our altitude. We've leveled off.

A second later we're in free fall.

"Well, that was a short trip," murmurs JollyBoy laconically.

"Enigmatrix…" I broadcast over chat.

"Trix here."

"Pull out. We're done. Bug out and slip away. Rendezvous at the next target in twelve hours."

"Roger that. We've pretty much ruined this place anyway. I wanted to blow it up… but hey… beggars can't be demolition engineers."

"I got this Reflex Cannon thing unlocked," shouts Hudson. "Power requirements say it's gonna drain our engines and batteries if we fire though."

"Everyone get to the dropship. We're abandoning ship," I announce over the chat. "Apone, tell the other Marines to bug out."

"Done, sir. We outta here!"

Hudson persists. "PQ. Sir. If we can get the bow angle vaguely on target, I can stay behind and pull the trigger."

"If you don't mind, PQ," says JollyBoy, "I'll hang out with my new best friend, Space Marine Private Hudson, and steer the ship for a shot. As ye know… captain goes down with his ship and all. I've grown fond of the old girl."

"You've only been captain for like a minute and half," I argue.

"I know… but I hate to toss her aside when we've been through so much together. And after all, I'm just a player. You're the head cheese around here."

I hate to lose Hudson and JollyBoy, but they're right—we can't pass up a chance to take out the *Yamato*. "Just don't miss," I say.

"Hudson…" says Apone as we leave the bridge, "that's so… outta character for you. You know… game over and all. I mean you know we all try to stay in character for the clan. Just sayin' and all, Bill."

Bill. I guess that's the real name of the guy who plays PVTHudson.

There's a long pause. We're racing for the dropship docked three decks below. The falling ship groans as JollyBoy adjusts the flight thrusters to get the bow angle just right for a shot against the *Yamato*. We reach the hangar deck and the waiting Colonial Marine dropship.

"Not really, Sarge," says PVTHudson. "He really went out a hero. Remember? There at the end?"

The Marines all murmur their agreement over the chat. Private Hudson did go out a hero in that old movie that had brought them together as friends. Now, he won't be going on with them. Rashid's bankers made it clear that if any of them got killed again in *Civ Craft: Mars*, they couldn't respawn as part of the clan. The Colonial Marines were already repurchased in once—at extreme expense after the last time Rashid killed everyone—and a second respawn would be astronomically more expensive.

"Yeah," murmurs Apone as we lift off of the massive falling starship in the Colonial Marine dropship. "He was a total hero, Bill."

The dropship races away. The *Yamato* is close. Missile trails compete with a sea of angry turret fire from both ships. Above and coming in fast, the *Yamato* is launching even more missiles and torpedoes right into the smoking and falling SDF-1.

"Firing!" says PVTHudson.

A searing multicolored beam of enormous dimensions erupts from the SDF-1 and hits the *Yamato* dead center. And then goes right on through as the massive space battleship detonates outward in a glorious kaleidoscope of endless destruction that shows off *Civ Craft*'s dazzling graphics to their fullest.

I'm already planning to rewatch that clip several times when this is all over.

The bow of the SDF-1 drops off sharply and the engines flare. And I see why. JollyBoy is aiming it for the Cylon Basestar.

"Good for you, buddy!" I shout to no one because my chat isn't engaged.

And then everything explodes.

Chapter Forty-Two

I walk out into the midnight gloom that surrounds the Cyber Warfare Center. The fog has come up and I can smell the salt of the sea in it. Tall lights on posts cast orange bursts of diffused light, turning everything vaguely ominous and menacing.

I have two messages. One from Kiwi. It's short and to the point. *If you're in trouble let me know. I will get you out.*

He was particularly quiet during the battle, keeping to the business of fighting our way out of there aboard a dropship getting harried by interceptors. And once we escaped, he logged out without a goodbye. It seemed odd, but I was busy organizing the next op. I thought we'd pick up later. But now I know his appearance, and that of JollyBoy, was a little intel gathering. No doubt everyone has been wondering how I ended up in Calistan working for Rashid.

The other message is from Chloe. I expect it's most likely from a burner. It reads simply: *I'll be in touch.*

For a brief moment I'm happy. Ecstatic even. And then fear sets in. I have a bad feeling deep down in my gut. Like somehow Rashid is on to me. That he knows about the message from Chloe, whoever she really is. She is, after all, out to kill him. And now he's going to turn on me. Things will get crazy and out of hand. Even Irv admitted someone found the trackers he'd placed on me. Things will definitely get out of hand. And though I want to blame someone else, in the end, I'm really the only one to blame.

I'm responsible for where I've ended up. Bad things are going to happen, and most likely, they're going to happen to me.

I soon find that I'm half right about that.

Too many generals and personnel are leaving the building all at once. As though they have to. As though they've been ordered to.

An armored personnel carrier pulls up in front, followed by a beat-up cargo van. Soldiers flood from the personnel carrier and race to the back of the cargo van with their weapons ready. The darkness mixed with the parking lot lights and the silence here along the water and far away from the party scene along the Gold Coast makes everything feel isolated. Alone. Surrounded. The way bullies always want to make you feel.

There's all kinds of harsh shouting. Men are being pulled out of the back of the van into the orange light of the parking light, kicked and pushed forward into a line. Every weapon trained on them.

Rashid comes out of the building and walks forward briskly like he's transformed from affable party prince to head of state and government functionary. He stops before them. The men who've been dragged from the cargo van. His hands are on his hips, feet spread apart. Like he's daring them to try and take him, never mind that they're surrounded by men with high-powered assault rifles. In Rashid's eyes they're cowards despite the fact that the odds are against them. That he, Rashid, holds all the cards.

To him, glaring contemptuously, they are nothing but stray dogs.

The men standing under the hellish orange light and swirling fog look bleak and afraid. They have no intention of challenging anyone. They're clearly aware of which way the wind is blowing and that it's blowing against them.

Even though the night is hot and still.

Rashid shouts at them in Arabic. It's harsh and guttural and I understand none of it. But I know things will not end well tonight and I suddenly just want to drive away because there's really nothing I can do about what's going to happen next.

I know it.

And I hate myself for knowing it.

There is nothing I can do about it.

Which is a feeling you never actually think you'll feel. And when you do, you understand how cruel the world really can be. You understand like you never did before. And you're forever changed after that moment. The world's a little darker after that. Maybe even a lot darker.

A moment later the men are being pushed against the wall of the building. Above their heads the Cyber Warfare Center's shimmering neon lettering drips with night moisture.

Rashid turns to me.

"This is the clan that screwed everything up tonight. Pigs."

I wasn't aware of any clan that screwed anything up. But Rashid's face is imperious with disgust. In the orange hell-light of the parking lot, his face is the opposite of the haunted faces I see behind him. He nods toward someone and a command is barked. Again in Arabic. A few soldiers rush into a line and stand shoulder to shoulder. Weapons at port arms.

No. I do not like what is about to happen.

I know they are about to shoot these men with their backs to the wall. To murder them.

How many people have I shot online?

I've never seen it happen in real life.

And I instantly know I never want to.

But Rashid is staring right at me. Like he knows everything. Knows about Irv, Kiwi, Chloe. Knows how badly I want out. His eyes are dull and somewhere else.

Like a shark.

Rashid doesn't live here anymore.

He nods only slightly, and that other voice barks a command I don't understand and don't have to. Bolts are pulled back and rounds locked into place within the assault rifles. The men with their backs to the wall begin to scream and cry and I know they're begging for their lives.

Then one word from that other voice. One word. Even though it is Rashid who gives the actual orders. It is all Rashid. The Arab prince who will never know anything but what it is like to live in luxury, to have everything that he has ever wanted. And to order the killings that he wants done...

The soldiers fire.

Chapter Forty-Three

I think I walked to the Porsche after the execution. I distinctly remember the feel of the fob in my hands. Pulling it from my pocket as though that were the most natural thing in the world. The brass casings that had fallen to the ground seemed to still be tinkling in the night though the firing had stopped minutes before.

It isn't until I start the engine and realize its massive growl is replacing the sound of the falling brass shells on the pavement that I really begin to think about those now-dead men across the parking lot.

I sit behind the wheel.

Rashid is getting into his car. They brought it around to the front, near the steps that lead up into the building. The dead bodies are still lying off to the side. The soldiers are organizing themselves into some kind of work detail to pick up the dead. Everyone is going home, except them. They will stay and clean up.

And me. I'm not going home either.

I have no home.

I think about the sailboat. If I knew how to sail, or even turn on the motor, I'd take it and head out to sea tonight. Straight into the dark and the fog. I don't care.

Anything to stop hearing the sound of all that falling brass as the rounds tore through bodies like sacks of wet cement. The screams that had clearly been pleas for mercy stopping suddenly once the firing began. The quiet moaning in the silence that followed. One of the soldiers walking forward and firing with a rifle into each body. He had to reload halfway through. Short staccato bursts. No pistol. No *coup de grâce*. Somehow the short bark of the AK was worse than the initial killing.

Much worse.

Like it was saying there are no second chances. That death is here.

I pull out of the parking lot behind Rashid. No one is on the street. Just the two of us and the fog. And the night.

I stare at his red taillights ahead and I want to…

My fingers grip the wheel. The knuckles are bone white.

And what?

What do I want to do?

And if I did it, how would I ever get out of here alive?

He turns at the next intersection. Beeping his horn twice. A cheery counterpoint to…

…like he didn't just murder twelve…

…people.

And then it's just me cruising north along PCH, following my high-beams through the fog. Looking for a way out.

Wondering if there is one.

Chapter Forty-Four

I find myself back at the sailboat. For a moment I just watch it from the dock. Watch the dark water around it along the harbor become a mirror, the fog swallowing everything the mirror doesn't reflect.

The sailboat is a world unto itself.

And on it things like what happened in the parking lot never happened.

That's why I came back here.

That, and I'm pretty sure there's no way I'm getting through the border. Rashid will never let me go. I know that now.

On the boat, I dial her number. The one she called from.

"Hello."

Her voice is soft. Like I've just woken her from some dream.

"Hello?" she repeats.

"It's me," I say.

There is a long pause.

"It's late. I saw the streams. Big finish. But that was two hours ago. Where are you now? Where have you been?"

"Driving. Along the coast."

"Did he give you one of his cars?"

"Yeah."

"I hate him."

I listen to the silence that follows her confession. Then...

"I do too."

And then there is a longer pause. Me realizing what I've just said. Her expecting me to say more.

"Did he do something bad tonight?" she asks finally.

I swallow hard. Hear the brass shells hitting the pavement of the parking lot. I want to scream at the night.

I pull a glass out of a cupboard in the galley. Fill it with two cubes from the ice chest. Splash some Clevinger's across the cubes, then think better of it and go ahead and drown them.

I stare at the glass.

"Yeah." My voice is dry. Or at least that's what I tell myself when I lift the glass of bourbon and toss it back.

I close my eyes and wait for her to say something.

"Things are getting bad out there," she says softly.

I think of the helicopters patrolling the rest of Calistan. Beyond the Gold Coast. I saw them on the way into the Cyber Warfare Center. And after. I've been seeing them all along. Ever since I arrived.

"I'm getting out of here," I tell her suddenly. "You should come with me."

"I barely know you."

And...

"This is my home."

I pour more of the Clevinger's. Hold the glass and sip.

"This is no kind of home. It's a nightmare."

"I know."

I want to be next to her. In bed. Wherever she is. I suspect some rich Arab prince's house. Or an apartment someone is keeping her in. Their own private plaything.

This is dangerous. I tell myself I should drive to the border and wave my passport and hope somehow I get lucky and get across. Get out now. While I still can.

And I also hope she's in some normal house. Someplace that's ordinary. I imagine lying down next to her like I did that night she tried to stab me. Falling asleep with her touching my face. The opposite of now.

"You're beautiful," I tell her.

"That's not why you called."

She's right. And now it feels like I used the memory of her body like some kind of cheap defense to paint her as something cheap, something similar to Rashid.

As if there could be anything else like the devil.

She murmurs into the phone, "Say it."

Except I don't know what to say.

That I feel something for her? Feel some connection that has been missing in my life with a girl who tried to stab me in a bordello somewhere on the neon side of the third world.

"You were there that night…" I begin.

I'm saying this over an open line. Who know who's listening. The CIA. Rashid's secret police.

But I continue anyway because maybe at two o'clock in the morning everyone who listens is taking their coffee break. Maybe they're tired and waiting for the sun.

"…to…"

I wait.

"Yes," she says.

And…

"I was."

I listen to her voice. I want to know everything about her. Because I'm sure everything I know is some kind of lie.

"You're not really one of those kinds of girls." That could be either a question or a statement. In my heart it's a statement.

"Does that matter?" she says.

I sip the Clevinger's. It burns like harsh wood smoke. Somewhere out in the night, the foghorn guarding the harbor wonders if anyone is listening to it.

"No," I answer. It doesn't matter to me.

"We should meet," she says, then adds, "Tomorrow. I mean…" And she gives a sleepy little laugh. "…today. I'll pick you up."

"Where?" I ask.

"At your boat."

Chapter Forty-Five

In the dream that seems like another life, I'm standing in the grand dining hall where the vampires were about to feast. The corpses of the once-nubile vampire brides hidden beneath their hijabs have turned to dry dusty old bones, each with its own smiling rictus that seems to laugh at me.

And the vampire is gone.

But the house, this castle, this... and I know this is the right phrase deep inside my consciousness... this old pile, seems to await my next move.

I leave the opulent dining room and enter a hall of gothic grandeur. The high walls are alive with stone gargoyles and dragons that seem to watch me. I blink once and find myself back in that inn somewhere in a haunted forest. I'm sitting across the table from Death. All across the table I see the castle in miniature. Rooms are alive with the undead. Vampires, zombies, and unquiet ghosts prowl ornate halls and shadowy passages rendered in malefic beauty. A tiny me, a samurai in miniature, stands on the lowest level of this impossible castle, a thing straight out of some madman's nightmare.

And now Death speaks, and I recognize the voice. It's that smoky barrel-aged bourbon and dry leaves voice that's been constantly narrating my journey since this, whatever this is, began.

"Which way will you go, Samurai?"

I watch the living hell beneath our eyes. Every path leads to a certain and horrible death. And I wonder if in that instant it will be me watching miniature me die… or me actually dying.

Because I'm not all that sure what this is. And what the stakes are.

"Will you pursue the vampire deeper into the depths of the castle, Samurai? Or has he perhaps gone on for some meeting, some appointed rendezvous?"

I feel frozen, and that is not good. Beneath me the statues above the tiny samurai come to life. Dragons and gargoyles move like liquid clay. Fantastic beasts made fantastically real. I marvel and know that I'm doomed.

Death pulls its bony hand out from within a hanging sleeve. Between finger and thumb bones it's holding a figurine. I look closely and see the murdered angel.

He leans forward, and I can hear his bones grinding one against the other. He places the figurine next to the tiny samurai.

Enemy or friend?

The tiny murdered angel comes to life.

"Up," I whisper, hearing the husky, dry grate of my own voice.

And now I'm back in the grand opulent gothic hall of living statues.

I turn to see the murdered angel. She's beautiful and familiar, but I can't tell who she was, or why she might even be tagged as familiar inside my mind.

Her face is a swirling mask of anger, pain, and victory as she pulls a blazing sword from a sheath on her hip. Her gray robes and raven hair swim and undulate as though she is underwater. She turns to me, eyes wide with terror, indicating some urgent message I can't understand.

The blurred movement of gargoyles coming at us like angry wasps fills the corners of my vision and I wonder if we will be okay. If we will live. If we will be all right on the other side of all this.

"Not at all!" she screams in some ethereal battle command, and then we are in battle, back to back, slaughtering flying demons coming at us from the heights of the room.

I pull Deathefeather in one swift motion and lop the arms from the first flying gargoyle to come at me. The screeching abomination goes flying past and two more come weaving and bobbing like crazed insects, except the size of a pit bull with wings and teeth and razor-sharp claws reaching out.

At my back I hear the angel's blade pass through the air on high soprano notes as though it is singing some song not meant to be heard in this mortal life.

Within seconds the battle turns desperate and the two of us are hacking and slashing for all we're worth. Cuts and slashes appear across my body and torn robe, and a long-bodied dragon circles the room above us.

The bodies of the dead gargoyles turn to crumbled stone pieces at our feet and we are left with the menacing dragon. And then it turns to black smoke and streaks off into other chambers.

In the yawning silence, the angel turns to me and beckons with her sword that we should go on. And up. Her face is one of desperate pain. And incredible beauty.

So I follow.

We go upward through winding stairs and moonlit galleries. Haunted enigmatic rooms where lone candles burn and corridors that seem an endless trek through a mirrored eternity. We fight corpulent spiders and shadowy specters. We pass a murdered woman lying in a grand bed. A book rests on her chest above the gossamer of her nightgown. Her face is ghostly pale as though she has been frightened into death.

We climb high into the dark reaches of an ancient tower, following stairs that seem as though they will forever climb upward and never end. But they do end. And at the top they open out onto a parapet atop a lesser tower. We are high above the surrounding forest, yet still merely at the base of the main tower that reaches its spindle far above. A tiny door leads into it.

It is here that a coven of witches cackles and gives battle on the scant space of the lofty parapet. Swords and spells do battle one against the other, and the clash is nothing short of titanic. Black cats screech and cross along the limits of the place with careless abandon as we trade blows and enchantments. The height on which the battle takes place is daunting, as though daring us to strike too hard, to rush too fast at the spider-webbed witches... and over we go.

It's a long fall after that.

The angel cleaves a witch, and the hag shrieks with unholy torment as it shrinks down into its shrouds. The other two come at me with brooms turned to sudden smoking torches, and I sense my moment. As though an opening has been granted, or some special ability unlocked in the dreamy game of this reality. As though it is time for me to reap.

I see autumn grain. Full and waving beneath a harvest moon. All of this transposed against the bloated moon of the midnight battle against witches atop the tower.

I embrace this moment of harvest and step forward between the two hovering witches whose faces are masks of wicked glee, voices muttering like the insane... and I harvest.

They barely move as first I give one cut.

Then two.

Three.

Four.

Five and six.

In the space of the upper lid of an eye falling toward the bottom, in the unmeasurable time it takes for just that and nothing more... I've delivered so many cuts with the remorseless Deathefeather—and I have so many more to give—that the witches have lost their arms and legs. One more strike clean through and I've severed both their throats and only the first black spurts of pumping blood have arched into the still air between us before I give them six more cuts from the razor blade that is Deathefeather's edge. I don't just kill them. I dissect them before one of them can even finish the final syllable of the first word of her muttered and final damning curse.

Deathefeather passes through its final arc as I draw a line from east to west across the curvature of the world. And when I am finished they are dead and dead. Dead. Dead. Very dead.

Some old song I heard long ago, in another life not this one, begins. Like rats or ghosts tapping on furniture in some distant room while I sit sleepless and waiting out the long night.

Something about someone being dead dead dead.

And as fast as the fleeting memory of something half remembered comes... it's gone.

I look out over that haunted forest I came through and nowhere in it is anything familiar. It is as though I've gone into another world. All I see is a vast dark ocean of twisted trees clutching like fingers at the mist and moonlight. Far below, mean torches gutter at the gate to the tower and the manor house I came through earlier in the evening. But that seems like a long time ago.

I turn to the angel, the murdered angel, who floats just above the stone of the parapet, her clothes still undulating as though she is swimming in a sea that isn't there. Looking at her and the dark forest, I wonder if there are indeed other worlds than these.

And where did I hear that line once long ago? In another life not this one.

She beckons me to the door of the main tower, holding out her cold fiery sword toward its tiny barrier, indicating we must go through. That we must go on. That we must enter.

I wipe the dark blood from my sword with a cloth and turn to the door. Its warped wood is bound in ancient black iron. Old text, all curlicues and half loops, litters its face like unholy graffiti. All of it is alien to me. And somehow, I know we've come to the heart of the matter. As though what lies beyond is some final moment to all of this.

I cast one last glance out over the hauntingly beautiful forest in the midnight moonlight. Whatever this world is, I don't want to leave. I want to go on exploring it forever. Finding all its secrets. Its adventures. Its wonders. Like an eternally promised childhood of adventure and terror intermingled.

But if feels as though things are coming to a close for me. That I am close to leaving.

And I wonder where I'm going next.

And if I will still be me.

We step through the door, and there indeed is the heart of the matter. It climbs up through the core of the twisted tower. It is horrible and wonderful at the same time. And it is so shocking that I...

Chapter Forty-Six

I wake with a start. A sudden start. My heart is pounding and I'm covered in sweat. I can't remember what I was dreaming about. I lie back, my heart thudding, and wonder if I should stop smoking.

I listen to the waves slap against the side of the hull. Right near my head. Then I light a cigarette and lie there for a while, and in time I can't hear my heart pounding like it was.

She shows up later that morning in an old sports car. But it's cherried out. I hear it from a long way off, its loud muffler tearing up the silence of the sleepy port. She gets out and waves from the top of the ramp leading down to the dock. She's wearing a red plaid schoolgirl skirt, short. Shiny metallic boots and a gray sweater. Her hair is in a ponytail. Her skin is alabaster with a little olive. And of course there's the body I have not forgotten.

But it's the smile I don't remember seeing that night in the bordello that seduces me from the start of what is to come.

I walk up the dock, and we stand awkwardly before each other. The last time we met she was naked, mostly, and she tried to kill me. Her smile falters as though she knows I'm remembering that desperate fight for the knife in that tiny room. Or the soft curves of her unmasked body as she tried to kill me.

She bites her bottom lip.

"It's okay," I say, not really knowing what's okay and what isn't. Just thinking something needs to be said. And that telling her things are okay is a good place to start.

Suddenly that smile is back. And that's when I realize it's what I was looking for. Wanted to remember. Would remember… about her. That smile that seems determined to be happy, no matter what.

"Where are we going?" I ask.

"Surprise." The soft purr of her voice in our late-night conversation is still there. But now she speaks with all the lightness of an easy breeze drifting this way and that along the old California coast.

In her car and headed back off the island and onto the mainland, we take the coast road. Any conversation that can't be yelled above the roar of the tiny engine is lost. Instead she turns on some music coming from the local official Calistani radio station.

She leans in close to my ear at a stoplight.

"We have to listen to this junk until we get beyond the zone. Plus, it helps when they do their state-mandated call to prayer."

I'm looking into her eyes. They're deep brown pools, warm and alive. She suddenly realizes I'm doing this. Then I lean slightly forward and kiss her.

And does she ever kiss me back.

Someone honks at us and she puts the car in gear, casting a glance at me. At first I can't catch if it's naughty or seductive, or some role she plays, but then the smile. The no-matter-what happy smile. And even though we're listening to all the lies of some terrible Middle Eastern cheesy crooner who's singing in a language neither of us understands, all sappy and over-emotional, we don't care.

We kissed.

And anything is possible.

We pass out of the zone, through the official boundary of the Gold Coast, the mustachioed angry guards casually murdering us with their contemptuous stares. A block later she pulls out a tape cassette because this old sports car has a tape player. Or some retro vintage version of one that plays things that look like tapes. She glances at the one she grabbed from a knapsack behind her seat.

"Perfect!" she screams with delight. Then looks at me and smiles.

Later I will find out it's a band called Social Distortion. From way back. Last century back. Before the Meltdown back. For now I only know they play searing hot guitar licks and driving beats while the singer thunders through a barrage of down-and-out anthems.

I know, heading into the old OC—she tells me that's what they used to call the area once known as Southern California, now known as Calistan—I know I will remember that sun shining moment and the girl next to me forever. And the music surrounding us.

Nothing lasts. No matter how perfect an unexpected moment can be. Nothing lasts in this life. In the end, everything burns. And if you know that... then that perfect moment becomes even better.

So I lean back and watch the third world while listening to some good music from a long time ago and being driven by a mysterious and beautiful girl on an afternoon date.

Buy the ticket, take the ride, someone once wrote.

We drive through the slums beyond the zone. Crushing poverty and despair compete with satellite dishes and clothing lines strung across streets. Business seems piled on top of business in some places. In others, not a soul is to be seen and I notice the scarred pockmarks along the bullet-riddled walls and the old rusty sprays of not-spray-paint. We cross over an old freeway long perma-frozen with dead vehicles. Only one lane is open. The rest of the lanes are the permanent residences of cars and trucks and the occasional motor home that has been turned into a house. There are even vegetable gardens in containers along the medians.

And there's always the constant hovering presence of Calistani helicopters. Old Russian Hinds and even the occasion Mexico war-surplus Cobra gunship. All of which must be at least a hundred years old. Somehow they still run. And still bristle with guns.

We weave through blocks of suburban waste that have burned down only to enter whole new blocks where gangs of children play in the street like small armies. Some neighborhoods are strictly Arabic, others definitely Hispanic, by what I can tell from the business signage. The Arabic neighborhoods seem generally better off, but only slightly so. It's hard to believe places like this still exist in the modern world.

We enter a Mexican neighborhood known as Santa Ana.

"We're safe now," she tells me at a light over the mutter of the engine. My eardrums feel like they've been beaten to death by the sound of the engine. And… I didn't realize we *weren't* safe. "This is my barrio," she says with pride.

A few streets later we pull up along an old Main Street USA from the last century. Brick-and-mortar buildings. Chipped gargoyles and crumbling scroll-worked stone. But every sign is in Spanish. Maybe it always was. Which seems odd considering the restaurant we've just pulled up in front of.

"This is my cousin Frankie's place," Chloe says. "They make the best pizza. And the Vietnamese mojitos are to die for." She laughs and sets the parking brake.

She tows me inside. Angry young Mexican men lingering on the street cast those same casual glares of murder that the Calistani guards at the border of the zone did. But Chloe smiles at them and they seem suddenly helpless to do anything other than smile back. As though she has broken them and turned them into bashful little boys.

Inside the restaurant, little red-netted hurricane lamps on the tables cast dim illumination. Massive paintings of regal bullfighters dominate the walls. In candlelit alcoves, somber candles burn softly. The place feels more like a cathedral than a restaurant. High above, a stained-glass window—an Aztec warrior holding a bloody heart atop a pyramid—casts the room in a wash of crimson. Somewhere, someone quietly seduces a guitar.

A short, squat woman who looks more Chinese than Latina leads us to a table deep within the labyrinthine maze that is the restaurant. We slide into a deep banquette of ancient red vinyl. All around us candles are like fading stars in a universe that is only the color red.

"Neat place, huh?" she says with zest and slides close to me. Now it is her turn. She kisses me hard and bites my lip after the woman leaves us with no menus. A few minutes later we come up for air.

"Let me order, okay?"

Buy the ticket, take the ride.

I nod that this works for me. For some reason I can't find my voice. And maybe that's for the best.

Frankie arrives from the kitchen. He looks like her, but Asian. His hair is slicked back in dark thick strands and his forearms are covered in arcane tattoos. His smile is bright and white beneath his enigmatic Asian eyes.

"It's good to see you, *mi flamenca*," he says and bends down to hug her.

She babbles to him in Spanish and he back at her.

I continue to smile and dig on the cathedralesque weirdness of the place. Each facet reveals some new enigmatic twist.

Frankie leaves and Chloe throws herself at the menu he left. It's as though she's reading some holy and sacred text that reveals the meaning of life, the universe, and everything, if one could but pick the right combination.

Frankie comes back. Chloe throws down the menu in mock disgust and commences to beg.

"Frankie... can you make us your Pizza Ravi? Please, please, please, *please*?"

The way she begs has *me* wanting to make her a Pizza Ravi, whatever the hell it is.

And again... it isn't the innate seductiveness she can't help but exude... it's something else. Some knight-in-shining-armor disease I have that makes me want to storm castles and slay dragons for her.

I really need to have that looked at by a specialist. It's gotten me into trouble before and if I could think straight for a second I'd probably realize it's going to get me in trouble again.

But she seems like fun trouble at the very least. At the most... something different. Something better than the last eighteen months. Something I've been looking for for a long time and didn't know it.

"Of course I'll make it for you, *mi flamenca*. Why else were such things created if not to offer to the most beautiful woman in Santa Ana? And of course... two Saigon Whores?"

Chloe laughs wickedly and clasps her olive-skinned hands together like a little girl who's just discovered candy.

"The extra-special kind," she purrs.

Frankie leaves as though on a mission. He isn't just a cousin. He adores her, and she probably doesn't know how much. Any man could see that.

She dives at me again. And when once more we come back up for air she doesn't pull away. Instead she prefers to remain close as though interrogating me for some lie I've already told.

"You're different," she pronounces. "Very different."

"Not so much," I reply.

She shakes her head slightly.

"No. That's a lie. But it's what you're supposed to say. So it's okay."

"What's a..." My voice cracks. I'm thirsty. I clear my throat and try again. "What's a Saigon Whore, exactly?"

She smiles devilishly and bounces her head side to side. "It's fun. Vietnamese version of a mojito. Made with tequila instead of rum. Mescal. Some say it can even make you see the spirit world. But only when the moon is full. Game? Or are you scared?"

"Me...?" I shrug. "I'm the bravest man in the world. And thirsty too."

Our drinks come out. They're tall and slushy. Thai mint springs from rims in jungle-worthy profusion. The sweet herbal taste competes with the hot jet-fuel-grade tequila.

We raise our glasses and smile at each other like we're daring the other to survive. And of course we laugh. The look in her eye is daring me to go for it. As though she told me a monster's tale on a dark and scary night. And now it's time for me to go touch the back of the cemetery wall all alone. A kid's challenge.

I put the drink down.

Her smile falters.

She puts hers down.

"I know…" I begin, unsure where I'm going, but knowing I need to say what I feel. "I know this is all fast… and weird."

Her face is suddenly sober and… still beautiful.

"I'm not with…" I struggle because I don't want to profane this place, this afternoon, her… with Rashid's name.

"Them," she finishes when I can't bring myself to say the name of our devil. I've gotten hung up on all the dead bodies from last night.

"No," I croak. "Not with them at all."

She murmurs those words back. But in another order, one she chooses.

"Not at all." Like she's in a dream. Or under some witch's spell. Or reciting some sacred text. Or a forgotten song.

"No," I say after I look around, checking the shadows for state-sponsored listeners. "I came because I was paid to. And…"

I gaze at all the enigmatic Hispanic beauty of this strange restaurant lost in the barrio. "And if I had known what I know now… I probably never would've come."

A small silence falls between us. And I know somehow we're each considering what that means. Or rather, that it somehow means we never would've found each other. Except we've just met. And that's a lot to think about. The guitarist dances along some chords, plucking them out individually. Like he's working on a moment that's nothing but gossamer. Coaxing it to come alive.

"Probably?" she whispers softly.

"Except…" I begin, "for this. For you. And I get that I don't really know you… but the other night when we just lay there… and now, with you, here…" I scan the crimson shadows and burning candles and the deep alcoves of strange paintings. "I feel like I would've done anything for… this." But what I mean is… for *her*.

Her lips part slightly.

She takes my drink from in front of me and holds it up to those full cinnamon lips. Staring at me, she drinks.

Then says, "This one is poisoned."

Chapter Forty-Seven

"We poisoned you..." she says as she sips from the drink that had been set in front of me. "I mean... we were going to poison you."

Her eyes begin to glaze over.

"Not... really poison. Just... get you to answer a few questions. Truth or..." she giggles, "...or dare serum."

She comes at me holding her drink, kissing me greedily, and suddenly she's all hands.

I bring her chin up after a few hot seconds of this.

"Why?"

"Why what?" she asks, all doe-eyed and innocent. Her pupils are huge.

"Why poison me?"

She stares at me blankly.

"Me," I prompt. "Poison."

Awareness blossoms on her face like the sun suddenly destroying a perfectly beautiful rainy day.

"It's not really poison." She's mostly in control of herself. A little... dreamy maybe. "We just wanted to know where Rashid will be tomorrow."

"Why?"

"Oh," she says with a sense of rapture. "We're going to kill that pig dead, dead, dead."

And then our meal arrives.

It's gorgeous.

The surface of the pizza is a burnt golden orange with small pieces of sizzling charred chicken. Atop this, chopped cilantro a vibrant green dances with diced green onions. The aromatic punch of curry overwhelms the senses as steam rises up from the pie. I smell ginger and smoked paprika. The garam masala has obviously been lovingly cooked down with garlic and chilies.

Chloe gushes like she's just won some major prize she didn't deserve as Frankie stands proudly over our table. A moment later she has a piece up with both hands and is ravenously devouring it and moaning with happiness.

I down my drink, the one originally intended for Chloe. I'm still wondering if it's poisoned too. And about that whole kill Rashid bit.

But I realize I'm starving and I pick up a slice and forget about everything that is the hellhole of Calistan.

The underside of the pizza is crispy. The top has bubbled and charred in places from the heat of the brick oven it was cooked in. As though the oven easily pushed into the thousand-degree range. The tangy tart bite of the tikka masala sauce hits me. It's the very essence of savory. But it's the dough, the crust of the pizza, that makes subjects such as being poisoned, and killing Rashid, seem like petty concerns read in some dime-store pulp ebook on a burner Kindle. The crust is both incredibly crisp on the bottom and chewy on the top. Thin, light, delicate... It's like chewing a cloud with a nice crunch.

We devolve into a world of pizza for a little while. She moans and I eat. After a few slices I start to get thirsty again.

"Poisoned?" I ask, holding a slice up.

"Uh-uh," she grunts between bites.

She catches someone's eye and orders two more Saigon Whores. This time she doesn't say "special."

She keeps looking at me. Smiling and hungry.

Then she giggles.

"You know you can ask me anything... right now. I have to tell you the truth. I basically just roofied myself. Sorta..." She giggles again and tries to inhale more pizza.

I find her incredibly sexy at that moment and asking her questions seems inappropriate. But one does occur.

"Why didn't you let me drink the poison?"

She puts down her pizza. I eye what's left of this incredible pie and count the slice she's just discarded as fair salvage once we reach the last division.

"Because you're so sweet," she says.

Our drinks arrive.

I drain half of mine in one go. Even the not-extra-special Saigon Whores are... special. The room swims and I feel... let's just say groovy.

She burps and holds up a finger as she picks up my slice.

"Don't worry... they're not poisoned. Just..." she burps again as though making room for more, like the scoundrel she is, "powerful."

Soon she leans back and sighs contentedly.

Our once-golden pizza is thoroughly done to death.

We order another round of the powerful drinks.

She leans in close, snuggling in as though a nap is in order. The unseen guitarist plays some melody that seems meant for an afternoon in a Mexican joint that serves the most amazing Southeast Asian fusion pizza ever. You know... that one.

"We're going to kill him," she murmurs. "We just didn't know if you were... with Rashid. We needed..." And she trails off. Her eyes flutter.

"I'm not asleep," she says after a moment. "I'm just dreaming."

"About what?" I whisper.

My eyes have closed and I didn't even know it.

I feel like we're the only people in the restaurant. I feel like the world is just... this. And I'm fine with that. And then I drift off...

* * *

In that tower, lost somewhere in a valley I know I'll never find the edges of, after the battle with the witches, we start up the inside of that spire. That spire that is more than a spire.

A large beating black heart fills the tower above us, suspended in space. A giant demon's heart. It pumps, its tempo strong and angry. As though it is seething with nothing but anger and insolence and pride. It beats as a heart beating on those vices could only beat: loud and wild until the sudden violent end that has been coming all along.

It is a frightening thing to behold.

I can hear blood swooshing through the arteries that run into it from the walls of the tower. The noise of it makes the same two-syllable sound every second, like a staccato backbeat to some song I should know.

Ra-shiid

Ra-shiid

Ra-shiid

From high up, from among the bloody red upper reaches, beyond the heart, a dark figure comes down a curving stair that runs along the outer wall.

It is William Alucard.

Ra-shiid

Ra-shiid

Ra-shiid

Billy Alucard, the sergeant of the keep called him.

The vampire and he are one and the same.

He wears black plate mail. Spiked boots and pauldrons. Beneath one massive mailed hand he carries a helmet. A bastard sword in the other. It is made of some dark metal I know is unholy. The opposite of whatever Deathefeather is.

I prepare to spend myself as a samurai must. I place one hand on the hilt of my katana and wait for him to come to me. The odds are

not in our favor here. On the stairs, only one of us can fight him
at a time. And he seems to agree that this is where things must end.
His swaggering stride, heedless of the edge and the height and the
manically beating heart, is careless of anything other than slaughter.

The angel rushes forward, away from me, flying up the stairs like
a sudden fury, seeming to still be in that odd slow motion her movements effected. Alucard dons his helmet and parries her first blow. The
clash of their swords rings out, deafening the backbeat of the demon's
heart.

I might have screamed no.

The ring of sword on sword resounds again and again within the
expanse of the tower's inner hollowness, competing with that infernal
metronome.

Ra-shiid

Ra-shiid

Ra-shiid

The angel is driving the unholy armored Billy Alucard back up the
stairs, past the heart, with a cascade of blows from her bright and
shining singing sword. He gives ground like a sure-footed pirate on
a rolling ship at sea. Deft and economical. Revenant sword always
between him and the fury that would have him dead. And then of a
sudden, he would unleash a wicked backstroke and stop her momentum cold.

I call out to her to stop because I know this can only end one way.
Badly. Very badly. It is I who has to face Alucard.

The samurai.

Me.

She lands a terrific blow and splits his helm in two. He dances away
from her, falling back onto the steps above. I can see his spiky blond
hair and a stream of blood coming from a jagged cut on his forehead.
But his mocking blue eyes and whiplash sneer tell me he is still in
control of the battle. Still dangerous.

Ra-shiid

Ra-shiid

Ra-shiid

She runs him through, but he just laughs in her face, spits blood across her gray shrouds, and pushes his own wicked black sword upward and through her stomach in the same moment.

The cry that comes from her is sudden and horrible. It is the end of all things. The end of love.

Ra-shiid

Ra-shiid

Ra-shiid

He laughs and begins to move, his sword sticking out the length of her. She pulls her sword from his body and drops it on the stone steps. It clatters and falls off into the void, tumbling away, past the massive beating heart, into infinite nothing.

Ra-shiid

Ra-shiid

Ra-shiid

I see the heart beating strong and hard. Triumphant. As it always will. And I know it is Alucard's heart. I race up the stairs and grab for an artery just below the lowest ventricle of the insane thing. Both hands land around its bloody slipperiness, but only one holds. With the other I draw my katana and drive it up into the black beating heart. Again and again.

Alucard and the angel are above me on the stairs.

Alucard sweating and pale, but not dead.

The angel is gone now. She hangs limply from his sword. Her eyes closed. But I can see that her mouth is moving. Saying something.

"No. Not at all."

She turns her head toward me and opens her eyes. Deep brown eyes like two pools pity me for what I will see, and live through, long after her going. And then seem to apologize finally as she summons the last of her strength to fling herself over the edge of the stairs… just after she grabbed onto Alucard's black breastplate.

I can only watch them go. Spinning away into nothingness. Because that's all there is down there at the bottom of the tower. Nothingness and the forgotten.

Above me the heart begins to heave spasmodically. Quickly. As though in sudden fear. As though it will explode.

And there is still nothing I can do.

Stones crash down from above as the heart begins a series of staccato seizures. The entire curving stairway collapses all at once, and the building shakes and trembles.

I look down into the swirling nepenthe of the void and I know there is no other choice. Except to try what I know is impossible and hope isn't.

I swing and throw myself at the crumbling remains of the stairway.

Deathefeather tumbles away and into the void.

My hands find the edge of a broken step and then lose it. I scrabble to hold on to something, anything, and after a frantic second I find myself with just fingertips clinging to a bit of shattered stair barely large enough to stand on. I try to pull myself up but it's beyond any strength I have left. The earthquake that is destroying everything is shaking my fingers loose. I try one last heave, willing myself to go up and over the edge...

...but I have nothing.

Nothing is left.

A stone glances off my chest, just beneath my shoulder, and I lose my grip with one hand. My scream is drowned out by the roar of the collapsing tower. It feels like I was shot with a gun.

Except what is a gun?

My other hand holds on in defiance of the inevitable. Telling all the world and all the rules and everything it could ever throw at me that they are wrong. My white-knuckled fingers seem to scream, "I'll show you!"

And then a dark and hairy hand, massive and leathery, reaches down and takes hold of my wrist. And I am hauled up from the abyss and onto the broken stair. I grab my shoulder and roar as my vision turns red with murder and pain. In the darkness behind my eyes I can see her looking at me as she disappeared into the void below. As she fell away… did she reach out for me?

"PerfectQuestion…" rumbles an animal growl above me. I open my eyes and see a massive minotaur standing on a stair above me. He snorts and smiles. His muscled chest heaving like a dark bellows.

"You know me. I'm Morgax. We have to leave. This tower is coming down all around us."

And then he pulls me to my feet and we flee the collapsing tower. I…

＊ ＊ ＊

"You. And me," she whispers to me from far away as we lie there in the red vinyl banquette in the Mexican restaurant that serves strange mojitos called Saigon Whores. "I'm dreaming about you and me."

I'd fallen asleep too. I wipe some drool away from my numb lips before she can see it. She's leaning against my chest. Eyes closed. Softly murmuring to someone in a dream.

After a moment I ask, "Is it a good dream?"

"Very."

"Sounds nice."

She's quiet. I almost thinks she's fallen asleep again. Then she speaks as though she's even farther away now.

"In a different world not this one anymore. No…" she says, and stops. "Not at all."

Chapter Forty-Eight

Later we wake again, though we haven't even really been sleeping. It was like the most wide-awake sleep I've ever had, and it was completely relaxing. I imagine the eventual hangover from all the Saigon Whores will be brutal.

I open my eyes and she's staring at me. Her big brown eyes are wet. Like she's been crying.

"I'm sorry," she says.

I shake my head. It feels like it weighs ten thousand pounds.

"Don't be. That was the best pizza I've ever had." I laugh to let her know it's okay.

"I mean," she says, "about trying to drug you in order to make you talk. That was…"

I hold up a hand to stop her. "You didn't. And it would've been worth it."

"Because of the pizza?"

"That too."

She leans into my chest once more.

Our bodies feel warm and electric. Like there's some wild current running through us unrestrained and ready to do anything.

"What if I make it so Rashid doesn't become sultan of Calistan?"

I don't whisper this. I just say it. In Calistan of all places.

She's up. Almost pushing herself away from me in shock. Her movement so sudden and abrupt it startles me.

"There's a way. Tomorrow night," I say.

"Tomorrow night?"

"Yeah. But then I'll have to leave town. And by town… I mean I'll need to get out of Calistan if I survive. And quickly."

Her face falls.

She leans in slowly. And this time there's no sudden attack. No desperate searching. This time it's that long slow kiss that means you don't want to say goodbye. Ever.

"You could leave with me," I tell her. "There's a lot of world to see."

＊ ＊ ＊

We leave the restaurant and I know we probably shouldn't drive… so we don't. She hails some sort of half-motorbike, half-wagon, and we climb in. Despite the beating engine and the smoke, it's rather comfortable. Or maybe I'm just still drunk.

It's too loud to talk, so we just make out for the hour it takes to get where we're going.

I asked just before we got in, "Where are we going?"

She smiled and said, "The Unhappiest Place on Earth."

Fun, huh?

Now as evening falls across what used to be Southern California and surrenders to some kind of burnt orange and purple that spreads out and away over the smog-and-smoke-shrouded inland sprawl, I smell cooking meat on the evening wind. As though a thousand fires have suddenly sprung to life. We pass dark streets where I see candles in windows. Ancient streetlights remain dark and only occasionally does some wan electric neon sign advertising dancing girls or liquor pierce the darkness.

We enter a ruin of collapsed businesses and apocalyptic streets. We thread these carefully, the *puttputtputt* of the motorbike wagon the only sound, and pull up in front of a sign that once announced a fantastic place called Disneyland.

We climb out of the cab, barely, and I gaze up at the faded graffiti-covered icon as Chloe forces cash onto the smiling gap-toothed driver. Then he's off into the night, and I can hear the music that is the only sound of this ancient monument to the world before the Melt.

Not really music. More like chanting. On the other side of a fallen mesh fence and long-trampled landscaping is the most massive parking lot I've ever seen. And in the distance, the ruins of the place. Half a mountain and half the skeleton of some ancient dinosaur that never was. And the hunched skeletal shadows of what remains of the rides. And in the dark among these shapes, the flicker of a thousand candles.

"C'mon," she whispers as though we're about to enter a cathedral, or some holy place. "It's safe."

Hand in hand like lovers, we walk across the ruined parking lot that is wider than any field I've ever seen. It's cracked and broken from countless burning days under the sun and long years of no one bothering to maintain the abandoned place.

I knew it never opened again after the Meltdown. But until now I never really put it together that the reason it never reopened was because it was no longer in Southern California. It was in that foreign nation now known as Calistan. Not America.

She whispers, as if in the presence of something sacred. "Disney Apple... back then it was called just called Disney... abandoned the park after the riots."

"The riots?" I ask.

"When the sultan and his mercenaries started airlifting in jihadis from around the world to take control of Southern California after the collapse, a bunch of my people held out here for two months against the sultan. There was a big battle. We call it *Las Lágrimas de Tomorrowland.*"

"What does that mean?" I ask in a whisper as we draw close to the ruin. Approaching the turnstiles. The old ticket booths. Some still bear the prices and the old characters even I recognize from Disney Apple's constant merchandising on the internet. But these are somehow different… as though I'm staring at ancient hieroglyphs from some lost civilization that once ruled the known world.

"The Tears of Tomorrowland."

A pathway illuminated by guttering candles placed in jars leads off through the wreckage beyond the gate.

"Tomorrowland was once a place inside. It promised us what the world was going to be like in the future. And it also happened to be the last defense of the freedom fighters. No one surrendered to the Muslims. They were all killed inside."

I look at the line of candles, a string of hazy specters guiding us from one realm to another. Across some unseen boundary.

"And what is it now?"

She takes my hand. It's warm and soft. There's a tenderness there I didn't expect. And I allow myself to be led along as she talks of all she knows.

"It is our memory," she begins. "And our hope. The Catholics, our priests, they have a secret order here now. Every night they chant from dusk until midnight. Offering prayers, solace, comfort… and hope for a better tomorrow."

"Why?"

She doesn't answer. We pass into the park. Above us an old-timey train station rises like a shadow in the night. The engine and some passenger cars have been pushed down into the courtyard. Upon these, and on every surface, graffiti has been written. And beside each is a date.

"We call this *el patio de los guerreros*. The courtyard of the warriors. Everyone who has ever died trying to bring back freedom to Southern California has been tagged here. The dates are when they passed into heaven."

"I'm sorry," I whisper.

She takes a slight detour and kneels near the bottom of one paint-covered axle. Down near the pavement is a name.

Luis Camerano.

She takes a small jarred candle and places it in front of the name. She lights it.

She continues to kneel, and I just stand there.

I can hear her sobbing.

And then she stands. "Do you have a cigarette?"

I shake one out. Light it. Hand it to her.

She takes a drag.

"He was my father."

By the glow of the ember I can see her face. It's cold and far away.

"I never knew him," she says. "He died before I was born. No one knows how. Except that jihadis who had become the official army of Calistan got him. After he was dead they crucified him on an overpass in Fullerton. As a lesson to us not to fight back. Not to believe in God. My mother's brothers found his body and removed it after curfew. They buried him at sea. This is only... this is all I ever knew about him. This place."

She's lost. There. Wherever there is.

"My mother said he was brave. That he believed in America. That he died for America. Trying to bring it back after the Meltdown. But it was all gone by then."

"I'm..."

She holds up a hand. "Don't."

Then...

"Don't say you're sorry. Everybody's said that to me my whole life. About him. About my mother as she drank herself to death on bathtub tequila. She died the day he died. She just didn't know it then. And everybody said they were sorry. My *abuela* knows what I do... and she says she's sorry even though she's ashamed of me. So please... please be different and don't ever be sorry for me. Promise me that. Right now. Okay? Please don't be sorry for me. No matter what happens."

She takes a long drag from the cigarette and stares at me as she blows the smoke out across the courtyard. Over her shoulder. Daring me to be different than everyone she's ever known.

I nod.

"I promise."

There are some promises you make that you never should. But how can we know?

She flicks the cigarette off into the darkness and reaches for me to take her. To hold her. I do, and we kiss like we've never kissed before. Like it is the last kiss before the end of the world.

"Why did you bring me here?" I ask.

"Because I want you to see some things. And I want you to meet someone."

"That's all?"

"No," she confesses. "Because if you're willing, I think you can help us. I think you can make a difference."

She looks at me as though she's asking me a question. Like it's my turn to answer. And she's waiting.

But I don't.

So she asks.

"Will you come?"

I nod, and she leads me deeper into the ruins of Disneyland.

We pass along a main street that looks half haunted and half shrine. It takes me a moment to realize there are other people here in the darkness with us.

"Who are these people?"

"The faithful. Catholics. Aztec Liberation Front. The grieving. The lonely. The ones who don't want to ever forget all that once was."

Everywhere I look, people are staring into the ruined stores and amusements. To my surprise, many of the displays inside have been meticulously reconstructed.

"The monks have tried to restore everything to what it once looked like," she explains in a whisper as we gaze in at a candy shop. "Isn't it beautiful?"

It's like looking into some old photograph of what America looked like long before the Meltdown. Except if you look closely you can see the damage. The chips and nicks. The glue and tape. The missing eyes in some of the dolls.

At the end of the street lie the half-burnt remains of a fairytale castle. Here is the source of the low chanting and the occasional mournful bells.

"They come here to remember why we fight. Why we want America back."

She leads me on, toward the castle.

Chapter Forty-Nine

We cross what was once a big park but is now nothing more than dead trees and shell crater holes. And this ruined landscape now hosts some kind of weapons bazaar.

I've seen all kinds of weapons in games. From the latest tricked-out HK Type-90 smartgun to even the old 1911 .45. But that was all in-game. Not real life. Now I'm seeing tables and stalls filled with antique guns and the occasional modern AK-2000 complete with a tri-dot target acquisition system. I know assault rifles like that retail for upwards of ten thousand. I checked once when I used one in a game and wanted to see what the cost was in real money.

"What's going on here?" I ask as we weave through the stalls like shapes among shadows.

"This is where the resistance gets their weapons. It's run by the Aztec Liberation Front."

"I didn't realize there was any real resistance actually going on," I say. "Seems like the Calistanis have things pretty well locked down."

She snorts. "Hardly. That's why the zone is so guarded. Truth is they're on the verge of losing it. All the barrios, us, the Chinese, the Thai, the Vietnamese, and even the Indians are ready to revolt. And it's only recently that we've started working together."

"So what happens if…?" I ask.

"What do you mean?"

"What happens if you revolt?"

She stops. Turns to face me.

"We go back. We join America again. We become California."

I've taken some history courses on the world before the Meltdown. It was a madhouse of grievance action and social justice. And all of it a scam for cheap power and wealth redistribution. That's what caused the old America to collapse. Grievance politics, out-of-control immigration, deficit spending. And when the power went off, everything just tore itself apart until the corporations stepped in to restore order so they could get the global economy going again.

I know that one of the facets of that time had been the resistance of minorities to assimilate into the classic American culture. Without assimilation, diversity wasn't a strength. It was a fracture. One that opened wide the second it got the chance.

So I ask.

"But... you're Mexican, right?"

"Mostly."

"Before the Meltdown, most Mexican-Americans wanted to return California to Mexico," I say. "I remember something about La Raza and all that."

She puts her hands on her hips. Defiantly.

"Listen, those *vatos* were crazy. They had no idea what they were talking about. They viewed the countries their grandparents had come from with some sort of blissful nostalgia that wasn't grounded in any kind of reality. They completely disregarded the fact that most of their ancestral countries were at best oligarchies and at worst totalitarian regimes that were nothing short of living nightmares. My parents and grandparents, they were second- and third-generation. Didn't remember first-hand what they'd fled. Why they'd fled. What they'd wanted to get away from. What they'd wanted to get to instead. But once they got a taste of what it was like to live under an oppressive government—fifty rich families governing everything in Calistan, no one gets a chance to better themselves and everyone is just a servant—they got over that *real* quick. They remembered just how great America was. I was raised with the truth."

"Which is?"

"America was a pretty great place. The old ones, the ones who were once Americans, they're proud of that fact now. They wear it like a badge of honor, and there is no one more committed to the restoration than them. And they'll tell you straight up that they weren't like that as kids. That the public school system and the colleges, which were run by a bunch of power-hungry leftist goons who tried to make everything they didn't agree with bad, made them that way. Tried to tell them America wasn't great. But it was all a lie. The elites, as they called themselves, just wanted power. The old ones like my *abuela*, she was just a teenager when it all happened. She'll tell you she was lied to. She'll tell you that when she's pumping water from the village well where she lives in Riverside. When there's no food to purchase in the market. When she remembers that she once had beautiful teeth. She raised me on how much America had and how great it was. And the one thing they had… and they lost it… was freedom. You could be anything in that America if you were willing to work hard enough. Is it like that still?"

She looks up at me with those deep brown eyes. Like she's just recounted some religious truth her whole culture faithfully believes in and she's asking me to tell her if it's actually the truth because I've been to the heaven they're all dreaming of going to.

And somewhere deep inside, I wonder if she's daring me to shatter everything she's ever believed.

"It is," I say. "It's tough. If your family works corporate, you probably start out with a leg up… but yeah… you can still make it. I did."

She looks down and nods to herself. And then back up at me. I see some weight come off her shoulders. The doubt. The fear that maybe she was wrong and every terrible thing she'd had to do had been for nothing. And now there's almost an otherworldly shine in her eyes. As though… as though I'm some monk who's been to the top of the mountain and told her that there really is something there. Something to believe in.

That's all she was asking for.

"That's all we want," she says. "A chance. Here… we have no chance. But in America you can have a chance." She takes my hand. "C'mon. I want you to meet Brother Chris."

We pass through the gun bazaar and come out the other side, directly in front of the castle. Across an old bridge covered in graffiti, she leads me to a door next to the main gate. From beyond that gate comes the low monastic chanting. It is both deep and peaceful. Above, the moon rides into the night sky and I realize I'm standing beneath it, next to a fairytale castle that is both a fable and a historical landmark. Next to a damsel in distress. All of this was important once long ago and now not so much. But it's something. Some place on the map of people's lives then and now. Something to believe in when belief is what is needed. And I am standing here, next to her.

And that is a good thing in a world that is anything but.

She knocks on the wooden door.

A tall man opens it. He is wearing cargo shorts and nothing else besides wire-rimmed glasses and a large wooden cross hanging around his neck. His hair is long and gray.

"Heyyyy, Chloe," he says. He reminds me of the hippies that used to sit in Grand Central all zoned out on F8 and selling knockoff SoftEyes. "Where you been, girl?"

He smiles expectantly at me. Like it's what he does. Like everyone in the entire world is a friend waiting to be made.

"This is…" She seems suddenly nervous. Aware of herself like she's never been. Like a little girl who has once taken communion and learned all the holy things that must be learned. "This is my friend, Brother Chris."

"Good to meet you, my man. I'm Chris. Humble shepherd to His children. I'm deeply, and I must say deeply because I've known Chloe for a long time, honored to meet you. Come on in." He opens the door and holds out his hand as though ushering us into some grand palace.

"He's the last Catholic priest left in the OC," Chloe whispers. "He's a very wanted man. The sultan would airstrike this place if he knew he was here."

The room beyond the door is tiny. A lava lamp undulates, casting red blobs of light and shadow. A long counter, where once Disney merchandise must've been sold, is piled with ancient books. Pulp novels. Old sci-fi books with fantastic covers of rocket ships, monsters, and beautiful women.

Brother Chris smiles. "I'm not the last, Chloe. I know there are others. We just can't find each other right now. But you're never the last. God reminded Elisha of that when he tried to tell God he was the last man willing to serve Him. Nay, nay, said the Big Man... I've still got seven thousand who haven't bent the knee. I like that story. I need it sometimes."

"And yet they would kill you if they found you." Chloe seems almost to be lecturing the old priest.

Chris busies himself with clearing a space for us to sit on a beautiful ancient leather couch.

"We are souls, not bodies, little girl. They can't kill a soul. So even then..." He laughs like a badly timed motorboat engine. "Even then they can't get old Brother Chris." He sits across from us and fixes us with a sober smile. "So why are you here, little girl?"

Chloe sits, knees together, leaning forward, eyes shining, her whole posture somehow now desperate. The priest takes a cigarette from a small tin and lights it. He offers one to each of us.

I accept.

"He's close to Rashid, Brother Chris," she says, indicating me.

Behind the wire-rimmed glasses the old man's eyes go wide.

"How close?" he asks.

"He knows where Rashid will be tomorrow. He will be with him."

Chris gets up and begins to pace.

"Baby girl, I can't condone a hit. I've told you that. Even if he wants to kill me, that's not the way…" He sighs and takes a long drag. "I know you and the Aztec Liberation boys don't get it… but that's not the way we do things. We'd rather die for our faith."

"Even if that means Rashid wins and becomes the new sultan," she says as though remonstrating some small and wicked child. "He'll be worse than his father ever was."

Chris casts sad eyes down at her. Then he kneels and puts a long gangly arm about her. "Even if," he says softly.

Her eyes begin to fill with tears. She shakes her head. Then…

"He says there's another way," she whispers.

Brother Chris looks at me hopefully.

"Tomorrow Rashid will lose the final battle," I say, "and his brother, who it seems might be a better fit as sultan, will win… by default."

"Rashid'll lose? How?" asks the priest.

"I'll throw the battle."

He shakes his head and laughs. "Yeah right. And then you'll be dead. We heard about the executions."

I finish the smoke and crush it out in a ceramic skull ashtray.

"I can do it," I tell them both. "But yeah… I'll need to get to the border and clear out of Calistan once it's done."

Chris thinks about this for a long moment.

"The Front has been looking for an excuse to revolt. Look at 'em out there. They're armed to the teeth and spoiling for a fight. If the world watched Rashid lose big-time tomorrow…" He rubs his bare chin. "Maybe things get crazy for a few days. We could get your boys at the Front to start some protests and even blow up a few power stations. No one gets hurt—and I mean that—but in the chaos I can get you some transport to get out." The priest looks at me. "But you've got to make it outside the Gold Coast first. I can't do anything for anyone inside the zone. You get outside after you stab Rashid in the back, metaphorically speaking, and I can get you across the border and into Mexico. Can't go to LA. Too hot. They'll be all over that border. But yeah… I can get you out through Mexico no problem."

Silence. And then…

"Get us out. I'm going with him," says Chloe.

Chapter Fifty

We make it back to Chloe's car at around midnight. We drive through the dark neighborhoods of Calistan, avoiding streets where bonfires are springing up. They look like they'll burn until dawn.

By the light of the dash I watch Chloe's face. She's lost in thought. Not even listening to the music coming from the speaker. I turn it down.

She nods toward one of the bonfires. Shadows dance around it. And yes. The shadows are holding guns.

"It's starting," she mumbles.

What's starting? A revolution? Civil disobedience? I didn't mean to do that. I've only wanted to ruin Rashid's day. And I've only just come to that realization. Maybe even ruin his life if I get lucky. But now this feels like something heading out of control.

Something I started.

Or something I'm going to start.

No. Not start. I didn't light those fires. But I'm going to fan the flames.

What else did I think was going to happen?

The truth is, I have no idea how I'm going to backstab Rashid. Game time is twelve hours away, and I have no idea whatsoever. But I do know that I'm going to do it. For a lot of reasons.

I text Irv. Probably not the smartest idea. No matter what Irv said. My text is probably being observed, noted, and filed under T for Treason before being forwarded to the appropriate authorities.

But I don't have a choice. I need to get out of here.

I need to get *her* out of here.

Need to get out of Calistan tomorrow. Things about to explode. Meet me at that pier we passed once we turned onto the coast.

"Is everything okay?" Chloe asks, casting me a quick glance from the dark road ahead.

I know what she means.

"Yes."

"Really?" She looks at me expectantly. "I can come with you?"

"Yes."

She smiles and places her hand on mine. She squeezes and doesn't let go.

Irv texts back.

Be there by four.

An hour later we're walking down the dock to the sailboat. Both of us haven't said a word. We know what's happening.

"Are you scared?" she asks me as we stare at each other in the galley after I lit an old candle I found in one of the cupboards. "About tomorrow?"

"Yeah," I say. My voice sounds dry and hollow.

"Don't be," she whispers.

She moves to kiss me. The night, what remains of it, is ours. And later we sleep.

Chapter Fifty-One

I was wounded badly in the shoulder when the minotaur pulled me
from the remains of the crumbling castle. Its destruction was ma-
jestic. It didn't come down all at once. It came down, apart, collapsed, in sections. Individual towers and walls and wings of the
great structure sloughed off in great sheets of stone. Ghosts and
spirits fled into the night sky as we made our way out. And as we
reached the bridge, the soaring slender tower that had housed the giant
demon's heart collapsed in on itself, its ancient stone walls turning
into a sudden waterfall of debris that drenched the rest of the castle.

The silence was devastating.

I can barely walk now. The pain of my injury burns like a white-hot
poker.

"We must hurry. This simulation is coming apart, PerfectQuestion!"
huffs the beast.

Simulation?

PerfectQuestion?

"What is this?" I croak, my voice dry and hoarse. We're struggling
along the road through the dark and haunted woods. The destruction
of the castle has faded behind us and all I hear are the mournful cries
of night birds.

"You're not ready for that yet," growls Morgax. "You're still in
danger. If we don't make it to the temple before the end, there's every

chance the programming will take and all will be lost. You'll be lost, my friend."

I don't understand.

I'm limping along now, following the beast man as best I can.

"And you can't," whispers Morgax. "Now is the time of greatest danger. We must make it to the temple before noon and confront the Raggedy Man. Those are the set parameters if you are to complete the resistance programming. It was all we knew about you. I'm sorry."

None of this makes sense.

"You remember him, right?"

I stop and search my mind, but all I can see is the beautiful murdered angel spinning with Alucard into the void at the bottom of the tower.

"In the Black. The Oubliette of Torment. The vampire," says Morgax.

Alucard.

The Priest of Chaos.

And…

The Raggedy Man.

"You must defeat him if you are to come out of this with your mind, PerfectQuestion. And he's waiting for us at the Temple of Elemental Evil."

We walk on through the night, crossing through the twisted dark forest and passing down into the north end of the Lost Valley. In the distance, within a great swamp beneath the jagged peaks, an old temple lies in ruins. It's dark and foreboding and my whole body feels cold and poisoned when I look directly at it.

"Tell me," I say to the minotaur as we rest at a bend in the trail that winds down into the mire. "Tell me what this is."

Morgax shakes his great bull's head.

"Not yet, PerfectQuestion. You're not ready to understand. But if you survive, then I can tell you what became of you."

The first bird of morning tries its song.

Poo-tweet.

It will be a long hot day down there. It feels like that kind of day. A day of slaughter and bloodshed. But a day with an end on the other side of it, one way or another.

"Trust me," says Morgax. "You saved my life once. And I'm here to save yours, PerfectQuestion."

But all I can think of is…

What became of me?

Chapter Fifty-Two

I hear Rashid's horn honking as I push off from the mattress. I've heard him honk that horn at vehicles that were too slow, or in his way, or not his. Now I hear it again.

Chloe lies next to me, her eyes wide. She sits up clutching the one thin sheet.

"Him?"

I nod.

I pull on some pants and go out. Topside. My arms and legs feel weak because all I can think is that I'm about to double-cross the guy. Which seems easier to plan and harder to do.

He's standing on the dock. Hair tousled by the light breeze that wanders across the idyllic harbor. And it's somehow all perfect. Him and his polo shirt and shorts and what look to be very expensive shoes, watch, and designer sunglasses. Like he should've been a model in one of the magazine shoots Sancerré used to work on.

Maybe she still does.

"Hey, buddy… got a breezy in there?"

The look on my face must not match the "don't blow it" mantra I've been repeating to myself over and over.

"It's cool," he says with a smile. "No need to look guilty. She bangin'?"

I nod.

"Still sleeping?"

I nod again as I repeat the mantra over and over again in my head. Along with an added *Be Cool.*

He laughs and says something about me wearing her out.

Then, "Listen, my father wants to meet you before we start."

That was an order. Not a request.

"Now?" I ask sheepishly, because that isn't part of the plan to double-cross him and get out of Calistan.

He nods soberly.

"I'll get dressed." Which is all I can really say.

"Hurry," he says.

I go below to grab a shirt and shoes.

Chloe is sitting on the bed, the sheet covering her gorgeous body. But it's the gun in her hand that draws my attention.

And the thousand-yard stare.

I take the gun from her hand and lean in close to her ear.

"We don't need to do this," I whisper. "We can ruin him worse than killing him. Living in the shadow of his brother as sultan will ruin him in ways we can never imagine. Trust me. And then we'll be gone."

She doesn't move.

I love the smell of her. I kiss her lips but they don't move for a long second. And then finally she kisses me back. Desperately. Like she's fighting for her life.

"Gather up my stuff and meet me across the street from the Cyber Warfare Center. There's a McBucks there. I'll text you. Be ready to leave because we're heading for the rendezvous from there. We're leaving."

She says nothing. Just watches me with her frightened eyes. And then nods once.

I stare back at her and know we're in way over our heads. That the possibility for all of this to go horribly wrong is getting larger by the second.

But if…

…just if we make it. Then by tonight we'll be free of Rashid and Calistan. And we can go anywhere after that. Anywhere.

I like that. It's something to look forward to even if at this second it seems impossible.

"Will you meet me there when I text you?" I whisper silently. Rashid is just beyond the hull and up the dock.

She nods again.

She would have killed him if he'd come down here. I'm sure of that. That's why she went vacant. Went to some killing place. She wanted to kill him. And then we'd never have gotten out of Calistan.

But wanting to, and actually doing it, seem like the opposite sides of some gulf she can't cross. Which is good. Because murder would make things much worse. Even if Rashid deserves it.

A few minutes later Rashid and I are blasting up through the hills toward a palace so grand that I now understand why Rashid calls his place a shack.

I have a very bad feeling.

I won the Super Bowl a week ago.

Now I'm double-crossing the leader of a country.

And there's every chance I'll get killed, or disappeared, doing it.

Of course I have a bad feeling.

Did I mention the CIA is involved?

But what can you do?

I light a cigarette without asking Rashid and take a long drag, the wind pulling the smoke and ash off behind us. Like I don't have a care in the world. Like I'm not going to double-cross him. Like I don't work for the CIA.

Like I'm going to live to see the end of the day.

Rashid shoots me a look.

I lean back and pretend I didn't see it.

Buy the ticket, take the ride. That's what I always say.

Chapter Fifty-Three

We slither through the ornate gate leading into the hilltop palace of the sultan of Calistan. Rashid's father. In many ways it looks more like an ancient medieval fortress than a palace. I'm sure the security and the troops are state-of-the-art. But it's also beautiful. The grounds are immaculate. Gray crushed rock contrasts against vivid green swaths of lawn and sprays of deep red bougainvillea. Giant terracotta urns erupt in profusions of tropical flowers, and below us, beside the rising drive, an orchard of ancient olive trees looks almost too picturesque to be real.

Beautiful girls in sheer silk and tiny veils stroll hand in hand, avoiding eye contact with all. Even Rashid.

We get out of the car, and Rashid and I are searched by guards who seem to care less whether Rashid is the number one son or not.

Once we're cleared, we're escorted inside. High marble walls covered in the most ornate tapestries I've ever seen give way to impossible ceilings and grand airy domes. We pass through halls and rooms that could fit Grand Central Station with room to spare. The farther we go the less we see other people, and in time the lush carpeted silence is overwhelming.

Rashid leans in close and whispers, "My father is not well. Very soon… I'll be the sultan."

He smiles like the cat who swallowed a family of canaries.

The seneschal, or whoever the guy is who's been leading us deeper and deeper into the maze, stops. We're standing before a pair of doors easily two stories tall. The silent man knocks twice, and the doors creak slowly open.

Beyond is the most fantastic room I've ever seen.

It's more a park than a room.

There's even a living lagoon at the center. Birds fly from massive palms rising from cyclopean urns. We cross a terrazzo, passing the silent emerald blue lagoon, and stop at another door. A smaller one. Two more knocks and we enter some kind of kinky motel of a bedroom.

Except super weird.

At first I think they're people. People painted in gold. People doing one of those art things where they pretend to be a statue. But then I realize they're actually statues. And not just statues, but golden statues. Golden statues of people having sex. Mainly one guy and a bunch of different women in just about every combination and position you can imagine. The statues ring a canopied bed of immense proportions. Flowing silks and the wafting scent of burning jasmine and sandalwood do little to mask the stench of decay and death.

On the bed lies a tiny, gray, shrunken man. Around him are what look to be three doctors.

Rashid strides forward and kneels at the side of the bed. The shrunken gray mummy casts pale watery eyes over him and seems to recognize him.

I don't really know what to do. So… I just stand there.

Rashid whispers something to the old man in Arabic. The man nods, listening, murmuring in the high yet scratchy voice of a small boy. Then he nods again and Rashid stand to move away and the doctors move in. A needle filled with something comes out, pills are administered, blood pressure is taken. They raise the little mummy into a sitting position, and when they seem completely satisfied with some sort of staged set of affairs, they back away.

The shrunken ashy gray mummy stares at me with vibrant burning eyes and an imperious mouth. He wanly beckons me forward with one shriveled hand.

"Leave," he manages in a husky whisper. "All of you leave us."

For a long second no one obeys.

"Now!" he growls like some lion that isn't as wounded as was thought. I notice his palsied hands are shaking. Trembling uncontrollably. But the doctors and Rashid and even the seneschal back away. Not totally leaving the room. But far away enough for us to have a private conversation.

I have no idea what we could possibly discuss.

Me.

And the mummy.

He motions me to come closer.

"My name," he begins, his voice even huskier now as though it might fail at any second. He swallows hard and begins again. "My name is Abdul ben Hasan. Do you see…?"

His watery eyes wander around the room.

I turn to look. Weak light struggles through the heavy silk curtains that guard his demise from the outside world. The smell of death is somehow more pervasive.

"That was me," he says, indicating the obscene statues. Then he giggles like that small naughty boy his voice seems to have been taken from.

I don't know how to respond. I mean, how exactly does one respond when the leader of a third world nation proudly shows you the golden statues he commissioned to celebrate all the sex he had? Life just never trained me for such a conversation.

I nod. A "neat" may have escaped.

He nods again, like a sage confirming some wisdom of the ages I have discovered.

He begins to cough and choke after attempting to laugh. He grabs my shirt and pulls me close. And even though he's old and frail, his grip is like iron. He holds on to me like some undead demon that's not yet ready to go into the outer dark.

"You could be very happy here," he manages through his coughing fit. Then after one particularly violent spasm during which something gray and bloody ends up on the silk duvet, he composes himself.

"My sons are good boys."

I think of the men Rashid had executed. And the story of the girl he fed to the sharks.

"One of them will take my place soon." His eyes bore into me like drills. Like he's begging me to believe every word he's saying.

"They need a real warlord. You…"

He begins coughing again, and I truly want to be anywhere but in his clutches as his mouth sprays disease and death with each shuddering hack. I would tear his hands from their death grip on my shirt if it weren't for the fact that he's the leader of the totalitarian Islamo-fascist regime I'm currently knee deep in. Not to mention all the guys with guns at the front gate. So I let him hang on and hack what's left of his lungs out.

"You," he begins again. "You are a conqueror, PerfectQuestion."

"No," I whisper. "I'm really just a gamer, sir. I was just hired…"

I probably should have called him "sultan" or "Your Highness."

"No," he protests weakly. "I watch all the games. Watch how you play. You could be the one in charge here. You could have the real power if you play the game the right way, my son."

His eyes are wild. Insane with some kind of reason only he understands.

"They are good boys, but my sons… they are spoiled. Not killers like you."

I could offer evidence, at least in Rashid's case, to the contrary. But I don't.

"You play online… like some kind of warlord. But here, if you stay in Calistan… you could be a real warlord. We have enough to take…"

More coughing. Ragged heaving. The doctors try to come forward, but the sultan glares at them and they back away like dogs just hit by a rock.

"We have weapons... many, many weapons. And so many fanatics who want to die for heaven... so many," continues the sultan. "We could take Baja away from Mexico with a real warlord like you," he whispers. "The generals know nothing but how to murder one another." His voice is seething and full of spite. He casts an eye filled with malice at the doctors and somehow manages to pull me closer.

"I can make you Rashid's right-hand man. You can have all this and more." His eyes wander lecherously about the room and the statues. "Pleasures unknown to mere men for a lifetime. Stay... and be Calistan's warlord, PerfectQuestion. You will live a life few have ever dared dream of."

I don't know why... but somehow it seems like he knows I'm ready to run. Then thankfully his entire body is racked by a coughing spasm so powerful it seems like he's going to die. The doctors swarm forward, and all the while he keeps staring at me with his burning mummy eyes. Willing me to accept his offer. Willing me to accept the destiny he foresees.

When we're out of earshot and headed quickly down a painting-lined passageway—I could swear we just passed a Picasso, an actual Picasso not some knockoff—Rashid murmurs, "Old fool."

I say nothing.

"I know what he asked you."

Again, saying nothing seems prudent. What with me about to backstab him and all.

Rashid stops. We stare out a tall window and a whole new garden of "delights." And of course more obscene statuary.

"He's a dying fool, but he carved all this out of the nothing that was America. Took it away from the weak who hated their country and thought tearing it down was some kind of virtue. But he's right.

I know what he asked you. I could use a tactician like you. We've almost won because of you. I'm not stupid. I wish I was as good as you. But I'm not. Instead, I know talent. And you're a great gamer, my friend. Which means you would be pretty useful once I'm in charge. If we win today, the generals will unite around me. We won't need the mullahs anymore. I'll be sultan and you'll be my right-hand man. And together we will do great things."

Out there, over Calistan, fires are burning down in what was once Orange and Santa Ana. Attack helicopters are swarming the skies. Rashid seems not to see any of this.

"Did he tell you his crazy idea about conquering Baja?"

I nod.

"I bet you could do it," says Rashid wistfully.

Things are getting out of hand out there beyond the zone. Down there. Out there. Calistan is on fire and they barely know it at the palace. The sultan is dying. And I'm being offered the keys to the kingdom. And Rashid is probably planning his own series of obscene statues.

I think of Chloe and the two of us getting out of here forever.

I see us on the Amalfi Coast. Which seems like a million miles away. Another life only dreamed of.

Then Rashid says, "Time to finish this, PerfectQuestion. C'mon."

Chapter Fifty-Four

I stand in front of the big tactical map at the Cyber Warfare Center. In real time I can see all the Calistani clans converging on our final objective. This will be our one last massive push against the most aggressive clan in the Geek League. Team Commando Joe.

Clan Joe has an insanely well-protected base on top of a high Martian escarpment. There's only one approach by ground. One road that's no doubt covered with artillery fire plot points and dozens of fortified positions.

Taking it will be ridiculously hard.

But I don't have to take it. I just have to lose *trying* to take it… and then pin the whole thing on Rashid.

"Hey, buddy." It's Rashid at my side. He's scrolling through something on his smartphone. "The networks are buying all kinds of bandwidth to cover this battle."

"Really?" I ask. This isn't a premier e-sports game. Then again, the stakes are high. Word has probably gotten out that the next leader of Calistan is being made today. Or broken. And that somehow a game is deciding the fate of a country. Along with millions of people.

When I think about it that way, it's one of the saddest thoughts I've ever had. At first it's funny. And then it makes you want to cry.

That sad. Know what I mean?

I turn and see that every general in the room is beaming. In their own mirrored sunglasses and busy mustachioed frown way. But they are beaming. You just have to look closely.

"Can we do this?" Rashid asks.

Gone is the overconfident spoiled rich kid playboy who seemed to never take anything seriously. Now, in this moment... he is very serious. Because if we win, he will be sultan. I'm sure there are ins and outs and eastern promises that go along the way, but somehow him proving he can lead will let his father green-light him to all his allies.

I study the map once more.

Doing this is even harder than he knows. But I can't tell him about the backstabbing part. Then it wouldn't be backstabbing, would it?

"We'll try," I offer.

Rashid puts his phone in his pocket and steps in front of my view of the map. His dark eyes stare into mine. He's taller than me.

"I have to meet with the mullahs before the battle." He says it as though that's supposed to mean everything to me. I don't know exactly what it means... but it doesn't sound like something he's too anxious to do.

"They want to know that... that I'll defend Islam if it's me over my brother."

He's talking low as though he doesn't want the generals to hear. But I'm sure they're listening. You don't get to be a general in a homicidal banana republic like this without knowing which way the wind is blowing at all times.

The weather report in Calistan is life insurance.

My five million in gold is gone. I realize it at that moment. I haven't been thinking about it much anyway. Not like at first. But now... looking into his dead fish eyes, seeing that the weight of everything is collapsing on him... that he'll have to make deals, offer power, and build a coalition of the willing to get the kingdom... I realize he'll never let me go. He'd kill me instead. But one thing is for sure: I'll never see that five million in gold.

I don't care.

Getting out alive with Chloe means more. Even if I can't get the revenge. I can get me and her out. I'm down to that. Down to bargaining with what I can get away with and live. In the end I just want to take her and get clear of this circus of horrors.

"Let's get started," I say.

He smiles wanly, like he isn't all there. Then he nods to someone and they all begin to bark orders and replies to one another in that harsh language they attack everyone's ears with.

"I'm going to strap into my suite now, Rashid," I tell him, like I'm all in. "I'll see you on the other side." And then to sell it I add, "Congratulations, sultan."

He barely nods. He has the entire weight of a country on his shoulders. And he's just moments away from having it all within his grasp.

Except compared to ninety-nine point nine percent of the rest of the world for all of human history, he's already had it all.

I'm on my way to my suite when Rashid's brother comes out of the blue shadows along the gray concrete halls.

"You realize he's a madman," he hisses at me. "If you go through with this and help Rashid—if you make him sultan—he'll kill us all. You and me first. I can get you out of here if you throw the battle today, PerfectQuestion. The mullahs are willing to get you to the border and hand you over to the CIA. They know about your agent."

I study him. He's chubby and businesslike. The opposite of his brother. In truth, yeah, with his modern ideas, Calistan would probably be better off under Omar. But right now I can't trust anyone. Not even someone who can get me out of here. This place is a madhouse. And everyone is lying in order to get what they want.

"Everybody's on their own." That's what I tell him.

His pale face and thick lips tremble. He's the literal definition of crestfallen. Like he's bet everything on this last-minute plea and is only now realizing what a bad bet it was all along.

He played the game, and he lost. Or at least, he lost the game that gets played by the rules. And he played badly. Maybe that means he wouldn't be a better leader.

But he probably isn't a homicidal egomaniac like his brother.

Probably.

He composes himself and takes out a handkerchief that matches his perfectly tailored suit. He mops his brow.

"If that's the way it has to be," he says, his voice trembling, "then there are going to be consequences. For all of us."

I push him against the wall and get in his face. It's for his own good.

"Listen, everything you're saying..." I can't admit it's true because what if he and Rashid are playing some weird loyalty test game? But I also can't let someone die. "If you really believe it, then get the hell out of Calistan right now. You can do that and live. Even if out there you'd be a nobody like the rest of us... at least you'd be alive."

Shock and befuddlement wash across his face. Not so much at the thought of fleeing for his life, I suspect, but at the thought of not being the son of the sultan. That... to him... is simply unimaginable.

If I knew right then how dangerous he really was... I would've killed him myself. Instead I merely watch as he tears away and stalks off into the suffocating darkness of the underground bunker. And I feel good about myself about having thrown him up against the wall. Like I'm a big man or something.

I make my way to my suite, swipe the card they gave me to access it, and log into *Civ Craft*. I bring up the tactical menu and start dropping my orders in the command channel. Clan commanders click "received" and "executing." I drag a giant cartoon arrow across the map to indicate the direction of our attack and then pull at the top of the arrow to make more arrows indicating positions I want knocked out and who is to take them out. And then I add... when in doubt attack whatever the Colonial Marines are attacking. Follow the dropship. Because it's got to be that simple. And it really is that simple. It's a pretty straightforward plan, and if I were playing it straight, we might win. Barely.

But I'm not. And I can't.

I have to lose. And then get out of here before they catch me losing.

And here's the really hard part. I have to stay alive, in-game, long enough to make sure Calistan loses this one. If I get killed early on... I'm out. And therefore useless to effect the outcome I want.

"Hey, Perfect." It's Enigmatrix over chat.

"Go ahead," I say as I finish getting my VR adjusted and dialed in. I tap in a quick message to MarineSgtApone asking how many Marines are left.

"I'm looking at your plan. You're sending everything into the cheese grater at the front gate. What's your game?"

"It's the only way," I reply.

"Sure... but that's not like you. I know you. I'm your biggest enemy. In every game back in *War World* you've always come at me from where I least expect it."

Noted.

"Now you're just dumping everything into their front. Where they're waiting. I'm looking at the sub-clan guarding that approach. Cobra Command. My op research algorithm crawl on all these players' online performance in other games shows them to be highly rated killers. Of the heartbreaker/lifetaker mentality. Why not air-drop or go up the cliffs and take the Commando Joe fortress that way?"

She's right.

"Because we have to make it look like a big battle—a devastating victory. We have to crush every asset they have today to make it look like a total win. No hit and run. This is for all the marbles. If we can convince them that the road leading up to their base is the battle, then they'll commit there and throw everything at us. Basically, we can win through attrition here."

"Yeah... but why?"

Because I want us to lose. And then I want to get out of Calistan fast. And suddenly that makes me think of her. She'll be left holding the hired-pro-players who-double-crossed-Rashid bag.

I could message her to run as soon as everything has gone sufficiency south. That's an option.

I watch as the first Calistanis throw themselves against the first line of emplacements. Within seconds we have multiple dead. The fighting is brutal and vicious.

"Look at them, Question. They're getting wiped out already."

"Use the artillery now," I tell her.

"How much?"

"All of it," I say. "I'm going in."

Chapter Fifty-Five

I'm with the Colonial Marines, or what remains of them, streaking above the combined clans of Calistan as everyone races for the objective, the front gate of the Commando Joe fortress.

Ahead I can see at least three defensive lines, and I have to admit they're pretty impressive. They've got reinforced concrete trenches where hundreds, if not thousands, of grunts are waiting to defend against our ground assault. Angular concrete towers with high-powered quad fifties are dumping copious amounts of digital lead into everything that moves. Hundreds of small machine gun pits rake the area with interlocking fire. And above and behind all this rises the massive Joe fortress. More towers. More turrets. High walls.

The ghostly tracers of artillery begin to fall all across the rising escarpment that leads up the enemy base.

I get a text from Irv. I've patched my phone to my VR helmet so it shows up on my HUD. That connection is scrambled, too. Encrypted.

I hope.

Kid, Calistan's on fire and melting. Having trouble getting across the border. Gunships everywhere. But I will be there. What's going on?

I don't have time to reply.

"Take us in all the way under the barrage," I order CPLFerro. "Sergeant Apone, we've got to clear a beachhead within their defensive works. Stand by for combat drop."

"Roger that, sir!"

"LZ in twenty seconds!" calls out Ferro.

Enigmatrix is sending everything toward us. We'll make a path right to the front door to make it clear we're coming at them head on. I need a steady stream of reinforcements to move forward from both sides. On private chat, I tell her, "No matter what… keep them moving. Got it?"

Long silence in which I hear only the ambient in-game sound of the dropship's engines spooling into a high-pitched whine, then roaring hard to brake and hover. And then Marines are shouting.

"Down and clear!" yells Ferro.

The back ramp drops and we're flooding out into a concrete yard at the very leading edge of the defensive works. Dead Geek Leaguers in some sort of wacky bright-blue tactical armor are everywhere. Others are surprised to see a dropship come in hot while artillery is still pounding everything to pieces all across the Commando Joe bunkers. Plumes of smoke and showering debris rain down as more strikes come in.

"Let's rock!" shouts MarinePFCVasquez, and I hear one of the smartguns cut loose on full auto. I'm engaging Joe troops on a parapet as they try to reposition a minigun to pin us down.

Somewhere in there, Enigmatrix manages an "affirmative."

A second later a missile streaks across the yard and takes out the dropship as it lifts off. Ferro and Spunkmeyer go offline in the HUD roster.

"We lost the bird, Sarge!" screams Frosty.

"We ain't leavin' today, Frost!" yells MarineSgtApone over the chat.

I rush the concrete tower with my M4X out and set it to full auto. Two Cobra Troopers—killers by Enigmatrix's assessment—are just coming out, and I engage as I close, putting hot smoke trails of 5.56 between them and me. Both go down and I'm in the squat tower darkness of the bunker. Artillery rounds from outside are falling indiscriminately all along the walls. The game rattles and shakes like an earthquake and my helmet speakers are both rumbling and screeching, even whining and popping. It's the full show up close and personal.

Concrete stairs lead up onto the roof where a minigun team raking the Calistani troops watches over the surge now pouring into the shattered first defensive line of Commando Joe's fortress. I follow the barrel of the M4X up, and at the top I land it on the minigun team. I ventilate them via mag dump and reposition the minigun toward the large support trench leading from the Commando Joe inner defenses toward this one. Cobra Troopers using what looks like some high-tech version of the ancient German grease gun are flooding forward, ready to retake our beachhead.

I hose them with the whining minigun and cut through dozens in seconds. Including a player. I'm rewarded with a tiny trumpet flourish and some dog tags. A player tagged Da'Baroness420 is down and out. For whatever that's worth. I'm sure there'll be a lot more logging on in the next few minutes.

A Cobra ground-attack dropship fills the top of the tower with suppression fire as it makes a pass overhead. I take damage.

If I get killed, I'm out. And then Enigmatrix will probably take over and do something smart to save Calistan. I can't let that happen. Because then Rashid gets to be king.

Sultan, I mean.

I ditch the heavy gun and fall back inside the tower for cover. The red Martian sky throws bloody illumination over the battle that's now turning into a real knife-and-gun show as all the Calistani clans stream for the front entrance. The Geek League is making its last stand.

A news crawl erupts over my comments feed. TWITCHNN is reporting that *Civ Craft: Mars* has broken some kind of record for gross micro-transaction velocity. And it's not just Calistan, but both sides that are paying to win. Though looking at the swarm, I don't know that money's going to make a difference.

This is a slugfest. Last team standing wins.

"Where's our air support?" I ask Enigmatrix over chat.

"Inbound in five. Can you hold your current position, PQ?"

I roll my head and sigh into my mic.

I've lost half my Marines.

"Can do."

The volume of fire coming from the access trench is overwhelming. I dash to the now-flaming wreck of the Colonial Marines dropship and low-crawl toward some clan Marines.

"Gotta push forward now!" I tell Apone over the chat. I dislike trying to get this guy and the rest of the clan killed, but hey, I'm surrounded by psychopaths with real weapons who will real-kill me in real life. Side note: If I ever make it back to America... I won't leave for a really long time. Freedom ain't free, and... it's pretty great.

"You mean... we just gonna attack 'em? While they're attacking us?" says Frosty.

"Yeah. Form up into two units and move forward. Keep up overwhelming fire. Most likely that'll force them to go into a defensive posture for a few minutes and that'll give time for our reinforcements to come up along our flanks. Cool?"

It's all about momentum. And only one side gets it. I'd like to be that side.

"If you say so, PQ," mumbles Frost. "But we about to die real soon."

"Probably," I mutter to a muted chat.

And then...

"Follow me!" on live broadcast.

"Affirmative," says Hicks over the comm.

I move forward, firing on full auto and crouching as I try to keep flaming wreckage and smoking debris between me and everyone on the other side currently shooting back at us. I'm about to find out if anyone followed. Cobra Troopers are swarming forward, firing and going prone. I knock down two more and shout "Mag out!" over chat as I duck behind a piece of the dropship's exploded turbine.

Hicks sweeps in behind me and lays down suppressive while I reload.

I hear MarinePvtDrake's smartgun off to my right. Or maybe it's Vasquez. A repeating mechanical blur distributing death in mass quantities. I see Cobra Troopers ripped to shreds. The walls of the bunker turn to dust and flying fragments as the heavy gun continues its destruction.

I pivot and move around the side of the turbine and surprise a Cobra squad trying to flank us. I drag the M4X down their line, hitting some. Others get waxed by Apone and Frost on my six. Cobra fires back and we lose Hicks in a hail of bright gunfire. But not before he smokes two and cooks a grenade that knocks out the rest of the cluster.

"Keep moving forward!" I yell over chat and check the time. Reinforcements should be on scene soon.

Suddenly the battle is up close and personal and no quarter is being offered by anyone. I empty the M4X and don't have time to reload. I pull my .45 Longslide and unload on a soldier carrying an LSX-99 heavy gun. I get off a headshot in the smoke and melee.

I see Frost go down off to my right. Apone empties his pulse rifle at point-blank range on some player tagged MajorBludd.

Someone tosses flashbangs into the concrete trench we're fighting for and everything on my screen fritzes out. I see only weird smoky ghost images of the Cobra Troopers shooting back, dying, and pushing forward. I target as best I can and fire because there's no other play here. I'm not even sure if I'm hitting anyone. But when in doubt… mag dump.

When I regain vision and integrity, the mouth of the trench is covered in shredded bodies and smoke. Only Apone and I remain.

Everyone else is very dead.

For now we have beaten back the counterattack. But as a unit we are no longer combat-viable.

"Hot damn!" shouts Apone over the chat. "We did it, sir."

Calistani reinforcements are swarming forward. Jihadis in clan battle armor moving through the wreckage. And also three skins I recognize from *WarWorld*. Kiwi, Fever, and Jolly.

I hear the distant chatter of machine gun fire and explosions as other Calistani clans are trying to destroy different objectives along the first line of defenses.

"Coming forward with more troops," says Rashid over command chat.

Good. I hope he gets killed. The thought of fragging him myself occurs to me. Except IRL I'm trapped inside the same building he and all the people who serve him are. And they have real guns. Whatever happens has to look like it just... happened.

And I still don't have an answer for that yet. But it's getting close to the disappearing hour. Soon I'll need to slip away and make it look like I'm still here. Chloe and I will need a head start regardless of which way we go. Either with Irv, or the priest's contacts Chloe has the loc on.

"Great," I tell the maybe-soon-to-be sultan of Calistan. "This is the breakthrough. Throw everything at this point and follow me. We're gonna win, Rashid!"

"For Calistan!" he shouts.

Yeehaw! I think.

"Perfect..." Rashid says excitedly over command chat. "We've got over half the online viewership watching right now. This is big... for me," he says like some actor who can't believe he just won some cruddy award no one cares about.

Of course it is.

"Great. I'll make sure you get in on all the action. We've got to punch through the secondary defenses next. Be ready, Rashid."

"I'm on my way in!"

He sounds so excited to win. Everything.

Chapter Fifty-Six

I get a text from Chloe.

Waiting for you across the street. It's getting bad. Calistan has declared martial law. Aztec Front took out a military convoy and blew up one of the oil wells in Huntington Beach. Gunships everywhere. We've got to move.

And then one last text.

Hurry.

For the last hour we've been trying to punch our way through a series of trenches to reach the main bunker that will give us access to the Commando Joe base. An understatement would be we are "taking heavy losses." Truth is, we're getting cut to pieces even with reinforcements. But somehow Rashid, and I, and MarineSgtApone, along with Fever, JollyBoy and Kiwi, have managed to stay alive despite the overwhelming casualties. Thanks in large part to Fever's excellent combat medical skills. The shock resuscitation paddles have been used. Heavily.

Jolly, Fever, and Kiwi are all officially Calistani clan, with full mullah approval. Jolly had to buy his way back into the game with his own money after blowing up on the SDF-1 yesterday. Guess he didn't quite lose all his Super Bowl winnings in Monte Carlo. Still, I owe him. I owe them all. Rashid has promised to reimburse them with a bonus if we win...

But of course I'm determined that won't happen.

So yeah. I owe them.

We're stacked and ready to go for breach. "Fire in the hole!" shouts Kiwi over chat as we blow the last bunker before the gate.

The planted charge goes off like a thunderclap. Jolly goes in first, spraying the interior with a candy-cane-striped Uzi, bright brass shells streaming in every direction. Rashid follows with an AK-2000 he's scavenged from the dead. He burned through all the ammo for his original primary to get up alongside us.

By the time I go into the bunker, checking right, with Apone checking left, the Cobra dead have been well-ventilated. Kiwi and Fever come in on our six, and it's a good thing they do because one of the Geek League players we missed comes out of the shadows with a ninja sword.

Kiwi's avatar pivots and unloads. He's rewarded with a kill for some player tagged ImYurSnakeEyez.

I need to leave and link up with Chloe but I can't figure out how to disappear and not have Rashid know it.

I DM Kiwi. Other than me thanking him for coming in and having my back, we haven't had time to communicate. It's been run-and-gun ever since.

I'm in trouble.

On screen we're threading the bunker that leads up to the wall of the fortress. It sounds like the end of the world out there in the battle aboveground. Enigmatrix is hitting the base with everything. More artillery. Purchased mercenary airstrikes. As many of the jihadis the Calistani bankers can get back online even though they're being slaughtered in bulk.

"We need that front door down, PQ!" she says over command chat.

"Roger, Rashid and I have taken the last bunker. Assaulting the main gate in five. Stand by to move forward with as much as you can. This is the last push."

"Roger," she replies.

I've got to tell her to get clear of Calistan.

We pass some graffiti along the tunnel leading to the courtyard before the main gate. It says *Destro is Kurtz, and I am his errand boy.*

That makes sense to someone.

Kiwi texts me back. *What can we do?*

No judgment. No *I told you so*. Or, *What were you thinking?* Like a good friend he knows exactly what's important. Helping me when I need it most.

I text back. *Need you to get Rashid killed taking the front gate. I'll hang back on overwatch. You'll probably get killed too. I'm getting out of Calistan. Will call once I reach the border.*

I wait. Despite Irv's assurances, I can't help but wonder if some Calistani secret policeman has hacked in. If right now he's telling Rashid what I'm up to at this very second. If a squad of soldiers is being dispatched down to my suite.

If the jig is up.

"What's next?" asks Rashid over chat. "Eyes on the main gate."

Four heavy machine gun positions and about a company of Geek League soldiers, all of them in identical red outfits, and all of them heavily armed, are positioned around the objective. If we can take the gate out, the fortress will be wide open for the Calistani clans to push through.

"Hudson is watching the livestream, sir. He tells me that's their cream of the crop. Crimson Guard," says Apone.

"Eyes on a chrome dome!" says JollyBoy. And then, "Oh my… I think I've just found my spirit animal. Note to self, JollyBoy… research how does one chrome plate their head for *WarWorld* skin. That would drive RangerSix absolutely bat bonkers."

Kiwi chimes in.

"Twofold plan. We flip that machine gun pit near the bunker exit. Then assault the gate with someone manning the machine gun position. I'll take breach. Question, you take the pit. Roger?"

"Hold on," says Rashid, and I feel myself break out into a cold sweat. "PQ is in charge. I know you're *WarWorld* teammates. But... this is his show."

I take a deep breath. I see Kiwi's plan.

"It's a good plan, Rashid. If I can flip that pit, you and the rest can go in under cover. The streams will catch you demoing the gate for all the glory."

Long pause.

"I'll be right there with you, Prince Rashid," says Kiwi.

Kiwi's legs were blown off by a "muzzie" land mine in Indonesia. He hates Muslims. But he's my best friend. So he's acting up a storm to get me out of something he knows is real bad.

If they gave out awards to real heroes, he'd win the Oscar.

I've just got to tell Enigmatrix to get out while she can...

"It really is a solid plan," I tell the princeling. "Toughest part is flipping that pit. I'll make it happen, Rashid."

And before I can say anything Apone adds, "Me too, sir."

And yeah, I feel like scum. I am not worthy of the friendship of the Colonial Marines no matter what it says on their blog site. Hopefully they'll understand. Someday.

"Okay," says Rashid cautiously. "If you're sure, PQ."

I say, "Hundred percent, Rashid," like a liar who tells lies.

We coordinate with Enigmatrix and two minutes later we go for it.

"Covering fire!" shouts Kiwi, and we pin the nearest machine gun position. Apone and I rush out. Our screens blur from the suppressing effects of enemy fire. I have a message composed to Enigmatrix in DM. I just need to hit send.

JollyBoy does a solid and fires a micro-RPG into the enemy position that's working us over. Flashbangs are lobbed and we storm the pit a second later, double-tapping the occupants.

Apone takes a sniper round that zeroes him out.

"No time for medical," he says over chat. "Get that machine gun locked on the other positions so they can move forward."

"Roger," I reply and hate myself a little more. "First Team in position," I call out.

Rashid will be busy now. Sensing his moment. All Calistan, the generals, the mullahs, and the entire world will watch him take the gate. And become heir apparent to the Caliphate of Calistan.

I send the composed DM to Enigmatrix telling her to get out of Calistan while she still can. Things are about to go real bad.

That's all I can do for her. And in the end, it's far more than I should've done.

Kiwi signals to move forward with Rashid and the rest. Rashid will be expecting cover fire from me, with the machine gun we've taken.

"Second Team moving!" calls out Kiwi over chat.

I note TWITCHNN's main channel is now livestreaming the battle at the front gate. The viewership is off the charts.

I open up on the three other pits, raking them with fire. Crimson Cobra super-soldiers, or whatever they're called, return fire despite the fact I'm ripping them to shreds. I even unload a full burst of fury on the shiny-headed chrome dome player running the local bots.

His head explodes in a metallic spray.

Kiwi and the team are dashing from cover to cover with satchel charges, moving closer and closer to the gate under fire. I'm covering Rashid as he moves. It's Rashid who will detonate the charges at the gate.

If I keep up the fire.

But I'm already out of my immersion gamer chair, messenger bag over my shoulder and exiting the suite.

Time to leave Calistan.

Chapter Fifty-Seven

I've got a small window to get out of the bunker. The shadows and subdued lighting and the fact that almost everyone is watching the disaster unfold as Calistan gets badly routed in front of the entire world... it all plays into my hands. The front door to Team Joe's fortress won't be open because Rashid's avatar is most likely dying on the Martian sand in front of it. Torn to pieces by three remaining heavy machine gun positions. Along with my friends who don't mind dying in-game.

Competitive gamers hate dying. Even if it's not for a ranked game. But real friends occasionally take a digital bullet for you so you don't disappear inside some third world country.

The important part is, the attack has stalled.

It's when I hear Rashid's screaming temper tantrum echoing down the halls of the underground bunker that I know I've got to get out the front door of the Cyber Warfare Center *now*. I fast-walk up to the ground floor level and then adopt a purposeful-but-unhurried pace toward the front door. The two guards who watch the entrance to the vault haven't been alerted yet. They don't know it's all going to hell in a handbasket down in the bunker. Online and in front of the whole world. That the ruler of Calistani, a dying old sultan who looks like a shriveled-up mummy, is watching Rashid lose everything. Including tens of millions in wasted micro-transactions. As are the mullahs. And the generals. The factions that allow someone to take the reins of power. The long knives will come out now.

I nod politely at the guards and act like I'm just going outside to have a smoke. Take a walk. Whatever it is they need to think as I walk past them.

Certainly I haven't just burned their soon-to-be leader's plans of future glory to the ground with a metaphorical Zippo.

They buy it and I push open the door, leaving behind the stale-smelling bunker that reeks of burnt ozone and warm electronics. I enter a hot smoke-filled afternoon that smells of salt, sulfur, brimstone… and rebellion.

Calistan is on fire. Literally. From IED attacks or out-of-control riots, I don't know. The air is alive with sirens and the sound of beating helicopter blades. And yeah… I hear automatic gunfire in the distance.

Out, I text Chloe. I'm starting to thumb *Be ready to move* when Rashid bursts out of the door behind me. He's screaming. Screaming that he knows what happened.

"Enigmatrix told me what you're up to!" he shouts raggedly. Like he's almost on the verge of tears. And homicidal in the same moment.

The big gold-plated Desert Eagle is in his hands.

This will end badly.

I am not a fighter. Not in real life. I really know nothing about guns. I'm just good at an online sport that involves digital versions of weaponry.

My fight-or-flight reaction kicks in as he screams for me to explain what just happened and why I betrayed him. As if that will make any difference. He's not pointing the pistol at me but it's clear this isn't going to end with him *not* doing that. Especially if he finds out what really happened.

So I run.

I cross the parking lot at a flat-out dead run, legs pumping, dive into a thin line of landscaping for cover, and burst through it, not having slowed my pace in the least. I'm cut and scratched and, yeah… he's just taken a wild shot at me. I hear a cannon roar and a nearby palm frond is slapped hard as the bullet tears through the shrubbery and goes careening off across the street.

I vault out onto a sidewalk and there's PCH. Pacific Coast Highway. There's no one on the road here in the perfect world of the Gold Coast. In the distance I can see military vehicles heading away toward the barriers that guard the zone from the rest of Calistan. I dash across the street and make the McBucks parking lot. The McBucks building itself has been shuttered with state-of-the-art anti-riot roll-down metal gates.

It's clear to me in that moment that Calistan is going seriously sideways. Corporations, even satellite outposts inside third world countries, have always been pretty good at smelling which way the wind is blowing. And McBucks has no doubt been ready for regime change since long before now. Has prepared for it. They smelled the wind, and right now the wind in Calistan is turning into a hurricane. A hurricane that's on fire, if such a thing is possible. And no, I can't believe I'm the cause of all this. Rashid and his family brought this on themselves. It was always going to blow… it was just a matter of when.

I was just the spark in an old dry forest full of deadfall and kindling waiting to burn.

I hear Rashid crashing through the brush behind me as my Docs thump against the hot pavement. And then I hear more footsteps, someone farther back, behind Rashid's ragged breathing and hoarse screaming. Someone following Rashid.

I make Chloe's car. She's in the driver's seat. But as I start to open the door, Rashid emerges from the brush across the street. His polo shirt is torn. His white slacks are dirty. His hair is a sweaty mess and gone are the expensive sunglasses. But he comes across the road screaming at me. His eyes are wild and murderous.

"Traitor!" he shouts. Which is true.

The gun is pointed right at me and he's following right behind it as he crosses the street swiftly. I know he won't stop or slow until it pushes against my cheek. Then he'll pull the trigger and blow my brains all over Chloe's car, the McBucks parking lot, and Calistan.

Chloe opens the driver's-side door and crouches down behind it. I see she's now holding the gun she was holding this morning. An old one. A revolver. I'd forgotten about that. She's staying behind the cover of the flimsy door, the car between us. But Rashid senses this and fires at her. His aim is bad and the windshield of the car explodes. I raise my hands to shield my eyes as flying glass goes everywhere.

This is nothing like a video game.

His enraged face cannot believe he won't be sultan of Calistan. It's like the worst day ever for someone who has lived a life of utter luxury on the backs of everyone else and always got what he wanted. He screams and fires the massive weapon again. He misses again.

She does not.

She shoots him from above the driver's-side door. Rashid goes down in the street shouting to no one who cares that he's hit.

"No!"

I said no. That was me. I remember this from that other place I see this all happening from. From the temple. The Temple of Elemental Evil I ended up at.

I stare at her, as if in a dream, as she stands and walks around the door of her tiny car parked in front of the shuttered McBucks. She crosses the hot parking lot and walks out into the street to stand over Rashid who twists and writhes from the bullet she has put in his gut. All of this like she's in some kind of trance. Or I am.

She doesn't see Rashid's brother, Omar, pull himself out of the landscaping protecting the Cyber Warfare Center from the Pacific Coast Highway. Doesn't see he's holding a small automatic pistol. It's not gaudy like something Rashid would carry. It's all business. It's an assassin's weapon. High-capacity mag. Snub-nosed for close quarters. Lots of bullets and firepower to make sure the job gets done.

I scream her name. And then Omar shoots her just as she's about to put the final bullet in the man who would've ruled Calistan.

Why?

I don't know. Maybe because Omar knew it would be him who would be sultan now and that it would cost him nothing to save his brother's life.

Or maybe because they were brothers. And that had meant something long ago.

I don't know.

Omar hits her several times dead center and she falls, dropping the pistol and twirling onto the hot pavement. Her hair covers her face, and everything in me says get the hell out of here. Except I don't.

I don't even think of that. I'm just running for her when Omar shoots me. It's like a hot burning pill I just swallowed that goes halfway down my throat and lodges in my collarbone. It doesn't fling me back or drop me because I'm hunched over grabbing the place in my chest where I just got shot when I kneel down next to her. I brush the hair away from her face and see her beautiful brown eyes staring up at something in the sky. I hope it's something beautiful.

I still do when I think about her. And that place.

I am dimly aware in the dream that Omar has slapped in a new clip for his murderous little business-like matte-black pistol. I hear that sound. Hear him pull back the slide and chamber a round.

Then I hear a heavy cannon go off.

An old-school hand cannon.

Like the kind Irv had in the door pocket of his old Porsche the day he picked me up at the airport and we got high-end hipster street tacos.

That day a long time ago.

Omar goes flying back against the hot pavement in the street. Literally he's been thrown from his expensive Italian loafers. I remember that detail.

The wound in my chest is starting to hurt. To really burn. And I can feel blood seeping between my fingers.

Irv, .44 Magnum in hand, crosses the street and pulls me to my feet. "C'mon kid! Gotta blow now."

He's dragging me across the pavement and I'm starting to black out. I remember thinking we should take Chloe with us. She was coming with me. I told Irv that.

"Nah, kid. She's gone."

I black out.

I see the ancient temple through the fetid reeds of the swamp. It is a decaying old unclean place that never knew joy. Or the smile of a beautiful brown-eyed girl named Chloe.

A few seconds later Irv is forcing me into his old Porsche. We're parked in an alley. He's telling me to put pressure on the wound when I fade away again.

It's an evil place. The temple. Silent and brooding. But Morgax is next to me. The wound is so bad I don't think I'll make it.

"You have to," Morgax tells me. "He's coming out. This is where you must confront him if you are to remain you."

I see that same man, spiky blond hair and vaguely homeless, coming down the front steps of the ruined temple. He's got that same crooked smile and unblinking vampire's stare he had when I first met him deep down in a dungeon inside the Black, as the Raggedy Man.

The buzz of insects rises up from the swamp like some chorus of the damned.

It's the engine revving up to sudden high speed that brings me back up to the surface of the dream I was swimming in. Chloe and I were swimming in. A blue-green tropical lake in an ancient primordial forest. This was one of all the places we were going to go.

Irv nods at me from the driver's seat. He has a sickly smile on his face. But it's a smile nonetheless. The big nickel-plated .44 Magnum is lying across my lap. I smell gun smoke. And burning tires. The sun is bright and a helicopter gunship floats overhead. Irv downshifts and I feel centrifugal force pulling at me as we corner. Tires squeal. He goes up through the gears and we're flying forward.

"There's gonna be hell to pay for this. Sorry, kid. I didn't see it going this bad. And you're gonna be in a lot of trouble… but we'll do what we can."

Who is we? I wonder. Is Chloe okay? We were going… going someplace nice.

I hear sirens out there.

And then I'm out.

I think I woke again and heard gunfire. Irv's gun. But I never really regained full consciousness until I awoke handcuffed to a hospital bed in Los Angeles. It was obvious time had passed.

But in between was the dream that told me everything about what had happened already. And what became of me. You see, this is the weird part. The dream came after everything. The dream is the present. Everything that happened in Calistan, that happened before. A long time ago.

Chapter Fifty-Eight

The insects buzzing in my ears, along with the heat of the day and suffocating nature of the ancient pile of stone that is the crumbling Temple of Elemental Evil, all combine to make me feel dizzy and on the verge of passing out. As though at any moment I will just collapse and die.

Blood stains my samurai's robes, seeping from the wound in my chest.

The Raggedy Man wears no armor. But he's carrying a long sword made of volcanic red metal. It's inscribed with strange angular runes. He's standing above me, atop stairs leading into the temple's gaping maw.

I draw DeatheFeather and find I am more leaning on it than ready to wield it in battle. My breathing comes in short, halting gasps. I cough, and see blood on my hand.

"Glad you finally made it here," says the Raggedy Man. "This is where the fun begins."

"Don't listen to him," huffs Morgax, who is carrying a massive double-bladed axe. He wears a hauberk of shining chain mail. A kilt. Large boots.

"Yeah," says the Raggedy Man in an almost friendly manner. Like a carnie selling dangerous rides, or a huckster ripping off the rubes for their last buck. "Don't bother with the truth. Let's just start slicing and dicing and see who comes out the winner, why don't we?"

I cough in the silence that hangs between the three of us. More blood.

"Because you're in shape for a fight right about now, aren't you, PQ, buddy?"

"What is this?" I ask… meaning everything. Not just here at this moment or the ancient evil temple looming behind the Raggedy Man vampire standing here beneath the sun at the blazing high noon in full. As though that too is somehow wrong. But all of it. The valley. Everything and everyone.

What. Is. It?

"Well now, PQ, that's the trick, ain't it? I can tell you. Sure. But if I do then you only ever know my side of the story. Or Morgax here can tell you, and you'll just have to trust him that he's telling the truth."

I say nothing and suppress a cough.

"Fun, huh?" says the Raggedy Man and shows his fangs. "Another game just like back in the Oubliette."

I turn to Morgax.

"Why can't you tell me what's going on?"

Without removing his animal eyes from the Raggedy Man, Morgax says in his gusty voice, "I can't until you reject the programming. Defeating him unlocks the parameters I'm constrained by."

The Raggedy Man laughs.

"See… what'd I tell you? Trust. And believe me you, that is over-rated these days. I'll tell yooooooouuu what, PerfectQuestion?"

He pauses. Rubs his stubbly chin.

Then…

"I'll give you a hint. And then you decide. You decide if I'm telling the truth, then you come into the temple and life begins anew. You get everything back. Fresh start. Upright citizen and all. You game?"

I say nothing.

My body feels paper-thin and fading. I have no idea what's real and what isn't. But the sword I'm leaning on… that's real. And it may be the only thing that is in all of this. Like it's some kind of truth in a make-believe world of lies.

"You, PQ," begins the Raggedy Man, "are currently asleep and riding in a giant starship as we speak. Destination: Mars. This is all part of the programming you're undergoing to teach you how to serve in the armed forces and... let me check my records here... fly dropships for close air support and infantry operations. Interesting."

The Raggedy Man walks forward, coming down the first few steps and dragging his massive red iron sword after him. It scrapes along the dusty pavement causing some sparks to fly up.

"You can't understand the particulars..." continues the Raggedy Man. "But all of this... everything you've undergone... has meant something in your real life. This is just a basic game-personality-interaction tool we've been using to turn you into a warrior. In real life, IRL as you call it, I'm your commanding officer. Call me Colonel Flagg. Friends call me Randy. And I am a hard man, PQ. I am your villain. I will not lie to you about that. No, sir. And you need to be afraid of me if you're going to serve on Mars. This is a war we're heading into. No-holds-barred toe-to-toe combat-to-the-death possibly involving nuclear weapons. You need to fear me if you are going to stay alive, PerfectQuestion. That... is for your own good."

He's standing right before me. Looming and leering like he's won everything in the world.

I've got nothing. Nothing in me can fight back. But the sword... the sword is real. I can feel it in my grip and so I concentrate on that because it is a known in a world, a sim, a game, full of unknowns.

But I cough up more blood because I can't stop myself. I feel weak and pathetic.

"So, we can do this the easy way, PQ," says the Raggedy Man. Colonel Flagg. Friends call him Randy. "Or the hard way. The easy way is to kneel down and we move on to the next training session.

Survival. Escape. Resistance. And evasion. We'll have fun with that one, PQ. Oh boy will we. It's set in a zombie apocalypse. And there're Nazis. Crazy stuff. But it works."

The Raggedy Man smiles, his eyes shining with gleeful delight at horrors only he sees.

"Or we can do it the hard way. In which I kill you here, and you start the whole sim again. Live through all that pain and horror that got you here. Spoiler... she dies again, PQ. Every time. She dies because she pulled a gun when you both should have just run."

I look at Morgax. It takes almost all my strength to do this.

"So what's it gonna be, PQ? You wanna be responsible for her dying all over again? Or accept the behavior mod and get a little get-out-of-PTSD free card?"

The giant minotaur shakes his head slowly.

"No, PerfectQuestion," he says. "You must fight him. You must resist."

There is no possible way I can.

"You saved my life once," says Morgax. "Now I'm here to save yours. Trust me."

I lower my head.

There's nothing left of me.

I cough.

"What?" asks the Raggedy Man. "I can't hear your answer, PQ."

I cough and say it again.

"The hard way," I mumble.

"All right, all right, all right!" erupts the Raggedy Man and steps back, raising the red blade with a grand flourish to strike me down.

And then it's on.

I get DeatheFeather up just in time to parry his first terrific blow. Hot sparks fly. The massive red iron blade glances off Deathefeather and sends me spinning away. Blood is running through the fingers pressing against my wound.

The Raggedy Man comes at me but Morgax attacks, slamming his great double-bladed axe through the air. Wily and lithe, the Raggedy Man ducks, twists, turns, and barely avoids being sliced in half. He laughs insanely at this, then swings his own blade, cutting the minotaur across the chest. The beast man roars and gives ground as the Raggedy Man moves forward with a sudden hurricane of cuts. Some find their mark. Some miss. But it is clear to me, even as I'm struggling to hold on to what little I have, to stand, to breathe, that one cut will soon find the fatal mark.

I can't summon anything within me. There's truly nothing there. Nothing.

Nothing.

So I tell myself to do it anyway and charge it to some cosmic credit card.

I scream and race forward, Deathefeather raised over my shoulder. Blood pumping from my wound.

The Raggedy Man knocks Morgax to the ground and spins on me in time to meet my cut. Except his blade, his red sparking iron blade, is in the wrong position to do much of anything.

"Ahhh hell…" he starts to say. And then his head is separated from the rest of his body. It goes spinning over the steps of the evil place, blood trailing after it. And a moment later his rag-covered body flops over.

Morgax stands, bleeding from a dozen cuts as I fall to my knees and know I am dying here.

The minotaur kneels.

"It's over now. Unlocking. Psychometric analysis complete. Programming rejection implemented. Behavior mod override."

The world of the Lost Valley is disappearing. And so am I.

"What-t-t?" I barely manage. *What is this place? Where have I been? Who am I?*

I have to know before I fade away. What was real, and what was the dream?

"W-w-was he lying?" I ask.

Morgax helps me up. We are walking down the steps. Away from the temple. He's carrying me really. There are mists ahead. Golden mists and other adventures.

"Yes. And no, my friend."

I look into Morgax's eyes.

"Yes. You are on a ship. The *Uruguay*. Part of a task force being sent to quell the Martian Rebellion. Currently you are in cryo being trained to serve in the military. Because you are a criminal, that comes with certain behavior mods that will make you more controllable. In other words... you wouldn't be you anymore if they had been allowed to implement. I couldn't do much for you, my friend. Couldn't get your sentence reduced or pull any strings to get you off the invasion force. I'm just a college professor looking for the truth.

"But you saved me. Saved my family and my career. So a colleague of mine, she works in Applied Game Psychology, wrote an experimental DreamVR program to counteract the effects of the military behavior mod. I know... there are side effects and there's that whole brain damage study. But we needed to save you. And this was the only way. We paid a hacker to run the program while you were in cryosleep aboard the *Uruguay*."

I look around at the Lost Valley. At the mountains and the smoking peaks. Grand castles and ancient dungeons. Ruin, mystery, and wonder.

"The program used an old fantasy game setting and integrated what happened in your real life to fight the programming being forced upon you. Everything, and I have no idea what you saw, was symbolic of something that happened back in Calistan before you were arrested. Maybe. Some stuff might have just been latent garbage being processed by your subconscious."

The forgotten book I found in Rashid's house.

The Priest of Chaos who murdered the young girl.

The mad hermit and the jungle cat.

The Lost Keep.

The manor house.

The trail of revenge.

The murdered angel.

"Chloe…"

I was going to ask if she was still alive. But I know she isn't.

"When you wake up, the military won't know you've avoided behavior mod. That's all we could do for you, my friend. I hope it's enough. This isn't even me. Just a low-level AI algo running inside the DreamVR program, placed to explain things if you managed to reject the programming. The program organized it all into something you could understand and fight. DreamVR gets a bad rap, but trust me, there're some practical aps. Look me up when you get back from Mars. And thank you, my friend."

Epilogue

Irv got me back across the border into LA. He took me to a hospital and disappeared. Never heard from him again.

But he was right. I was in a lot of trouble.

Calistan revolted and I was charged by the UN with attempting to destabilize a foreign government.

Which it turns out is a pretty big deal. I was looking at twenty years in a UN prison, or a colonization sentence to Alpha Centauri after a forty-year deep sleep. ColaCorp hired a lawyer and I think the "we" Irv mentioned was probably the CIA. They pulled some strings and got me military service.

I spent six months fighting on Mars and lost my right leg below the knee. The UN taught me how to fly dropships on the way there.

And I saw the *Uruguay* go down in the sand the day the invasion began.

The End

About the Author

Nick Cole is an army veteran and working actor living in Southern California. When he is not auditioning for commercials, going out for sitcoms, or being shot, kicked, stabbed, or beaten by film-school students, he can often be found working as a guard for King Phillip II of Spain or in a similar role in *Don Carlo* at Los Angeles Opera.

Visit Nick Cole at nickcolebooks.com and say hi.

CASTALIA HOUSE

SCIENCE FICTION
Superluminary by John C. Wright
City Beyond Time by John C. Wright
Back From the Dead by Rolf Nelson
Mutiny in Space by Rod Walker
Alien Game by Rod Walker
Young Man's War by Rod Walker

MILITARY SCIENCE FICTION
There Will Be War Volumes I and II ed. Jerry Pournelle
Starship Liberator by David VanDyke and B. V. Larson
Battleship Indomitable by David VanDyke and B. V. Larson
The Eden Plague by David VanDyke
Reaper's Run by David VanDyke
Skull's Shadows by David VanDyke

FANTASY
Summa Elvetica by Vox Day
A Throne of Bones by Vox Day
A Sea of Skulls by Vox Day
The Green Knight's Squire by John C. Wright
Iron Chamber of Memory by John C. Wright
Awake in the Night by John C. Wright

FICTION
An Equation of Almost Infinite Complexity by J. Mulrooney
The Missionaries by Owen Stanley
The Promethean by Owen Stanley
Brings the Lightning by Peter Grant
Rocky Mountain Retribution by Peter Grant
Hitler in Hell by Martin van Creveld

NON-FICTION
SJWs Always Lie by Vox Day
SJWs Always Double Down by Vox Day
Collected Columns, Vol. I: Innocence & Intellect, 2001—2005 by Vox Day
Collected Columns, Vol. II: Crisis & Conceit, 2005—2009 by Vox Day
The LawDog Files by LawDog
The LawDog Files: African Adventures by LawDog
Equality: The Impossible Quest by Martin van Creveld
A History of Strategy by Martin van Creveld

CPSIA information can be obtained
at www.ICGtesting.com
Printed in the USA
BVHW071254050122
625453BV00006B/500